REBEL FURY

Serg turned and threw his weight backward into his enemy.

As Thyne fell, Serg rotated his hold with a viselike grip. The move should have stripped the cannon from the rebel's hand. Instead, the woman pulled the release.

A thunderous roar filled the room. Serg found himself surrounded by the acrid smoke of a discharged cannon. He started at the energy blast that had obliterated the floating dust into glowing specks just under his right arm.

Thyne didn't waste the moment. She swung both legs up around Serg's neck and with a single pull, threw him free of his hold against the back wall.

He recovered slowly, breathing heavily through the pain in his ribs. Then he rose to face his adversary.

Thyne frowned behind the steady muzzle of the handcannon leveled at his head.

"Now you die, Pax devil."

SONGS OF THE STELLAR WIND
BOOK 1

Requiem of Stars

TRACY HICKMAN

BANTAM BOOKS

New York   Toronto   London   Sydney   Auckland

Contents

Galactic Overview

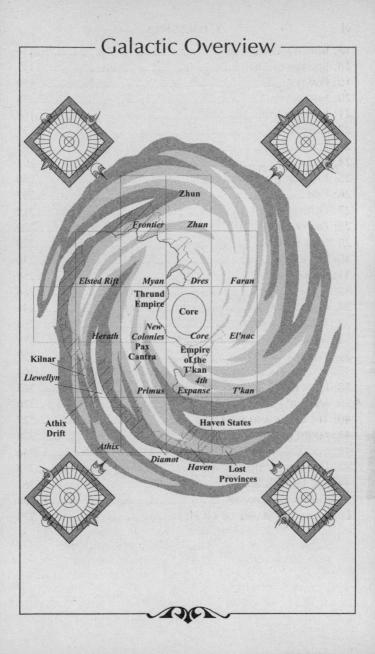

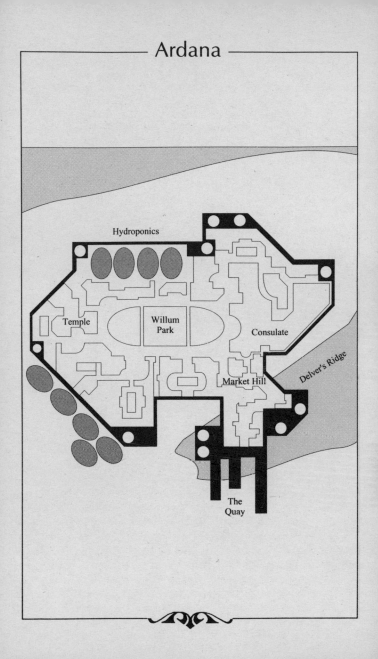

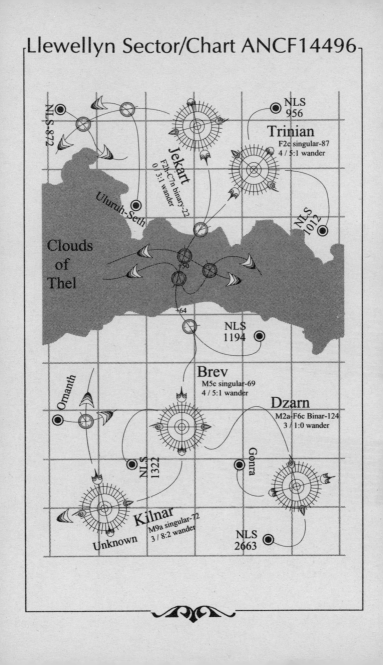

Llewellyn Sector/Chart ANCF14496

NLS-872

NLS 956

Trinian
F2c singular-87
4 / 5:1 wander

Jekart
F2b-C7n binary-22
0 3:1 wander

Uluruh-Seth

NLS 1012

Clouds
of
Thel

·80

·64

NLS 1194

Brev
M5c singular-69
4 / 5:1 wander

Ornanth

Dzarn
M2a-F6c Binar-124
3 / 1:0 wander

Genra

NLS 1322

Kilnar
M9a singular-72
3 / 8:2 wander

Unknown

NLS 2663

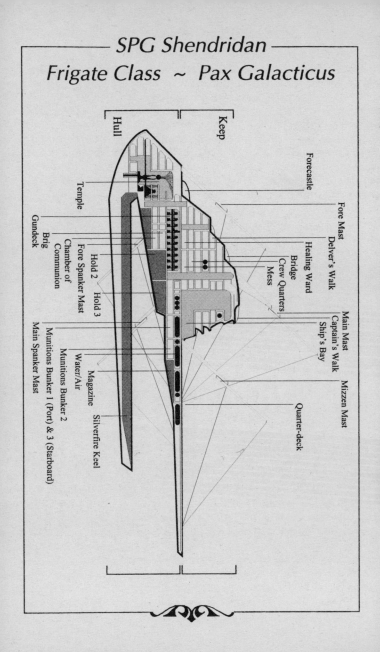

SPG Shendridan
Frigate Class ~ Pax Galacticus

Hull

Keep

Forecastle

Fore Mast

Delver's Walk

Healing Ward

Bridge

Crew Quarters

Mess

Temple

Brig

Gundeck

Hold 2

Fore Spanker Mast

Chamber of
Communion

Hold 3

Main Mast

Captain's Walk

Ship's Bay

Mizzen Mast

Munitions Bunker 1 (Port) & 3 (Starboard)

Water/Air

Munitions Bunker 2

Magazine

Silverfire Keel

Main Spanker Mast

Quarter-deck

Requiem
of
Stars

Prologue

The Calling

Oh, the siren of the night sky! What is there in that bright scattering of light that calls to us? Is there not some part of us that looks to the furnaces of space and sees our own beginnings? What is this longing to return to that darkness from which we came? Do we not see, as we gaze down eternity, the depths of our own soul?

Worlds get crowded. Never mind the distance to your neighbor or the height of your wall. No measuring rod nor breadth of hand nor even the light of the stars themselves sets the limits of the soul or the constraints of the spirit.

Are you a Groundling? Do you walk the surface of your world blind to the grand scale of creation itself? Look into the faces of all those who mill about you. Their world extends to the point of their nose. They are lord and master over all they see. Their vision is most limited. Their backs are bent; their faces toward the dust. Their existence is the cobbled stone beneath their feet.

Ah, but look up! There, then, is majesty! There, then, is perspective!

Walk the shore of any ocean on your world. Reach down for

a handful of your universe. With great care, separate a single grain of sand from all the others. Gaze on it. This, friend, is your world. This is your precious ball of stone weaving its place in all creation.

Quickly, now! Take that grain and drop it over your shoulder. Turn around, friend, and find it! Find your one special, precious world there among the millions of grains on which you stand. A Groundling might walk to his neighbors and return to his home without thought. Yet take him to the very next star and ask him to point out the light of his own home star—he cannot do it. Its previous importance is dwarfed by the sheer grandeur of the galactic mosaic.

Do such thoughts depress you, Groundling? Your art, your literature, your powers and possession; such achievements are trivial when weighed on the scale of the firmament.

The physical world is only as large as our hand's grasp. But the mind and spirit! There is no limit to what it can command; no boundary to hope.

The Pax Galacticus spreads its influence and settlements on over a thousand new worlds each day. The Pax ships sail the darkwind between these worlds, weaving the fabric of a new order among the stars. The Pax has reigned over peace and order for nearly five hundred years. Yet you shall know that the true power to rule the galaxy lay not in the might of the empire's warships, but in the hearts of its inhabitants.

Leave your one-world thoughts, Groundling. Let go with your limited hands and serve with your limitless mind.

Join us—and the stars shall be yours.

A Jezerinthian Tract pamphlet
for recruitment on new worlds

1

Heroes

❦

"*Sankt*, how I love being a hero."

Windcaptain Carth Mandrith again reached desperately for a handhold and missed. His helmet slammed against the blood-brown lampgrids overhead before his flailing hands closed around the gun deck's maze of conduit.

Thank the Nightmother this isn't my ship, he thought. The raider corsair certainly had the look of death to her now. Most of the port side hull was staved in here. The huge iron guns had sheared from their mounts, scattered as though they had been carelessly tossed about the deck by some powerful hand. The power optics that had fed energy to the guns and their crews were now an indistinguishable mass of twisted carnage. The smell of boiling varnish mixed with seared flesh drifted with the haze that filled the compartment. The starboard cannons, still lashed to their rails with gleaming cables, danced in their mounts as the floor quivered. Fascinated, Mandrith watched the arm of one of the dead raiders. It raised, flailed ominously with each roll of the deck, beckoning Mandrith on. The windcaptain knew the gravity was stuttering, a sure sign that the keel was beginning to unravel.

When the keel went, everything went—beams, spars, sails, rigging, air, and life.

Through the shattered hull, the nebula's light painted swinging columns of warm pastels in the smoke-filled room with regular precision. The Thel nebula was a breathtaking sight, its iridescent colors transforming the diamond-studded velvet of normal space into diaphanous patterns of brilliant light. Mandrith watched it swing past as the ship spun slowly. He knew the nebula's beauty was a siren's call. It was, he thought ironically, breathtaking, for if his ship fell into it, the nebula would certainly take their breath. Its glorious patterns lay outside the reach of the darkwind. Beyond the darkwind lay the Void, a place where no wind blew and from which ships never escaped.

He ought to get out. Many years experience told him he should, but he was in the chase now—and a driving part of him loved it dearly. Heroics was his breath of life. It was why he was there. It wasn't just the fighting or the conquest—those things were rather hollow to his way of thinking. No, it was the *cause* that made the fight worthy. It was the sure knowledge that Mandrith carried with him wherever he went. Above all, Mandrith loved to be covered in the holy sanction that put a seal of good on his heroics.

One other thing pushed him on—a brilliant crimson anger at having been dragged into this horror at all.

The capital ships of the Pax Galacticus, as with all interstellar craft, danced the stars to the beat of the darkwind. Its invisible currents spun outward from the heart of stars, swirling along each system's ecliptic plain into the reaches of space. There, amid the darkness, these tendrils occasionally intersected. In such places the optical sails, woven of silverfire from the ship's temple deep in the hull, would catch the change in the unseen winds and bring the ship to new stars and new worlds. Sometimes the darkwind currents were strong and wide. In some places, they were only wisps of force, narrow and treacherous. Regardless of its strengths or attributes, all darkwind streams made their shores against the forceless doldrums called the Void. The Void was where the darkwind was not; it was pure space where no sail could find motion and no keel could find purchase. All ships that drifted into the Void were becalmed forever, their crews sentenced to death without appeal or recourse.

Mandrith could have done little about the attack even if it had been expected. The loyalist captain and the corsair-class starship he commanded had trapped him cold, dropping down on him in the narrows exiting the nebula.

Mandrith normally would have preferred a safer passage, one with a strong and wide current. Yet some desk captain had decreed that the world of Kilnar would be accepted into the greater glory of the Pax Galacticus on a certain day. An emissary from the Pax was necessary to attend. The darkwind passage through the Thel nebula was the only route that could have delivered the emissary to Kilnar in time.

The Strait of Thel was also the most treacherous passage on the chart, with only a single filament of wind connecting to the other side. The unseen river in which their silverfire keel found hold had only a feeble current there. Mandrith's own ship—a Pax frigate normally swift and sure in the darkwind—had handled like a slug, even in the center of the channel.

The corsair, on the other hand, was a smaller ship but of equal sail to his own. It rode far outside the center channel on the fringe of the faltering darkwind, weaving its wake like a shadow between titanic clouds of interstellar dust. Even with the barest sigh of a wind, the enemy overtook his ship. Not a soul on watch ever saw their approach until their first pass.

He was congratulating his crew on navigating the center of the nebula, when the alarm sounded. Running for cover in the nebula was impossible. Navigating blind in those clouds would have been a hazard even in a solid darkwind; here it would be suicide. Without a wide-enough channel to turn and insufficient wind to run, he had no choice. Fighting was all that was left.

He'd lost over thirty of his crew in the first two passes by the corsair. The enemy guns fired a port broadside first, then swung sharply around, raking his ship again on the same side before his own guns were ready to open fire. Most of the guns Mandrith would normally bring to bear were suddenly rendered out of commission by the volleys. Worse yet, the foremast had collapsed as well, slowing Mandrith's frigate perceptibly. The corsair was coming around for a third pass when Mandrith ordered the keel locks released and pulled the helm hard over. The keel, momentarily free of the darkwind, answered the helm crazily, slewing sideways and rolling sickeningly over nearly a hundred and twenty degrees. It was just enough to bring the frigate's starboard guns to face the on-racing corsair. Mandrith ordered the keel locks slammed home again just as his own cannons fired in unison. The corsair slewed sideways against the assault, firing its own guns a third time. Ultraviolet bolts ripped between the two ships, splintering the main rigging of the corsair. Mandrith knew he outgunned the corsair and was preparing to finish the battle, when the opposing ship suddenly rushed forward, looping over his aft deck and turning suddenly into him.

In the end, the corsair had rammed him, tangling the optics lines of both ships. He watched with rage as the wrenching hulls merged, twisting the raider's masts flat against his frigate's boat deck. Mandrith's own masts and rigging were hopelessly tangled with those of the corsair's. The silverfire keels fought against each other until both lost their footing in the darkwind. Both ships then began tumbling in a dance that is every delver's worst fear. Unchecked, the ships would both soon drift free of the darkwind plain into Void. There, beyond the darkwind, rescue was impossible and no ship could ever return.

There may yet be time, Mandrith thought, to save his ship from that fate, but all he wanted now was the neck of whoever had cost him and his ship so much.

The dim green glow of the emergency lighting wavered for a moment. The corsair had paid the ultimate price for the ramming. He finally found a secure hold and his muscles ached from alternately hanging from and standing on his hands. The gravity seemed to steady itself without much enthusiasm. Mandrith pulled himself quickly aft, swinging to lay against the bulkhead next to the rear hatchway. Through the rainbow-colored smoke he could see the shadows of his boarding party moving up with him.

Four rungs up a stair-ladder and down a long corridor, he could see his objective.

"Jarj! Finth! Forget the side ladders and corridors. Cave that aft hatch." Mandrith smiled grimly to himself. "I have an audience with the captain."

"*Allai*, Captain." Finth was already moving like a spider down the twisting corridor with Jarj—a silverfire Acolyte—scrambling after him. Mandrith smiled. It actually looked as though his deckmaster was using the shifts in gravity to his advantage. Well, he thought, that's a true delver for you. He himself hadn't been all that long there on the Athix Drift—he had earned his own braid commanding full fleet maneuvers during the continual war with the Haven States in the Argo Drift. Still, that was over a thousand pardymes away.

He was suddenly struck with the distance that represented. Pardymes were all anyone in the Pax Galacticus thought of anymore. The Pax had somehow lost all track of real distance, or so Mandrith thought. When on occasion he was moved to think about the good old days on the frontier, he also realized just how very far away they were. After all, the light reflected off his own great conquests for the empire would not reach his current area of service for at least another hundred thousand years.

His boarding party painfully made its way up the long corridor to take what little cover they could find and still have a clear shot at the hatchway ahead. Fighting corsairs with boarding parties was far different from the stand-up and more civilized combat of sovereign stellar nations. War was tactics—this was vengeance and blood. Mandrith moved into the hall, tucking himself into a closed hatchway that offered some protection. He judged himself to be about halfway down the corridor.

Through the dust and dim lights, Mandrith saw Jarj finish the careful painting of the rune symbols on the great metal hatch that closed off the end of the passage. It wouldn't be long now. Mandrith pressed the back of his left glove twice with his right hand. One by one, soft symbols appeared glowing at the edge of his vision. Five green. One red. He recognized the symbol as that of Sequeth. It was the kid's first time "over the side," and he was still having a little trouble with the battlesuit. At least he's still here. They'd lost Urdin and Polk just getting below the main deck and three more clearing the gun deck. Now Dresiv's symbol failed to respond at all. Mandrith had known Serg Dresiv for nearly a year under his command. Serg was badly overqualified for a third-master of the ship but had fought against any promotion harder than most of his crew for it. Now he was probably dead. Well, poor Serg always seemed a bit careless. . . .

Sequeth's symbol turned green. Finth stood suddenly before the door and glanced back at the captain.

Mandrith tensed, flexing his gloved hands. At his will, the armor field on his left forearm activated, its clear refraction swinging forward to cover him. The shield and the handcannon were ready. Looking directly at Jarj, he nodded.

Jarj turned, starting to recite the words that would collapse the metal within the silvery runes. Once the recitation was completed, the silverfire would do the rest. Then all the Acolyte would have to do is get out of the way while all *Demoni* broke loose from the captain's assault team behind him.

Jarj almost finished the chant.

The hatch suddenly opened. A driving rain of energy erupted from the breach. Jarj, standing full in the path of the shattering violence, never knew anything but surprise. He was silhouetted against the column of energy one moment—gone the next.

Mandrith screamed his worst oath as he pulled himself tightly against the side hatch. The corridor was ablaze with brilliant bolts, lighting the hall in stark whites with blue shadows. Screams punctuated the roar of evaporating metal. Pressing back flat against the sealed hatch, nearly blinded by the light, Mandrith watched four more symbols at the edge of his vision turn flashing yellow and then disappear from view. He turned and saw Sequeth, filled with rage, leap into the hall, his handcannon erupting against the energy pouring down the hall. Sequeth's shield flared a blazing red against the onslaught and held for three full seconds before collapsing. The young delver exploded, what was left of him being carried away into the now-burning gun deck by the continuous barrage.

Mandrith turned his face away, just as Sequeth's symbol also faded from his vision. That left Finth, still up by the now-open door, Huelmar, and himself. *Dinch!* The team was falling apart.

Falling apart.

"Finth, listen hard!" Their skull-helmets carried their voices well, but the captain still had to shout over the circuit for the delver to hear him above the blast.

"*Allai*, Captain! Host in *Herac*, what's this pirate got under his bed?"

Rods of lethal energy continued to slam past the captain. "Ya, odd weather we're having, isn't it. Look, what's at the other end of the gun deck behind us?"

"Gotta be one of the keel bulkheads—nothin' else would take this kind of rain or else he'd have vacated to open space before now."

"Right. So they have to stop soon or they'll blow their own keel. They'll shut down the blaster and try to close the door again."

"Yes, sire, that makes—ah, *Dinch*! You offering me a job, Captain?"

"You got a job, Finth, I just want you to earn your pay. The moment the blasting stops—you rush the door."

"Captain?" The ominous groan of a melting bulkhead rumbled against the continuous bombardment.

"Yes, Finth."

"I definitely want a raise."

Suddenly the blaster fire ended. Mandrith swung out into the corridor just as the hatchway slammed shut. There was no sign of Finth.

The bulkhead far behind Mandrith groaned horribly as it cooled, twisting again, and sending another gravity flutter through the ship. It was now or never. With a single glance, Huelmar pulled himself free of his own hiding place and the two began frantically clawing their way up the shattered wreckage of the hall.

They reached the hatch. The remains of Jarj's runes drawn on the doorway could still be seen, though they would be useless to them now. Swaying from the gravity shifts, they stood for a moment, staring at the circle of metal.

"Well, Captain, what do we do now, sir?"

"I don't know—knock?"

Suddenly the hatchway slid open. Mandrith flung himself sideways, out of the line of fire. Huelmar panicked and fell backward, losing his footing. He stumbled, the fall to his back knocking the wind from him. Horror-struck, he stared straight through the now-open hatchway into—

—Finth's smiling face.

"Gee, Huelmar, I didn't know you were so quick on your feet."

Adrenaline coursed through Huelmar like a thundering river. "Oh, yeah," he sputtered. "*Joz*, Finth, don't do that! I might have cut loose or something—"

"Yeah, kid, sure. Thanks for not blowing me apart by accident." Finth turned to Mandrith and offered him a hand. "Sorry, Captain, but we got all wrapped up. Come take a look."

Mandrith took the delver's hand and swung into the room. There was the strong smell of ozone and a thick pall of smoke hanging in the room from the dust particles that happened to be in the field of fire. Mandrith could see the squat, hulking machine in the center of the room.

"Rapid pulse plasma gun? *Joz*, Finth, how do you think they got hold of that one?"

"Don't know, sir, but it looks like they have it tied directly to the keel power. He could have fired that weapon all day except—"

"Except I see you persuaded him otherwise." Mandrith looked at what was left of the figure on the floor. "Expensive cloak. The body armor is custom-made—I think. You didn't leave me much to work with, Finth."

"Sorry, sir. Ol' Darni just couldn't help herself, and you seemed to want to get this done with quickly."

" 'Ol' Darni'?"

"My handcannon, sir." He patted his weapon arm. "She isn't much at conversation, but she does keep me warm whenever I—did you hear something, Captain?

Mandrith froze suddenly, his eyes casting about the room. The smoke was clearing. Arched beams supported the low ceiling. The lush carpeting was ruined but did little to spoil the incredible sight out the half-dome window spanning the full end of the room. There, the nebula continued to tumble, its new suns burning hot and blue in their infancy. It would have been beautiful if the quarterdeck of his own ship didn't hang at an odd angle in the view. There was a huge table and the usual chart cabinet. Even short trips along known routes required a tremendous number of maps. Navigating the darkwind between ports of call was not a gambler's game. No captain's quarters would be without such a cabinet to keep safe the rare and valuable charts that were as easily sold without questions. Next to the table stood an astral globe repeater for determining the ship's present position. But other than these necessities and the simple bed swinging freely in one corner, the only decorations in the room were the black scars of the recent battle.

The captain gazed once again down at the charred figure in the flamboyant crimson robe. Flashy costume but a plain cabin. What an odd pirate, he thought.

Then he heard it—the muffled pounding underfoot.

"Lift that deck plate, Huelmar." Mandrith took three careful steps back and leveled his gun arm. "We don't need any more surprises."

Huelmar carefully reached down and grasped the edge of the deck plate with both hands. Setting his feet, he crouched, and, after a moment, sprang back with his legs. The massive plating swung free, falling back to the deck with a heavy slam.

A figure, cowering from the sudden light, shivered in the corner of the cramped compartment. Mandrith saw the dirty blanket lining the floor of the hole. The space couldn't have been more than four feet square and five feet deep. The face turned up to blink at the light.

Her eyes were great watery pools of gray set in an otherwise plain face. They looked up from a tangle of matted hair. Her large square jaw was set, though her lower lip trembled slightly.

How long had they kept her there? Mandrith wondered. He spoke quietly. "Bring her out, Huelmar. Be slow and gentle. Don't alarm the lady."

"Allai," Huelmar said quietly. He offered his hand down into the hole. The girl took it hesitantly.

Even Mandrith was surprised. She was tall, a good hand's-width taller than the windcaptain. She was obviously not a Pax descendant, for she lacked the frail structure common to the Coreward worlds. Other than that, it was difficult to tell anything about her. She wore leggings and a loose blouse, both somewhat torn and soiled and neither of which looked to fit her very well.

The floor fluttered beneath them. Finth looked quickly at the captain. It was time to go.

Mandrith quickly lowered his handcannon. He moved hurriedly to the girl. "M'Lady, may I ask your name?"

Her large eyes blinked. "Th-Thyne. My name is Thyne."

Finth moved quickly toward the forward hatch. "At least she speaks Paxish." Urgency was welling up in his voice. "Come on, Captain, this ship's done for!"

"Right." Huelmar was right behind Finth. Mandrith turned to the woman. "Please come with me, M'Lady Thyne. We'll get you back to where you belong." He took hold of her arm and moved her toward the door.

They were in the hall when he felt her suddenly stiffen.

"Jekanth! Sroi Jekanth!"

"Lady"—Mandrith was startled—"what is it?"

"Jekanth!" She shook her head. "Jewelry. My jewelry!" She suddenly ran back into the room.

"LADY!" Mandrith and his men turned in the hall. "We don't have time for . . ."

The girl grabbed the handles of the plasma gun and fumbled

to open the ordinance release. Mandrith cried out—there was no
time for formal orders. Instinctively, Mandrith fumbled for the
shield activator, but he knew it was too late even as he reached
for the pad.

Flaming white rage filled his vision for an instant: then his
thoughts evaporated with his body before the pain ever registered
in his mind.

"*Aros,* I hate being a hero," she sniffed.

Thyne Haught-Cargil, captain of what was left of the Kilnar
free corsair *Justar* stepped from behind the gun. Reaching under
the blanket lining the still-open floor compartment, she pulled
out a short-cut plasma repeater and two light fusion grenades.
Now properly armed, she walked slowly into the corridor.

One of the men had been their captain, she thought—though
by the look of things, they might never have been in the corridor
at all. They may have been blasted apart to the molecular level
for all Thyne knew—or cared. It was better not to concern oneself too much with one's prey.

Standing in the twisting corridor, she saw the charred and
shattered remains of those who hadn't had the fortune of taking
the full plasma blast.

A tear traced a line down her dirty cheek. She drew a single,
shuddered breath, then straightened up. She hated it. She hated it
all. There were a thousand pains she would have suffered more
readily than those her calling promised. Yet if she didn't right the
wrongs done to her people, who would? Where were those who
would rise up and fight off the yoke of the Brotherhood and the
Pax they served if she did not? Her people needed a hero to
champion their cause. Their pain cried out to her—or so she had
named those cries she heard in the darkness of her sleep.

She remembered suddenly who she once was and, for a moment, was able to connect with that bright-faced, confident girl.
Yet that girl had died years before; the Pax had seen to that. She
mourned for the loss of her own innocence and for the bright future that would no longer be her own. All that was left was a
hero—dedicated, relentless, and whose brightest future included
only a swift death.

A shadow crossed over her. She turned and saw the dark figure of a man framed in silhouette against the open hatch and the
nebula in the windows beyond.

He had surprise over her, but raw adrenaline was on Thyne's side. She raised the repeater sharply, pressure already coming to bear against the release. . . .

The world suddenly went blinding white inside her eyes. Her mind tumbled, shattered into disjointed filaments. On instinct alone she raised the weapon again.

Once more the sun exploded in her head and consciousness blurred darkly. She couldn't see, but instead heard the deck overhead splintering. The massive figure moved toward her. It swung her over its shoulders. She heard the creature say only one thing before her mind slipped into the safe bliss of unconsciousness.

"Ugh! I hate heroes!"

2

Abandon

～❦～

Pol Vidra, Second Master in service aboard the Pax frigate *Shendridan*, surveyed the ship and decided it would be one of the shortest commands ever. He'd seen his captain's life indicator disappear from the command patch on his left arm and was fairly certain that he was now the senior officer aboard the rebel corsair. He looked around and wondered quickly if his first order would be his last—to abandon the vessel.

Two of the corsair's three mainmasts still swept forward from the corsair's quarterdeck, but even those were shattered short of the gallants. The gallants and the top gallant were either stripped clear of the hull or lay crumpled beyond recognition over the deck itself. Optics cables and filaments were strewn across the general carnage of the deck. The entire mess heaved and buckled like a living thing in torment. The cables writhed about the deck in the fluctuating gravity, undecided between the intermittent attraction to their own ship's keel and the keel of the frigate which hung almost upside down and to one side overhead.

Pol looked up and shook. His own ship's masts and conduit cables meshed hopelessly with those of the corsair. He could see delvers and priests struggling to save the frigate and somehow mend her. It looked like a hopeless task and was proceeding without much organization or direction.

Joz, what a way to end it. He'd seen a lot of the empire. He'd fought in the Bestran Tyrannies and survived to claim reasonable fortune and honors. There had followed a period of comfort and pleasure that he had never quite gotten tired of.

On the other hand, of course, there was ALWAYS Serg Dresiv. Just when you thought things were going well, you could always count on him to show you how wrong you were.

Pol never understood Serg and doubted now that he ever would. He'd served under him for years and had risen with him in acclaim and stature. Serg had captained their old ship, the *Scylan*, into war and glory. The Oyunth Campaign, under Dresiv's command, had become a textbook example of Pax policy—might, restraint, and mercy. They had all been honored and decorated by the Pax Command personally. Honored? *Hesth*, Dresiv had become a legend. There wasn't a place in the Core worlds where Pol's friend and leader wouldn't have been hailed as a Hero of the Pax rivaling the Emperor himself.

Pol once wondered why people used the phrase "meteoric rise," since every meteor he had ever seen was plunging down at incredible speed. Serg, somehow and for reasons of his own, suddenly plunged himself. When their captain revoked his rank and set out for the frontier, Pol and Genni had both gone with him. Not that Serg hadn't given them opportunity to abandon him. He'd as much as tried pushing them away. Yet Pol and Genni both knew that somehow their former captain needed them here. Their once-gallant and cheerful Captain Dresiv had fallen— or, perhaps, jumped—from grace, becoming moody, quiet, and, somehow, deeply sad. Neither of them understood the change in Serg, though it had been the subject of many a long conversation when their former commander wasn't within earshot. Only one thing was certain between Genni and Pol—if Dresiv was to fall, he would not fall alone.

Pol's reveries were shattered by a sudden jolt from behind.

"Yo, Pol! Wake up! We gotta clear this rig!"

"Hey, Genni." Pol smiled suddenly at his friend, then instantly puffed himself up and raised an eyebrow in a great show of over-acted authority. "You have to treat me with respect. I'm captain aboard now."

"Oh, *allai*, sire!" Gennithna Parquan was just a kid when he joined the Pax fleet. Pol met him when the boy had hardly cleared the Academy. They both served side by side out to the Tyrannies. Genni, in Pol's opinion, had seen too much too soon. It had forged him anew—tempered him to a fine edge. Though he was two decades younger than Pol, Parquan hardly considered himself anything less than an equal. "Look, your captaincy, I'm forced to point out that this ship of yours is diving straight for the Void. How about dumping this hulk before it dumps us. What's left of the rebels have been put in the brig by now—and any below decks are done for anyway."

Pol took in a deep breath. "The captain went below with a team—"

"Yeah, I see your command patch has changed. Look, Mandrith is gone and so's his Second and Exec." Parquan's mood changed as he stepped up to Pol Vidra and grasped his shoulder with a firm hand. "Besides," he said quietly, "Dresiv went below and now we've lost him too. We stood with him to the end, which is just as we said we would. He found his fate below . . . and I don't think we should wait around for it to find us."

Pol looked down away from Genni's eyes. "Ya, I just wish it weren't so . . ."

The deck exploded into splinters behind them with a terrible roar, the debris carving strange arcs in the fluctuating gravity. Pol and Genni both fell flat against the deck more due to instinct than thought, activating their shields and swinging them protectively over them.

"What the *Hesth* is that?" Genni yelled.

"Those are handcannon bolts!" Pol replied as the wooden decking continued to rip open, shattering from a hail of fire below.

A sudden silence followed as the cannon fire ended. The two Pax officers, still flat against the deck, glanced at each other and then slowly drew their own handcannons. Both of them kept an eye on the huge, smoking hole now open in the decking. Pol fingered the release on his weapon.

A loose tangle of dirty blond hair, clothing, arms, and legs rolled limply from the hole onto the deck. *A woman!* Pol thought. *These scum are going to use this poor woman as a shield?*

A head of short curled black hair rose out of the dark opening. The eyes were slate-gray with a power all their own. Pol had always thought those eyes capable of warmth, but they always seemed to have an edge of ice about them.

"Master Dresiv, sire!" Pol scrambled to his feet. "The scepter is thine!"

Serg grunted as he struggled to pull himself out of the ragged opening. He couldn't be thought of as tall, but with his fine build no one seemed interested in calling him short either. He finally rolled over with his back on the deck. "You might have waited until I could stand up, Pol."

"I wasn't sure you'd have a ship to command if I waited that long. She's all yours, Captain—"

Serg's head snapped toward Pol, his eyes glaring a warning.

"—er, sire. That is, what's left of her. Captured loyalists have been transferred to the *Shendridan*. There's only the boarding party left."

"I see."

"Sire, we thought you were gone."

"Some *dran* pirate jumped me. Knocked my helmet off and tore the com-patch from my suit in the scuffle." Dresiv squinted as he lay on his back, looking up as though inspecting the *Shendridan* rigging, but his eyes didn't seem to focus. "Mandrith got heroic—I couldn't get to him in time. The rest of the team below decks is done for."

"*Joz*, sorry, sire."

Dresiv sighed and then, in a single motion, rolled to stand on the deck. "Master Parquan, do you see anything that might be salvageable here?"

"You gotta be kidding." Genni grinned. Noting Dresiv's raised eyebrow, however, he straightened to attention and responded more formally. "Oh, uh,—sirc, in my estimation there is nothing to be profited the Pax by salvage."

"So be it in the record." Serg slipped easily into his command voice—a voice that could carry the length of the raider ship's open deck. "Hear me! Abandon vessel! Hear me! Abandon vessel!"

The delvers quickly moved to the boarding lines, sliding up the cables with an agility that would have surprised a Groundling. Each delver moved easily from the deck as the ropes swayed in the conflicting gravity fields. Pol watched them, moving to his mind much like dancers suspended between two impossible floors, then turned toward the sound of Serg's voice.

Serg was stooping over the large woman he had unceremoniously sprawled on the deck. "Help me get her aboard the *Shendridan*, Pol. I think she's the last one. Where is the rest of the crew being kept?"

"There were quite a few of them, sire," Pol said as he moved to the other side of the woman's limp body. "We couldn't keep them in the regular brigs so we've locked them up in the third munitions bunker aft of the gun deck. Is that all right?"

Serg replied as the two of them picked her up. "That's fine for the others. See that this one gets put into brig cell number two. Don't put her in with the others, regardless—understood?"

"*Allai*, sire," Pol replied, but thought, *What's the captain up to this time?*

Genni groaned trying to move the limp form. "*Joz*, Dresiv, what did you hit her with?"

"Standard-issue neurolizer, Master Parquan. Nothing fancy. Still, it did take two bolts before she dropped."

Pol looked up suddenly. "Two? If you'd wanted to kill her, Serg, you might have just as well used your handcannon."

"Look, she's still breathing, isn't she?" The comment had irritated Serg. "It's not like she gave me much choice in the matter. Besides, I thought someone might want to have a chat with her later."

Pol and Genni secured the heavy limp form of the woman to the boarding lines and began hoisting her up toward the deck of their own ship. Dresiv kept his silence for a time. It wouldn't do to have the crew know he's captured the murderer of their captain. Keelhauling was an ancient tradition that stemmed from the days of water-borne ships. In the days of the stardelvers, the practice took on a special horror when beings who had displeased the crew of a ship were dragged slowly from the ship's bow aft along the silverfire keel and brought up the stern. Water was bad enough. Void vacuum was far worse.

"Who's senior master aboard now?" Dresiv asked with studied ease as he watched the woman lowered to the *Shendridan* deck above them.

Pol continued to haul the line but winced as he spoke. "That would be Master Bivis, sire."

Out of the corner of his eye, Pol saw Dresiv let out a long breath and shake his head. Pol had worked under Bivis over several watches. He knew what Dresiv was thinking. Surviving combat was easy. Surviving incompetence was not. It appeared their worst danger still lay ahead.

3

Passions and Policies

Water broke against the bow, slapping with a slight off-rhythm as the boat cut through the water. She could feel the gentle gallop of the deck as they moved; smell the freshness of the shoreline. The sun burned softly through her closed eyelids. She struggled with herself for a moment, unable to decide whether to continue warming in the sunlight or move to shield her eyes. She was afraid of breaking the perfect spell of the moment. A shadow crossed her eyes.

"Thyne!" The baritone voice chimed softly. "Thyne-mine! You need to get some lotion on or the cook might just mistake you for some gigantic sea-claw."

Her father's voice. She opened her eyes.

He towered over her, blocking out the sun. His great barrel chest was bare, showing a remarkable physique for a man of eighty-seven. The brilliant white hair, whipped by the wind, was a glorious nimbus, long and luxurious. It was his greatest and possibly sole vanity. His square face was set on a thick neck. His eyes were black, shining coals set deep into his skull. He stood with his legs wide on the deck, knees bent slightly to take each roll of the ship without complaint. Everything about the man was solid, permanent, and eternal. So Thyne believed with all her heart.

Thyne's smile flashed almost as a reflection of her father's face. *Argos*, how he loves me, she thought, and basked in the warmth of that thought.

Cargil Aps-Delthin, son of Delthin Aps-Sonth, was the latest in a seven-generation-long line of West Province Governors. The world had changed since those early days of frontier-breaking and conquest in the name of King Sarth. Mind had replaced might; compassion was seen as more acceptable than conquest. What had decades ago started as a bloody and rather heartless conquest of expansion by a deposed king had turned into a great beacon of republic thought and action. The Sarth Kingdom had evolved into the Sarthian Dominions after two rather bloodless palace revolts and the March of the People.

Cargil was himself only a boy at the time of the March but had often told Thyne the tales of that time. Through his eyes she had seen the people of the Dominions taking to the streets as one, after news of the Lonket Famine and its devastation of the Northern Free Estates. Her father—the twelve-year-old son of Chancellor Delthin—had stood next to his own father on the Forum steps and looked down on the sea of candlelit faces that stretched beyond sight in the Great Plaza. The Governors and Councillors then struggled for months thereafter and forged a new form of government along republic and representational lines. The new government was born where first her grandfather, and later her father, became Governor.

Now, Thyne thought warmly, times really have changed. She was Cargil's only child. In decades long past, that would have meant finding a young man from the lines of aunts and uncles to take the position of governorship when his time to pass from the world came. No longer. This was a new and more enlightened age. When her father was gone, she would become the governor. And, she knew, she would be a fine one.

Thyne stretched out, pulling her swimwear tight over her large frame, then curling to sit up. "Where could the cook find a pot big enough to boil me in? Besides, I doubt that he knows the recipe. What's for lunch today?"

"Ah." Cargil looked to the sky. "I believe he said something about Sanfish Pockets."

Thyne curled her lip.

"His father cooked for us for years, Thyne-mine, and he will too. It's just taking him a little longer to get the hang of it."

Thyne looked away, squinting hard across the radiant sea. The water was capping ever so slightly over the aquamarine below. Clouds rushed eastward over the water to the great pinkish-orange of the shoreline cliffs.

"I know, Pampa," she sighed. "All I have to do is be patient and—"

"—everything will find its own truth." They said it together, the completion of the ritual. Both of them laughing, Cargil helped his daughter up from the deck. They made their way back beneath the great triangular cloth sails that pulled them through the sea to the tiller of the ship.

"You'll be a good Governor, Thyne. Just remember that people have their potentials—it just takes time and effort to find them on occasion." His great bronzed arm shook her a little. "Tell me, are you entered in the regatta? You haven't let the deadline slip again, have you?"

"No, Pampa, I haven't let the deadline slip. Still, I wasn't sure I wanted to enter this season. It's a long way for you to travel."

"With a third standing from last season's race? Am I so old?" He started yelling aft to the ship's pilot. "Yuran! Get me a wheeled chair! Get me a physician!"

"PAMPA!"

Her father's smile broke like sunshine over her. "Well, you do what you think best. I rather suspect you have something else in mind for this season than sailing. How is Phylip these days?"

She could feel her face redden, hoping suddenly that the tan would hide it. "Pampa, there really isn't much between the two of—"

"Governor! Governor!" The uniformed man came up from below decks. Thyne recognized him as a wireless operator. She crossed her arms and looked at the deck. *Hergist!* A message from the mainland. So much for the rest of their day.

Cargil read the filmsheet. His eyes widened and he looked up. He didn't move.

"Pampa? What is it? Is it the Southern Reaches?"

Cargil looked down again.

"Pampa?"

"No, Thyne. No, this is something—different." He turned to

the officer. "Prepare to strike sail, Marc. Get the furnace stoked up, we have to head back at once."

"Wait!" Thyne ordered in the flat, firm voice she had learned as part of her tutelage for the governorship. "Pampa, the wind is good and quartering. I can get us back to port a lot faster with the sails than you can with your mechanical mess below decks."

Cargil looked at his daughter and smiled. "Yes. Yes, I believe you can. Marc, give command to my daughter, the next Governor of the West Provinces. It looks like she'll be running her regatta a little early this year."

He loved her, she knew. He trusted her, she knew. She closed her eyes to remember the moment, the warmth, the joy, to somehow make it last for all eternity.

"Thyne-mine?"

Her father's voice. She opened her eyes—

—to pain and slammed them shut again. The dream of that day—her last perfect day—dissolved into the terrible reality that was her life.

The men from the stars had landed that day. They were small and frail. Their language was bizarre but their attitude spoke of pride and arrogance. The War-marshals were all for wiping out this "alien menace" but the Forum Council chose a more diplomatic approach. Some hoped that an alliance with these "creatures of the deep sky" would gain them some permanent advantage over their enemies of the Southern Reaches. Others, it was later said, hoped only to call attention away from some of the Forum's own dealings. For whatever reason, the talkers and diplomats established communication. The off-worlders were discovered to be emissaries of a great union of worlds that was sailing into the far reaches of the galaxy. They had come—this "holy crusade"—to persuade new worlds to join with them.

In retrospect, Thyne had wished the War-marshals *had* blown them down to individual cells on the spot.

This "union of stellar worlds" was an alluring trinket on first viewing but—as with all good things—there was a catch.

The habitable worlds in the galaxy numbered in the trillions. The enormity of bringing so many diverse worlds and cultures into harmony under the Pax Galacticus chevrons was a nightmare of government. To have to deal with multiple sovereign nations on each of those worlds would increase the depth of the problem exponentially.

To this end, the men from the stars explained with patient smiles, it had been decreed that the Pax Galacticus would deal only with those worlds who had evolved into unified world governments. When her world had finally settled its own affairs among its sovereign nations and had developed a unified world government—then the Pax would return to Kilnar and welcome the world into the galactic neighborhood with all the promise that star-faring technologies and magic could provide. In that same plaza where once her father and grandfather had stood and brought about new peace and order, representatives from each of the kingdoms across the face of Kilnar heard the stirring message. They witnessed as the star-men set a shining sphere on a pedestal—a silverfire signal device. To each representative they gave a single key. Only by inserting all these keys at once would the device signal the Pax that their world was of one mind.

The star-men opened their great gossamer sails and rode their rainbows of light back into the sky. They would return, they said, with the riches of uncountable civilizations. All Kilnar had to do was achieve world government.

Yet in the absence of the star-men, as each representative eyed another, the question arose: *Whose* government?

So it was that the world set about achieving world unity in the only way it knew how—conquest, war, and oppression. Each nation believed it was its destiny to rule the world and represent it to the stars. Each nation fought to maintain its own identity and supremacy. And each knew that, in the end, whoever forged and controlled the government of the world was also required to have possession of the silverfire sphere by which they could communicate with the departed star-men.

The Sarthian Dominions, where the sphere had been placed— *her* home, *her* land, *her* people's blood—became the vortex of a world plunged into the chaos of final and unrestrained world war.

In the end, when the resources of the world's nations were squandered, when their youth had bled oceans until there were few youth to be found in any land, when the factories stopped from lack of material and chaos alone reigned across the world, then—only then—did the Brotherhood act.

They called themselves the Brotherhood although rumors said that they called themselves by another name among their own orders. They were as old as society itself and could be found across the world. They were thieves, murderers, and conspirators. They dealt in vice and death for their own profit. In a world of chaos, they were also the only organization that even looked like a government.

In the end, then, it was they who sent the message to the stars. The star-men soon came in their great ships, trailing light through the heavens. How sad, they replied, that this should happen so often—so often! Yet, they said to the cold, maimed, and dead, things will be better as soon as the stars began trading— *with the Brotherhood!*

Thyne opened her stinging eyes to the nightmare and forced herself to run. She was a dark figure dwarfed by the Great Plaza, its buildings now cold with more than winter's touch. The capital was the only city that had remained free of the destruction of war though not free from crime. Now, with its light rationed and government dismantled, only gaping darkness could be seen where once windows had blazed with life and purpose. Her rapid footfalls cracked against the frost-hardened grasses of the Plaza, taking her closer with every step toward the Forum. Part of her knew what was there and wished her legs would stop or turn. But the nightmare continued and she was powerless to change it.

Her steps echoed in broken glass as she climbed the great wide stairs in the frozen morning air. The Forum was dead and gone for everyone—except her father. When, on occasion, he disappeared, she knew where to find him. The Forum was unused now, for the Council had been dissolved under the new king, a member of the Brotherhood. She pulled her fur-lined snow coat tighter around the hood and continued to climb. At last she passed the great columns and stepped inside the huge open doors.

The leaded-glass dome over the Forum floor was shattered in places and frosted with the morning cold but still admitted a soft light from the cheerless dawn. The benches that circled the tiers about its center also had a light covering of frost, for the building was long out of use, unkempt, and unheated. There, huddled in the center of the audience floor, where often he had spoken with power and eloquence, sat Cargil Aps-Delthin, ex-Governor of the West Provinces.

"Oh, Pampa."

She walked down the great flagstones that led to the audience floor, her breath drifting in clouds around her in the chill air.

"It's time to go home, Pampa. You can't stay here—I never understood why you always came back." She stopped for a moment and sighed. There were ghosts here: the dead of wars and of her own future.

"It's over, Pampa. It's all over."

Her father didn't move. His back to her, he simply sat on the ground. She compressed her lips and moved quickly to the floor to help him up. The touch of him was as cold as the empty benches that circled the hall. Eyes wide, she dropped to her knees beside him, shaking him by his shoulders.

"Pampa?"

No sound disturbed the moment. Her father slumped gently toward her. For a moment she thought it might have been through some act of her father's own volition, but at the moment she knew that it could not be so as she gathered him into her arms.

"Then it truly is over, Pampa," she sobbed quietly. She slid her legs beneath his head, ignoring the biting cold of the stone. She stroked the long wisps of his iron hair just as he had caressed her own tresses so many times before.

There, in the hall, her memory stirred and called up her father's voice from the past. In her mind it echoed as though it sounded in the hall.

It's never over until you give it up. You don't win a regatta by crossing the line first; you win it by coming back every time you finished less than first.

She looked up where her father's eyes had so long stared even after death. At the edge of the Forum floor, where the benches were parted, she could see an engraved phrase. OUR DREAM IS THE VISION OF THE PEOPLE. It was a vision now as dead as her father's eyes.

She looked up higher through the broken dome. The frost was thinning with the dawn. Through the glass she could see the last stars of morning high overhead. The stars had destroyed her world and taken her father. The stars must pay.

As she watched, the prismatic arc of a starship's wake cut across the thin blue sky. They were regular these days. The sight held no beauty for her, stirring only hatred.

"Very well, Pampa, then it isn't over." And she knew that it never would be.

It's never over until you give it up. She heard the voice in her mind.

Her father's voice. She opened her eyes—

—and saw the cold light of the holding cell. The Pax had finally caught her, but not before she'd crippled their own ship and taken their captain from them. She doubted that they would get her under way before they all fell into the Void. The thought saddened her, not because of the loss of her ship or the slow and agonized wait for death that would follow. No, she was saddened because the fight would be over for her. She wanted to live; she lived to fight. She wanted to take the world—her world—from the star-men and the Brotherhood.

She did not care for the people or their adulation for such an act. She did not care for vengeance.

All she wanted was to remember her father. All she wanted was to hear his voice laugh again in her memory.

4

Nature of Command

~~~~~~~◆~~~~~~~

First Master Serg Dresiv crossed over last. He had waited until
he was sure Genni and Pol had both managed to get the unconscious woman back aboard the *Shendridan* before he started his
own climb between the ships. As he stood on the writhing deck,
he thought for a moment of Captain Mandrith, how he had died
just below where he now stood. He would have brought the body
back to the ship—if there had been a body to bring back. Serg
had been too late to save his captain. He sighed. Too late again.
He pushed down a rising anger within himself, grasped one of
the boarding lines, and began pulling himself upward.

Moving from one gravity field to another was habit more than
thought. You either get the knack of it or you find yourself floating into Void. The first thing they taught Groundlings when they
entered into fleet service was that "up" and "down" were entirely
dependent upon what was bigger and how close it was to you.
Serg often thought that this might apply to relationships between
people as well.

He moved gracefully in the battlesuit, a second skin to him after too many campaigns. Indeed, with the exception of the padded tunic torn in the scuffle below decks, he had come through

fairly well. He had lost the helmet, but it was standard issue and held no sentiment for him. The breastplate, however, he had carried through several campaigns. He was relieved that it had come through relatively unmarked. There were marks, however, where he had ordered the crests and ornaments of honor removed. Even so, he could still see where they had once been, wondering, from time to time, if others could see them also. He fervently hoped that they could not.

Hand over hand he pulled his body along the cable, using his legs as a brake whenever the gravity decided to turn the universe upside down around him. As he moved, suspended amid the careening nebula, he was at last able to shift around and point his feet with some confidence toward his own ship's deck. With that gravity asserting itself more strongly by the moment, he was at last able to lower himself rather than climb to the flat stern of the *Shendridan*.

Serg looked forward to surveying the ship. The quarterdeck was a chaotic tangle of optics and rope stays, the bent shaft of the miz'gallant mast had turned under the debris, hopelessly trapped. Farther forward, the various levels of decks rose above the main deck—known as the keep—looked fairly intact. The main gallant mast at the top of the keep even looked serviceable. The atmospheric envelope had obviously held—since they were still breathing—but smoke drifted up from somewhere near the prow. It curled inside the envelope, obscuring the glowing clouds of the nebula beyond.

Genni had already secured the prisoner and had returned to the deck. Like Serg, Genni was examining the wreckage with an eye toward work. He shook his head as he turned toward Serg. "I suspect there's plenty to keep everyone occupied, sire."

"*Allai,* that it will." Serg nodded. "Where's Pol?"

"Here, sire," Pol said, his head suddenly appearing from behind a mass of unrecognizable conduit. "I'm wondering how we'll ever make sense of this mess."

"I'm not sure that sense is what's called for right now, Pol. There certainly isn't any reason to . . ."

The sound of a dozen trees breaking caused Serg to look up and crouch at the same time. Overhead, the corsair was bursting open. Sections of the outer hull writhed like a living thing, tangled in the web of its own rigging hopelessly tangled with that of the *Shendridan*. His own ship rocked with each tortured pull

as the doomed raider threatened to take its enemy with her into
Void.

*Bad enough to be tied to that, but the thing I dread is right
here,* Serg thought as he turned his attention back to the *Shendridan.* Delvers were climbing frantically over the debris on the
deck but with little direction and less success. Most of the tangled lines were caught between the fallen miz'gallant mast of his
own ship and the main gallant mast of the corsair which refused
to let go of its own hull.

The whole of the mess was centered in a debris mass lumped
rather unceremoniously along the center line of the *Shendridan's*
large, open quarterdeck. It was a trick of the *Shendridan's* design,
normally useful, that was now threatening the very lives of its
crew.

The quarterdeck itself was normally deceptive and disorienting to Groundlings that first came aboard. Gravity aboard the
Pax ships was generated as a product of the silverfire keel that
runs the length of the ship far below decks. The center of gravity
aboard the ship was most easily thought of as a line drawn the
length of the keel. Since all things aboard the ship are drawn directly toward that line, most of the decks of the ship were curved
around it. Groundlings found it disorienting in the extreme, feeling that they were walking on the outside of a barrel turning
under them whenever they walked large, open decks. Delvers
tried to explain to such novices that it wasn't any different on
their own worlds, where they were walking on the outside of
what was essentially a huge ball rather than a barrel.

The quarterdeck, however, normally reversed things to its own
advantage. It looked flat to the eye—indeed, was built flat by all
normal standards. However, because the line of gravity in the
keel was within a hundred feet of its deck, a delver could stand
perpendicular to the quarterdeck in the middle but, as he walked
out toward the edge, the floor would seem to gradually tilt more
and more toward the center. The farther out he walked on the flat
deck, the more it seemed he was walking up an incline. This little illusion normally was used to great advantage when bringing
the smaller ships' boats in from expeditions and the like. If the
skiff was a little off the centerline, then the gravity of the ship
would drag it gently back to the middle of the quarterdeck.

Now, however, it had become a major hazard. The debris was
all being dragged naturally by the gravity in toward the centerline

of the quarterdeck, pinning not only their own wreckage under tons of debris from both ships but also holding the lines tangled with the hull and keel of the corsair as well.

The *Shendridan* deck heaved under Serg as the corsair lurched again, this time toward his own deck. The gravity wavered as the corsair's keel swung closer. The shattered deck he had just left threatened to fall on him from above. The corsair lurched in the lines overhead and finally slowed to drift back until the lines were again taut.

"*Dran!* Pol! Who's the watch QDO?" Serg yelled.

"Evan, sire. But I don't think . . ."

"EVAN!" Serg dragged himself up and began running along the edge of the debris field. Pol and Genni were caught unaware and scrambled to catch up with Serg. It was a disquieting sight— Serg ran along the edge of the deck, seeming to lean out toward open space but never falling. At least, with the debris pulled toward the middle of the deck, this left his path relatively clear.

"Master Evan! Serve and report!" Serg was at last coming to the two doors at the aft base of the keep. An officer stood there, inspecting the remains of the miz'gallant mounting with one of the silverfire Acolytes from the ship's temple.

The officer turned his smooth face toward Serg's voice. "The duty quarterdeck officer is in the healing ward. I, Third Master Nereth, hold the scepter of the QDO." Nereth spoke clearly and distinctly but couldn't hide the fear that burned sharply in his eyes. "Master Bivis has asked that we clear the damage and repair the miz'gallant mast. I have two details working on debris, but it's taking time to sort out which optics are ours and which belong to the raider."

You look green, Master Nereth, thought Serg. *Probably third sailing and the first with any rank. You'll do.* "Delver, cut away all lines that aren't where they belong. I don't care where they lead, just get your crew cutting."

"We can't save the mast without the optics."

"Dump the mast and clear this deck of lines." Serg looked straight through the eyes of the new QDO and pointed up. "The longer we drift tethered to *that*, the more likely it is that we go for a long swim in the Void. Cut those lines and prepare to clear this deck."

"Sire," the young officer responded, "I don't have the manpower to clear this deck of all that debris."

You had to give him credit, thought Serg. *The kid didn't even blink.* Dresiv's eyes never left those of Nereth as he bellowed, "Delver Pol!"

Pol arrived in moments. "*Allai,* sire."

"It seems to me"—Serg still had Nereth locked in his gaze—"that the captain's gig on this ship projects a rather remarkably sized sail, does it not?"

"Yes, sire," Pol answered quizzically.

Serg spoke directly to the officer before him. "Master Nereth, use the captain's gig to clear the deck. Cut the lines and attach some cabling to the gig; activate its sail and have it drag this mess clear of the ship."

Nereth swallowed, then blinked. He was the captain's pilot and was nominally in charge of the elegant, small-sailed craft used to make important calls on planetary governments. "But—but, sire! We just—painted it," he finished weakly. He looked plaintively into the stone face of Master Dresiv. "Yes, sire. We'll have it done."

"Look here, Third Master Dresiv!" The Acolyte had followed the conversation thus far without comment. Serg had seen him occasionally working down in the temple but couldn't recall his name. "We have orders directly from *Captain* Bivis"—Serg stared coldly at the emphasis on the word—"which you, being only a Third Master, may not yet be aware of. We need this mast if we are ever going to . . ."

"Father, I would normally agree with you, but . . . well, it's quite simple, really." Serg suddenly flashed an easy, iron smile. "You see, these *are* the orders of Master Bivis."

"What?!"

"I repeat, Captain Bivis just gave me those orders and I—as you will understand—as a lowly Third Master intend to carry them out."

Pol didn't move but looked sharply toward Serg. Genni started to take in a long breath.

"Master Vidra! Master Parquan!" Dresiv's easy, pleasant manner continued though his vacuum-cold eyes. "I want you to go forward on the starboard side and convey Master Bivis's new directive to the crews there."

Pol snapped to attention, but by the look on his face he wasn't sure why. "*Allai,* sire! Er—uh—just exactly what *were* those . . ."

"Have the officer on deck position delvers around the tangled areas with cutters. Then have him arm the EMS squibs and blow the starboard main and spanker masts clear of the hull. The delvers will have to cut any remaining tangled lines as the corsair swings free of us." Serg looked again at the mess on the quarterdeck. "We obviously don't have to blow the miz'gallant, since it is already free of the deck, but we don't want any loose cables holding up this separation. Maybe if we amputate we can save the patient."

"*Allai*, sire!"

"Once that's done, have the senior officers who can disengage themselves from damage control meet me—" He turned suddenly on Master Nereth. "What's the condition of the bridge, Nereth?"

Nereth shook his head. "The bridge was raked by cannon fire on the second pass. We don't know if it's habitable."

"Okay." Turning back to Pol, Serg said, "Have them meet me in the ship's bay in half an hour."

The Acolyte spoke smoothly, but there was oil in his voice. "Did you say to meet *you* in half an hour?"

"Why, yes, Father." Serg's voice was like bright ice. "The new captain is a very busy man. Nereth, clear those lines at once and get your crew clear. We don't want anyone dragged overboard, do we? Oh, and, Nereth?"

"Yes, sire?"

"Do it NOW!"

As Serg turned, he could hear the electrified Nereth start barking orders to the deck crew. He smiled to himself. We may be moving in the right direction after all. He walked purposefully toward the gangway hatch that led to the ship's bay beyond.

Pol tried to keep up with his former captain but could manage only a few steps behind him. " 'Bivis's orders'? Have you gone dustminded? You haven't even *seen* Bivis yet!"

"Ah, Pol, it's just a technicality. They *will* be his orders in a few minutes." Serg reached the door and turned the latch free.

"Serg." Pol grabbed the man's shoulder. "I don't know what you think . . ."

The fury, never far from the surface, surged up unbidden from deep within Serg Dresiv, red, dark, and powerful. He swung his arm crisply up, knocking his companion's arm free of his shoulder with such force that if Pol's grip had been more serious, he might have broken his arm. It was beyond his own control, a surrender of his conscious will to that dark pain that was always within him, longing for peace and release. He grabbed Pol by the battlesuit breastplate he still wore and slammed him abruptly against the bulkhead. For a moment he saw the focus fade in Pol's eyes and then steady again.

"This ship is dead"—Serg spat out the words—"unless you get your ass forward and get those lines cleared! First Master Bivis—oh, *excuse me*—*Captain* Bivis doesn't know how to save his own spit let alone everyone on this ship. I'll do my job if you do yours. Now, *move it*, delver, or we're dead."

The fever in his eyes suddenly quieted and he released his grip on Pol. He hung his head and then looked away. He couldn't explain to them. He barely understood the hollowness of his own life or the fear that occasionally overwhelmed it. If there were a way, perhaps, he could bring that dark center within him out into the light and examine it, then he could deal with it. Perhaps then he could conquer it. He knew where it lay in his soul, just behind a door that he could never bring himself to open. How could he explain that to his loyal shipmates? "It'll be all right. Just—just get forward, follow the plan, and it'll be all right." He suddenly smiled tiredly to himself. "*Hesth*, gentlemen! Bivis is about to become a hero!"

Serg pulled open the hatch and slid with practiced ease into the ship. Then, when he was sure he was no longer within sight of his companions, Serg leaned weakly against a bulkhead and tried desperately to collect himself.

Through the still-open hatch he could hear Genni and Pol converse as they moved away. He felt the sadness in their voices as they moved forward to carry out his orders. Their words fell on his soul like molten rain.

"He ain't no better, Pol."

"No, Genni. No better."

5

View from Above

———❦———

Serg sucked in a deep, shuddering breath. Pushing himself away
from the wall, he moved quickly to cross the ship's bay. It wasn't
easy. Delvers from every watch swarmed over the floor of the
bay, each intent on his assigned duty station or task, as often as
not getting in the way of several others who were equally intent
on their tasks. A dozen delvers were already forcing open the
great fitted doors that led to the quarterdeck. Serg glanced aft as
he pushed his way across the deck. In that instant he saw Nereth
climbing over the side of the captain's gig. Serg grinned to himself. The finish on the small gig was, indeed, mirror-bright.
Sorry, Nereth, he thought. *I hate to think what you're about to do
to that pretty little boat.*

Halfway down the bay, Serg glanced up. The great wooden
beams arching overhead were partially obscured by a thin haze of
smoke from the fires he had seen forward, but they still looked
beautiful. Used to house the ship's emergency boats and captain's
gig, it was the largest open area in the ship. Brass-fitted lanterns
of firecrystal lit the bay in a gentle blue light, casting a strange
pall over the swarming crew of the *Shendridan*. The vaulted ceiling opened into a towering shaft three more decks high. There,

slung on great hoists, the remaining small boats of the *Shendri-dan* still looked serviceable. Serg had heard tales of ships' crews having to take to the small boats and sail the darkwind to the next habitable world. He knew, too, that there were far more ships that had simply disappeared than crews that had saved themselves in those boats. If he moved fast enough, they might not have to take so desperate a gamble as fighting deep space in a wooden hull and single sail twenty feet long.

Just as he reached the ladder to the upper decks, five delvers rushed down the stairway toward him. Serg threw himself to one side, pressed against the planks as the delvers thundered passed him. The way now clear, he reached for the handrail and began his rush to the upper decks. His arms and legs worked together, pulling and pushing him higher into the ship's keep.

Four decks later, he reached the top of the gangway. Serg could now barely see in the choking haze. Dim flickers of a smoldering fire cast dancing shadows from the bridge forward. For a moment he wondered how he would find Bivis in all this mess.

A voice edged sharply with hysteria floated down the staircase behind him. The captain's walk was located at the back of the keep just up those stairs. It afforded quick access to the bridge as well as a literally commanding view of the quarterdeck. It was, in fact, Mandrith's cabin up until a few minutes before. Bivis had apparently wasted no time in occupying it. Serg smiled grimly to himself. *If he wants it that badly, he can have it—so long as he doesn't get the rest of us killed.*

Climbing the stairs, Serg stepped onto the captain's walk. The smoke was thinner here but noticeable. The massive polished desk of the captain and the furnishings that such rank commanded were much in evidence. The arched ceiling, however, extended only partway aft over the deck. The last third of the room was formed by a low wall and railing, the entirety of which was domed in glass. Blower tubes for communicating with the lower decks were arranged along the aft railing of the deck. Bivis had the blower for the quarterdeck in one hand and was rapidly working his way past command voice into full scream.

"Who in *Hesth* ordered out the captain's boat?! No! I want it put it back!" Bivis had to stop now and again to get the reply through the blower. He had been forced to yell in order to be heard over the chaos on the decks below. Whoever was answering him felt obliged to return his end of the conversation in the same way. As a consequence, the two people at opposite ends of the tube could barely understand what was being said by the other. That Bivis had never even considered leaving the prestige of the captain's walk to actually DO something about the damage merely confirmed Serg's own estimation of the man.

Serg had long ago taken stock of Bivis and found him to be of that type which was all too easily classifiable. Bivis was even shorter than Serg and strong as a bull. Serg suspected that Bivis had had a difficult childhood because of his height and had compensated for it with something of a bully mentality. Somewhere along the way he'd found service in the Pax and the discipline to make it work. He always wore the uniform of the Pax— sometimes with full braid—and was the type of perfect example that pleased superiors, irritated peers, and gave those serving under them cause for any number of jokes. He looked good in parades, was a stickler for following the book when it came to anything not covered by the book, and was—in short—the very type of person who could get you killed in a crisis.

A great crack had started on the port side in the dome and had worked its way up nearly to the top. Serg glanced from the dome to Bivis. From the looks of him, the newly fashioned captain had a lot in common with the dome. The man was definitely both cracked and in over his head.

Serg drew a breath. It was time to get this over with. "Third Master Dresiv reporting, sire."

Bivis, still red-faced from shouting, turned and stared back at Serg, who was doing his best attentive-delver act. Captain Bivis dropped the blower—which was still pouring out a hollow stream of noise—and landed both hands on the huge desk.

"Dresiv, who the *Hesth* ordered the captain's boat out, for *Jeth* sake? Here we are with a mizzenmast that *must* be reset and those delvers are playing around with a *dran* yacht!"

"Sire," Serg replied as formally as possible. "I beg to report that the optics to the mizzenmast are not salvageable. I recommend, sire, that we cut away the remaining lines and clear the—"

"Dresiv, that's the biggest barrel of *krava* I think I've ever heard! We *need* that mast. Without it we limp around the stars like a dog on one leg. It's come down to speed, man, speed! Speed and maneuverability! Didn't they teach you anything on Pax Prime?"

Serg winced at the reference. Apparently the former Second Master Bivis had been rummaging through the ship's files and had read his service scroll. He'd have to remember that in the future—if they had one. "Yes, sire. Speed and maneuverability were taught in our tactical courses. I would point out, *sire*, that the battle is now over. Surely we can afford some time to make our way to the next port, effect proper repairs, and—"

Bivis uttered a single explosive laugh with a hysterical edge to it. "Sure—sure we survived this assault! But what about the next one! They aren't going to let up now, Master Dresiv! Have you any idea how important this mission is?"

Serg's eyes narrowed. *The next one?* What the *Hesth* was he talking about. Dresiv tried to reply. "Well, I—"

"No! Of course, you don't! We've got a major diplomatic mission aboard our ship."

"Yes, sire." Serg kept his eyes locked on Bivis. "Emissary Hruna and Farcardinal Sabenth. They're here to welcome some world or other into the Pax Galacticus."

Bivis sneered. "That 'some world or other' is Kilnar—an important acquisition for the Pax here in the Athix Drift. *Hesth*, man, the celebrations of an entire planet have been arranged by the Brotherhood government there! If we're late, it will be a major diplomatic incident. A major embarrassment to the new government there! And, Third Master Dresiv, that is *exactly* why these Loyalists have attacked us here and why their second wave may be expected at any moment!"

"Uh, sire"—Serg shook his head—"this was just a raider vessel. I really don't think . . ."

"No, I don't suppose you do, Dresiv!" Bivis's voice was moving higher and higher in its panic. "You don't think that they just come one at a time, do you? *Hesth*, man, no one attacks a frigate of the Pax without planning. They certainly don't come alone. Sure! Send one in to cripple us, and when they know we're down, finish us off. We'll need all the sail we can muster for a fight."

Serg shifted slightly. He had hoped that Bivis would understand his arguments, but now he saw that their new captain had slipped a bit past reasoning. Serg's left hand reached for the neurolizer at the back of his battlesuit. *Some people,* he thought, *just never listen to reason.*

Bivis jabbed a finger toward Serg's nose. "Get below, Dresiv, and tell that QDO to stop playing with boats and get that mast repaired. There's been enough slacking off on this ship! Then get forward and see to the mainmasts. I want this ship battle-ready before—"

A dull succession of quick explosions rumbled through the ship, followed in an instant by a sudden listing of the gravity center to starboard. Serg, having expected something like this, quickly steadied himself against the large desk, but Bivis was caught unawares. He tumbled hard across the floor and against the low wall. The deck bucked and swayed in the rippling of conflicting gravity waves.

Serg gaped at the sight overhead.

The corsair's hull began to slowly pinwheel. The silverfire keel glowed brilliantly, writhing like a living thing as it tried to shake itself free of the splintering frame that held it in check. The main deck of the corsair was broken almost beyond recognition. As it turned, it streamed behind it a tangled web of optics, cables, and broken masts. The view of the wreck nearly filled the dome as it spun aft toward freedom.

Serg was so absorbed in the sight that he forgot, for a moment, why he had the paralyzing weapon in his hand at all.

"No!"

Serg turned toward Bivis's sudden cry.

Bivis had clawed his way up to the rail, his face all horror at the sight. "We've gotta stop it! We need . . . salvage. Yes, salvage. We can get the parts we need off the . . . you know! Fire the grappling hooks!" Bivis, suddenly pale, clawed at one of the blowers, his words almost incomprehensible. "Port weapon's master, stand by . . ."

There was a sound of something hitting thin metal as the neurolizer went off. Captain Bivis sighed as the wind left him. He collapsed with the blower still in his hand.

"Sorry, Master Bivis, but I think you need a nap." Serg stepped over the limp Bivis to look quickly over the rail. He could see Genni with the delvers far below desperately cutting snagged lines. Wherever the bucking derelict pulled a cable or line suddenly taut, the delvers leaped forward to cut free. The job was fearfully dangerous. The lines, straining with the weight of both ships, whipped furiously when cut. Men had been cut in half by such suddenly released lines but the delvers were quick to avoid them. Genni seemed to have the situation under control.

It was the debris still lodged on the quarterdeck that worried Serg. Nereth had lashed the whole of the mess to the captain's gig. The small boat was now under full sail with no one aboard and straining against the bulk of the wreckage. The crew on the deck, though slashing recklessly, couldn't seem to cut away enough snagged optics cable to get the wreck free.

Serg looked up again. The great hulk was now swinging downward. The cutters hadn't been able to clear the optics quickly enough. The corsair fell backward, still tied to the rigging of the frigate, and suddenly swung down toward the quarterdeck. Serg gripped the railing hard and crouched slightly against the impending collision. His eyes widened.

The remains of corsair slammed against the *Shendridan* quarterdeck. The collision thrust the deck downward with incredible force. The *Shendridan*'s own gravity field couldn't compensate for the tremendous impact. Serg gripped the railing against the plunge of the deck. As he watched, most of the deck crew had managed to do likewise. Those who hadn't were flung into the air—seemingly suspended there for an eternity.

The *Shendridan*'s long and elegant quarterdeck shattered into broken deck planks and timber. The wreckage lashed to the gig broke free, and, with the captain's boat, suddenly rushed into the clouds of the nebula. The remains of the corsair, now loose of all ties to the *Shendridan*, tumbled astern of the frigate. The airborne crew members, no longer caught between conflicting gravity fields, fell painfully to the broken deck. The gravity again righted itself. A heartbeat later Serg heard a dull thud behind him.

He suddenly remembered Bivis, and turned. He had left the captain lying unconscious on the deck. The new captain had been slammed against the dome headfirst with the impact. The glass overhead was now further cracked, as was the now-bleeding head of the short-term commander of the *Shendridan*.

"*Dran!* Sorry, Bivis." Serg stepped quickly over to Bivis and knelt beside him. "Looks like you may be sleeping longer than I really intended . . . I'll send you up a healer as soon as I can, *bungko*, but I've got to save your ship first."

6

Pressing Matters

"Captain Dresiv?" Trevis Fel leaned cautiously over the gaping hole in the bridge decking. With the cascade of noise around him, he wasn't all that sure that he was being heard. Even if he was heard, he wasn't sure he was being listened to. He felt awkward and out of place there, a priest kneeling next to a hole in a world of ships' captains and star delvers. Lately, however, he had become increasingly aware that he was awkward and uncomfortable wherever he was.

His entire life seemed to be an apology. Trevis stooped slightly in a constant repentance for his height of just over six feet. He tended to move his frame a bit awkwardly, as though he never had quite gotten use to his own size. His hair was a wispy white, as with all his people, but had a tendency to stick straight out from his head in places regardless of the care he took with combing it. He had tried to grow a beard, hoping somehow that it might add some dignity to his bearing, but it had come in a rather dirty blond. The effect was more comical than empowering—he had remained clean-shaven ever since as something of an apology for not being able to grow one effectively. His eyes were a shallow, brilliant blue set like diamonds beneath his heavy brows. This gave Trevis a rather hauntingly desperate appearance that often startled people who first met him. His robes draped straight down over his thin frame, which further added to his spectral aspect.

The robes, of course, were a necessity, as he was a Jezerinthian Localyte, servant and assistant to Farcardinal Sabenth of the Holy Union. It was a high calling and a cherished position for which he had worked many hard and long years. Assisting a Farcardinal was generally recognized by those in his order as the most advantaged situation from which to gain stature and position. Service as a Farcardinal's Localyte was the surest way to leadership in the Jezerinthians, and, once obtained, brought with it comfort and power for as long as one drew breath. It was the most contested assignment to which any of his peers could aspire.

Trevis wasn't sure it was what he wanted.

It hadn't always been so. There was a time when the lure of the stars called to him and the Jezerinthians had offered him the possibility of worlds and stars, cultures and opportunity unbounded. It had offered him a say in how the entire universe was run.

Having a say was Trevis's greatest dream. He had lived a life of being heard but never listened to. He had grown up a prince of his world, heir to the Nendrith Dynasty—a worthy title but in his case without much force. The truth was that he was the fifth in line for the throne (assuming none of his elder sisters contested it), and therefore, few in the court took him very seriously. They heard him politely but they never *listened* to him. Why should they? He would never be in a position to make a difference in any of their lives.

So he decided one day that he would make a difference, that he would set out into the great breadth of the galaxy and make himself heard there. The Jezerinthians served the Holy Union as an order whose talents and training made them the voice of communication across the galaxy. The prestigious Farcardinals, it was true, were the ones who actually communed with one another, but it took the Localytes to translate the thoughts and images they received into words. Why, theirs was the voice of the entire Pax! He would be a Jezerinthian and then his voice would be heard.

So he bade farewell to his tearful mother and his proud

father—he had at last gotten the old man's attention!—and boarded the Pax trade ship for the long trip to the Lyceum of Localytes.

The trip was, as all Groundlings first experience in space, both exciting and tedious at once. There is a tempo to shipboard life which is entirely its own, hurried and lazy at the same time. As they stopped at differing worlds for supplies, his senses were bombarded with the difference and sameness of each successive culture. As the number of worlds he knew grew from one to a dozen to a hundred and more, his attitude transformed from amazed to charmed to critical and finally apathetic. The uniqueness that was the spice of each world soon blended in his mind into an overpowering and unsavory mélange.

He was, in the end, relieved to arrive at the Lyceum and begin his academic training. He schooled. He practiced. He studied. There in the dim, ancient halls of the order he faced down the fact that their order was concerned primarily with the mechanics of their craft rather than the spiritual elements of their faith. He accepted. He compromised. He struggled. At long last he had mastered that craft and had been given his assignment: the highest, most prestigious posting of anyone in his class.

Now, with the best of all possible assignments of his order securely his, Trevis made a horrifying discovery. He was, indeed, being heard as he spoke many great and important words—but they were not *his* words! As a Localyte, his task was to interpret what the Farcardinal received—never to embellish or interpret. His opinions and thoughts were—irrelevant! He had learned the crafts and arts of the priesthood, only to become a puppet with a ventriloquist's voice.

After three years in the Lyceum and another year sailing from star to star with the Farcardinal, his burning enthusiasm for the great mission of the Union had cooled to embers. When the occasion permitted, he would ask an officer on the various ships on which he had sailed if he might—please—just look at Herath Sector Chart ANBZ84785. If the map cabinet held that chart—which, as they moved farther out in the Athix Drift they increasingly did not—then he would gaze at it for hours. His finger would trace the Ergo Downdrift slowly and stop ever so gently at the world of his birth. On such occasions he would long for that world, where, he knew sadly, he would prefer to be taken for granted by those who at least he knew loved him.

Now, adventure, battle, and conquest had visited themselves upon his ship, endangering his Farcardinal master and his very life. It was a time for action and valor. What had he done? He had waited dutifully with the Farcardinal as they both sat locked in their cabin. Only when the delver guarding them had said it was all over did Sabenth allow him to leave—and then only to deliver a message to the captain about meeting with the emissary and Sabenth.

So much for the romance of the stars, thought Trevis with a sigh.

Now he stood on what had once been an ornate and beautiful bridge. The compartment was now a shambles. What damage had not been done by the cannon fire from the renegade corsair had been finished by the crew trying to patch it back together. The great crystal dome that had once graced the bridge had vanished. It had been replaced by a framework of fitted glass panes. The once-polished deck was torn up all the way from the flying bridge to the foremast railing. The wheel, blowers, repeaters, and other various control mechanisms had simply been removed for repair elsewhere in the ship. Now delvers who had been working over two days without rest continued to crawl, hammer, shave, saw, and measure their way through the ruins.

Two heavy boots were all Trevis could see under the maze of cables and wide planks. Stark light cast strange shadows across the legs from somewhere near where the head connected to the feet should be. A muffled voice shouted out of the hole.

"Pol! Three-quarter spar, five and four-fifths hands long!"

Trevis glanced up at the delver kneeling on the other side of the great gash in the floor. "*Allai*, Serg. Ah, while I'm doing that, would you mind stickin' yer other end out. You have company." Pol returned Trevis's own look and grinned. "Go on, Father, give it another go."

"Captain Dresiv?" He had meant to make it sound firm and steady, but the voice came out more like a loud squeak.

The boots squirmed for a moment amid the dust-hazed gap in the deck. Then black hair filled with wood chips appeared.

"C-Captain," Trevis stammered. "I have come . . ."

Dresiv's gray eyes flashed once over the Localyte's robes. "Ah! A temple priest." In one fluid motion Serg pulled himself out of the hole in the deck. He stepped past Trevis to a pile of short cut timbers at one side of the bridge, talking all the while.

"I see that Mistress Ordina has finally graced us with a report. No matter, you're here now. I suppose they sent you up to report on the shrine." Serg grabbed a thin length of beam almost as tall as himself and pulled it free.

"Ah, er, well, Captain, that's not . . ."

"Not captain, boy." Serg turned abruptly, raising a warning finger. The gray eyes smoldered dangerously. "Call me Master Dresiv if you insist on being starched formal. I'm just temporary here until Captain Bivis can get back on his feet again."

"Er . . . *Allee*, Capt—eh—Master Dresiv."

"That's *allai*, boy, and I can only assume you've just fallen out of your planetary cradle if you can't even pronounce that." He had just set the timber on a rare clear space on the deck, when something caught his eye. "Hey! Delver K'Tahx! Yah, I'm talking to you. I need you to spin those control cables longer than the specification lengths in the ship's plans. The whole keel seems to be out just a little since we lost the quarterdeck."

"*Allai*, Captain."

Serg grimaced. "Don't call me . . ."

"Please, Master Dresiv," Trevis squawked, vaguely wondering what it was about him that somehow *forced* people not to listen to him. "I have come . . ."

"Right!" Serg reached for a wood plane and began working the plank smooth. "Look, Brother . . . ah . . ."

"Fel, sire. But . . ."

"Look, Brother Fel, I appreciate the concern of you and your brethren regarding the sacred silverfire source." Serg never looked up from his work, more curls of wood flying with his speed, some landing to add even further texture to his hair. "I need to know how stable the shrine is and how much sail does Shipwright Ordina think it safe to project."

"But I don't know."

"What do you mean, you don't know."

"But, sire! I'm not from the temple."

"You're not?" Lightning flashed again in the gray eyes. Dresiv set aside the plane and stood suddenly facing Trevis. "Well, who the *Hesth* are you, then?"

"I am Localyte Trevis Fel. I'm a Jezerinthian prospect in service to . . ."

"Yes, yes, yes—Cardinal, ah, whozits." Dresiv waved his hand limply in front of his face as if to dismiss the subject. "Why am I wasting air talking to you, Brother Fel?"

"The Cardinal is assisting . . ."

"Emissary Hruna." Dresiv rubbed his temples.

". . . yes, on a mission for the Pax and desires greatly to meet with you. I have been sent to find you and convey—"

"Fine!" Serg cut Trevis's discourse short with a single hand motion. "Pol, I guess it's time to practice diplomacy. Think you can keep us out of the Void until I get back?"

Pol gave a tired smile. "Serg, the main gallant sail is projected and we're slipping back into the center channel just fine. You go play politics . . . I'm going to get some sleep. Genni's rested and we've just set up shifts so that the crew can get some rest too."

"Nice piece of work. Maybe we can get the starboard main rerigged before tomorrow. We'll cast some wake, then, Pol!" Dresiv's smile faded as he turned to Trevis. "Okay, son, where's this party being held?"

"The only suitable place was your cabin, sire."

Serg frowned. "You mean the captain's cabin."

"*A-allai*, sire."

"I see you take the captain's cabin, Master Dresiv—most fitting." Pax Emissary Hruna Nruthnar purred her words in multiple harmonics as she deftly laid a large, soft tapestry in front of the desk. In fluid grace she then folded her six legs under her to sit on the beautiful rug. Though seated on the floor opposite him across the desk, Serg was still constrained to look up at the large Thrund.

Despite the vast number of worlds encountered in the galaxy, the Thrund were one of the few truly alien races that had been assimilated into the Pax. The Pax made no secret that it was primarily a humanoid-centric organization. Early history of the Pax conquests distilled down to three tenents: if it's human, convert it; if it isn't, conquer it; and if it won't be conquered—kill it.

Yet when the expanding Pax empire had finally come against the Thrund at the time of the Fourth Expanse, they would neither be conquered or killed. The Thrund fleets—thousands of beatific radial-designed ships reminiscent of trees—were graceful, natural, swift, and deadly. The Thrund were arboreal, naturally used to thinking tactically in three dimensions and unfazed by the lack of gravity beyond their world. They were, therefore, formidable deep-space opponents. The war was fought viciously on both sides. In the end—so the official Pax history recorded—it was the honor, understanding, and diplomatic skills of the Thrund that finally won for both sides. The peace that was forged allowed full citizenship to the Thrund: the first remarkably nonhumanoid race admitted into the Pax.

Thrunds stood nearly three meters tall when angered—few have survived an encounter with an enraged Thrund long enough to take the measurement. Their body was a humped torso from which radiated nine appendages; six legs and three "necks." The main of their body was supported by the muscular legs. Those who have seen the Thrund moving among their native trees have told of the remarkable ability the creatures had to move gracefully overhead with their legs fully extended in many directions at once. When moving along flat ground, as most humans saw them, Thrund naturally squatted down, carrying the torso low toward the ground much in the manner of arachnids. Each of their legs ended in long-fingered feet—normally gloved. Thrunds were dexterous enough to do fine manipulation with these appendages, each of which had two horizontally opposed thumbs working with four additional fingers.

The three additional appendages seemed to defy anatomical description. They were neither head nor tail nor arm, although they performed a combination of the functions of all three. Thick at their common muscular base, they tapered toward the ends, where they split into two branches. One of these branches was another set of manipulator "hands" with an additional set of two fingers and an opposing thumb. The second branch was a sensory pod containing a large, featureless eye of shining black. Each of these appendages shared a common base near the "back" of the Thrund—at least it was commonly perceived as the rear lest the creatures were in the habit of traveling backward. All three normally curved gracefully over the main body of the creature, arching forward rather formidably. As there were three of these appendages, the Thrunds appeared at first glance to have three heads. Early in the wars, jokes had been made about individual Thrunds being unable to make up their minds. The truth was that the Thrunds' single brain pan was located under the well-boned hump on its torso back. Indecision was never a problem for the Thrund.

Most remarkable of all, however, were the flexible diaphragms and several smaller versions of the same which covered the boned hump. This proved to be one of the most magnificent sound-producing organs known to nature. The Thrund "voice" was capable of simultaneous harmonics at various pitches that exceeded any human ear. It had been speculated that this remarkable anatomical feature may have evolved when the Thrunds were in trees and could use such sound to lure their prey. Serg had once even heard a Thrund musician reproduce an entire symphony in all its various instrumental parts as a solo work. He remembered the sound as being the most exquisite rendition of the piece he had ever heard.

Much of Thrund anatomy was, of course, guesswork, as Hruna and all her kind wore traditional robes that covered most of the body features when among strangers. Only the sensory "faces," triple manes running the length of the Thrund "necks," and the vocal diaphragms were ever exposed in public. Thrunds had their own ideas of decency and modesty, to which they adhered strictly and which made little sense to anyone but a Thrund.

As Serg looked at the Thrund squatting in front of him—covered with fabric and ornamental jewelry—he was suddenly struck with the thought that Thrunds must occasionally be mistaken for a piece of overdesigned heavy furniture. The only thing that he could be sure of was that the Thrund was female. Thrund society was exclusively matriarchal in organization and custom—the only Thrund one saw in any official Pax position was female.

Dangerous as the Thrunds were in battle, they had a far more effective set of weapons for obtaining what they wanted than raw strength and armament. The Thrund ability to bridge cultural gaps became legendary. Their service as ambassadors and emissaries for the Pax had been so successful that over half of the imperial diplomatic corps was soon comprised exclusively of Thrunds. This, coupled with the deeply articulated and harmonic voices—Thrunds even in one-on-one conversation liked to affect their speech as though they were multiple voices—made them far more dangerous as negotiators than as warriors.

Serg sighed and tried to prepare himself. Enter into polite conversation with a Thrund, so the saying went, and you'll either buy something too expensive, sell something too cheaply, or lose something before you're done. He hadn't yet finished with the greetings, and it was already time to consider his words carefully.

"It's the only place on the ship left where all the communications still function. I don't have much choice." Serg leaned back in the great captain's chair and set his feet up on the desk. Considering the number of ship's plans, navigation maps, and notes that covered it, it was remarkable that he could find room enough for them. His posture probably offended Farcardinal Sabenth—seated in a chair to the right of the Thrund—but the gesture was one of courtesy to the Thrund. "I have other reasons for taking these quarters—all of which have to do with running this ship and nothing to do with the captaincy."

The Thrund let that point slip by easily, gesticulating toward the other two entities that had accompanied him. "You know my Farcardinal Sabenth, and I believe you have met his Localyte, Trevis Fel."

Serg crossed his arms and eyed the two. Sabenth appeared to be a human of the Berdin type, for the angle of the jaw seemed to follow that line. The shock of golden hair at the back of the neck, however, was a certain giveaway to some recent crossing of his genealogy with humans of the Haven States. That would make him an outcast among his own people. No wonder such a person of an obviously propertied and powerful family was rambling about the extremes of the galaxy.

He still hadn't been able to place the boy's origin. The white hair could be an aberration, he supposed, but he rather favored the odds that it was a new strain of human he had not yet become familiar with. The galaxy was just too *dran* big.

"Yes. I met the Farcardinal once at the captain's table. Localyte Fel has just introduced himself." Serg turned to the young man. "Father, you are of the Jezerinthian order, are you not?"

"Why—yes, sire."

"I thought so." Serg nodded. "I believe your order has some training in temple work and silverfire mysteries, doesn't it?"

Light flashed in the Localyte's eyes. "Yes, sire, although we—well, we seldom are given opportunity to practice that art."

Serg turned to the Farcardinal. "Your grace, might I impose on you. I would ask to borrow your Localyte to assist in the temple. Mistress Ordina—our shipwright priestess—has just informed me that she is in need of additional assistance in getting the ship under way. Father Fel here could be of great help to us right now."

"Well," sniffed Sabenth, "I don't know that I can spare my aide at this . . ."

"Please, your grace!" Trevis interrupted. "May I please go? I've never actually had the chance to work in a temple, let alone a temple of the Pax fleets."

Sabenth turned to the boy with an answer, but his expression changed when he saw the eagerness in the Localyte's eyes. An understanding smile crossed Sabenth's wide face. "Yes, my son, go and work in the temple for a time. I suspect you'll be of little use to me until you do."

"May I go now, your grace?"

"Of course."

Trevis nearly knocked over his own chair in his rush to leave. *One down, two to go,* Serg thought to himself, and then said, "Good sires, I am aware of your mission from the captain's logs and his Writ of Charter. You are both en route to Kilnar to represent the Pax in their acceptance into the empire, a most important mission indeed. I apologize for not being able to meet with you sooner, I've been somewhat preoccupied for the last few days."

"As we have heard, Master Dresiv." Hruna's voices purred in silky harmony. "A most impressive rescue and the capture of the renegade leader as well. Indeed, it is the woman that concerns us at this time."

"The woman?" Serg questioned.

"The captain of the privateer."

"Ah, of course, go on."

The Cardinal spoke suddenly, his voice sounding thin and reedy. "The Ether has granted us knowledge concerning her from our brother on Kilnar. She is—"

Serg held up his hand. "You have joined communion with the Farcardinal on Kilnar? When did Mistress Ordina give you access to the silverfire?"

Hruna smoothly spoke. "Sadly, Captain, we were not aware that permission was required. Our communion was cut off by your good mistress shipwright while it was still in progress. It is, in fact, why we wish to speak to you."

"Of course, Madam Emissary, but first things first." Serg turned back to Sabenth. "What about our prisoner?"

"She is of the house of Haught-Cargil and still fights the unification of her world." Sabenth leaned forward, replying rather too conspiratorially for Serg's liking. "The World Brotherhood on Kilnar seek her out as a traitor to their common cause and wish to make an example of her. Inasmuch as Kilnar is our destination . . ."

"Brev is our destination, my lords," Serg said abruptly, "not Kilnar."

"But, Master Dresiv!" Sabenth blustered.

Serg swung his feet down and sat forward across the desk. "My lords, we have barely been able to clear the Clouds of Thel on the single sail that remains operative. Unless this crew can rig a new sail on the starboard side, it may take us weeks to make Brev when a day should do. Passage for you to Kilnar can be arranged once we make planetfall. Until that time, my only concern is making one destination, and that destination is Brev."

"Surely," said the Thrund, all three obsidian eyes flashing at once, "you realize that these are the farthest outpost worlds of the Pax. Interstellars are not just rare but often are not seen on some of these worlds for months. We journey to Kilnar to welcome that world into the Pax Galacticus. The ceremonies and festivals have been scheduled for over a season's time."

"That schedule was also, no doubt, known to our prisoner and her crew." Serg smiled to himself and sat back, shaking his head. "*Lorn*, what a delver! She must have sailed the whirlpools of the nebula for weeks, waiting just for us.

"I also understand your mission perhaps better than you think. The Rule of One was formalized some four thousand years ago under the influence of the Disciples of Nar but more accurately parallels the Pact of the Knights' Rebellion. The Rule of One states that no world without a single world government is sufficiently advanced for interstellar contact. Through the Second and Third Expansions, the Rule of One has made galactic consensus manageable, government of the Pax possible, and planetary warfare relatively unnecessary. The policy hasn't worked very well with the Zhun, who are highly territorial in all things large and small. It has also failed to stop the secession of the Haven States from the Pax. It would apparently also have caused problems here on your precious new world of Kilnar. Still, it seems to be a good policy if you don't look too closely at individual worlds. No need to look surprised, *Hsthanish* Nruthnar. I was born on Cantra Primus. I've seen a lot of the galaxy to get this far."

The Thrund's cupped ears on each head swiveled forward at

the sound of the most distinguished form of address in her language.

The Farcardinal was not used to being put off. "Couldn't the required repairs to the *Shendridan* be made at Brev to allow us continuance of our journey?"

Serg stood. "Yes, your excellency, but that is a matter which you will have to take up with the captain—when he recovers. Now, if you will please excuse me, I have a ship to tend."

"Master Dresiv!" the Farcardinal blustered.

"Indeed," the Thrund smoothly interrupted, "we have not yet concluded our business, good Master Dresiv. As our communications were interrupted, might you at least allow us to complete them?"

Dresiv's eyes narrowed. "You wish to complete your communication with Kilnar? "

"Yes," the Thrund chimed in a perfect chord.

Serg needed to communicate with Brev. There was much that the ship needed to get her back in shape again. If Brev were aware of their condition before they arrived, it could cut down on the refit time considerably. More than that, it was dangerous to be aboard a wounded ship too long on the frontier. Predators were always more eager for wounded prey.

However, asking the Farcardinal to contact Brev rather than Kilnar would just result in a longer argument, one he wasn't sure he could win. Perhaps, he thought, there was another way.

"Emissary Hruna, I shall be glad to honor your request on one condition."

"Yes?" Hruna purred, though something inside Dresiv told him the Thrund's voice was a little tentative.

"That you first ask the Kilnar Farcardinal to pass a detailed account of our condition to Brev before concluding your own conversations." Serg smiled his response. "It will allow us to get the ship repaired sooner—and, I would point out, get you all the sooner to Kilnar."

"Why, Master Dresiv! Such was our intention from the first!" hummed the Thrund in a sound that filled the room. "Now, I am curious about your home world. I have never been there, as such, and was wondering—"

"Some other time." Serg stood abruptly. "I have much to do. How long until you will be ready to commune with Kilnar?"

Sabenth blinked. "About three hours, I think . . ."

"Please call me when you are ready. If you will now excuse me, there is much to prepare." Without further explanation, Serg left.

As Dresiv disappeared toward the bridge, the Farcardinal spoke. "A son of Cantra Primus! What is one of the Highblood doing out here on the frontier?"

"Indeed," murmured the Thrund in soft, low voices. "What drives a man from the center of all civilization so very far into the night?"

7

Below Decks

LLEWELLEN SECTOR / ANCJ14496 / UPDRIFT BREV /
CLOUDS OF THEL THE SHENDRIDAN

"Krith! Thyne abroad—I sure it now. When strike?"

The old delver, swaying in his hammock, looked down his iron-gray, bristled beard past his feet at the girl and sniffed. Krith Sonath-Paun, as anyone who knew him would confirm, could smell any and all advantages and profit in all times and circumstances—even in the heart of a Pax lockup. It was a gift, a kind of inner light and compass. It had kept him out of more than one prison and had freed him from many more. The gift told him when greed had pushed a man past sense—that was the time to swindle him. The voice whispered to him when a ship was filled with wealth—that was the time to redistribute it among his own mates. Now, swaying gently in his bunk, it served him still. Deep inside his massive frame, Krith knew that the time was not yet ripe to strike.

The willowy child swaying with the rest of creation between his feet was all wet eyes, full of dreams and glory. Her edge hadn't yet been tempered with too much blood nor sharpened by a companion's treachery. They called her Snap—as much for her swinging temperament as her staccato voice—though she was a first-rate Weaver of Spirit. Her enthusiasm knew no boundaries and far exceeded anyone else's desires. Still, she was inexperienced in the ways of the stars. She was small as humans go, with slight features and a rough tussle of blond hair that never seemed in order regardless of the care she took—when she bothered. Her magic was her love and the Loyalist cause her conviction. She was, in Krith's eyes, an idealist ... and therefore a dangerous person in dire need of a quick education.

Besides, he thought as he shifted slightly in the hammock, she was stirring up the rest of the crew. The Pax keepers had crammed them all into a single large compartment at the aft end of the lower gun deck. While the support posts and beams provided a delver with sufficient opportunity to rig his hammock, the nearly twenty of his shipmates stuffed into the compartment made it stiflingly tight. The effect of all the hung bedding was more like stacking wood than proper sleeping quarters. It was close and hot. Even with the ports to the ships' atmospheric envelope open, Krith still had the uneasy feeling that he was breathing too much of other people's air.

"Soon enough, Snap. When 'e's Mistress's ready and the time be right, then we move. Be you sure the Lady's aboard?"

"Sure I!"

"Eh, how 'about it, Krith?" Wethen, the weathered delver, swung slowly in his bedding near the floor to Krith's right. It seemed almost an effort to work himself up to the thought as he spoke with his eyes closed. "D'ya think we might spring free from this net?"

"I've seen worse and lived for the telling of it, chummer. It ain't a matter of *if*—just when, that's all."

"Eh, Snap!" said Yantha, a thin delver leaning against the corner of the compartment. He was still a beardless youth but had eyes that had seen too much for such an age. "Give with the magics. Whammy-jammy the lock-keep and let's make for it."

"Ah, batten yer trap, Yantha." Krith settled deeper into his hammock and pulled his cap down over his face. "Snap'll do her job when the time gets its coming and not afore. Get some sleep-shift, will ya. You'll be no good to the captain with smoke in yer mind. Our Lady Thyne will give us the word when the time comes."

"Ya, but how we gonna know, Krith? Maybe the captain can't shake the lock-keep on her own? Maybe she dying? Maybe she ain't even aboard the—"

"You heard the kid, Yantha. If the little Weaver's picked her up, then she can't be all that far . . ."

"Maybe"—Yantha frowned—"but that don't mean she's walkin' the decks. I'm thinkin' she could be in need of our assistance."

"Ah, the brave picture of heroic action," Berana, the gunnery officer, sneered. She squatted next to the wall, though, Krith could tell, by habit she wasn't leaning very hard against it. She was all steel, cold and hard. No one knew where she came from, although everyone had an opinion, none of which agreed. Berana herself was quiet on the subject of her past. She took only standard delver pay although she rated more as an officer. Berana still wore her battle armor, cobbled together pieces of different sets and styles that somehow fit. Two of the Pax dolts had insisted that she remove it when they brought her aboard. She refused, claiming that it was all she was wearing. They had demanded a search for weapons. One of them got away with only a broken leg. The other had probably not yet regained consciousness. In the end, the courageous Pax guards had decided to simply force her back into the prisoner compartment with the business end of several handcannons.

Berana turned her face up toward Yantha and smiled dangerously. "Yantha's looking to come to the Lady's rescue, mates! I can't imagine the reward he'll be asking next."

Yantha flushed at the laughter from the rest of the crew. He turned hotly toward the young Weaver. "You got the Light or not, Snap? These fish seem to think you're shy of the mark. You gonna show the Grounders who's got the way, or no?"

Snap nearly trembled. "Snap juiced high. Snap show grounddelvers Weaver magic! Show delvers free-walking!"

His low grumble escalated into a roar by the time Krith rolled loose of his bunk. In the small compartment he needed to take only a step before reaching Yantha. Krith was huge. Those who didn't know him often thought that he was in poor shape. It was a mistake never repeated by anyone who thought him an easy mark. He lifted the thin delver off the deck and tossed him— overhand—into the mass of hung hammocks filled with delvers. The stays gave way under the impact, the whole of the mess falling to the floor in a seething jumble of tarpaulin, rope, and enraged delvers.

"We move when it's time, boy, and not before." Krith bellowed. "You have the need to get yourself cut down by the *karks* at the door, that's your mindspin, but I have a thought to keep my hide stuck to my meat until our Lady the captain tells us it's time to move on! This ain't no yacht, farmer! Move wrong on this barge and your frozen skull might float home before the end of the next millennium."

The iron latch grated at the single planked door entering the room. Krith froze instinctively.

The door swung inward. Two battle-armored sentries stood blocking the exit, their handcannons leveled into the room. Behind them, almost completely hidden by the gargantuan guards, a high-pitched voice sounded out. "What goes here?"

"Ah, begging your great pardon, sire!" Krith smiled the most polite smile in his rather large arsenal. " 'Twas just a disagreement between shipmates as to sleeping accommodations. The men are a bit tired after so sorely fought a battle. They also be most disheartened to bear the loss of their great ship. There'll be no further difficulties on this account, sire."

"Well, then, see to it and no more disturbances. The word to you is to keep your peace until you can be brought before the tribunal. We are ordered to maintain the peace and have the authority to enforce it."

Officious little tick, thought Krith through his smile. Still, he replied, "You can be sure we will keep that in mind, sire. We surrender ourselves to your ship and its justice." Krith gestured widely through his open arms and bowed. He could see that the little officer hiding behind the armored goons was lapping his performance up like cream.

"I am sure that your cooperation will be a factor taken into account when your case gets its hearing." The voice squeaked.

"My thanks, and that of my grateful men, sire! We shall be more quiet so as not to disturb your sleep further."

The officer blinked but retreated. In moments the bolt was again thrown and the room was theirs alone.

Krith picked up the dazed Yantha, this time setting him upright. "Snap says the captain's aboard, and that's enough for me. She knew she couldn't stop this wagon with our fine little craft, so she had another trick in mind. Don't be blowin' away the entire haul just for a few more hours in stir!" Krith turned to the rest of the crew. "Well, stop yer gawkin' and get them hammocks back up. We have a long haul ahead of us, and you'll be no good to the Lady if you're snoozing upright."

Krith swung himself back into his own bedding and was just settling in, when the thin voice quivered near his ear.

"Snap sorry. Snap hero yet if be good."

"Ya, kid, now, settle down and get some sleep-shift. We gotta be ready when the captain gives the call."

Krith rolled slightly and found his favorite place in his tarp. Heroes! Everyone wanted to be a hero these days. The Loyalists in exile all wanted to be heroes in getting their dustball planet back. He understood the Brotherhood better. They, at least, were out for the power and wealth that a unified world government made possible. Now, *there* was a motive he could understand. *There* was a motive he was in complete sympathy with. The only problem Krith had was that he didn't fit into the closed circle of the Brotherhood and, therefore, was denied what he believed was his due—and rather large—share of the wealth and power.

The Loyalists, on the other hand, retained their rather provincial view of right and wrong in a galaxy that was more vast than they could possibly imagine. They couldn't offer wealth that was really worth anything. Their real assets had all been taken by the new world government. The Loyalists had, of course, appealed to the greater good in all their fellows to right a terrible injustice. This had netted them but a handful of followers. It hadn't been enough.

So they offered something else that in the end garnered to them a tremendous—if somewhat undependable—following. They simply gave their moral sanction to steal.

Actually, the more proper term historically was "privateer," and by thus condoning such piracy they had stumbled on a high moral ground from which to hire mercenaries and add to their own coffers at the same time.

Krith was firmly in the camp of whoever was paying the highest. And, he smiled to himself, if the Lady Thyne pulled this one off, they would be living well for quite a while yet to come.

Thyne stared silently yet again at the guard at her door. Standing with her legs set wide and her arms folded solidly across her chest, she stood motionless—her large eyes fixed precisely on the forehead of the young humanoid guarding her. Now and again she would move suddenly, pacing the small and featureless cell with all the intensity of a caged and obviously dangerous animal. Then, with an equal abruptness, she would again stand in the same pose, staring for minutes at a time.

Her gaze told her all she needed to know about the pup guarding her. He had told her his name when he had come on shift two hours before. Her question had been more a command than a request: her first and only words to him. Since then she had repeated unerringly the routine of pace and stand, pace and stand, for this Delver Kilfnan and watched him unravel under her gaze. Her mind considered him closely. *Does a single river of molten sweat make its way down the middle of your back, Delver Kilfnan? Do your dry eyes burn? Is your throat dust-dry, Kilfnan?*

Each cycle brought her a little closer to the boy by the door. Each cycle brought the boy closer to panic. It was a dangerous game—turn the tail of the kid too much and he was likely to do something stupid. Something, she reminded herself, like splitting her with that handcannon his fingers moved over a little too nervously. However, if she played him well, she'd get what she wanted.

She raised her head slightly. Yes, she thought, this looked like the right moment. She took a single step toward him.

The boy's eyes widened at once. With a jerk, his handcannon swung down level and the bolt was slammed shut.

Thyne laughed suddenly, bright and gay.

The guard stared at her. *He's wondering if I've lost my mind. He's off balance now.*

"You're good, I'll give you that," Thyne said, her voice sparkling like sunshine.

The tension of the moment before shattered like glass. Suddenly, Thyne was relaxed and personable. Confusion mixed with relief danced openly on her target's face. Kilfnan had taken the bait, his perceptions reeling, plunging from sharp-edged fear into a sea of confusion.

"M-ma'am?"

She set her hands on her hips, but it was with her eyes that she held his attention. The iced hatred those eyes had projected a moment before suddenly melted into a warm laughter filled with the distant memory of summer. She saw the handcannon waver.

"Delver Kilfnan, don't be so modest with me. I sadly admit

that I have had occasion to be guarded from time to time." She filled her eyes with sadness the boy could swim in. "I was once guarded as a princess of my people. Now I am an outcast in a just cause. Being of the Pax, however, I don't suppose that you would know much about such things."

The story was partly true. She wasn't a princess by any real sense of title, but the tale sounded better for it. Lies are always easier to believe when they are liberally seasoned with truth. She hung her head slightly but her eyes never left him. Thyne gave every evidence of being relaxed—but she didn't take a step back. She coiled the power deep inside her—preparing to release it.

"No, ma'am, I don't know a great deal about the local stellar group. Where're you from?"

"Kilnar."

"Really? That's where we're—uh—"

" 'That's where we're going?' I know." She laughed sunlight once again. "Oh, come now, sire, surely I already knew that. It's hardly a secret, now. Let's see, you're heading for Kilnar as representatives of the Pax for the acceptance of the world into your galactic order. I only wish that we had been able to stop you."

"Ma'am, I just don't understand that. The Pax offers trade with uncountable new worlds! The empire's knowledge and learning spans almost a thousand pardymes of intelligent life— nearly half the galactic disk! Its fleets keep order among world nations. Why would anyone want to stop such progress?"

Thyne knew that the boy was belching back lines to her right from page one of the *Pax Delver's Manual of Trite Phrases*. She'd heard the argument before—she had experienced all too clearly consequences of the policy.

"You ask why? Your law may be just in many places in the galaxy"—another lie as far as Thyne was concerned—"but it has failed my world. Unjust rulers oppress the great—uh—oh, what is the word for 'many people'?"

"Majority?" the delver offered.

"Yes! Thank you—majority of the people." Thyne smiled thinly. "I am sorry, I am afraid that your language remains rather difficult for me." Another lie, but the smile seems to cover it well enough, she thought.

"But you speak the Paxish very well." Kilfnan smiled gallantly. "Well, there are places, I suppose, where tyrants rule. In time, however, the influence of many thousands of worlds asserts itself. The right prevails."

And by that time all my people will be dead, thought Thyne. The dead have little consolation in being right by history. Extinct nations and cultures have no use for apologies. Thyne reined in her emotions under a surface of calm and a face filled with false hope.

"Do you really think so? We've fought for so long!"

"Surely, M'Lady, the Pax would never allow unjust rule to triumph over time!"

Bold words, delver, but your handcannon's been dropping to your side. Thyne's mind raced. Time about her slowed.

She took a small step toward him. "Perhaps I could appeal to your captain." *If I hadn't personally blasted him down to his chemical components,* she completed to herself. "Perhaps he could do something that could put our people at peace."

"I don't know—the captain . . ."

"Please, Sire Kilfnan! Please give me some hope!" she begged as she took another step forward. Thyne stood within inches of the cell's iron bars, close enough now for her arms to reach the delver. Her eyes held his in their steady gaze.

"But the captain is . . ."

Thyne never looked from his face, her hands moving slowly through the bars toward the guard's handcannon. *Sorry, Kilfnan, this is gonna hurt.*

A new voice, cold and quiet, intruded on them.

"Hey, Wenther, why don't you just ask her to dance while you're at it?"

The delver shook himself loose from Thyne's gaze. His handcannon snapped back up to threaten her. "Sorry, Master Genni, we were just talking, and . . ."

"Reported and on record, delver." Genni drew his own handcannon and turned his attention to the tall female. His wary eyes were on her, though he spoke to the delver. "Get to a blower and tell Master Dresiv that the Loyalist captain would like to see him."

Thyne once more had become the wall of ice. No emotion crossed her face as she again stood stiffly tall.

Genni eyed her cooly. "You *do* want to speak to the master of this vessel, don't you?"

"My concern is for the well-being of my remaining crew. I demand to inspect them and their quarters." Her words fell like ice from her lips.

"That you will have to take up with Master Dresiv—when he has the time to hear you." He turned to the returning Kilfnan. "Delver, you are relieved of this Scepter. I now have the Scepter of watch on the prisoner."

"*Allai*, sire."

"What did Master Dresiv say?"

"His word was that he would call for the prisoner sometime before the end of the next watch but was occupied at present."

"Thank you, Wenther. Go and get some sleep, will ya? You don't look so well."

"It's been a difficult shift, sire."

Genni checked his own handcannon, ignited the standby chamber, and took a good look at Thyne.

She again stood in the middle of the cell, her legs apart and her arms folded over her chest. Her large eyes stared at him. She would try again. She would do whatever was necessary. She might fail a dozen times, but she would eventually succeed.

Genni cleared his throat.

Delver Genni, she thought, *you're going to have the longest shift of your life. If I'm lucky, it will also be your last.*

8

Enlightenment

~~~~~

Llewellen Sector / ANCJ14496 / Updrift Brev /
Marker +65 The Shendridan

Trevis crossed the raised threshold from the anteroom and stood
breathless on the temple balcony. A wave of dizziness passed
over him from the height—in his eagerness he had entered the
compartment at the High Vaulting level and thus found himself
gaping down from the top of the largest compartment in the ship.
Due to the forced perspective of the vertical compartment, it
looked even taller than the five decks it already was. He steadied
himself against the railing and grinned broadly. Usually shy and
reserved, he harbored no hope of disguising his excitement now.
This was the temple—it was the center of worship for every
Jezerinthian Priest, though few of his order ever were offered opportunity to enter its sacred confines. To work in a temple—even
a ship's temple—was a hope that Jezerinthian Localytes only
dreamed of during lapses of humility.

Trevis was awestruck, nearly moved to tears. The nave of the
temple extended down from the balcony where he stood through
five decks to the polished marble floor below. The young
Localyte knew each level by its name—from the High Vaulting,
where he now stood, through the Vaulting, Clerestory, Triforium,
and, finally, the Arcade floor itself. Iron buttresses sprang up

from the deck of the Arcade along both walls to form the vaults above, giving strength to the compartment. Yet it was not the vastness of the open space contained in the prow of the ship that moved him, but the beauty of its fixtures.

At a casual glance, it appeared that an impossible great tree—a glistening lace of light for its leaves—had grown to fill the compartment. This brilliant trunk branching into the nave was, in fact, the Transtator. The Transtator was the means of distributing silverfire throughout the ship. Its optical filaments were both veins and nerves to the *Shendridan*; the basic motive power for virtually every main system aboard.

The Transtator, as with most things in the temple, was more than just functional—it was a religious icon beautiful to behold. The base of the Transtator was a massive gleaming disk on the main floor of the nave. This disk supported five exquisite statues: the Sisters Ga'alna. The sisters represented the spirits of time and distance who first harnessed the power of the silverfire spirit to the greater glory of Elim—the god of all. The graceful arms of the sisters arched upward to support the Transtator sphere itself, a tumble of opalescent light. The trunk of the tree extended up from this sphere: a massive optics conduit that then proceeded to split and branch again and again into the vaulting open space of the compartment. Each branch of this brilliantly glowing tree entered the walls of the temple at various places, carrying with it the power of the temple—giving life to the ship. At each terminus of the optical trunks, by means of the magic with which each member part was imbued, the silverfire was transformed into that which was needed. It wove itself into the great darkwind sails that turned nature around and sailed their craft among the stars. It drove the keel hard into some invisible place where the ship could be stable and have a reference on which to chart its course. It nourished the atmospheric envelope that gave breath to her crew. It lit the halls. It warmed them. It protected them.

Yet it was the three-level altar immediately aft of the tree that drew his attention. Four ornately turned granite pillars towered up into the nave, supporting the main dais at a level parallel to the Transtator Sphere. On that dais, the Great Altars of the temple were tended by the Temple Priestess—known aboard ships, Trevis reminded himself, as the shipwright.

Directly below those altars, Trevis knew, was the Ark of Transent. Silverfire was generated by the Transent, a crystal structure that some heretics claimed had life of its own. It was never static, never the same. It constantly changed and grew, feeding off itself. Early legends told of how those who even glanced at the simultaneous growth and destruction of the Transentstone could be driven mad by its changing patterns. No one in modern historical times had tested that legend and lived to challenge it. As for his own order, Trevis's faith was firm: the power of the seething crystalline structure was linked directly to Elim, the god that made all things.

The religion of Elim was interstellar, pancultural, and all-encompassing. As each world entered the Pax, so, too, was the religion of each world brought slowly in line with Elim. This was not as difficult as it might seem, for Elim never asked any culture to give up any native belief. Elim philosophy and teaching accepted all the diversity of creation as a part of the great reality of Elim. If that meant occasional odd contradictions between two vastly different cultures—well, that contradiction was itself part of Elim.

Transentstone was Elim among them. It was the power of creation itself: the heart and soul of Pax worship and religious thought. More than that, to Trevis and all the different orders of the Union of Spirit, it was a complete mystery of the most compelling sort. Transent, Trevis breathed to himself, is as close as a priest could get to touching god.

Trevis literally shook himself from his reveries, the grin still spread across his face. It had taken a conversation with the shipwright herself to allow him passage into the temple at all. Now that he was there, he wondered if he could ever leave.

"At last, something worthwhile," Trevis whispered as much to Elim as to himself. He moved quickly to the thin staircase spiraling down to the main dais. He could even now see the shipwright gazing up at him impatiently. "Please," he prayed, "help me do this right."

Master Shipwright Ordina was wondering just how much help the Localyte was going to be to her. She'd been weaving reflective magic around the Transent core for over a hour now. Ordina had initially been relieved to have collared the young cleric come to assist her. Now, after an unending stream of questions, she despaired of ever filling the vacuous brain of this backwater boy.

"The center of its power shifts from time to time with the

structures that surround it." She felt like she was giving a devotional lecture at the seminary. "Look, there. Those eight-sided structures on your left are indicative of a four-factor shift in the mean core position. By drawing the field back and polarizing it to this twelve-faceted structure, we can continue to build power in the core and allow for more growth yet."

The boy remained undeterred by the technicality of her explanations. He seemed to Ordina, somehow, to revel in the lyric without understanding the words. "Where did it come from—I mean, I know that it was a gift from *Elim* to the children of the stars—but what is its history?"

Ordina nearly lost her concentration, snapping a look at him of total incredulity. "You don't know the tale of Lord Merik of Candus? Great *Hesth*, kid, what rock have you been living on?"

Trevis just stared eagerly at her. *Jez,* Ordina thought, the boy's so eager, he can't even be insulted. "Lord Merik was the ruler on a fragmented world known as Candus. He was a good and just ruler, but there were kingdoms bordering his own that threatened him with destruction. His lands were rich where theirs were poor; seemed that was reason enough to be disliked. One night, as Lord Merik prayed, Transent fell from the sky into his lands. It was an answer from *Elim*. With the power of the—hey! Loose your grip on that phase pattern again, boy, and you set us back several hours work!"

"Sorry, Mistress Ordina. Please—please continue!"

She sighed. "So Lord Merik used the power of the silverfire that came from the crystal and unified his world. In time, he desired that the peace he had established on his own world be shared with all creation. Thus the great Crusades began to the stars." Ordina was reciting a rather condensed but official version of the tale. She personally had considerable doubts about it. Merik may or may not have actually prayed, and the fact that the stone fell in his little parcel of land may have been chance rather than in answer to his supplications. As for the peace he had established on his world, that was simply conversion through superior firepower. She occasionally wondered just who they would be honoring with this tale if the Transent had fallen a few kilometers across Merik's border.

"Ah, I see!" said the boy in reverent tones. "So, where *is* Candus?"

Ordina rewove another reflective structure and shuddered. This boy hadn't lived on a rock, he'd lived under one.

"Mistress Ordina, my pardon, but Cardinal Sabenth has asked that I bring this Localyte to him for assistance," a quiet and warm chorus of voices sounded behind her.

Ordina turned and actually jumped. The sight of a Thrund was enough to unnerve people who were expecting them. It hadn't helped that the Thrund, thinking it more polite, had moved behind Ordina with absolute silence.

"Of c-course, Emissary Hruna. I shall manage without the assistance of your Localyte. Please give my thanks to the Cardinal for his diligence in offering the help." She turned to the crestfallen Trevis. "Sorry, dearie, but we all have our duties. Perhaps we'll talk later?"

As the Localyte left, Ordina turned back to the main altar, smiling to herself. "The kid has promise," she murmured to herself. "If only he wasn't such a vacuum."

Trevis followed the Thrund aft through the temple doors exiting the dais and into the antechamber. In the ancient of days—and in many more civilized parts of the galaxy—the temple itself—known as the Sanctuary—was a holy place where common people were never allowed to tread. Shipboard, however, things were of necessity different as, for that matter, was the function of the ship's temple. In cities or communities the temple's purpose was support of the population and, to a large extent, weather control. Such concerns did not often require hasty action, and the luxury of privacy was assured. Aboard ship, however, things were considerably different. So, while the protocol of just who should and shouldn't be allowed in the Sanctuary were not as strictly enforced as some of the more stiff and officious leaders of the sect might wish, the net effect was a more efficient and safer passage for the entire ship's compliment and much happier working conditions for the clerical shipwrights that worked on board.

The antechamber was brilliantly lit by both wall and ceiling panels set in ornate white wood. Trevis glanced up at the delicately etched glass overhead. It was breathtakingly beautiful. A glint of light refracted through the panes caught in his eye and he was momentarily blinded. Peering through the blinking squint of his eyes, he stepped forward and walked directly into the soft robe of the Thrund.

"Brother, IF YOU PLEASE!" rumbled the Thrund. It reached up with its center legs and brushed the robe smooth. "You are below rank and station."

Trevis tried to look apologetic through his watering eyes. The Thrunds were among the strangest-looking sentients yet encountered in the galaxy. They were also, by reputation, the most prudish, modest race known. Touching a Thrund was permissible so long as the touch was not considered morally offensive. Just what *was* considered morally offensive, however, was often a mystery to humanoids that encountered them. The Thrund had a very strict code among themselves and there were humanoids that understood it, but only after considerable study. The Thrund's statement about "rank and station" was actually intended as both a rebuff and a warning that he had offended the creature's sensibilities and had somehow come near the moral equivalent of molesting it. There were two things humanoids are first taught about the Thrund. First, never touch them. Secondly, how to say . . .

"My station and rank are low and my offense is great. I beg mercy," Trevis said, grateful that his vision was finally clearing.

"The Chamber of Communion is aft through those doors at the end of the corridor. Perhaps you should proceed me."

"As you wish, Madam Emissary." Trevis stepped carefully around the Thrund—who apparently still considered the Localyte a threat to decency—and opened the ornate double doors to the stairwell landing. Upward, he knew, was the gun deck and the keep. Farther down he had never gone, though he had learned that access to the lower temple levels, the brig, and various storage compartments were to be found in that direction. He crossed the landing and opened a second set of ornate double doors that led to the Farcardinal's suite.

The corridor before him was luxuriously finished and remarkably wide for a shipboard passageway, most of which were only wide enough to be serviceable. Delicate lanterns on the wall lit the space less harshly than the anteroom they had left. Doorways on either side of the corridor led to meditation chambers for the Localytes such as himself but were seldom in use during the voyage: Two of these had, in fact, been converted into quarters for the Farcardinal and the emissary. Localytes by definition dealt only with short-range communion over distances of only a few miles in the initiates, to ten thousand miles or more in the higher orders. While such communion is important planetside and when fleets of ships are working together, it is useless to a single ship between the stars.

Stellar and galactic distances are the province of the Farcardinals. Such talents are rare and wonderful and discovered only after a Localyte learns his craft and finds within himself the ability of farsight. He hears the murmur of life that hums throughout the galaxy and learns to tune it out. Millions of the Farcardinals may be projecting their communion out into the void between the stars at any given time. Farcardinals learn to push the constant babble that enters their mind to the back of their conscious thought. They are always aware of it, lest at any time they should hear the call from some other part of the galaxy and know that their eyes, ears, and knowledge are needed by one of their brothers. Through them, all communication throughout the Pax was handled. It was only by this means that the Pax could be governed at all.

While the Localytes used the meditation chambers on either side, it was the Hall of Communion that was the province of the Farcardinals. Trevis opened the second set of double doors at the end of the corridor and entered the chamber.

Farcardinal Sabenth sat in preparation for communion on a raised, circular dais. The room itself was roughly circular with great wooden arches supporting the ceiling. There were chairs arranged around the room, a quiet statement as to the humanocentricity of the priesthood in the Pax.

Trevis noticed, as he walked into the room, that none of the surrounding seats were in use. The Thrund emissary that followed him in had the chairs on one side of the room removed so that she might sit comfortably on the tapestry laid out for her. The only other person present, aside from the Farcardinal on the dais, was Master Dresiv, who was the captain regardless of his protests otherwise. He stood leaning casually against the wall in near defiance of the sanctity of the place.

Trevis would also have to do without the luxury of sitting. His own place was next to his Farcardinal during the process of the communion. Not that he actually participated in the process directly. Such dangerous acts were far in his future, after long study and discipline. His purpose in being there was only to act as voice in the communion and for the protection of the Farcardinal himself. As voice, he would read the thoughts of the Farcardinal as they were received through the communion and form them into words heard by everyone else in the room. As for protection, the Farcardinal's task of hearing and holding on to the voice of one mind out of millions requires great concentration and effort. The great links of mind, if not cut cleanly once used, can snap back and damage the mind that forged them. Trevis's sworn duty and the focus of much of his training to date was to recognize one thing—when it was time for the Farcardinal to stop.

"Is there sufficient silverfire to do this?" The Thrund asked the question generally, either being officious or just not knowing who in the room might have the answer.

"We've managed to navigate out of the nebula and are in the center of a comparatively strong darkwind spur surging up from NLS-1196," Dresiv answered. "It links with the downspur from Brev. That allows us to fold the mainsail and drift for a short while without having to worry about the Void. The power we save by folding sail should be sufficient for communion, I would think—is that right, Farcardinal?"

"Yes, I should think quite sufficient for this communion. As I understand my lord emissary's wishes, I am to commune with the bishop of Kilnar. I am to inform them how and why we are delayed—and offer our apologies."

"That is correct, Farcardinal," purred the Thrund.

"You will first tell them,"—Dresiv spoke a little louder than may have been necessary in the confined space—"that we are making our way to Brev under heavy damage and are in need of repair assistance there. I would have preferred you conducted this communion with a Bishop on Brev rather than Kilnar . . ."

"But, my dear Master Dresiv!" The Thrund sounded hurt, though no one in the room actually thought that she was. "We were agreed on this! Our mission was and remains on Kilnar. It is they who expect us, not Brev. Our first priority in communication is to inform Kilnar. The Bishop there, of course, is in a much better position to contact Brev for us rather than squander our precious silverfire in repeated communions."

"Yes, Emissary Hruna, I understand all that, but, with all respect, M'Lady, the Bishop of Kilnar cannot possibly know what our damage is or what materials we will need once we get to Brev."

The Farcardinal spoke up. "I shall endeavor to inform the Kilnar Bishop in as much detail as possible, Master Dresiv."

"Lord Father Farcardinal, again, with respect, you don't know a topgallant from a piss pot." The Farcardinal reddened. "Neither does the Bishop of Kilnar. How can you possibly expect to tell Brev what we need—"

"This really isn't getting us anywhere." The Thrund's voices were quiet but carried through the room remarkably well. "Kilnar is the choice for communion. The Farcardinal will endeavor to communicate our needs to Brev through the Bishop on Kilnar. Please, Farcardinal, proceed."

Trevis took his place standing directly before the Farcardinal, studying his face, and through the words of his own magic establishing the short link of minds between the two. As he did, Sabenth nodded and sat against the high back of the chair. His hands reached out to rest on the glowing spheres to either side of the chair. Trevis could see the words forming on the lips of his master, rolling in endless progression as his mind merged with the collective conscience of a universe. The power of the silverfire, conducted through the optics cables radiating from the Transentstone in the Sanctuary, consumed the Farcardinal in a blue light that was difficult to look at and impossible to focus upon. The light writhed in living branches around him, dancing about the body with a will seemingly of its own. Through it all, Trevis watched the words forming again and again on the Farcardinal's lips and the communion link was forged.

Trevis spoke. "The communion is established. The bond is made."

Long moments passed as the Farcardinal, lost to the world that was around him, passed the knowledge he had been instructed to give on to the Bishop of a faraway world and star.

Suddenly, Trevis blinked and then spoke. "Father Sabenth has informed Kilnar that we have taken prisoners in the attack. The Brotherhood of Kilnar wishes to know if we are still holding the Loyalist captain."

"Yes," Dresiv replied. "She's in the brig directly below us— the Farcardinal knows that."

It was a moment before Trevis passed this information on through his link to the Farcardinal. "They believe her name to be—" Trevis narrowed his eyes. Concepts were easy to translate, but new proper names were complex and difficult. "Thyne

Haught-Cargil." Trevis glanced at the captain. "Perhaps the word 'believe' isn't quite right. 'Hope' may be a better word for what they mean. They also caution great care if she is aboard."

"More good news," Serg chuckled. "Tell me something I *don't* know."

"What of the Acceptance Ceremonies?" the Thrund asked.

Trevis frowned. "That information has been given in detail to Father Sabenth, and he will discuss it with you at length later." Trevis then reached forward and placed both his palms on the head of the Farcardinal. The field of living blue collapsed around him as though it had never been. Sabenth's eyes flickered open.

"Oh, thank you, my son. That was most properly done." Sabenth struggled up from his chair with Trevis's assistance. "I shall need a little time for rest in my quarters, I should think. No, Trevis, that's quite all right, I think I can make it from here. Would you care to join me, Emissary Hruna?"

"With great pleasure, if you do not think you are too fatigued." The Thrund was already lifting herself up from the tapestry.

"Not at all. We have much to discuss."

The two left Trevis to secure the silverfire linkage and shut down the power to the room. He had just started the routine when Dresiv—who hadn't moved from his place against the wall—spoke to him.

"Brother, what did the Kilnar tell the Farcardinal?"

"I don't know, sire."

"I thought you heard what the Farcardinal hears?"

"Not exactly, sire," Trevis said. "I hear the thoughts that the Farcardinal passes on to me during the communion. There are often private messages which the Farcardinals get that the Localytes are not privileged to hear."

Serg frowned. "I see. Thank you, Brother."

With that, Dresiv left Trevis to finish his business.

Serg closed the doors to the Hall of Communion and walked in slow, measured steps down the wide corridor.

Farcardinals communicate with others of their ilk through the magic of the silverfire and their own minds. When a Localyte acts as voice in the process, it is as though the Farcardinal is communing two people at once: He mentally talks to the Localyte, who is in touch with the real world around the Farcardinal, or he can mentally talk to the mind of the Bishop circling a distant star.

But he cannot talk to both at once. More important, the Localyte acting as voice cannot hear what the distant Bishop is saying, nor can the Localyte hear the thoughts of the Bishop. It's all rather like talking into blower tubes with only one person able to hear what everyone is saying.

That the Farcardinal had neglected to tell his Localyte the details of what was going on was of little importance; it was that in doing so he was keeping something from Serg. He also knew that if the Farcardinal and Emissary Hruna were plotting something on their own, he wanted to be as far from it as possible.

He wondered vaguely just what message the Farcardinal sent to Kilnar and if there was more to their reply than appearances gave. The thought made him mildly uneasy.

9

Delvers Walk

———❦———

Serg leaned against the railing and sighed inwardly. The great main sail that filled the view through the clear dome cast shifting patterns of opal light over him and the darkened room behind. Stars, normally starkly bright in the intrestellar vastness, flickered beyond the shifting sail, an effect of its shifting patterns of force. Only one of the stars seen through the kaleidoscopic sail held steady, its brilliance growing with each passing hour as his ship wound its way down the darkwind toward it.

This is where she belongs, Serg thought wistfully. He gazed down from the railing to the forecastle dome below him. He knew every inch of this ship as though it were an extension of himself. He was the ship and the ship was him. Again he sighed. *This is where I belong too.*

The *Shendridan* was huge, as Pax ships went. She seldom deigned to lower herself into an atmosphere—such travel was undignified to her even in the best of circumstances. Her true beauty was in the element that was her home. Darkwind space was where she burned like a light of hope to the worlds below her. Such was her promise—if not one that was always kept. In his mind, Serg could see her lines clearly, the physical symbol of everything he loved and hated.

The foundation of the *Shendridan*, as with all silverfire ships, was its keel. The *Shendridan*'s keel was fixed to the hull at its extreme forward end. The rest of the keel ran straight aft nearly the length of the ship above it—a skater's blade biting firmly into the invisible darkwind ice.

The hull of the ship began at its deep prow and then sloped back away from the keel at its forward mounts. The hull's wide bow tapered waspishly and then flattened to a rounded stern. This shape created an open space between the bottom of the hull and the exposed keel, where cargo could be easily stowed and removed from the *Shendridan*'s lower holds. The forward, wide section of the hull, directly above the keel mounts, held the temple spaces, where the power of all the ship's magic was either tapped or created—Serg wasn't sure which. No amount of explanation by any of the shipwrights he had served with could satisfactorily explain this to him.

The hull generally referred to the sections of the ship below the main deck. These were the brutish and uncivilized areas of the ship where the work was done. Here were the machines, conduits, and altars that made everything happen.

Rising above the forward expanse of the main deck, however, was the keep—an ornate and hospitable structure. The ship's keep was where life was carried on in a finer degree. Quarters, mess halls, libraries, and command found their province here. Here were the rewards for the work done below.

Three great domes stood in procession up the forward edge of the keep as it raked back from the bow. The first was the forecastle, where the crew could walk an open deck and stare into the night that was their home. The third, much higher than than the previous two and farther back, was the bridge, from which the ship's course was set.

But it was here in the second, between the other two domes, that Serg preferred to be. Smaller and almost an afterthought in the ship's design, the delver's walk was rather inconvenient to the main courses the crew took through the ship. The room's dome was small but elegant, offering a wide and expansive view of the mainsail and space beyond. The vibrant colors of the shifting darkwind sail framed the stellar light in an aurora that seemed almost alive. At speed, the mainsail was brilliant.

Now, as the ship settled slowly through the Brev system toward the single habitable world there, the sail was soft and pastel. Serg looked up again from the polished rail and stared out at the great approaching crescent that was their destination.

Yes, he knew the ship well, as well as any other on which he had served. He could command her with that sure hand with which he had . . .

That sure hand of command.

He could feel himself sinking yet again. The images floated like a black sea around his feet, always threatening to rise up and engulf him. Never when he was busy about the ship's routine. Never when he talked or moved or read or did any of a thousand meaningless tasks with which he busied his mind. All these things kept the blackness at bay, yet still it lingered there at the fringe of his life.

It was only when all else was done and there was nothing left but to wait that the visions came upon him. He could watch them approach and knew that he was powerless against them. It was in those times when he knew no one watched him that he was dragged silently into the despair that broke over him in surging waves. He never closed his eyes in such times—he feared somehow that the further darkness would only sharpen the unbidden images.

There! A shape formed from the blackness in his mind, dark on dark and without color. The arms and legs spread awkwardly from the body. He knew that the features of the face were there to be seen, but his mind shrank from them. Warm and cold. Blood, *Hesth*, the blood, it covered him. He couldn't get the stain out—he would never get it out—

No! He shuddered and turned his head away from the dome. Unbidden, there it was. Not a vision, but a feeling. No sight, but sound and pressure and bitter taste. Someone held him in his arms. Someone spoke the words and— No, please no!

Then another voice floated down from above. It called him back toward a life he couldn't face.

"Master Dresiv, sire?"

His head snapped forward, his eyes focused. The blackness slid again to the edges of his perception as his mind hurried to catch up with the real world steadying around him.

"Master Dresiv, you asked for the Loyalist captain, sire?

Delver S'knan has had her ready for some time but couldn't find you."

"Yes, Genni, uh—sorry, my mind was somewhere else. Yes, I would like to see her." Serg smiled weakly and looked away from the delver. "Thanks, Genni. How did you know where to find me?"

"Oh, just a hunch, sire," Genni said quietly. "I'll bring her right up."

Serg looked up again. *He knows,* he thought, *but he won't say anything. What would be the point? What would it change?*

Serg thought of saying something about his pain, thought better of it, and, instead, said, "Genni, when you bring her in, close the door but stay on the other side of it. This Loyalist is both cunning and heartless from what I've seen of her so far. She played the innocent to the captain and then spread him the length of a corridor within a heartbeat. I may need company very quickly, *allai?*"

"*Allai,* Captain." Genni smiled and then winced at his own words, rushing from his mouth out of habit unbidden. He looked at his old friend but got no sign except for the sadness still playing in Dresiv's eyes.

"Who's on the bridge, Genni?"

"Pol, sire. You don't want to make landfall, do you, sire?"

"No. Pol has instructions to high-anchor the ship in orbit. We'll use the gigs to get whatever the shipwrights need to put her back together." Serg patted the rail. The *Shendridan* was a good ship, and Serg knew that she was listening. Ships that are mistreated never give back more than they got when the time comes. "Thanks, Genni. Go get the Loyalist now."

"*Allai,* sire. Do you want anything else, sire?"

"Do I *want* anything, Genni?" Serg said as much to himself as to his friend. He smiled and shook his head. "No, nothing from you, Genni. Let's get on with it."

Serg waited until Genni left, then turned back toward the window. The ship's healer said that Bivis would be around in a day or so. Depending upon what he remembered, Serg knew he would either be in deep trouble or completely forgotten. Either way suited him just fine. It meant that he could give the ship back to someone else—anyone else.

Serg Dresiv, he thought to himself, *former ship's captain in the service of the Pax, one-thousand four-hundred and thirty-*

ninth recipient of the Galacticus Order of Gallantry and, for a time, one of the most honored and respected commanders in the entire empire. Do you want anything? The hero of the galaxy wants nothing more than to disappear from everyone's sight— including his own.

Thyne heard the door close behind her as she surveyed the room. An observation room of some type, she thought. Only one obvious door. That could be either a liability or an asset, depending upon how it was used. The exercise came naturally to her. Evaluate everything tactically first and you tended to live longer as a Loyalist.

The room was brightly lit through the great glass dome, the interior lanterns of the room turned completely down. A great bright crescent cut through the glow of the mainsail and starlight beyond. They were in-system somewhere and coming down the darkwind, but what system and where?

"A beautiful sight, is it not, Lady Thyne?"

Thyne started visibly and turned. Without conscious thought she crouched swiftly to face her adversary. She had not noticed the man leaning in the darkened corner of the room behind her. Now the animal part of her took control of her higher mind. Yet, by the time he finished his sentence she was again in control of herself and flushed, angry at the frightful pose her body had taken.

The man stepped into the light and walked past her with a studied casualness. "My apologies for startling you. Permit me an introduction of myself."

The shadow-cloaked delver moved past her. He continued to speak as he walked, his eyes fixed not on her but on the panorama in the dome beyond. Soon his back was to her. "I am Master Serg Dresiv, stardelver in service of the Pax Galacticus and holder of the Scepter aboard what is left of this vessel. First Master Bivis holds the current captaincy, but I hold the Scepter until he recovers from wounds suffered in battle." He leaned against the railing with a studied casualness.

He's either brave, sure of himself, or stupid, she thought to herself. *Probably all three.* Thyne responded in a voice that was a study in the Pax officer's own coolness. "What an inspired speech, Master Scepter-holder. Was that out of a manual, or did you make that up all on your own?"

The officer half turned his head toward her and smiled. "Actually, that particular one comes pretty much from the *Delver's Codex of Stellar Rights in Passage*. It isn't quite rote but close enough for the ship's log."

Thyne folded her arms in unquestionable defiance. She looked absently through the dome to space beyond. "So we're here to write the ship's log. Fine, butcher. You ask and I'll deny."

Serg turned to face her, leaning back against the railing. "We'll start easy and work our way up: Who are you?"

"I'm Thyne Tarenc-Thei. I am a hired mercenary for the Loyalists of Kilnar who are fighting the tyrannical and self-possessing expansion of an unjust empire." Her words were delivered with a calm that belied their content. As she spoke, she walked in measured steps to the railing and turned to lean against it as Dresiv had. "We ranged around the stars, pirating commerce to fund their counterrevolution against the Brotherhood. We also line our pockets until we are fat—surely you can understand that, oh, mighty warrior of the Pax?"

Serg's eyes narrowed as he now looked straight at her. "Greed? Yes, that I can understand, although I certainly can't understand what the Loyalists hope to gain. Kilnar resolved its own world government—a problem for Kilnar and Kilnar alone—and now the Pax simply comes to welcome it into communion with other sovereign stellar nations."

A laugh exploded from Thyne's lips. "Oh, right!" She sneered. "The great Pax comes down all pure and light and deigns let poor, backward Kilnar join their empire. Pax Pure says, 'Just one little thing, everyone. You can't come play among *our* stars—so sorry to tell you they are *our* stars—unless you slit the throat of your culture and launch the world war you've been working to avoid all these centuries.' 'Thanks, Pax Pure,' we respond, 'we will gladly draw and quarter our world for you.' Millions died in the flesh. Billions watched their dreams and spirit die as well. Pax Pure stands watch in the heavens, never soiling their hands in the rivers of blood on our backward little world below. Then, when all the dying is done and the children have no more tears to weep, you fall again from the stars and everything is going to be all right!"

She looked into Dresiv's eyes: cold stones both intense and shining. Her voice had risen with her passion. Now, suddenly, silence hung between them as they looked warily at each other.

There was a short series of taps at the door.

"Come," Serg barked as his eyes remained locked on her own.

"Sorry, sire," said the delver bursting through the door suddenly, his handcannon drawn. Thyne recognized him as the one who had escorted her there. "You wished to be informed when we had been placed at High Anchor, sire."

"Yes, thank you, Master Parquan," Serg said. "My compliments to Master Pol. Have the shipwrights begin transport groundside for supplies at once."

"*Allai*, sire." Genni left as quietly as possible.

Thyne turned and gazed at the large crescent of a world beginning to fill the dome beyond them. She took a few steps up to the railing, gazing at the world. The view was gaining clarity as the mainsail was fading out of existence. The ship settled to drift in its orbit. "You'll not make planetfall, Dresiv? Are your ship's injuries so bad?"

"No, Lady Thyne," Serg said factually, "but using the ship's smaller boats is much easier and less risky than taking the *Shendridan* down all at once in any condition. It's easier to stay here at High Anchor and let the small craft do the work."

"What is High Anchor?"

Dresiv's surprised look made her uneasy. She was vaguely reminded of being a schoolgirl and having just asked the headmistress a question to which everyone else already knew the answer.

Serg smiled knowingly and explained. "High Anchor is a point in the skies above a world where a ship may orbit and remain over one place on the geosphere. The world turns below and we turn with it. We are just close enough and slow enough for the gravity of the world to keep us circling the globe, yet we are just far enough and fast enough so as to stay over the same place all time." Serg turned to the woman suddenly. "Ma'am, I suspect that you have some beautiful shores on your world, am I right?"

Thyne's gaze was a mixture of disdain and curious amazement. "My world has no ocean, no shores!"

"Of course it does." Serg chuckled. "Permit me to say that your navigation of the Clouds of Thel was a tremendous feat. There's not a delver in a million who could have pulled it off. The Loyalists of Kilnar—if memory serves me—haven't had stellar ships more than a year or so. You were sailing long before then and in gentler winds than blow between the stars. Your world has seas. Those seas have shores of sand."

Serg stood quietly for a moment, then spoke. "When things were happier for you, perhaps you walked those beaches and enjoyed the warmth of your home star. Did you ever pick up a handful of the sand and look at it closely?"

Thyne still wasn't following this turn of conversation. *What was this Pax stooge driving at?*

Serg held up an empty hand, pantomiming as he spoke. "Reach down into that hand full of sand and pick out a single grain. Examine it closely. See how beautiful it is. See how rich its color and its crystal structure." He pinched his finger and thumb in front of his face as though examining the imaginary grain, but his eyes were locked on her face. "This, Thyne, is your world.

"Now drop it behind your back." Serg's hand flipped over his shoulder to release its supposed grip. His eyes remained steady on her own, making her again uncomfortable. "Where is that most precious piece of sand, Captain Thyne? If you were to turn around and search through the thousands of grains that were behind you on that beach, would you find it, that very same grain of sand?"

His face moved closer to hers even though she was a good half-hand taller than he was. Thyne felt the distance between them uncomfortably close. "You're out to save your precious grain of sand, Captain Thyne. The galaxy has more stars and worlds than there are grains of sand on all the possible beaches of your world combined. I know, I've sailed the darkwind past thousands of worlds. Each one is precious to its inhabitants. Each one is special. And, ultimately, each one sees the advantages to it in the Pax and its emerging order and law in the galaxy . . ."

Thyne laughed, but there was an annoying quiver in her voice. "Order? Law? You talk of stars and greater things, but what is greater than one soul's freedom or one person's life? Is it given to the great and all-powerful Pax to give and take life at its whim? No—I know well the Pax, Dresiv. You will wait up here among the stars and keep your hands and souls free of the blood—"

"I did NOT bring you here to discuss my culpability in your petty wars, Captain!" Dresiv's words shot out at her, loud and clipped. Each syllable was a dare to contradict his position, each dare an assertion of its own. "If your MINOR race among a thousand other races decides to commit social genocide, *it is not my fault*—nor that of the Pax, which offers only knowledge, trade, and interstellar security and peace!"

Suddenly Serg turned away from her to gaze into the star-filled night. *What nerve have I struck,* Thyne thought.

"Thyne—I'm not unsympathetic to you or your cause. I, too, have seen injustice in the Pax and understand its personal pain. If I don't know your world and its history, it is only because there are so many other worlds I have walked which have histories of their own. Many are glorious, many are tragic—and all of them get lost in the mosaic that makes up a galaxy and the minds that perceive it."

"Well, this is one part of the mosaic that won't fit properly," Thyne said. "Your emissary and Farcardinal were killed in our attack! There will be no Acceptance Ceremony!"

"M'Lady, you are mistaken. Both are alive and doing well."

Both are alive and well! Thyne gave the Pax dog her best surprised and shocked look. "What?" she squeaked.

He turned again toward her. Was there sadness in those eyes? "Lady Thyne, accept it—you have failed."

Silence hung between them for a time.

At last, Dresiv spoke. "Captain Thyne, you and the remainder of your crew will be transferred groundside within the half hour. The Governor General of Brev will take jurisdiction and see to your extradition and possible trial."

Brev! she thought. *Her own world was near—Brev offered her great possibilities. Things may not be so bad as they seem!* She masked her excited interest and responded as evenly as she could. "And my crew?"

"You'll be taken down in a separate boat from them," Serg explained?" You can see to their condition after you have made planetfall."

"Wonderful news," Thyne responded through a yawn. "What about you, Master Dresiv? I suppose, having dumped us and all of our Loyalist sentiment off on Brev like so much of your ship's garbage, you shall then sail away—Pax Pure—into the night?"

Serg responded with only a tight smile.

"I rather thought so," Thyne purred as she made her way across the compartment to the door, then turned casually toward him. "I like your little story about the beach. Just be careful as you run across the sands that you don't trip on a rock."

She opened the door. "Hello, Genni, it's time to take me back to my cell." She lightly touched his nose with her finger. "The captain's had his way with me and now he's tossing me aside. Who do you suppose will *ever* want me now? It's so tragic!"

Genni glanced at Serg and tried to speak, but the words just didn't seem to come out.

"Don't answer, Genni—don't even try." Serg grinned and shook his head.

Genni closed the door and motioned back down the narrow gangway. Thyne smiled, licked her lips, and began walking.

She thought feverishly. The emissary's aboard—the dolt captain had just confirmed it—and this ship's his only transport. She hadn't counted on the ship not landing, but, on the other hand, they were being turned over on Brev, and that definitely had its advantages.

All in all, Thyne thought as the cell door clanged shut behind her, things were going pretty well.

Serg looked back out the dome. He'd get all these people off the ship and then get her repaired. If he made Bivis look good enough, perhaps he'd keep his rank long enough to get transferred again.

As for the Loyalists—their leader was good but without real experience in the darkwind. She didn't even know what High Anchor was. She was determined, but she lacked experience. She shouldn't cause him too much trouble.

All in all, Serg thought, things are going pretty well.

10

Prison Walls

———❧❦❧———

The Loyalist crew was transferred one at a time from their holding cell into the waiting gig. It was a slow and a tedious process, carefully supervised. Dresiv himself had outlined the procedure for the detail. The ship's shuttle boat lay at the far end of the broken fantail, just barely within the ship's atmospheric envelope.

Krith stood between two guards who had been assigned to him. Both of the guards were fingering their cannons rather nervously. Krith smiled to himself; they certainly had every right to be nervous. If the order had been given, the two of these fine little fellows would be over the side by now and breathing vacuum. But the word had not been given and he understood why. The game still had quite a while to play. The Lady—as Krith was fond of calling his captain—was taking quite a gamble, but everything seemed to have worked just as she said it would. And if they took the prize—this time he smiled broadly.

Krith stepped over the side of the *Shendridan* and onto the open deck of the shuttleboat. It wasn't a small craft; indeed, Krith guessed that it was the largest kept aboard for such things. He'd guessed she was a thirty-footer with a good eight feet to the beam. The main deck was open clear to the prow. The ship's pilot and a Temple Priest stood to either side of the tiller atop the small altar housing aft. A single sail was projected from the mast, the optics pulling it into a curve that extended nearly to the keel itself while the keel raked forward rather than aft. Both these things reminded him strongly of his Lady's last ship now torn to kindling amid the Clouds of Thel.

Krith shook himself and grinned again. No time now to be morbid, he thought. He had been the last taken aboard the craft. It was time to rally his shipmates.

"Well, lads, it looks like we'll be Groundlings for a while. Nothin' quite like a few days at the bottom of a gravity well to cheer your outlook." Krith grinned again, this time at the Pax guard with his handcannon leveled at the crew huddled on the deck. He waved at the guard, saying, "Besides, we'll not be here for long."

The shuttleboat's pilot moved at once to clear the side of the frigate. A Temple Priest stood beside him on the quarterdeck, and, raising his hands, brought the small boat's sails alive. Opal pastels shifted from the mainmast and formed themselves into a great expanse of curved energy. The boat swung sharply from the ship, the residue from the sails streaming backward to form their brilliant wake through the darkness.

Krith watched the *Shendridan* intensely as it fell away behind them. "Say farewell," he said. "She was a good ship and a proper one."

And she'll be a fine and fitting home for us when we're done, he thought.

The shuttle drifted easily down toward the great glowing crescent, rotating slowly around its axis to bring the horizon level with its keel. The blue blur at the planet's dawning edge offered the promise of a free atmosphere and watery shores. The swirl of clouds that could now be seen in the shadowy face of night were a welcome sight to a nightdelver like Krith.

"Master Pax Guard, sire! Might I have a look over the side without being smoked by yer cannon?"

"Granted," came the iced voice, "but be cautious. I've orders to blast your entire crew at the least sign of trouble."

"Oh, never a care, you have my word on that!" Krith grinned at the helmeted guard again and strolled quietly over to the side rail of the boat. "You Pax devils sure are a bloodthirsty lot, aren't you?"

The stays for the mast were well secured to the hull. Krith reached up casually and caught hold of one as he leaned slightly over the rail. The touch of it thrilled him, for he could feel the vibration of the moving ship singing in the line. There was life in the ship, indeed! It cheered him just to experience it once again.

He gazed down over the side. The stay lines for the articulated keel, he could see, were taut and the optics lines to the sail well ordered. Say what you would about the Pax and its politics, they had beautiful ships, Krith thought. Then he gazed harder past the wires to the flattening curve of the world far below him.

For a time he thought that his eyes were failing him. He could make out the dim reflection of the cloud tops in the scant starlight, but no other features of the world presented themselves to him. Try as he might, all that appeared were those clouds against a flat and undistinguished background.

He turned his eye forward toward the rapidly approaching dawn. The clouds were brilliantly rimmed by the world's sun as they moved ever farther around the globe.

"What look-see, Krith?" Snap piped brightly next to him.

He almost leaped overboard. *Shakt!* He wished she wouldn't sneak about like that!

"She's a world, Snap, just another world. I can't say that I've ever been here though. It's close enough to Kilnar, that's sure, but the Loyalists spend most of their time dancing the winds around Orananth or Uluruh-Seth. It's a longer route but a safer one from which to raid Jekart. We've had occasion to run trade with Gonra and Dzarn, but everyone knows there's nothing on Brev. From what I've heard, they don't even have land."

"No land! Where Snap stand?!"

Krith looked at her. "Don't worry your little head, Snap. I said that they didn't have *land*—but there's ground to walk. What I hear, the continents float on the seas. Some sort of buildup of dying cells or some such thing over a long, long time. That ought to be something to see, eh, Snap?"

If the small girl saw any wonder in it, she didn't seem to show it. Her large eyes were now fixed forward. The boat was settling down into the atmosphere now. The blackness that was the delver's siren call was giving way to a deep purple of the upper atmosphere. The stars, his constant companions, were thinning. Soon the towering caps of great cumulus clouds were not below them but about them as the shuttle skimmed on light through the great billowing white. Now and then, through breaks in the clouds, they could see the capping waves of the vast ocean—a body of water that covered the planet in its entirety. Such a wondrous sea was filled with its water-borne life. Without dry ground, however, the world had never developed sailors who might enjoy such a vast place to practice the craft.

The shuttleboat settled down over the waves at an altitude of nearly ten meters, skimming over the surface effortlessly. At a nod from the pilot, the cleric raised his hands again and the envelope of atmosphere that had surrounded them on their passage through the cold space above dissolved.

Krith caught his breath, shook slightly, and pressed down the wave of emotion that swept over him. He, too, had been a sailor of seas before the coming of the star-men with their promise and doom. Now the fresh breeze swept full force over him like the memory of a lover returning. This air was alive and gentle. It filled him with thoughts of his youth and swept away, for a moment, the bitterness of years past. If he had known how, he might have thought to cry.

He looked about him. His crew had all gotten to their feet and were at both rails. Even Yantha was silent. They may have been delvers, but they were from the first men of the sea, not of the sky. It was a taste of home, bitter all the more because it was not home.

The ship soared slightly up into the sky and turned once more over the waves. In moments it was obvious why.

"*Avats!* Landing!" a voice cried.

Sure enough, Krith saw the great darkness on the horizon gaining in size by the moment. He could smell the shore now—a sure sign of land for any sailor—and see the great towering mountains in the center of the island. He wondered what type of plant and growth would cause such an upheaval on land that had no geological structure whatsoever.

They lofted over the impossible mountains, covered in deep plant life of the most beautiful green. There they found themselves soaring toward a great bowl in the center of the island. A vast lake shimmered under the sun just rising above the mountains. They were close enough now to see the green was dotted with color. Flowers brought a brilliant counterpoint to the green.

There, next to the lake, stood great spires of gleaming white rising up from within the high walls of a city. Its delicate architecture was a magnificent counterpoint to the sprawling green and blue about it. As they drifted over the city, the Loyalist crew looked down on the wide avenues and ordered parks. Life moved about those streets. The bright gaiety of their clothing were only drifting dots on the broad avenues. The harbor for starships was situated just inside the walls to one side. The clean towers of the central government complex rose majestically beyond the marketplace, representing by far the largest single building below.

Once again the captives were silent. The glistening, delicate city dropped behind them as the ship sailed on. All the prisoners' eyes except Krith's were fixed on its receding spires. He looked forward again and spoke.

"Well, lads, we've seen heaven—so, I wonder what their idea of hell is?"

The ship slipped between the walls of a towering mountain canyon and began to settle toward the far shore. A large clearing surrounded by flowers of brilliant red, pink, and white appeared to be their destination. Beyond it, rising above the trees, a gray and austere tower stood. There were few windows in the structure, and it looked about as comfortable as a cold, sharp stone.

The shuttle crew hauled the keel up into the hull and the ship settled in the mossy meadow. Within moments Krith's entire crew had been forced down the ship's gangway out onto the splendid moss. As the last stepped off the plank, it was hauled up and the ship again began to lift quickly into the air.

Krith looked about and was suddenly confused. "Hey!" he called up toward the departing boat. "Where are the guards? Who's gonna keep us dangerous criminals now?"

"I suspect I'll have to," came the distant answer from the edge of the clearing.

Krith turned toward the meadow's edge. A tall figure swaggered out of the brush.

"Glory mine! Hey, lads, it's our Lady who's come for us!"

Thyne smiled. For the first time Krith really believed it was going to work after all.

"How did you manage it, M'Lady? Gettin' us let free in the country like this and all. I was sure they'd be lockin' us up in that gray tower more than likely."

"Krith, we aren't free—this is the lockup."

"Oh, jolly right, M'Lady." Krith winked. "We'll be after the guards right as soon as we can find 'em."

"Sorry, Krith, it just isn't that simple." Thyne pointed to the forbidding tower just past the end of the field. "That tower is where our keepers stay. *We* stay out here."

"You mean they're lockin' up the guards and lettin' the prisoners run free? Seem to me there were some kind of joke ..."

"This is no joke." Thyne fanned her arm grandly out to encompass the island. "You like this tropical paradise we're standing in? The truth is that there isn't a single plant on this floating dirt-ball that's edible to Kilnarans—or the Pax, for that matter. Worse still, since the island is comprised mainly of moss and other organic matter, the ground isn't all that stable. You've been looking at the mountains, Krith, and saying to yourself, 'We could climb those and be in the city inside a week.' Yet nearly every step you took, you'd be risking breaking through the moss where it isn't as stable as it is here. Prisoners who wander away from this place usually never come back. You can't survive except for that gloomy tower which provides you with food. Even if you had the food, you'd fall through to suffocate or drown in the moss. Further, I'm told that the wall around the city is as hard to get into as the one around this tower.

"No, Krith, on Brev they lock the prisoners out and keep the nice people safe inside."

Krith thought on that for a moment. "Captain, there's plenty of trees growing in this moss. We could build a ship and sail away ..."

"Where to?" Thyne pronounced each word distinctly.

"Why, anywhere, we could—uh—"

"That's right, Krith, there *isn't* any anywhere else to sail to. This little island is all there is. It's the only starport planetside and no other floating island has ever been discovered to have anything but inedible plants on it—not that you could find it more than once since they all drift around rather randomly with the currents."

Krith blinked. "You mean we can build a boat but we've nowhere to sail. We can go where we want but there's nowhere to go. We're in the open country and trapped all the same?"

"That about covers it." Thyne nodded.

"*Hesth*, Lady, this really *is* hell!"

Thyne laughed and grasped the big man's shoulders. "Come on, Krith. There's shelters on the other side of that tree line we are being permitted to use. They have a lovely view of the ocean, although one can never tell from day to day whether it faces the sunrise or not. Don't worry, Krith, the cards really are all falling our way. We're about to play a big one right now."

11

Tales of Paradise

―――――⚜―――――

The sweet breeze rustled off the breaking waves, carrying with it the clean scent of evening. The low thunder of the surf rumbled under a clear, cloudless sky of vibrant lavender fading into an impossibly deep blue. A star or two was just making itself evident in those dark depths above the tall trees just back from the soft, mossy beach.

The clean wind then passed through the undergrowth, mingling with the full blossoms of vibrant color which were just then closing up for the night. Their soft fragrance was subtle and unobtrusive yet somehow conjured up visions of places long forgotten.

The old delver sat on the cooling grass and gazed with an unfocused stare through the great fire they had built. It burned as hot and furious as the conversation that surrounded it. The Loyalist delvers had been only a day there and already they were beginning to ship vacuum at the seams. Still, Krith's mind remained as unfocused as his vision, adrift in the paradise around him.

He gazed out across the grass and through the trees onto a perfect sunset over a perfect beach on a perfect day.

He hated it.

He hated it for its perfection—for the memories that it called up. He hated it because it reminded him of home or what he had come to convince himself home had been. Distance and time had changed much in his memory. The days were much more pleasant in his memory and the people much kinder than he might once have believed. It wasn't that the people had changed, but his memory had certainly sweetened them considerably.

This perfect place might be a paradise to one whose conscience would allow him to reflect on his past in serenity. For Krith—and he believed for the rest of his crew as well—memory was not a fond companion. It was the flight from their own recollections that often drove them on in a fight. Somehow they all knew that if they had to stand still long enough, their own memories would catch up with them and they would have to face who they were.

So here in paradise they were confronted with nothing to do. Their food was provided for them from the tower. The most demanding thing they had was the ten-minute walk to the tower and back to collect their food each morning and night. Without anything to fight against—not even the cold walls of a prison—they were left to fight only against each other.

Nothing could pull a crew apart faster, Krith reminded himself. He shook visibly and tried to return his mind to the course of conversation around him.

". . . without so much as a single word, Captain Kaga pulled that ship about and drove her straight for the black hole." The delver called Wethen continued his tale with far more enthusiasm than anyone wished to listen to. "It were their only chance, what with that Zhunni Task Force on 'em like bark on a tree. There they were, staring straight into hell itself, mates!—the dark that's forever. Only the black hole's turning and old Kaga figures on taking a pass on total oblivion. He sets course off the center and down they go in a darkwind gale more fierce than any you'll fear to sail. When they come out of it . . ."

"What's that?" The dark delver—known only as Yunta— rumbled with a quiet voice that cut razor-sharp into the story.

"When they come out of the plunge into the black hole, they found themselves in the strangest of ports . . ."

Yunta opened a single skeptical eye. "You're tellin' us a starship sailed a black hole? Well, lads, this ought to be a short tale!"

Wethen reddened at the laughter that followed. "I'm tellin' you, lads. I got this straight from a mate who spoke with one of the crew—*spoke* with him, mind ya! They found themselves in a place where the silverfire is born! A place where none sail lest they find themselves caught up somehow. A place beyond knowin' and beyond space. They'd have been rich as the Primus himself if . . ."

"If they could have gotten back." Yantha stuck in, and most of the assembly laughed. "Now you'll be telling us that they used the power they found to turn time about on itself . . ."

" 'Tis true, they did!"

". . . and came back before they had left . . ."

"Aye, that they did indeed!"

". . . with a cargo hold full of rock that had once been silverfire but had all been used up in coming back." Yantha shook his head. "Wethen, that tale is as old as delvers rode starlight. If you ask me, there weren't no black holes then and there ain't any now—unless you want to count this resort we're guests at."

"I got it straight from . . ."

"Right! Straight from the man who slept with someone who had slept with someone else who told this great truth in his sleep." Yantha kicked at a log on the fire, sending sparks into the darkening sky. "Bah! Great delvers conquer the stars! I've heard it before."

"Damn you!" Wethen reached down and pulled a flaming brand from the fire. "Eat them words, boy, or you'll be eating these coals! By *Ornth,* I'll take no such nonsense from the likes of you!"

Yantha jumped to his feet just as Wethen lunged. The fiery stump slammed against his rib cage, the sizzling of his robe and flesh louder than the fire before them. Yantha cried out and, in two moves so swift that they seemed as one, kicked the legs out from under Wethen and slammed his elbow into the older man's side. Wethen collapsed onto the dust with a wheezing sigh as the air left him. The rest of the crew struggled to react—unsure whether to stop the fight or just enjoy it.

The old delver scrambled—even without breath—to get up again. Yantha smiled savagely, hauling back a fist for a crushing downward blow.

Sudden, blinding pain whited out his vision.

"Discipline problem, Master Yantha?"

Thyne held the back of the delver's neck in a viselike grip. Her hands were large and notoriously strong. Yantha was in a poor position to do anything about it even if his mind were clear enough of pain to consider it. With a single motion, the Loyalist captain pressed the wide-eyed delver to his knees, then pitched him forward into the dust beside Wethen.

"Master Krith, why do I have rabble in my crew?" Thyne's voice was almost bored.

"I'm sure I don't know, M'Lady. We were just sharing tales."

"Ah, well, my *kidikers*, if you are in need of a bedtime tale, then I have one for you." Thyne looked down at the two former combatants to make sure that their enthusiasm for killing each other had cooled. Then she sat on a log near the fire and leaned forward, resting her forearms on her knees. She paused, gazing into the fire and then began speaking as though to someone who was just beyond them all.

"In the Isgaum Sea there once sailed a long ship, tall of sail and clean lines along her hull. The waters of the Isgaum were often as cruel as they were beautiful, for storms would boil up over the eastern mountains in Thilis and spill with rage onto the sea. Yet when the gods of Thilis were quiet, that sea was the most beautiful for sailing. Its ports were fair and its shoreline the most inviting.

"In that time there was a seaman who mastered that long ship and called on the port of Kamar-than. He marveled at the great arch over the harbor and watched the children play along the sea-wall. Happy were the children of Kamar-than in their clothes of the brightest colors." Thyne gazed across the fire into the glistening eyes of a crewman. "Is this not so, Master Ounthnar?"

Ounthnar blinked through the water-filled eyes and answered only a quiet, "Yes, M'Lady." Ounthnar had lived his youth in a village near the once-great city of Kamar-than long before the wars.

"Yes, this Captain Lundei walked through the great bazaar there and happened upon the face of his true love. His heart was lost to her at once but her father would not give her up easily. He was a man whose heart was set on wealth and power. Though he possessed much of it already, he would not give up his daughter without gain. He decreed that he would consent to the marriage only if the captain brought back that which was most precious in all the world.

"So it was that Captain Lundei set out to fulfill his quest. He traveled the nine seas of Kithnar and called at many ports. He walked the white sands of Paythal and entered into the great forests of that nation. He smelled the flowers of the Gardenry and their scent was Ornth blessed." Thyne turned to one of the figures still prone at her feet. "He found joy in the beauty of those forests, did he not, Master Wethen?"

Wethen smiled gently. "Ay, Lady Thyne. He found great joy."

Thyne spoke quietly but with a firm and compassionate voice. Each port she named, each land of which she spoke, was home and heart to the men of her crew. In the dying light of the fire, she pulled into their minds visions of the world which they had known—and was no more.

"At long last he turned course for home, but the storms of the Thilis mountains caught up with him. His ship was torn asunder and the waves took him into their depths.

"It was not long thereafter that the captain's beloved walked again the seawall as she had done each day to watch for his ship to return. Evening wore into night and still she watched. As she gazed across the water, a great ship of tall and shimmering sails glided atop the crests of the waves.

" 'I have brought you the greatest gift of all,' said Captain Lundei. 'I have brought you the gift of freedom from your bonds.'

"The girl reached up and took his hand—and was never seen among mortals again."

Thyne paused and looked at each of her crew in turn. Few of them were truly devoted to her cause, she knew. Most of them were there for the excitement and plunder. Yet the stories of their childhood homes had reached them somehow and caused them to feel something deeper again.

Thyne looked into the sky as she continued. "These stars look much the same as they do in our own sky, *kidikers*. We, too, have been cast into cold, dark seas. But like our fated captain, we, too, shall return and offer our people freedom—even if it costs us our own."

She stood and surveyed the quiet faces of her crew. She was satisfied with their apparent thoughts. "Master Krith, I need your assistance. Master Yantha, do you think you can get yourself off the dirt and see that everyone turns in? The wait is about to end. We strike in two days."

Thyne turned and walked into the jungle. The thudding footsteps behind her let her know that Krith was not far behind.

"Beggin' yer pardon, M'Lady, but why are we traipsin' off into the woods in the night—not that I mind any, now."

"Don't worry, Krith, your virginity is safe with me."

"Ah, now," Krith smiled shyly, "and me being so inexperienced and all."

Thyne smiled. Enough portmasters had complained about Krith to make it certain that he was anything but inexperienced. "No, Krith, I just have a few details left on which I need your advice."

They made their way down a path that seemed to lead farther into the island.

"M'Lady—how can you be so sure that all of this will happen in two days?"

"I'm very psychic, Krith." Thyne led them into a small moss clearing. The tree cover overhead made it almost impossible to see, and even Krith was unnerved when what he had mistaken for a stump suddenly stood up. Though he couldn't make out any other features, he couldn't forget the hair—long and brilliantly white even in this light.

"There's someone I want you to meet," Thyne said. "This is Wyath Sonai-Feth—a brother of Kilnar and the man who can give us the *Shendridan*."

12

Piracy

The ship hadn't even settled into her berth when Pax delvers began scrambling over the side and running down the quay. Serg smiled to himself and quietly shook his head. The Pax delvers had made planetfall and, as it had been even in the most ancient of times, making port was cause for celebration.

Serg waited until the shuttle boat was properly moored and the keel secured before sliding over the side. He noticed that the remaining delvers—detailed to take the first shipments of lumber and fittings back up to the *Shendridan*—had a good deal more energy in their step than they had only hours before. They, too, would find themselves relieved of duty and free to share in the beauty and entertainments of the port—after they completed their allotted shipments. Visiting the port had renewed interest for them in their work. After all they had been through this last week, a few days planetside would be a welcome and stable relief.

Serg ambled down the wide quay. Starflight had developed too fast, he thought. When the silverfire brought the first powers of expansion beyond the worlds of the Cantra, it was just as easy to travel a hundred pardymes as it was to travel one. Once you mapped out the currents of the darkwind, it mostly became a matter of how many times you had to tack to get where you wanted to go. The consequence was that the ships of the Pax had flown into the night and, in their haste to conquer the galaxy, had left much of it behind. The Pax claimed to be the great force in this section of the galactic disk, but the truth be told, they really held only a smattering of worlds among those that actually existed. Their commerce was far-flung but passed many possible ports of call along the way.

This was partially due to inertia and partly due to a certain slothfulness on the part of the Pax and its rulers. When faced with a choice between a nearby world with a superficially difficult climate and a faraway world with idyllic weather, the nearer world always got left behind and forgotten. Their positions were charted only so far as their system's darkwind currents would aid or hinder navigation and often barely rated the Sector Navigational number that was assigned to it.

Of course, in the early days the explorers gave actual names to their discoveries, but as time wore on and new systems were being discovered each week, even the explorers got tired of naming things and soon resorted to the number system used today. They saved their good names for the discoveries that were more interesting.

Brev had seemed at first appearance to be worthy of some sort of name. Its telltale blue-marbled atmosphere was a sure sign that here was a place where humankind could live easily and freely. The initial survey teams were also quite excited that there was no indigenous animal life on the planet let alone intelligent sentients. As a frontier world it seemed the perfect place for the Pax to establish its regional governorship—a neutral planet with no native population ax to grind.

So word was sent back to the Senate and made its way to the Quorum of Governor Generals and eventually the planet site was approved as the local Pax government seat. The process required an inquiry be sent through the Farcardinal at the closest Pax embassy which, by the time it arrived and was responded to, took nearly two months.

Unfortunately, while the Pax explorer ship awaited the response, they discovered something they hadn't expected.

The land was moving.

At least, it had appeared to be land. True, the sea covered almost the entire surface of the planet—even at the poles—but there were plenty of apparent island land forms to support this area as a government site. Unfortunately, the explorers discovered that the land they were tracking far below was shifting with the currents.

If the Senate was informed of this, then the site might be disapproved. There was a considerable bounty for vacant, paradisical worlds. The crew of the explorer made what they felt was the only possible decision.

They didn't tell anybody.

By the time the vanguard of the Pax fleet arrived to establish the government of the stars, the explorers were well away and, of course, their bonus payments long gone with them. Fortunately the appointed Governor was of the type that rather enjoyed a challenge. Rather than ask for a different world, Garan Stryne, Tribune of the Pax, set his craft in the center of the largest island and began to build.

Serg looked down from the quay over the city below. Stryne had done himself and the Pax proud. The docks were built atop the southern city wall along the top of Delver's Ridge. The great wall itself seemed to make the city an island. It surrounded the city and kept the lush and deep jungle all around it at bay. He could see the defensive towers sprouting up occasionally from the surrounding wall, but even they had a certain elegance of curve to them that gave them grace and beauty.

The city itself was a marvel within the walls. The graceful spindles of the temple spires could be seen rising above the clean buildings at the west end of the city. They faced the curving lines of the consulate towers on the east side. Though obscured by the businesses and dwellings that towered around it, Serg could make out a great open space between temple and consulate, where he knew an enormous park to be. In all, the city was a beautiful contrast of order to the wildness and chaos of the world that surrounded it.

Serg made his way through the throngs of merchants, delvers, and officials down the great ramp. The freeform walls of the shops along the street were sculpted in pastel whites, blues, and salmons of the lightest shades, highlighting a bright and clean appearance. Even the slate-gray fitted cobblestones of the street seemed well kept.

That wasn't to say, however, that order presented itself in all forms, Serg noted. The wide street—the sign proclaimed it Market Hill—would have wound its way down the ridge as a wide path if it were clear. Word had gotten quickly about, however, that a Pax ship would be making port here. Shops and stalls had sprung up from the roadway as though by magic itself (in some cases, this was literally true) and now the wide avenue was choked with merchants hawking their wares. Even those whose business was elsewhere seemed to have gotten caught up in the frenzy of the merchants and had turned out onto Market Hill all the same.

Serg was in the middle, putting off his third most persistent shopkeeper, when the thin and rather officious-looking man tapped him on the shoulder.

"Master Dresiv? Ah, excuse me, Master Dresiv?"

Serg turned in the crowd, his face clouded with bored frustration and irritation. "Look, kippy, I told you before . . . oh, your pardon, sire! I thought you wanted me."

"But I do, Master Dresiv. I am Djan Kithber, Secretary to the Tribune Consul here on Brev. I have come to escort you to the consulate. The Tribune is most eager to see you."

Serg stared at the thin man in the crimson cape and tunic that stood before him. The secretary's hair was carefully trimmed, as was his beard, which gave his thin face an even longer look. The smile was gentle and natural, but there was a fire that burned deep behind his eyes. "Thank you, Master Kithber. I was just on my way to see your Tribune. There are a few additional items we need crafted, and I was hoping that your city might provide them. I seemed to be having a little trouble . . ."

Serg let his voice die off without finishing his thought. The crowd that had been pressing him so close was suddenly several paces back from him and his visitor. Indeed, what had once been a sea of people filling the street had seemed to part now, leaving the way clear for him to pass into the heart of the city.

Serg looked again at the man he was addressing. Kithber stood with both hands clasped casually in front of him. There was an ease about him that seemed incongruous to the tension that he so obviously felt around the two of them.

"Not to worry about it, Master Dresiv. We are honored by your coming here and most eager to help you in any way that we can." Kithber took a step back, inviting Serg by his motion to continue down the street. The rumble of the marketplace had been replaced by a quiet murmur. "Please join us, this way."

Serg followed Djan Kithber down the hill. As his host moved, the crowds parted before them and silenced at their approach. The tall and beautiful buildings passed by as he walked down Market Hill and was led into the side door of the consulate building.

The beauty was lost on Serg, however, for his thoughts and attention were turned toward the quiet man with the burning eyes. A man this comfortable with so much obvious power was, Serg knew, dangerous in the extreme.

"Most impressive, Serg Dresiv. Probably one of the finest space delving tales that I have heard in a long time. You are a remarkable commander."

"I serve only the Pax, M'Lord." Serg shifted uncomfortably on his feet. He'd come down expecting to hear the Consul complain about their requests for materials and assistance. It was something of an unwritten law among the interstellar communities that you always helped star captains, crews, and their ships with whatever they needed. Those that didn't weren't visited again very often by any type of trade. Better to just put up with it than complain and risk losing a few shipments or protection from the warships.

Serg knew that his own requests had been pretty excessive. The damage the *Shendridan* had taken was unfortunately heavy, and many of the optics cables and glass filaments had to be rewoven, let along the massive shaping of three new masts complete with stays and couplings. The priests of the Brev temple had worked long hours for the entire week. They had shaped the final pieces—which Serg knew were ready for shipment—but at the last minute the shipment had been held back. He supposed that the Tribune had gotten word of his extensive requests and now Serg would be called on the carpet for them. The protests of the Tribune wouldn't change much in his life—but he still didn't look forward to facing them.

Now he stood in the great office of Garan Stryne himself and was being praised by him. Above all, Serg distrusted praise. Worse still, he found the Thrund emissary and Farcardinal Sabenth in the office as well. He'd sent them planetside as soon as possible, knowing that they would both be happier and—more important—out of his way. He certainly hadn't expected them to get involved in what he thought was a matter of ship's supply.

No, Serg suddenly realized, this was something else—and he had somehow walked right into the middle of it.

"I apologize for holding up your shipment, but Madam Emissary Hruna informed me that there may be no other way to get you to pay me a visit." Garan Stryne sat behind the great workspace desk, his arms folded across his barrel chest. Garan's race was broad and square, his wide-set eyes flashing under the close crewcut of his blond hair. He wore a casual open tunic and pants rather than the usual Tribune robes. He looked almost out of place in the overdressed formality of his own office. Garan leaned back in his chair in a way that was relaxed, friendly, and assertive all at once. "And I most certainly wanted you to pay me a visit. What do you think of this little outpost of ours, Dresiv?"

"It's a remarkable achievement, sire." Serg stumbled a little over the words. He was on uncertain ground here and afraid that anything he said might somehow send him down a path he wouldn't like. "I have never before visited Brev. The catalogue entry accompanying the local charts did not do justice to the beauty of the city."

The Tribune turned in his chair and gazed out the tall window behind him. Far below, the great expanse of Willum Park could be seen in its ordered beauty. The spires of the temple at the far end framed him perfectly in the window as he stood.

"Yes, Dresiv, it is beautiful, but it is only the half of it. We have much grander plans here than you see on the surface—literally. Tell me, delver, what do you think of our park here?"

"It's quite charming," Serg said a bit warily. It wasn't anywhere near as great as the Forest-parks of Manthius or the Grottoes of Iphtan, he thought, but what is this local driving at?

"Charming? I suppose so. I shall miss it. You see, we are excavating the island directly under the park—constructing an open core of thermocrete straight down to the bottom. It's quite a sight to see, really. We've already drilled a small shaft down all the way through. As each section is completed, the bottom is sealed off with a dome and the water and diggings are pressure-flushed out the shaft."

Stryne turned back to Serg. "Each level is fully designed for housing, shops, markets, and industries all planned around the core. Each level's pressure dome is optics-linked to the surface so that each level gets sunlight. And when we hit the open sea—we'll cap it off and begin colonizing the sea floor as well."

Garan paused, but Serg was still wondering what all this had to do with him.

Apparently not getting the reaction he expected, Garan continued. "Quite an achievement, eh, Master Dresiv? We've taken a worthless mistake on the part of a few explorers and are turning it into a living world. We'll be more than just an outpost, sire, we'll be a world."

"I see," said Serg slowly. He suddenly understood more than they probably realized. "It is a most impressive undertaking—one worthy of the praise you shall garner from the Senate if not from the Imperium itself. Sire, I am just a delver in common service to the Pax. What has this to do with me?"

"Well, Captain Dres—"

"Pardon, sire, but I am a ship's master only and do not rate captaincy."

"Then let me be the first to congratulate you, Captain Dresiv. I have just signed your ascendancy and, as Tribune of this sector, have given you the *Shendridan*—"

"NO!"

"—as your first command. Is there something wrong, Captain?"

"Sire! I respectfully remind the Tribune that the *Shendridan* already has a captain who holds the Scepter of that post." Serg began to sweat. Of all things that they might have done to him here, this was the last expected—or wanted. "It would be an act of treason and mutiny for me to assume a post that was rightfully someone else's."

"I'm not certain to whom you are referring, Captain." Tribune Stryne was as calm as a lake in early morning. "If you are thinking of Master Bivis, I'm afraid that his injuries require that he remain here. If you are considering Captain Mandrith, your own report confirms his loss to the Void. With no further clear succession in command, I am exercising my own rights to appoint you to the post."

"Sire, I *cannot* assume the post."

Stryne's voice was almost a whisper, but it carried through the room. "Captain, why?"

"Lord Tribune, I . . . I am unfit for command."

"Your modesty does not serve you well, Dresiv. I already have the report of Farcardinal Sabenth and Emissary Hruna. You have shown not only laudable bravery but commendable skill in bringing the ship safely into port." Stryne walked around the desk and took Serg's shoulders in both hands. "Delver, you've earned it and, if you are as intelligent as I believe you are, a great deal more."

Just what does he mean by that! Serg thought. *What more do they want of me?*

Hruna's melodic voice inserted itself smoothly. "In any event, there is little choice. We must be on Kilnar within the week for their acceptance ceremonies into the Pax. Their celebrations are already under way and cannot be postponed. Further, the World Brotherhood on Kilnar wishes to make a public demonstration of their unquestioned authority over their world. They've asked that we also transport the prisoners with us at the same time—"

"What? Are you people insane?" Serg felt as if he were swimming in a nightmare. "That crew nearly threw away their own lives to sink our ship in the Void—and you want me to bring them back on board for another try?"

Hruna hated to be interrupted. Her trio of voices responded in a slightly discordant harmonic. "Your security has proved to be more than adequate to the task, Captain. Besides, the Kilnar government feels that by making an example of this crew, they will greatly strengthen their own position."

"Meaning that their position may not be all that strong?" Serg countered quietly.

The Tribune turned with studied serenity to his secretary. "Kithber, I rather think that all of this has taken our new captain by surprise. Please escort him to the assembly hall and explain the details to him. I'm sorry to have to cut this meeting short, but there is little time and much to do to prepare your ship for departure. Your supplies will, of course, be sent up to your ship at once. Thank you, Captain, I trust that we will be able to meet again soon."

"Kithber, you can tell your boss that I'm *not* taking the Scepter of command and I am certainly *not* going to play whatever little game he has in mind."

Serg's words rebounded forcefully through the vast, dark hall. Only pools of illumination could be seen highlighting various campaign banners that hung from the ceiling. The rest of the hall was in deep shadows, making it difficult to gauge the true size of the auditorium. The two men stood on a polished stone platform at one end next to a large and ornate seat. Serg stood with his hands on his hips. The other leaned casually against the great throne.

"Ah, what an interesting role you play today, Serg Dresiv, and you seem to move between them with such ease." Kithber's voice affected an oily disassociation as though he were watching an enjoyable performance from the safety of a theater seat. "First you are the poor and humble delver of the stars who modestly did nothing more to save your ship and crew than any other right-thinking delver might have done. You are undeserving and unprepared for the position. Now you are the enraged and indignant man of honor who refuses to get involved in anything that isn't as pure as the Code of Stars. Really, Serg, you should settle on one role and make it fit the facts."

"Look, you irritating little *kilth*." Serg spat out the words. "I wand nothing to do with you or your little problems on this fleaspeck world. You want to go build yourself a kingdom on Pax coffers, that's your problem. Me—I just want to go back to the way things were."

"That's an interesting idea," said Kithber. He stood and cocked his head to one side. "Do you think that it's possible to go back? If you could, what would you change?"

Serg answered only with silence.

"You know, it took quite a bit of doing to find out about you. Fortunately, we now have a Farcardinal on Brev and that has made things a good deal easier. You know"—Kithber began tracing patterns on the arm of the throne with his finger—"the funny thing was that when we finally did reach someone who could tell us who you were, they thought we were looking for historical texts rather than living biographies."

Dresiv stood still, waiting. Djan smiled easily, then stood erect, clasping both hands behind his back.

"Captain Serg Dresiv, Hero of the Mnemen Campaigns, Honored of the Galactix Order of Gallantry, and Tribune Exemplar of the Pax—also the only known man to have renounced, at his own request, the Exemplar Scepter in life. Legend has it that you did so out of honor and modesty, although standing with this 'legend' it seems a bit difficult to believe. You are, in some parts of the Pax, still honored in song and a variety of popular pseudo-historical entertainments—does that surprise you?"

Kithber is a dangerous man, Serg thought, *of the most dangerous kind.*

"What is it you want? Just cut to it."

Kithber arched his eyebrows. "Ah, a man who likes to come to the heart of the matter. It is really quite simple. We need the help of the World Brotherhood and you need anonymity. You don't need to know our reasons and we don't care what you are running away from. Your reasons will be left your own—so long as you work with us."

Kithber smiled broadly, but there was no warmth in his expression. "Just get this ship to Kilnar and you can do whatever you like. Give the *Shendridan* to another if you wish or take it as your rightful command—I don't care."

"And if I should skip out on you?" Serg asked.

"Ah, but you wouldn't do that," smiled Djan. "Not when I'm coming along, would you?"

"And you'd stop me."

"And I'd stop you."

"I see."

Kithber walked around the throne, taking hold of the back of it with both hands. "Dresiv, we need a captain we can trust and you need to be left alone. I never trust anyone I don't have by the throat and I'm always sure of my grip before I move. In one week's time you can go back to being nobody."

Serg looked out into the blackness of the hall. "Inasmuch as the Tribune, authorized commander of the Pax fleets in this region has ordained it, I—I honorably accept the Scepter of commanding the *Shendridan*—"

"Ah."

"—for this week. May I submit my request to be relieved of command at the earliest possible convenience . . . say, in a week."

"I am sure that the proper processing alone will take that long."

Serg sighed, then glanced around the dark vastness of the assembly hall. "How do I get out of here?"

"Just walk off the dais, then up the aisle to the end of the hall. The double doors there open out onto the park. I trust you can find your way back to the quay from there?" Kithber purred.

"Many gracious thanks—we should be ready to leave by tomorrow dawn over your city." Serg took several steps down the dais stairs before he turned and spoke again.

"By the way, Kithber, while you're so intent on holding others by the throat . . ."

"Yes?"

"Best to be careful that they don't manage to get a harder hold on some lower part of your own anatomy. It will make it tough for you to maintain your grip for very long."

Kithber only smiled broader. "I love a challenge, Dresiv."

Serg turned again and walked down the hall, the sound of his steps rebounding of the distant walls.

Great, Serg thought, *I survive one pirate onslaught only to be boarded by others.*

13

Loose Threads

—◦◦◦◦—

The shipwright floated free, the runes of life glowing on the mantle she wore. She drifted freely at the end of a gossamer tendril of light a thousand yards from her ship. Keri Ordina seldom was given the excuse to "walk the Void," and she reveled in it each time it came. Such action was most often called for during the most dire of emergencies. She never let the pressing need of such moments get in the way of the sensation any more than she would let her enjoyment get in the way of her doing her work.

Still, from her vantage point, she could look gratifyingly upon her handiwork. The *Shendridan* was again patched back to an image of its former self, floating above the disk below and bathed in the light of yet another sun. True, the fireoptics for the gallant spanker sail were a bit out of line and the new starboard masts were rigged a good deal differently from the rest of the sail projectors. Even so, the ship glistened where it could. The new masts shone with their fresh stain and varnish and the decks were clear and clean. Floating serenely above the great blue crescent below, the ship faced the sun and had the look of determination about her bows.

"She'll fly proudly now," Keri whispered to herself.

With a sigh, Keri formed command symbols with her hands above the chord. The glowing magic pulled her back along the great loop of its length and she drifted ever closer to the ship. She could easily make out the side rails of turned and finished wood that had replaced those taken during the collision with the Loyalist ship. It might have been easier to have replaced those with square sections rather than take the trouble to turn each post and rail to match. Still, it was *her* ship and *her* vanity in her work—one of the few indulgences which a Temple Priestess might freely engage in.

Not that her position was all that restrictive. Shipwrights are from the Proscedics sect, which have traditionally serviced the temples of ships since the beginning of space flight. Their sect deals primarily with the practical uses of silverfire as opposed to the more spiritual side. As a result, their sect is not particularly demanding along strict moral behavior lines. They weren't so much concerned with acts and deeds—a situation that suited Ordina just fine.

The ship seemed to drift toward Ordina. Her excursion was ending too quickly. She wondered how she might prolong it. A number of rationales came into her mind and she settled on a reasonable excuse: The hull might have been breached between the keel and the main body of the ship. Of course, she would need to inspect it personally to make sure that the hold hatches were secure and that there were no holes in the hull itself or in the atmospheric envelope the silverfire had woven around it.

With a slight series of gestures, the glowing cord that tied her to the ship lengthened and twisted, wrapping itself at a loose distance around the ship, bringing her now in a spiraling descent to the deck. There were apprentice shipwrights who would have lost their last meal in such a maneuver, but Ordina reveled in the swinging spin deep in free space. To her, the ship, planet, sun, and stars were all whirling around her and moving to her whim. In that moment all creation moved to her command.

The great superstructure of the ship drifted below her as she soared over the decks from the port to starboard side. She frowned. The damage from the second collision with the bandit ship had removed a large section of the fantail and landing deck for the shuttle boats. They had managed to control the damage there but were still far shy of completing the refit on the deck itself. The jagged sections broke the clean lines of the ship, and that annoyed the shipwright. She noted it in her mind as something she would have to rework as soon as the last shipments from Brev were aboard.

Ordina sailed down the far starboard side. There was plenty of damage yet to be seen. The starboard hull had taken the brunt of the attack. Both the fore and main spanker masts had been completely shattered with the first impact of the enemy hull. Even the couplings were so badly torn as to make them almost unserviceable and the optics were little less than a glowing tangle of light and heat bleeding energy into the Void.

Now, however, all seemed well ordered. The crews had worked hard and had managed now to get both masts reworked and refitted. Four crewmen now stood over the side within the atmospheric envelope of the deck, finishing the paint on the hull repairs there. They swung tethered by ropes alone—as was the delver's custom when working near the ship for as long as men sailed the stars. The hull gleamed with their work and the pride they put into it.

Ordina continued to glide along the glowing path the magic prescribed until she drifted under the keel itself. The great arm of layered hardwoods reinforced with rawhide straps held the optics of the keel in its framework. The keel arm extended from the prow, mounting backward like a knife blade, its light illuminating the bottom of the *Shendridan*'s hull sloping away above it. The keel optics glowed with soft shifting light. Ordina smiled, for it seemed to her that this most important part of her ship was sleeping after a long ordeal.

Her eye caught something odd.

Not odd really. Just something that was out of place—something that wasn't right. She murmured the words of magic almost without thought to bring her progress to a halt—her concentration centered on the vast expanse of hull above the keel. There was some scarring, but that had been expected. Interior checks of the hull had shown it intact except for the stern, and those hull repairs had been among the first to be completed. She could still see unpainted wood where many of the patches had been made, but that certainly wasn't it.

Then she had it. The third lower magazine hatch was sprung. The designers of the ship had originally thought to put hatches for both the holds and the cannon magazines in the bases of the hulls. The hold hatches were placed there more to be out of the way than of any convenience: The *Shendridan* was an instrument of policy—not cargo. The magazine hatches, however, were supposed to be a safety feature. If certain power elements of the broadside cannons were to go unstable, it was thought that the entire magazine could be cleared by releasing a lower hatch and flushing the entire contents of the hold into the Void before any real damage could be done. The magazine hatches were angled in pairs so that any such emergency evacuation of the munitions magazines would angle away from the keel of the ship. Still, the idea of blowing already unstable elements out the bottom of one's own ship somehow went against sense. So the magazine hatches were built dutifully under the ship and quietly forgotten by their crews as being at best a nuisance on their checklist and at worst another possible way of blowing oneself up by accident.

So if the hatch was sprung—why wasn't the atmosphere of the ship gushing into frozen crystals? The envelope woven around the upper decks didn't extend down to the keel. It should be setting off any number of alarms on the ship.

She again spoke the words but this time signaled her arms in different motions. The great stream of light that she rode around the ship tightened and shifted. Now she drew closer to the odd hatch and, in the soft, glowing light of the sleeping keel, could see it in much better detail.

This section of the hull was pitted with odd marks. While the silverfire brushed aside inconvenient small masses when they sailed the darkwind, cratering from orbiting matter around worlds was something ships of the stars took as part of the normal course of life. But these marks were different—deep, angled gouges at regular intervals and all spaced near the skewed hatch.

The latches on the hatch were torn loose. Those fasteners were designed to hold under the worst of battle conditions—they hadn't given up their hold easily. One of the six catches still held its closing ring which had torn loose from the hull before the latch gave way. All of the latches showed signs of damage and the hatch itself was slightly bent—which accounted for the poor fit with the opening in the hull. So warped was the hatch that she could see into the darkness of the compartment beyond.

Now there was a mystery. Blinking, Ordina reached forward to catch hold of the hatch and swing it open. Her hand tentatively slid into the opening between the hull and the sundered entry.

She gasped in astonishment.

So unexpected was her discovery that she lost concentration on the woven silverfire that sustained her. The great glowing tendril flared and wound in on itself. The great mass of the ship reeled beneath the shipwright as she spun crazily closer and closer to the deck. . . .

Ordina opened her eyes, trying in vain to fix her eyes on something steadily.

"Mistress Ordina! Mistress, are you all right?" Her assistant held her head in his hands, gazing at her eyes. They continued to involuntarily track repeatedly from left to right as though she were a child who had spun around too many times before falling. "Mistress?"

Ordina clasped hold of the assistant's arm suddenly and shook her head. The world was settling down for her but not quickly enough.

"Maxim! Is the captain aboard? I've got to . . ." She struggled to get up but hadn't yet regained her internal balance. Her arms flailed around her.

"Please, Mistress, stay here. I shall see if the captain is aboard. I don't think that you should be going anywhere for a while. Sometimes travel in the pseudo-self can be disorienting."

Ordina bristled inwardly. As if this little pup of an assistant knew more about sensory projection than she did! You could send an object that represented yourself through the magic of the silverfire and it was the same as if you were there. This kid was telling her that she couldn't drive her own senses—as if she were some old woman in a pony cart holding up a chariot race.

"You do that, Maxim. I'll just wait right here quietly."

Maxim smiled. As Ordina heard his robes rustle out of the room, she sat up again and, checking her movements more carefully this time, stood up.

"Scrud!" she swore mildly to herself. "I'd better get down there. The captain isn't gonna care for this one bit."

The damage to the door had been too specific. There weren't any battle scars around the opening—only the specific damage to the hatchway securing latches and the door itself. Still, that wasn't what had surprised her into losing control of the projection.

There was an atmosphere envelope woven about the broken hatch. That particular design was made without a backup atmosphere shield so that it *could* evacuate the hold into space. There was no way that could happen unless someone specifically put it there.

She knew that she probably should wait for the assistant, but the idea angered her. She left the meditation chamber and climbed down the gangway toward the aft munitions magazines.

Some thief had broken into her ship.

"Captain on deck!" squawked the unprepared quarterdeck officer, his young voice breaking.

Serg bound over the side of the shuttle before the yeoman pilot could quite bring it to moor on the quarterdeck. He landed in mid-stride, still moving toward the forecastle of the ship without missing a beat. There was defiance in each step and a fevered brightness to his eyes set in a face devoid of any other expression.

"Master Kilfnan! You are the QDO?" Serg locked his eyes on the boy as he passed without slowing his pace.

"Yes, sire!" The young man straightened to attention so sharply that it looked as though his back might lock. Both arms snapped upward, then crossed his chest in the reflexive salute that Serg's voice seemed to require. Dresiv motioned as he passed, however, and Kilfnan fell into step behind him.

"Tell Master Nereth he's now the QDO again, then find the commander of the Pax Legioners that took care of our prisoners. Have her report to me in my quarters at once. We will be reboarding the prisoners within the next six hours. I want you to then find each of the shift masters and have them report to me individually at their convenience—so long as it is within the next three hours . . ."

Kilfnan didn't manage to navigate the hatchway quite as deftly as the charging Dresiv. The top of the low opening grazed the top of his head as he passed through, blurring his mind and vision for a moment.

". . . all weapons aboard are secured in the weapon's locker. Then I want you to report back to me. GANGWAY!" Serg suddenly shouted as he dragged himself up the ladder three rungs at a time. Kilfnan scrambled behind him, struggling to keep up with both his directions and his blur of motion.

"One last thing, Master Kilfnan; I must see the shipwright at once. After you finish with the others, find her and bring her back to me in person." Serg stopped so abruptly that the gamboling delver nearly ran into him. "Do you have all that, delver?"

"*Allai* . . . sire!" Kilfnan gulped. "But, sire . . ."

Serg turned again and plunged through an opening.

Kilfnan followed him and was surprised to find himself on the ship's bridge.

"Master Parquan." There was no question in Serg's tone.

"Master Parquan is off watch, sire. I stand in his place."

"Hear me!" Dresiv's voice itself was a command. "By will and grace of the Imperium and by the hand of his Glorious Tribune Garan Stryne, I, Serg Dresiv, take the Scepter of captaincy of the Pax frigate *Shendridan*. Master Vidra, so note it in the watch log."

Serg turned from the astonished faces of the bridge watch to his old shipmate. "How stands the watch, Master Vidra?"

"The *Shendridan* stands ready, sire . . ." Pol Vidra moved a bit closer and lowered his voice considerably. ". . . with a few exceptions I'd like to talk to you about."

Serg didn't miss a beat. "Master S'Knan, the Scepter of the bridge watch is thine. Master Vidra, come with me."

Serg turned and might have run over Kilfnan if the delver hadn't been so quick to move backward into the access corridor.

"Sire, please!"

Serg stopped and stared at Kilfnan as though wondering why the delver was still here. "What is it, delver?"

"Sire, the shipwright is missing."

"Missing? What do you mean, the shipwright is missing?"

"He's right, sire." Pol Vidra spoke up behind the captain. "Her assistant came looking for you half an hour ago, then came back saying that he'd left her somewhere but that the woman was no longer there. I suspect she's just in one of the obscure spaces of the ship inspecting it before sailing."

"Delver Kilfnan, if the shipwright is lost, then I can think of no better person to find her than you." Serg spoke from a face that was calm but with a voice that could not be mistaken. "Carry out your orders at once."

"*Allai*, sire." The young delver hurried away.

When Kilfnan moved out of sight and hearing, Serg turned to Pol. "What's this about Genni not being on watch?"

"Oh, he was attacked by a huge martak on the planet," Pol

said somberly. "I suspect he'll recover, but not for a while longer yet."

"A martak? What kind of beast is that?"

"No beast—it's a fried sweet cake."

Serg allowed himself a smile, then shook his head. "Not to change the subject but ... did you ever play cards with a Delphan?"

"Of course not!" Pol snorted. "They always cheat!"

"So you'd be stupid to play cards with a Delphan, right?"

"Right—I don't follow you, Serg."

"So what do you do if you have to play? What if someone is holding a knife at your throat, saying 'Hey, you're gonna play cards with the Delphan'? What do you do?"

Pol blinked for a moment as he thought. "Lose?"

"Yes—or cheat better than a Delphan. The local Tribune here is playing a Delphan game with Kilnar and we've been dealt in, knife and all. Both the Farcardinal and the emissary are backing him up. I suspect that the prisoners also sit at the table somehow. We've got to find a way to cheat better than all of them. If nothing else, perhaps we can change the rules to the game."

With a large sigh, he climbed another ladder-stair toward the captain's quarters. He hoped he was up to the game.

14

Into the Bottle

Things were slipping from his control. The one thing Djan Kithber could not tolerate was the loss of control.

It wasn't that the smug captain of the Pax frigate had given him the wrong coordinates for the ship's orbit. Djan had expected something along those lines from such an officious little *drig*. He would have been greatly disappointed if Dresiv had just rolled over and played ball. He was in part glad to see there would be some challenge to their grand workings. No, not finding the ship at the captain's coordinates didn't bother him.

Not finding the ship at all—that bothered him.

Djan hauled in the spanker. The arm fought him initially as it bore the force of the darkwind around it but surrendered itself quickly as it aligned with the force of the invisible gale. Kithber sensed more than saw the ship slow in the darkwind that surged around it. This far from the surface of Brev, such changes were not sensed by the eye alone.

Twenty thousand miles below his glowing keel the world of his present home hung like a great bright arc lit by a far more distant sun. Above him, somewhere in the great diamond-dusted void, the *Shendridan* floated quietly, preparing for her voyage to Kilnar.

Yet where was she?

That the *Shendridan* had departed early was not possible. Ships that sail the darkwind leave a magnificent wake. As the energies of the stars locked within the darkwind are released, they trail the ships in great arcs of shimmering colors. The glowing spirals of the silverfire wake swing through the sky like brilliant tendrils and then fade to transparent rainbows before they dissipate and can no longer be seen. Delvers often sing songs or spin rhymes about the great swaths of color they paint through the black heavens. All delvers comfort themselves knowing that the light of their ship's wake will one day fall on their home world—though they would never live to see that day.

If the ship had moved, then its wake would have been seen by many of his own people whose eyes, ears, and thoughts he had purchased. Yet no word had come. The ship should be where it had always been.

Yet where was that? The first coordinates had obviously been given to mislead him. No doubt some sort of "error" which would be apologized for profusely once he figured his way aboard. Once he had dutifully gone to the false location, he turned his mind to his magic—that eye that never failed him. He drew from the well of silverfire within him. The ship itself would emanate the magical essence, and like finding like, would show him the way.

Then the eye failed him, or so it seemed. He exerted his powers and guided his craft to where the magic seemed to be. Blank space was his only discovery. Yet, there, not afar off, was another place where the power of silverfire seemed to burn not more than a few hundred miles away. Again, only emptiness was found.

Hours passed as Kithber flew with increasing frustration. Each new place seemed all the more promising. Each was as empty as the last.

Less than empty. Djan Kithber was a sorcerer supreme. He walked quietly confident in his ultimate power over those who surrounded him—equally confident in the whispered legend of his ruthlessness that proceeded him. The tales of his power had often served him better than the magic itself. Still, he had not arrived at his position without having taken some precautions—one of which was to never trust anyone.

The skiff that he flew was his own. Its sails and keel were powered by no external source that might be tampered with. The well of his own magic drove the ship into the sky and had always been sufficient for such orbital trips as he occasionally needed. Now, with each passing empty destination, that magic was draining just as his pride was being battered into a flaming rage.

Kithber always won. He had worked his way from one place to another along the galactic arm. He'd always traded up—he'd always found the better position. Now it looked like he had an entire system of stars and their rich new worlds just outside his grasp and here he was, drifting around like a novice from pointless space to pointless space.

At last, weary and left with little reserve, he let the skiff drift around. He thought of his failure in this simple little task and how it might affect his reputation.

A shadow fell upon him. Looking sunward, he saw the dim glow of the darkwind sails pull the silhouetted hull toward him. The *Shendridan*, it would appear, had found him.

That drig *captain is in my book,* thought Kithber. *He's an account I'll balance soon.*

The *Shendridan* grew in size quickly and then hove to presenting her flat quarterdeck. Kithber's skiff settled gently into her gravity envelope and onto her deck. Several delvers secured the little craft as Kithber jumped over the rail and onto the deck of the frigate.

"Master Kithber, we have been searching for you for the last hour! Where the *Hesth* have you been?" Serg Dresiv wore all the belligerence of a captain who had just been inconvenienced.

Kithber's face was red, his voice barely controlled. "I have been sailing from one blind location to another since your staff had the incompetence of giving me improper coordinates for your High Anchor location."

"Nonsense." Dresiv dismissed the argument. "We stood on station for two hours waiting for you."

"You told me to meet you elsewhere!" Kithber fumed.

"Hmm. Perhaps there's been an error in your coordinates."

Kithber calmed himself. *Another time and another place,* he thought, but then spoke smoothly with only a hint of a snort in his voice. "Of course."

"My apologies, Master Kithber. Would you care for a tour of the ship?" Dresiv still seemed annoyed but calmer.

Kithber sighed. "No thank you, Captain. I would like to be shown to my quarters. The experience was unnerving."

"Of course. I'll show you the way." Dresiv turned to one of his two flanking officers. "Master Vidra, would you command the crew to stations three and prepare to get under way?"

Pol Vidra blinked. "Stations three, sire?"

Dresiv began to walk casually forward, motioning Kithber to follow. "Yes, Vidra, stations three—and would you then be so kind as to join us on the bridge?"

"*Allai*, sire."

". . . and the crew are all stationed two decks below. This deck and the deck below it are the officers' areas of the ship."

Kithber grunted an automatic agreement. The truth was that his mind was numb with the captain's endless and pointless prattle about his beloved ship. All he wanted as to get to his room, quietly tap into the ship's silverfire lines, and gather strength while he rested.

"This corridor forward leads to the offices and guest quarters. Master Parquan, how many officers do we have aboard at this time?"

"I believe that we have nine officers and three general officers, sire, with a compliment of twelve sub-officers," said Parquan, following behind Kithber.

Dresiv moved down the narrow corridor, followed closely by Kithber and Parquan.

"At the forward end of this passageway is a beautiful observation dome just below the bridge, where—"

There was a sudden burst of light surrounding the sorcerer. Dresiv saw Kithber's eyes flash wide as he prepared to defend himself, but gravity was quicker. The floor had opened under him and the tall figure dropped quickly out of sight into a brilliant room below. In an instant the door slammed shut.

"Station three, Genni!" Dresiv commanded as he quickly wrapped his arm around the corridor railing.

The delver didn't wait to question but grasped tight to the same railing. "Do you think he might . . ."

The ship thundered. Decks heaved and bucked like a living thing and the timbers groaned under the strain. Eventually the ship began to right itself again.

Parquan tried to speak again. "I suppose that he wasn't . . ."

Another great roar rocked the ship. Globes shook loose of their fittings and rolled, still glowing, between the moving walls and the floor. Quiet decanted slowly and the world settled again to its natural place.

Moments passed. No further calamity seemed forthcoming. At last Dresiv released his hold on the rail and stood up.

"I think he's probably finished for the time being," Serg said with a calm that was edged with relief.

"Who the *Hesth* was he?" Parquan was still a little dazed from the sudden assault.

Serg walked aft toward the main stair shaft. "His name is Djan Kithber. He's a sorcerer and he's here to help those Loyalists in the hold take this ship."

"What?"

"Look," Serg said. "Here's how I see it. The Thrund, Farcardinal, and the Tribune are all working on some sort of scheme. They're the ones who insisted on putting the Loyalist crew aboard. Why bring them along unless you need them?"

Parquan blinked. "You expect trouble?"

Serg smiled. "If they arranged to bring their own crew aboard, that means that they are figuring on *not* needing ours. I suspect Stryne is trying to set up an independent kingdom here. I don't know. Whatever the reason, Stryne put the Loyalist on my ship and that can mean only—"

"That they'll take the ship!" Parquan whispered.

Serg's smile broadened as he turned to walk down the corridor, Parquan following him as he spoke. "Not anymore. They need two things in order to take a ship: weapons and a wizard with the firepower to back them up. We've just bagged their wizard. It's possible that they expected to use the sorcerer to get to the weapon's locker and use our own weapons against us. Otherwise, they must have a cache of weapons around here somewhere. If they do have a cache, we'll find it."

"When do we tell the Loyalists we're on to them?"

Dresiv stopped and turned toward the delver. "We don't—and that's very important. No one is to know that we've secured the sorcerer, especially the Thrund or the Farcardinal, at least for the next few days. I want the Loyalists to think that everything is working according to their plan and stop them when they make their move. That won't be for a couple of days and it gives us a chance to find their weapons."

"Besides," said Dresiv, "without their wizard, they haven't much of a chance. Let's get the ship under way."

Dusk colored the warm sky over the city, bathing the streets and pristine buildings in a soft pastel light. The inhabitants gathered together amid the rolling green of the park, grateful for the cool short grasses that cushioned their steps and drained their cares from them as they walked. The tallest of the city spires were still ablaze with sunlight—the last vestiges of a day of work and struggle to master this new world's environment.

Though the stars themselves were far yet from appearing in the deepening purple of the sky, a single fleck of diamond light hung almost directly above the city walls. It had come into their sky just a week before and now it had come time for its leaving. The word had gone about the city and everyone who could possibly be spared had come onto the park to enjoy the experience together.

As they watched, the star began to glow brighter and brighter in the darkening sky. Just when the brightness of its light seemed unbearable, the great star began to move, trailing behind it a wavering stream of iridescent colors. Suddenly the brilliant fleck of diamond light shot beyond sight. Those that were delvers knew that the ship was now no longer where they could see it. Still, they followed the trail of the ship through the sky. The great arch of opal light continued to follow the course of the starship, leaving a great trail in rainbow hues. For many nights that wake of the starship's passing would hang in the night sky, as if to follow at light's speed the course of the ship that had long since left its own wake behind. There it would be a great arch of beautiful light, tracing slowly the path the ship had passed seemingly swifter than thought itself. It was, in the heavens, a sign of the starship making its way across all creation.

Through the great windows of the consulate general of the city, however, two figures stood side by side and watched the wake trace its way into the heavens. From their vantage point, they could take in the full grandeur of the spectacle—both that happening above and that which was below. The great glowing arch of color cut across the deepening sky above as the cheers and awed voices of the people welled up from the great green below them.

"A great moment, Tribune."

"Yes, my fine adjutant, a great moment indeed, although I wonder at the wisdom in putting the prisoners aboard."

"Regrettable, indeed, but unavoidable—the Farcardinal dispatch from Kilnar was most specific in demanding the prisoners return at once. Besides, I doubt that such a rabble will be of any trouble to the crew of the frigate."

Garan sighed. "I suppose you are right—you usually are. Did you see Loremaster Kithber aboard?"

"No, Tribune, I did not. I do not care for space travel, as you well know. I did see the loremaster to his skiff, however. As we have had no other word, I can only assume that his journey was completed as planned."

"Excellent!" The Tribune turned from the great window and walked to the sideboard in his office. Pulling an ornate crystal carafe, the Tribune began to pour. "A toast, then, to this mission—ah, I forget—you do not drink."

"A habit I have avoided since youth."

"Here, then, sweetwater for you and a little something more for me. A toast to this ship and her mission. May she bring a new world into the Pax and a new peace to her people."

Garan Stryne, Tribune of the Pax, raised his large goblet and smiled. It had come off pretty well, he thought—not that he could talk about it with his adjutant. The man was a competent administrator and kept all of the occasional required reports in order for the Office of Inspection, but he had no real vision. Besides, the man was from one of the local stars and might have some objection to helping build a base for plundering his own world.

No, thought Garan, it had been best to keep his little secret among those who could profit by it most. The Farcardinal was easily brought into the deal. The Thrund had her own reasons for wanting to establish a law that was outside the Pax. With the deal about to be finalized with the Kilnar Brotherhood, nearly all the pieces were in place.

By the time the Pax got wind of what he was up to, he'd have his own province set up. He was too far from the Core worlds to send a fleet out here—besides, the Pax already had its hands full with the rebellion in the Haven States. By the time any real pressure came this way, he would either be strong enough to resist them or prepared enough to move farther out. Either way, he'd be wealthy and powerful beyond the hopes of any man.

So, Garan smiled at his adjutant and raised his goblet. The man smiled back at him with equal fervor, his face framed by luxurious long white hair. It mildly troubled the Tribune.

After all, what would Wyath Sonai-Feth have to smile so about?

15

Patterns

———— ❦ ————

A single lamp shone from the middle of the circle. Its dim yellow light shone uniformly on the faces of the captives. Each eye glimmered unfocused in its light. Each mind concentrated on a single subject.

Krith stood to one side of the circle, his boots firmly planted wide apart on the deck of their now-familiar cell. From time to time he would stride across the circle with great steps, casting long shadows across his fellow delvers. So began the quiet litany. So it had begun for many nights planetside. So it continued tonight until the litany was put to use.

"Weave the song, *kidikers*," Krith began, the light casting strange shadows up onto his face. "Tell me the lay of it. Tell it to me as if our captain herself were here. *Where be the captain now, my friend?*"

> The Captain's nose is in a book
> Unbending backs do break
> We'll walk the decks in humble bow
> We'll sleep the bunks in dreams
> but on the walk betwixt between

We coil tight our razor claws
The Time is in flower
We wait the word to cut the fruit.

"Aye, well, my lads, tell me more of the lay of it. *Is this the way to hell?*"

So on they murmured among themselves the words in the morning and at night, excusing themselves to their captors as a crew praying to their own gods of the sky.

"Captain, the Loyalist leader, sire."

"My thanks, Master Parquan. Please show her in."

Thyne exploded through the double door, bounding up the wide stairs in the captain's walk. "My men are being treated for horrors, Captain, and I demand that you do something about it at once."

Serg quickly bit his lip rather than laugh outright. "Treated *for* horrors?"

Thyne charged on despite her mistake. "Yes. You have them stacked below decks in a hold like so much cargo. You keep them in the darkness without proper ventilation . . ."

"Ah, you mean treated horribly. Madam, there isn't much light or air between the stars. I don't know how I am denying them that which they couldn't have anyway."

Thyne blinked but remained otherwise unmoved. "They are delvers, like your own crew, being kept in a confined space without benefit of movement. Don't your regulations speak something about freedom of the deck or exercise for captives?" In fact, Thyne could have quoted the exact paragraph out of the Pax manual but didn't care to let him know how far she had gone in her study of his empire. *To know the enemy is to defeat them,* went the old axiom, *while to deny them knowledge is to conquer.* It was a small thing, but she never gave even small advantages away to her enemies—certainly not to this short Pax captain.

Serg leaned back in his chair. "Yes, in fact there is. I'll grant your crew freedom of the quarterdeck only—and only in groups of six at a time. Each will have half an hour on the deck under guard. Will that satisfy you?"

"When will I be allowed to see my crew?"

"You'll see them—if you see them—planetside at Kilnar. On my ship you'll remain separate." Serg spoke evenly.

"Perhaps, in time, I might change your mind on this?"

"I rather think not. Is that all, Lady Thyne?"

"Yes, thank you, Captain." Thyne cocked her head roguishly. "You know, you're not half bad for a butchering lackey."

"Nor you for a self-rationalizing anarchist."

They smiled at each other the tight, polite smile of hunters before the kill.

It began in the morning of their second day in the darkwind. Krith lay in his bunk and awaited his turn on deck. The great iron door to their shared cell—the same empty munitions bay they had occupied before—swung slowly open. The first group trudged into the room. Two guards flanked the door, their handcannons leveled. Standing behind them in the hall, the officer of the watch began calling out names.

"Yorki Sauth-Endr! Yantha Candith-Surath! Yunta Vishan!"

With enormous effort, the named Loyalists began to roll out of their hammocks, move away from the wall, or rise from the floor.

"Emilithia Haught-Soeshalbi!"

Krith watched Snap break into a sudden angry blush. As Snap had confided to Krith many times before, Emilithia was no warrior's name and she hated that she had to drag it around with her through her life. Snap was a quick name and a worthy name for a heroine. She considered it more her name now than the title given her by parents, who were now long separated from their wealth and status. At least the rest of her crew were polite enough to seem not to notice.

". . . Ardo Pelin! Krith Sonath-Paun!"

Ah, thought Krith as he hoisted himself slowly from his hammock, so the Lady has worked it out this far. It's time to work out the last of it.

The six - Yorki, Yautha, Yunta, Emilithia, Ardo, Krith were motioned into the access corridor which continued aft to the remaining magazine compartments and forward toward the gun deck. The two guards backed aft to allow the prisoners into the hallway, then motioned them forward toward the two additional guards waiting for them.

Quietly, like the others with him, Krith shuffled forward. His eyes were downcast, yet he was terribly aware of all that was around him. He knew there were ten magazine compartments in

the ship. His glance aft as he came out of the compartment told
him there were three more iron hatchways on each side aft. That,
he thought, would put them in compartment three—a little farther
forward than they might have hoped but not as bad as it might
have been. The hall itself would barely fit two abreast with difficulty. Narrow enough, he thought, for what they had in mind.

They came to the end of the corridor. The vast gun deck
opened there before him. Rows of cannon were tended by a crew
of twenty or so, each moving over the maze of machine and fiber
conduit like spiders through their own webs. Down the center of
the compartments overhead was the main conduit for the silverfire feeds. Its segmented shielding gave it the look of a giant
spine pulled from some horrific beast. The illusion was supported by the image of curved ribs from the great arcs of optic
conduit that branched from the spine down to the individual guns
on the main deck as well as a second battery of guns on a deck
above. The crew moved through this great rib cage, keeping the
massive fibers clear of flaws.

By the look of the spine, which thickened noticeably forward,
Krith knew that the temple must also lie in that same direction.
The main power trunk on this craft almost certainly ran directly
to the temple of silverfire. This ship held her heart in her bow
and, as any stardelver knew, the man who holds the ship's heart
can own her or kill her.

Krith then considered the costs of gaining control of the ship's
bow. The gun deck was a wide space with no fewer than six access hatches—four of them at the far forward end. If they were
fast enough . . . strong enough . . . bled enough . . . they might
make it.

The guards motioned their still-acquiescent charges to continue. The prisoners climbed the access ladder up two decks to
yet another pair of cannon-wielding guards. The ladders were
steep. Krith made a small show of laboring up the rungs, as if his
great bulk were a burden. He noted the arrangement of the ladders as they climbed and silently counted the steps. There were
airtight iron doors at the first landing and an airtight overhead
hatch at the top. That, he thought, would have to be number two
on the list of things to do. Sealing off these hatches could keep
the response to their little piracy down to a manageable fight on
the gun deck.

Krith continued to slog up the ladder. The overhead hatch

opened into the great ship's bay. It looked larger from there on the deck than the exterior of the ship would have seemed possible to contain. Directly overhead was a five-deck-tall mooring, where four handsome little craft were secured. Davits for a fifth were empty and Krith vaguely wondered why.

A rough hand shoved Krith. He meekly gave no resistance to the push but marked the man in his mind as one with whom he would settle later. He and his group were escorted aft through the great bay doors onto the fantail. The four guards took up positions at the forward end of the expansive flat quarterdeck while their prisoners walked aft without enthusiasm.

Krith stretched and walked about. The great opal sails of the ship curved in a translucent glow around the bow, fading into black night and stars aft. He looked but saw none of it, for his thoughts were elsewhere.

The plan firmed up in his mind. The mage and two others hold the access forward while the remaining two free the crew. Press forward into the gun deck; seal the hatches in the ladder shaft; take the gun deck and drain the main power trunk through the ship's own guns. When the lights drain out, then press forward again and take the temple. It sounded so neat and proper in his head, but he had lived enough to know that it never was quite that clean in performance.

Krith looked at his shipmates on deck. They talked about the ship they were on and talked to each other about her rigging. They stared at the stars overhead or ran in easy measured strides in great circles around the now-clear landing area.

And when it was time to return below, they each seemed to sigh in their own way the sigh of disappointment and resignation. Each prisoner shuffled back through the ship's bay, down the ladders, and halfway down the long access corridor to rejoin their fellow prisoners. Krith followed with equal apparent resignation.

There was a chance that it would work. If they succeeded, they would cause a thundering flash that would send ripples all the way to the center of the great Pax itself. If they failed . . . well, you can only die once.

Krith watched as group after group was taken up on deck. All through the ship's first watch the prisoners were brought up six at a time. Each time they were quiet. Each time they were docile.

Each time they ran the litany given to them by Krith over and over again in their minds.

> ... but on the walk betwixt between
> We coil tight our razor claws
> The Time is in flower
> We wait the word to cut the fruit.

The second night wore on and again the circle was formed. Again they chanted ever quietly among themselves. Again the lay was told and retold.

"Aye, well, my lads, tell me more of the lay of it. *Is this the way to hell?*"

> The way is now a'fore and aft
> Them with the fate must hold the rushing prow
> The Spirit Weaver in their aid

Snap's eyes flashed at this. This was her part and she relished the celebrity of being so much a part of the lay.

> While others stove the stern
> A dead-man's run to win the prize
> Them that hesitates then dies
> But them that lives takes blood for blood
> And strikes out for the Lady's heart.

There was silence for a time. Each person sat on the floor, gazing into the single lamp, lost in his own thoughts.

"When do we play, Krith?"

The huge man towered over the lamp, his face speaking from a shadow as deep as the night. "Two days, lads. We be docile little *Mumar* for two days more at least. Then the captain will be ready—and we'll follow her to death or glory."

The muffled sound of the creaking lines and stays were all that were heard for another count of time. They all sat still once more. Then Krith sucked in a great breath and walked across the circle as he had done again and again the night before.

"Weave the song, *kidikers*. Tell me the lay of it. *Where be the captain now, my friend?*"

The captain's nose is in a book
Unbending backs do break
We'll walk the decks in humble bow
We'll sleep the bunks in dreams
but on the walk betwixt between . . .

16

Silent as the Night

"Thank you, Master Parquan, you may leave us now. Care to join me in a game of chatur, Lady Thyne?"

Thyne looked about the observation deck. The shifting pastel glow of the mainsail fell through the forward dome, bathing the compartment in soft, warm light. Two large chairs had been brought into the compartment, though how they had been brought through the small access door was something of a mystery to the Loyalist. Between the chairs, a cube with glowing images sat on a low table, the faint lines of a cubed grid glowing from within.

"I'm afraid I haven't much interest in games. Life is more of a challenge and less a waste of my time."

"Still," said Serg as he sat with ease in one of the chairs, "you must admit that games can put an edge on one's strategic skills while providing a pleasant diversion from the unpleasant and otherwise dreary aspects of life. It's important to let go of one's troubles from time to time."

Thyne moved to the table and gazed for a few moments at the cube in silence. "I never let go, Dresiv. To let go is to forget who I am and what I must do." Her gaze then settled on Serg. "Do you let go, Dresiv of the Pax?"

Serg smiled, but there was a thoughtful sadness in his voice. "When I can."

Thyne sneered. "I just bet you do. Playing games is probably what you do best. It's probably what you're doing with my entire world right now. Oh, it'll be a fine little prize for you, won't it? The great and mighty Pax brings toys to the backward little worlds of their frontier. Sad to lose a few pieces, though, isn't it? It's all right, though. It's only the blood of fathers, the hearts of mothers, and the tears of their children. What's that to the great Pax? Just so many acceptable losses, I should think."

Thyne sat down stiffly. "So you fly your mighty silverfire ships from game to game, winning and losing with as little care as a boy bored with his old toys. You walk on the bloodied ground with soiled soles without even understanding what you have done."

"Understanding?" Serg whispered. "You want *understanding*? There's no such thing on a galactic scale, Lady Thyne."

Serg leaned back, both his hands on the table as he continued, his eyes looking toward the game but focused on something far beyond as he spoke.

"Our own minds are almost beyond our comprehension. Humanoid races have the capacity for about a hundred trillion pieces of information in each of our brains. Only about a tenth of that we use to make each of us who we are: hopes, dreams, passions, art, talents, and thought. Yet if we could use a brain for nothing more than memorizing the galaxy—not for eating or breathing or thinking, just for storing facts—we couldn't come close to comprehending it. There are over one hundred billion stars in this galaxy alone. I once figured out that if you limited your description to five sentences for each star, you just might be able to cram all that information into your head.

"*Five sentences* for each of those civilizations that grew and flourished for over a thousand years. *Five sentences* for all the kings and queens and paupers and lost loves. *Five sentences* for all the blood in all their wars and conquests. You couldn't even give a description of its location in five sentences that was accurate enough to just *find* its star, let alone even touch upon the richness of any civilization there.

"Write your own life in five sentences. That's all the space you have for your entire world and the combined thoughts of all its people. No single mind can come close to comprehending the vastness of the galaxy, let alone infinite space that surrounds it.

"No, Thyne." Serg looked suddenly into her eyes. "I don't understand what we have done. All creation is too vast for any understanding except of great principles which might encompass all the vastness of the incomprehensible. If that means injustice on a personal scale, that, it seems to me, is of little consequence in the vastness of the empire's harmony and the progress of law and higher order among the stars."

"Whose law? Whose order?" Thyne smiled behind sleepy eyes. "You're speaking in high moral terms, Captain of the Pax, but your words are meaningless when it comes to actual life and lives. Besides, as you say, you really don't understand anything."

Serg didn't reply at first, leaning forward and pressing his finger against the top of the crystal cube. The grid lines receded, scaling downward and revealing small glowing ships of light floating strictly in the center of their cubed places.

"Well, I think I understand a good deal more than you think."

Thyne had been seeing the Pax captain as a boy with his toys, but something in his voice suddenly echoed darkly in the back of her skull.

Serg continued to play with the chatur display, turning the grid of light around its axis and rolling it into various configurations. Thyne waited.

"For example, there will be no piracy today—or any other day, for that matter. You see, Lady Thyne, my shipwright was touring the ship before we left High Anchor and found one of our under-hull magazine hatches had been forced open from the outside and resealed. I'm afraid that Priestess Ordina takes such acts as a personal assault. Unfortunately, she ran off to investigate before anyone could follow her. The interior access was, of course, trapped as well.

"She found herself caught in a dimensional fold spell and disappeared for a few hours before her own Acolyte stumbled on it as well. Amazing thing, a dimensional fold—it rotates space around itself so that things within it have a dimension of zero to outside observers. Absolutely invisible and undetectable to those who don't have any knowledge of such things. Remarkable what she found."

Serg looked up from the glowing game field. The chords of the midwatch hymn sang distantly through the hull, almost a vibrant whisper. Thyne watched him critically but with unblinking eyes.

Serg sighed and again leaned back in his chair. "Weapons, Thyne; she found weapons. Not just any weapons either. They were definitely of Pax construction and aren't supposed to be obtainable by revolutionaries. And they just happened to be secreted in a supposedly empty hold just a few compartments aft of where your people have been kept all this time. We've moved them, of course, and you might still have been dangerous with your—what is it you call them—Spirit Weaver? We also have taken care of your Spirit Weaver."

Thyne's heart went cold. How could he have known about Snap? How is it he could have so perfectly ferreted out her plan? Everything turned around—ruined. She had gambled on seizing this vessel and the emissary as well. She might have forced the Pax to its knees and freed her world. Now she would be delivered by this Pax *skrud* to her enemies. Death would be the kindest fate but not the destiny the Brotherhood would have waiting for her. Still, she had one card left to play—and it was sitting right in front of her.

"Clever game, Master Dresiv." Thyne's voice was quiet. "Now we sail quietly on to Kilnar to be handed over and executed almost in the same breath. You value life too cheaply, Captain."

Serg's head jerked upward suddenly. A cold rage formed in his eyes. "Wash your own shirt before you complain about another man's smell, Lady Thyne. A week ago you valued the lives on this ship with less thought than I might give to an old rag. In any event, I will have to disappoint your expectation. We are stopping at Kilnar so that our illustrious Farcardinal and the Thrund ambassador can make planetfall and do their duty either by the Pax or themselves—I personally don't care which. You, however, and your crew will remain aboard due to an unexpected emergency on Ornanth—our next immediate destination. There you'll be handed over to the local Pax Consul ... we have a small supply station there that should be able to keep you out of mischief until I can find a magistrate in this sector that can sort out this entire business." Serg sighed, holding both hands open as he gestured toward the cube. "Look, I brought this game from the Core worlds and haven't found anyone worth playing it with me. I have to keep an eye on you while they search your cell ..."

Thyne bristled.

". . . so we might as well make the most of it."

Thyne sat stiffly for a moment and then shrugged. A supply station was certainly better than being handed over to the Brotherhood, she thought. Besides, it also depended on just what kind of supplies the station stocked. There might be something she could use. She would need the Spirit Weaver back to make it work, however. Thyne thought of Snap and wondered just how hard she had fought. The slight girl might have done herself more harm in resisting than in just giving up, and giving up wasn't like Snap at all.

"My crew is safe?" It was more of a statement than a question.

"Your crew is safe, Lady."

"And my Spirit Weaver?"

"He is being held comfortably."

"He is?"

"The fellow put up quite a lot of resistance, but the containment magic held. I'm sure he'll be quite all right once we let him out."

Thyne's mind suddenly raced. While her own language had no gender structure, she had mastered the language of the Pax well enough to understand its masculine and feminine structure. The only mage she had was female. The captain clearly stated the Weaver was male. If she understood . . . then the captain had neutralized the wrong Weaver.

The plan was to go off sometime during this shift. When she got word the captain wanted to see her, she thought herself lucky—it would be a pleasure to kill him herself. It was this Pax captain's image she now saw whenever she thought of her father dying, just as it had been with all the others she had killed. Krith would make the attempt, not knowing that the weapons wouldn't be there. Yet, apparently, he would have a Weaver with him— something that the captain and his crew did not know or expect.

Thyne leaned forward and considered the cube. "You're right. I suppose we should at least make some use of our time. Would you mind teaching me your game?"

Thyne returned Serg's smile as he leaned forward. *With any luck and a little bit of time,* she thought, *I might have a shot at killing you yet.*

17

Into the Darkness

~~~•~~~

Krith had counted down the shifts just as Thyne had instructed him before leaving Brev. He knew it was time, but the knowledge of it didn't make it any easier or offer him any comfort. This kind of action was tricky and he never much cared for it. Still, the plan was bold and everything was in place to make it happen.

Snap was ahead of him as they walked forward off the quarterdeck. Krith glanced starboard and grimaced. The stars weren't right for the course they should have been taking. Still, there would be time enough to correct that. He growled and gave Snap a shove.

"Hey, *Kotk*, watch step. No stop you, choke death on Snap feet."

"I'll break yer feet into four, ya little *Shith*." Krith's lips parted but his teeth had remained locked tight.

"Silence!" The Pax guard was showing his amused attention to the prisoners. "Get below in order and stop your talking. Order of the captain."

It would be, thought Krith. The Lady sure had that stiff read properly. *The captain's nose is in the book.* So far, the little tyrant had followed the Pax procedure manual down to the letter of the law. You could always count on the Pax to set up a routine and stick with it.

Krith trailed behind his crewman as they trudged their way into the great ship's bay. The giant Loyalist gripped the railing of the access ladder and began hauling himself down after his companions. "Sorry, yer lordship, but that little squeak of a kid has been gettin' on my nerves."

The guard above him gave a quick snort in humored agreement and waved him onward with the muzzle of his handcannon.

. . . but on the walk betwixt between, we coil tight our claws . . .

"Not that it would be so bad, mind you," Krith continued almost to himself, "If she weren't such a high-pitched piece of steel on slate."

"Big man speaks with whistle of hollow brain!" screeched Snap, now red-faced and all but proving Krith's point.

. . . The Time is in flower, We wait the word to cut the fruit . . .

Krith reached to bottom of the ladder with a quick glance forward. The gun-deck crews stood relaxed on their watch. The guards at the bottom of the stairs held their autocannons loosely . . . as he had hoped by now they might. He knew there were two other guards forward by the cell door, but they weren't his problem. Yantha could handle them without trouble, and though Yorki was young, he was surprisingly strong for so slight a frame.

. . . We wait the word to cut the fruit . . .

"Well," sighed Krith as he drew the guards into the corridor after him with his words. "I guess it's back to the cell and another shift of listening to this rat spit. What think ye, mates? Is this the way to HELL?"

The final word was a yell as in a single swinging motion the great Loyalist bent his knees and brought both fists upward. The autocannons wavered a moment too long. Krith's hands slammed upward like anvils to catch the hollow between the guards' necks and jaws. The screams of both men were muted, their jaws shattered as the huge Loyalist's swing hammered their mouths shut and lifted both men off their feet. Their heads collided against the overhead with a shivering thud.

Krith let both guards fall to the floor, wrestling a handcannon from one of them even as they collapsed. He slipped his hand into the cannon's metal gauntlet and, gripping the haft, swung it upward to cover the end of the corridor.

"Skak!" Krith looked forward into the gun deck. The gun crews were nowhere in sight, but the great delver knew they were out there somewhere—both alert and waiting for him. No doubt word was already spreading as well. He didn't dare look away. It was only a matter of time now.

"Snap!" Behind him, the cries and blows had died down and he could hear his own crew pouring from the now-open cell door.

"Allai, Krith! Aft solid now. Yunta and Wethen strike hard, work fast. Pax guards sleep the long one. Door staved. Crew aft."

The ship's alarm abruptly cut the air with a call to boarding quarters. He yelled back over his shoulder. "We're going to have company soon, friends!"

Yantha suddenly appeared at his side, grasping his shoulder. *"Dran*, Krith, the hold is empty!"

"WHAT?!"

"There ain't no weapons cache, Krith. We searched the hold—*Hesth*, we searched all the holds back there. They're all as empty as the Void."

"That there fellow on Brev took care of it. I seen them papers myself!" Krith bellowed, not wanting to believe what he now knew must be true.

"Maybe he crossed us, Krith!"

"Nay, lad! The Lady herself vouched for 'im. Them Pax dogs must have gotten wind of . . ."

Plasma slivers began tearing the air from the gun deck. The first shots were high to the left, raining splinters from the wall and ceiling. Yantha and Snap fell prone, more from instinct than desire. Krith crouched away from ear-splitting shrieks until the volley ended, then turned his own cannon forward and pulled the trigger grip.

Nothing happened.

A second volley ripped down the hall. Better aimed, it narrowly missed Krith as he threw himself on his back behind the motionless bodies of the Pax guards. As the plasma slivers shredded the air above him, he pulled the handcannon up and worked feverishly to fix it.

"Hesth farquan kotk sequath! The *dran* gun's empty. These *kotk* Pax have been holdin' us at bay with unloaded cannons!"

A third volley of the blinding slivers ripped overhead.

"Shisk, Krith, what now?" Yantha was flat against the deck to one side of the huge man.

Krith turned to the frail young Spirit Weaver. "What's above us, Snap?"

The girl's eyes were wide and watery.

Krith gathered the top of the girl's tunic in one hand and pulled her face within an inch of his own. Perhaps the sight of his face filling her vision would help her forget the fear that surrounded them.

"Snap! What's overhead?"

The girl blinked and her vision focused on his eyes. "Over— overhead. Water stores overhead."

"And below?"

"This deck bottom. Planks only, then open space."

The corridor fell suddenly quiet. Looking past his feet, Krith could see that his crew had taken cover in several different munitions holds. There were no exits aft—it had been a critical part of their plan that no one could get behind them. Snap could open a passage through the hull, but to where?

"Fine fish! We open a hole up and we drown. Go down and we suck vacuum." Krith thought furiously aloud.

Yantha's voice sounded as though it came from the grave. "So what do we do now?"

A voice echoed down the hall from the gun deck. Krith turned slightly on his back to try seeing where the voice came from, but the guards still lay in the hall and incidental smoke from the plasma bursts had caused a haze to settle through the area.

"*Awas*, prisoners! Submit and abandon your weapons!"

Snap and Yantha both looked questioningly at Krith.

"No, *dran*, we'll hold to the plan!" Krith growled through clenched teeth. "Snap, can you shield us long enough to get out on the gun deck?"

"Snap strong. Krith no worries here."

Krith looked at the slight girl and estimated her chances. There was no doubt that the girl was sincere and confident in her powers—but Krith also knew what raw power she would be facing. In the end, he knew he had no choice.

"Snap, ready yourself, gal. Yantha, when it starts we have to be quick. *A dead-man's run*. Remember, *them that hesitates . . .*"

"*Allai*, Krith. Get to it, man."

"Far as I can tell, there be a single gunner on the right behind the first cannon. That one's yours. I'll take them on the left. Stay behind the shield wall, then take 'em any way you can. Get a weapon and fire till she's dry. There should be mates there to help you by then." Krith turned to Snap. "Be a good gal, now, Snap, and put the wall in front of us."

Snap had already closed her eyes and was falling into the mystic sight she used in her magic. Suddenly, her eyes opened, focused as though on another place. A ball of transparent blue, crackling and alive with lightning, appeared before them. The tendrils felt the extremes of the walls and shifted to fill the space. The ball thinned into a wall and began rushing forward down the corridor.

Krith leaped to his feet and ran after it. In an instant, the sun-like streaks of plasma leaped toward him from behind the deck cannons. He ducked instinctively, but the bolts smashed against the mystic shield, exploding in blinding flashes without reaching him.

He passed the end with Yantha off his right arm. He heard rather than saw the handcannon rip loose its load from the access ladder above. A rain of plasma drilled into the floor behind them as they passed. The wall continued to run before them, conforming itself around anything that did not move but still holding off the deadly bolts leaping toward them. Krith's eyes went wide as the shield began to fade in front of him. The power of the on-slaught was taking its toll on Snap and the young mystic was losing her strength. The bolts began pressing into the shield as they flared, each hit seeming to drain the color and intensity from the shield even further.

The thinning shield folded over the mounted cannons. Krith leaped with it, falling behind the cannon just as the shield cleared it. The Pax gunner stood there with his handcannon locked, facing the giant Loyalist. In that instant, however, the shield passed over him and the plasma in his handcannon was held in stasis. The gun failed to fire for a fraction of a second and it was all the edge Krith needed. In a single sweep Krith knocked the handcannon aside and grabbed the gunner's throat. His momentum carried him as he had intended over the man. They both rolled to the ground, Krith stopping them both by using the man's head as a brake.

Yantha's screams cut through the sound of more plasma dis-charging. Krith pulled the handcannon off the arm of his now-limp opponent and began firing even as he turned toward the sound. Yantha had not fared as well as Krith, but the Pax gunner wasn't experienced enough to recover. Krith's bolts tore a line across the decking and through the gunner before he could even face his new enemy.

At that instant the air was filled with sound. Krith glanced over the top of the cannon and saw several of his crew trying to run out of the corridor, but only two made it past the continuing fire from the access hatch and ladder above them. Cries from the forward end of the gun deck seemed simultaneous with more fire from the forward hatches. Krith ducked down and then raised up, firing his handcannon forward for a series of shots before ducking back down again before a murderous hail of plasma bolts.

Well, he thought, *I have their attention.*

This wouldn't work. His crew pinned in the chambers around a single corridor were making no progress against the guns facing them. It was only a matter of time before they'd be overcome—or dead to the last soul. Krith needed a weapon and found it on the man he had just killed. With an easy toss aft, the small implosion grenade detonated at the base of the ladder by the corridor.

Thunder rocked the deck. Krith felt himself pulled back toward the blast area as the air around him collapsed toward the point of implosion. All other sound was lost in the reverberating collision behind him. As the air settled, he rose up again, firing a covering hail of bolts forward and then glanced aft as he dropped back down under cover.

The implosion had been rather more effective than he had hoped. The gunner from the access ladder had been silenced, as he had intended, but the implosion field had shattered the floor and, worse, the ceiling. The great spine conduit that supplied the ship's guns with the silverfire magic had pulled free of its housing and ruptured. Silverfire—potent, powerful, and chaotic—gushed from the single optic cable, no thicker than a child's wrist, writhing free of the housing. The silvery torrent spun tendrils out about the deck, warping space around itself into existences and possibilities that threatened the reality around it. The deck below Krith's feet shuddered under the strain of the magic rushing to be free of its constraints. The drain on the conduit would certainly soon be noticed by the Temple Acolytes and the power to that optic cut soon, but by that time the entire ship's company would be set to stop them.

"Shisk!" Krith swore.

Another spray of fire passed overhead as he leaned his back against the cannon protecting him. He swung his own hand-cannon around the end of the large deck cannon this time and fired down the row between them. As he turned back around for protection, his jaw dropped in wonder and horror.

"Snap! No!"

The slight girl leaped from the end of the corridor and, with both bare hands, grasped the snakelike cable of silverfire.

18

Streams of Life

"Here, then, to the success of our mission. To the success of our cause."

The emissary raised her glass with her leftmost appendage to the fifth of the Farcardinal's toasts in strict observance of the human custom, though again she did not drink. Eating and drinking were, by Thrund custom, as private an affair as any other bodily functions and not to be observed publicly. Still, the human wanted to celebrate, and this seemed as good a time as any. Their mission was well under way and, barring any mishap, the Thrund and all her race would be one step closer to their destiny.

"Yes, my lord Farcardinal, my congratulations. All things seem to have worked for us as originally planned. You have brilliantly played your part." A little flattery went a long way with humans, especially with Sabenth, thought Hruna.

"Credit as due, my Thrundian friend. A new world is being brought into the Pax with all its promise and commerce . . . not to mention our own slight incentive in this matter as well."

Hruna blinked furiously at this, her three faces all paling visibly. She turned to Trevis. "Perhaps you could be so kind as to bring us some additional pillows. I feel myself a bit uncomfortable on the hard floor."

Trevis seemed not to have heard him. He remained standing, arms across his chest and sharp eyes on his master. Sabenth had been a little too free with both his drink and his tongue. Now the Localyte was hearing far more than was ever intended for his ears. Hruna watched the boy's jaw clench. Certain political subtleties of the situation had not been explained to Trevis. Now the boy could bring them real trouble.

"Brother Fel!" The Thrund's quiet voices echoed slightly out of phase like quiet thunder cutting the Localyte free of his own thoughts. "Might I trouble you for some additional pillows?"

Trevis shook once and then bowed stiffly, his robes rustling against the polished wood floor. "If my lord has no further need of me . . ."

The sentence hung like a question in the air, but the Farcardinal failed to pick it up. His holiness blinked for a few moments through watery eyes. His toast had being rolling along splendidly, but the conversation had somehow slid into pillows and he wasn't sure he had caught up with it yet.

"My lord?" Trevis repeated pointedly.

Sabenth closed his eyes laboriously. "Of course, my Brother, attend to the wishes of our guest. I may do without you for a while yet."

Trevis bowed again and walked a little too quickly from the room. The finely grained door had barely sounded closed when the Thrund turned on the Farcardinal.

"Really, Sabenth." Hruna's three heads bobbed about either side of the Farcardinal's head. It was a Thrundian posture of threat and warning. The meaning, however, appeared completely lost on Sabenth, which irritated Hruna even more. "Bad enough that you should need such a child along on this mission, but to bring one that isn't even aware of our plans is more than foolish . . . it's dangerous."

"Bah!" The Farcardinal waved his hand emphatically, but as the action was unbalancing him, he quickly stopped. "The boy's a Jezerinthian Localyte green from his first meditation retreats. He does well for mind translation of the Farsight and is a diligent chronicler of all my communication. He's new to delving and depends on me for everything."

"You should have told him," Hruna repeated, her heads pulling back and closer together.

"Told him what?" Sabenth snapped, and flushed red. "Told him that his precious Presidium is allying with the Barons of the Outer Tyrannies? That the great priesthood of which he is a part is threatened in its autonomy by a group of politicals? The boy's barely two months travel time from his home world. How can he comprehend the problems of Pax Prime over three years travel away?"

"You said yourself," Hruna rumbled, "he's an excellent translator."

The Farcardinal sniffed and looked up at nothing in particular, his tone becoming increasingly reflective. "Yes, he is an excellent translator. He hears every word ... but he had no idea of their meaning or scope. He doesn't hear the entire empire as I do. He cannot be tuned to over a million minds as I am. I hear the song always in the back of my mind like a tune waiting to be remembered. He cannot know the galaxy, for he cannot hear the song. If only ... did you hear something?"

The Thrund's ear cups swiveled upward, her heads angling away from each other. "No, I don't think ... wait. Is that it? Sounds like someone beating on the conduits. Look, the boy may be from the rim worlds and without experience, but that doesn't mean we shouldn't worry about him. I think perhaps you should explain just what is going on to him. If you don't, then he could make trouble for us without ..."

The closed portal resounded with a heavy thud. As the two occupants looked up in amazement, the latch rattled frantically for a moment before releasing. The freed door crashed open, swinging Trevis Fel into a sprawl on the floor. The boy was pale, sweating, and obviously out of breath.

"Ca–ca–ca–" the Localyte gasped.

"What?" The Thrund slid all four legs effortlessly beneath her to stand on her feet. "Slow down, lad, make it clear."

"Can–cannon! Handcannons! There's a ... a big fight ... battle ... toward the back just one deck up. Can't ... can't tell how many."

"*Dran!* Oh, get up off the floor, boy." Hruna turned her heads sharply from the repulsive sight of the young Localyte's wide-eyed fear. "Well, Sabenth? It looks like our prisoners are less than docile after all."

Sabenth returned the Thrund's stare, his eyes wide with fear. "They'll come for us, Hruna! They must know of our plans and our mission and—and they'll come straight for us!"

"That rabble?" Hruna's right appendage seemed to flick the argument away. "Oh, be serious, Sabenth! They barely can see up from the mud of their home world, let alone involve themselves with the affairs of the heavens."

"You don't know them like I do! They're a lot more cunning than you give them credit for—cunning and absolutely ruthless. I tell you, Hruna, they'll want our lives!"

"Shut up, Sabenth!" Hruna was suddenly aware that the Localyte was still listening and no doubt hearing a good deal more than might be for his own good. Besides, the Farcardinal's fear disgusted the Thrund's deep social prejudice against cowardice. It was obscene to her. She thought for a moment and began to wonder aloud with her left voice only, as was her habit. "Why did the World Brotherhood demand that we return these prisoners at once?"

Sabenth, still wide-eyed, thought the question was directed at him. "I . . . I don't know! Can't imagine! The ambassador on Brev was most emphatic about it."

There was much here to ponder, thought Hruna Nruthnar, and little time to do it. Certainly this was something the hot ears of the Localyte did not need to hear discussed.

"Trevis Fel, get up at once and be of service to your master! Find the captain and, in your master's name, ask him what has happened and if he is in need of any assistance from us. Offer our services as negotiators." There was as much chance of negotiation now as drinking sand, thought Hruna, but at least the boy would be out of the way for a while.

Again Trevis looked at Sabenth for confirmation.

"Yes! Use all haste, Master Fel, and do as the Emissary directs," Sabenth urged.

Trevis shuddered. "The captain is probably several decks above us," he offered feebly, but drew no reprieve from either the Farcardinal or the Thrund. The pounding overhead was now punctuated by the distinct thud of handcannons discharging. Trevis drew an unsteady breath to steel his resolve and then ducked out the door once more.

•　　•　　•

The sound of cannon fire above was far more pronounced in the corridor than in the Farcardinal's quarters. Dim light flashed in the overhead hatchway at the end of the short corridor accompanying the sound of the handcannons. As Trevis reached for the railing, a brilliant light, blue shifting occasionally to golden hues shone down on him from the hallway above. The ship quivered and the guns silenced. Trevis began to climb.

"What kind of missionary work is this?" he muttered to himself through chattering teeth.

Emilithia Haught-Soeshalbi, the frail Spirit Weaver of the Loyalists, had heard tales of the silverfire. It was the power she used in her magic magnified a thousand times. It was dangerous. It was glorious. To tap directly into the source of creation and all possible existence, to harness a thunderous waterfall of power rather than take the dewdrops that came to her grudgingly from the universe around her, was the stuff of daydreams and fantasies. It was carnal and terrible all at once.

But the slight Spirit Weaver who would be called Snap had only heard the tales of concentrated power. She had no experience with it directly. Weakened by the shield she had formed, she was lying on the deck, watching the ruptured silverfire line and was seduced by its thundering chaos.

Her people had once been a proud race of warriors. Their gods were the gods of war and justice. Yet her own frail frame and meager talents had long betrayed her to that destiny she so fondly imagined for herself. She had always been pushed to the back, left there to aid her companions with her meager magics. Now, in the heat of battle, she watched her friends die under the murderous hail of cannon bolts. She'd seen combat before, but her friends had then been armed and dealing with their enemy on more equal footing. Now they needed her. Now was the time of her warrior proving.

Snap can help, she thought with conviction. *Snap save friends and captain.*

The brilliance was unbearable. Krith turned his face from the searing cascade of light. At least, he thought, the guns from the forward deck had stopped. Krith's eyes adjusted slowly, but still he was forced to take only fleeting glances aft from behind the protection of the shielding on his own arm.

The normally dim gun deck was now ablaze with light and color. Snap stood in the center of its flaming aurora, both hands seeming to merge with the conduit itself. An avalanche of magic rippled down her slender arms, the power making them transparent. Fire erupted around her feet as the power burned deeply into the wood of the deck. Most fearful were her eyes. They blazed, full of the silverfire light, a window to a soul being consumed with the power.

"Snap!" Krith bellowed, but his own voice sounded small to him amid the cacophony of the gun deck. "Snap! Cut loose, gal! Get clear o' the line!"

Waves of blue light surged through the compartment. Snap released the conduit with her left hand, but it was difficult to tell where her right arm ended and the conduit began. Ragged streams of phosphorescence gushed from her outstretched free arm, leaping over Krith to the enemy beyond the intervening guns. Screams punctuated the waterfall of sound and light. The streams began to shift wildly.

Krith fell hard to the deck. Water welled up in Krith's eyes. He screamed, "Snap!"

The eyes that turned to look at him were blinding white and without features. The voice thundered through the compartment not with any great volume but with a depth that seemed eternal.

"Krith . . . Snap save . . . Snap stop cannon."

"Durnadis Hesth, Snap!" Krith raged. "Stop it! Let'r go!"

Her entire figure had become translucent with the power flooding into her. Her form began to lose its cohesiveness, one minute appearing as Snap and the next changing to a gold, shining image of a warrior-god.

"Snap victorious! Snap save . . . save . . . power of all . . . sight looks over all . . . all creation . . . Snap all . . ."

The tendrils of silverfire were enveloping her now. Her form was being tossed about in the center of a terrible maelstrom of force, each blast losing a little of herself to the chaos that had seduced her. Her free arm became two, then three, then a myriad of appendages snaking from her body and tearing at the planks, bulkheads, and hull. Snap was fighting to maintain her self-awareness and identity against the onslaught of pure magic, and was losing the fight.

"NO! *Dran!* NO!" Krith leaped to his feet.

Without a thought, Krith threw himself at the center of the

magical storm. His huge body ached as the magic enfolded him, but the effect was as he desired. He struck Snap squarely mid-body.

The darkness that followed was so suddenly complete that Krith wondered if he had, indeed, died. No lights shone anywhere. In the midst of the darkness, however, a single voice from the darkened corridor was heard.

"*Them that hesitates then dies!* Now, mates, now!"

In the blackness, figures poured from the aft corridor and rushed forward. The darkness then was suddenly lit by the muzzle flash of handcannons, each flash etching a frozen moment of the battle now turned in the Loyalists' favor.

And each flash revealing a huge man kneeling at the back of the shattered deck, holding the limp figure of a slight girl in his arms.

19

Powers

Mistress Ordina went rigid, her long hands wrapped like iron around the Distribution Altar. In her mind she held a picture of herself as she knew herself to be. She concentrated on that with fierce determination as the third wave of searing blue chaos erupted through the Transentstone and surged through the temple.

The great optic tree rising above her writhed in its mounts, straining like a shackled slave. Reality flashed into and out of existence at once under the expanding sphere. For a moment she was aware of the power in the chaos and its seductive allure. The tempter called her to lose herself and her identity in the raw force and majesty that it offered. Still, she held the image of herself in her mind though the magic clawed at it.

Suddenly the expanding wave had passed. Ordina blinked furiously and shuddered. She was still herself. The magic had failed to change her, but she wasn't sure how much more of this she could withstand and still remain the person she had always been.

Ordina looked around. The temple walls blazed with blue-white light. The random magic suddenly took the form of a whirlwind around the main trunk, the air roaring around the shipwright. She saw shapes begin to form and then disappear around the Central Altar. Voices like a thousand dead whispered to her and then were silent.

Ordina blanched. There was a major disruption of one of the primary conduits somewhere in the ship. It might have been the keel, but other than the backwaves of chaos that the Transtator was now occasionally kicking free, the gravity seemed pretty steady. That left the power optics to the sails, rudder, and the gun deck. Each of these was actually three separate optics trunks which carried the silverfire force out to its final destination. If any one of these was severed, the other two could carry the burden without difficulty. The broken line would then have sealed itself within a few moments, and everything should have been fine.

Yet the line had not sealed. Something had prevented the automatic mechanism woven into the conduit optics from severing their link. Whatever had compromised the system had now invaded it. Resistance in the line was hammering back down the optics. The Transtator was randomly translating the feedback into waves of chaos. If the waves continued, then the Containment Altar of the temple would eventually unravel, freeing the Transentstone and the silverfire within it. If the Transentstone ruptured—well, thought Ordina, at least it would be quick for her and her temple workers.

Ordina was not, however, ready to die just yet.

"Tsara! Maxim! Ithilan!" The shipwright had to yell to be heard over the continuing rush of air.

"Allai!" Two of her assistants called back in a ragged chorus. She could see them now through the brilliance, clinging to the Altar of Knowledge on the opposite side of the temple.

"Where's Maxim?" The shipwright's voice barely carried over the gale.

Ithilan blinked furiously, shook her head, and turned away.

Dran! Lose your concentration in chaos feedback and almost anything can happen—with a high certainty that none of it is any good. Maxim was at the Stasis Altar to her right, just before the last wave, trying to isolate the conduit that was at fault. Now through the brilliant haze she couldn't see him. She wondered if he had forgotten himself in the wave or had not been braced enough when it hit. Her mind screamed at her that Tsara must have seen something—must know what had happened to him but couldn't say.

Ordina clenched her teeth. She would have to think about her assistant later. Right now all reality around her was breaking loose.

"Tsara! Help me isolate the main feeds! If we can . . ."

The shipwright turned to the Stasis Altar and stopped. Maxim's face grinned at her from the surface of the altar. The jewels of its normally cold surface shone back at her as the eyes of her friend, burning with a red light.

Ordina took a step back and then rushed across the room to where her remaining crew clung to the Knowledge Altar.

"The Stasis Altar is lost to us. What about the optics weave?"

Tsara's eyes concentrated fiercely on Ordina's face as she spoke, her loud voice barely carrying over the few inches that separated them. "The weave keeps shifting. The automatics and safety weaves are altering themselves in the system—probably the feedback. We have tried to reweave them from here, but they keep shifting on us." Tsara paused. "What about isolation? Can we isolate the temple from the general system?"

"It would mean bringing down all the mains and then pulling them up one at a time to find out which one is dysfunctional. If we shut down the keel . . ."

"Then we'd be sucking vacuum moments after the gravity cut out with the keel."

Tsara grinned as the fierce wind whipped her hair about her face. "Well, if the fault is in the keel distribution, then we're all dead anyway, right?"

"You're so cheerful," yelled Ordina with all the sarcasm she could convey through the storm. "I've already thrown the keel off line. It's working on its residual silverfire charge and should hold for about an hour. You commune with this altar while I take the Distribution Altar. I'll bring down each of the other lines and you tell me what you get. Got it?"

Tsara nodded and shook Ithilan from her stupor. Ordina lunged back across the dais. As she moved, shades of some unspeakable horror began to form before her. Her eyes widened as she passed through it, feeling the chill watching over her. It was an existence that was not real and a life that was not alive.

Just as she reached the altar, the world around her dimmed

again. Another chaos wave! She pulled herself together, strengthened her inner resolve and focus . . .

She saw trees and distant peaks. The walls of the temple were there too, but were somehow transparent. It was as though neither image was real, as though both were equally abstract. There was space too, and the Void and worlds and . . .

The wave passed. The walls of the temple wavered and twisted. The shadows and voices she heard were becoming more real and clear. The Ark was losing its grip on the Transentstone.

"Shut it down! Shut it all down NOW!" Ordina commanded as she reached for the main altar of the temple. The fields suddenly collapsed. Light seemed to fall from the walls into the single point of the Transtator globe. Darkness fell as a crashing wave behind it.

He knew he was in the bottle.

For the uncounted millionth time, Djan Kithber swore. Containment of an enemy wizard was the first rule in security. No single element could so powerfully affect the outcome of any conflict than the presence of a magician. Their ability to sway and alter the physics of the world around them left politics and diplomacy at risk. It took a great many nonmagicians to equal a magician in any contest of power or authority.

As a result, every palace or official building of state was carefully constructed with a bottle—a magical containment field in a slightly different dimension that held the magician and his powers in check. Bottles, to those who were in them, usually resembled a room with whatever furnishings the designer had woven into the field when it was created. Some torturous despots had created bottles that were unfurnished and without gravity fields or sensations of any kind. These bottles were especially vicious, for the wizard, devoid of any sensations, would often be driven mad if he were left in there too long. Such bottles were seldom ever opened again.

This bottle was reasonably well detailed—as bottles go. There was a sitting room complete with shelved books. The rugs on the floor weren't the most sumptuous, but they were comfortable. The walls were a bit utilitarian—more like the ship the bottle was a part of—but not unpleasant. There were also separate rooms for dining and sleeping, and a bath. The illusion was of a comfortable apartment area, except, of course, there were no doors or windows leading out.

When he fell into the bottle, he knew he was trapped. He was surrounded by a column of light and then his feet found solid floor beneath him. His rage found effect in the next instant. Power exploded around him, smashing the stuffed chairs into kindling, throwing the table crashing into the wall. The walls themselves buckled under the onslaught, gravity faltered, and the ceiling came crashing down. . . .

An instant later, all was as it was before. The chairs and table had reformed in their previous place.

Kithber howled and lashed out again. A shock wave of blue light flashed from him in an instant. The room dissolved into a maelstrom of superheated fire. . . .

And returned at once to its former serenity.

Spent, the wizard swayed back and forth, his vision blurred momentarily from the effort. Djan turned, panting, to the bookshelves. The books were burning cheerfully though their heat seemed to have no effect on the shelves. At least the books are real, he thought as he used his remaining meager power to snuff out the small, crackling blaze.

There was a fountain in the dining room. Through its illusionary water trickled the only source of magic in the shielded room. It was enough for him to live on. He could create his own food and water. He could even afford to recall some music now and then in the sitting room as he occasionally read a somewhat sooty book. Enough to let him know that he would be treated well and, possibly, someday, released—but no more.

Now he sat holding yet another book before him, but his eyes were not focused on the text. How could he have been so stupid. He had allowed the captain to lead him on a chase around the orbits of Brev to the point where he was weakened. Then he'd walked right into the bottle. He'd mostly come out to the frontier of the galaxy on commerce shipping. Such craft had little use for a bottle. He should have known that a frigate of the Pax would be outfitted with such precautions.

He drummed his fingers again against the arm of the chair and tried to focus his eyes and concentration. He had little choice but to wait and keep his mind active in the meanwhile. He knew that his time would come, and when it did . . .

Darkness surrounded him, and for a moment he suddenly felt

himself falling. Hard planking stabbed into his back with a jolt just as a cascade of books fell about him. He recognized from their smell that they were the remains of his own charred library.

He moved at once to stand up. Instinctively, he created a glowing sphere of light in his hand. It wasn't until the light filled the compartment that he suddenly realized that the spell shouldn't have worked.

The bottle had collapsed! He glanced quickly at the emitters for the field that were now clearly visible in the corners of the barren room. Their once-glowing cluster of seven cones continued to dim even as he watched.

He reacted at once. His own reserve of magical force, garnered meagerly from the fountain in the now-nonexistent suite, was not much but perhaps enough. He concentrated, carefully hoarding the force within him and began to float up to the ceiling of the room.

A part of his mind wondered, as he floated upward, why the bottle had collapsed. He then realized that he could not sense any flow of the silverfire through the ship. It was a source that he could absorb quickly to his own use but didn't seem to be near him.

That meant, he concluded, that his Pax hosts had lost power throughout the ship. Something must be going terribly wrong.

Reaching the ceiling, he found the hatch through which he had fallen days before. He quickly sprung the simple mechanism open and pushed hard against the door as the last of his powers began again to fade. Frantically grabbing hold of the edges, he heaved himself panting onto the deck of the corridor above.

Djan dragged himself to his feet. His sight returned slowly in the dark corridor lit only by the dim glow of the phosphorus emergency globes set in the walls. He wasn't sure where he was. The ship's plans hadn't been available to him before he left, and he had little experience in the design of Pax warships. He knew that their design followed somewhat the general layout of most planet surface ships, deriving their basic form from the watergoing vessels of ancient times. This meant that the crew, machinery, optics, and temple of the ship were below him— toward the keel. Officers and command centers would be up— away from the keel.

He was for a moment astonished that gravity was keeping everything natural. That alone told him a great deal about the condition of the ship. If gravity was still exerting its evidence of up and down, then the keel was still intact and functioning. There was no other evidence of power aboard, however, and that could mean only trouble in the temple. The ship felt stable, another good sign. The silverfire in the temple altar must have remained contained, otherwise the ship would be tearing itself apart.

More good news, Djan thought. If the keel is intact and the temple is stable, then the ship could be salvaged.

So what the *Hesth* happened?

The ambient magic of the galaxy again began to seep into him as he stood on the deck, panting. If there was something wrong, then he would have to fix it. First, he'd need to have some idea of what was wrong.

In the dark, his face twisted into a wicked smile.

There's only one man, he thought, *I'd like to have him explain this to me. He's got quite a bit to explain.*

Djan could hear the distant sound of men calling out over the low thunder of their feet against the decks. The sounds were dull and faraway. The wizard looked down both directions of the corridor. He took a tentative step to his right, paused, and then turned suddenly toward the clearer sound of panting and steps behind him.

Trevis threw himself at yet another ship's ladder with flagging enthusiasm. Holy Crusade? Mother of Night? Star Spirit? All these high ideals that he had honored . . . the spiritual enlightenment of the backward people among the stars . . . had brought him to be a lackey in some political contest of wills and might very well get him killed. Profit or prophet? Which did the church really espouse? He'd had enough little petty intrigues as a prince in the house of Kendrith. The small minds of power-hungry men were one of the reasons he had turned his back on his own world in search of a higher purpose. He found not so much a higher power in the galaxy as a great deal more of the same old power. For all he could tell, it was all that was aspired to, both inside and out of the church, by the same small minds as before.

Now he climbed through the dim decks of a crippled ship in search of a captain to save those same small lives. The petty contentions of rebels and Loyalists and schemers and dreamers—he didn't have a full picture of what was happening but he sensed enough. They argued over small points like a pack of starved *keran* over a single bone. Not one of them would let go until the ship itself was sundered and the only pride left would be the pride of the dead.

Each passing rung of the ladder lifted his anger higher. *So I'll die out here in the cold black like some martyr or, worse, sacrifice to their ambitions.* Him! A prince of his world! A dedicated follower of the stars! Dead because some Farcardinal wanted to hide a little ill-gotten wealth beneath his robes!

Yet he *had* heard the call. Tears stung his eyes sharply in the darkness around him. He had felt the peace in his heart and heard the wordless voice give answer to his prayerful supplication. He had never known such joy as he had at the revelation. It was a peace beyond any which he had ever hoped to know.

So if the spirit was right, why, then, was the church so wrong?

He pulled himself up the next deck, wiping the fiery tears from his eyes. The dim markings on the walls told him he was on C deck, just two decks above the battle. Two more decks and he'd find the captain. What he would say to him once he found him was . . .

The hair on the back of Trevis's neck stood suddenly on end and he turned.

Black against black moved toward him from the well of the corridor. Trevis suddenly sucked breath, but the powerful hand covered his mouth before he could cry out. He stared wide-eyed into the dark-bearded face that too quickly moved too close to his own.

"My name is Kithber. I've business with the captain. You will show me the way."

Trevis could barely nod under the pain of the man's powerful grip.

20

Interrupt

LLEWELLEN SECTOR / ANCJ14496 / BREV UPDRIFT TO KILNAR
THE *SHENDRIDAN*

Interrupt. The continuum of time focuses to a single frozen moment. The universe hangs in the balance. All that has happened before is counted as part of one past existence. All that happens after is never again thought of as it once was.

Serg Dresiv moves his arm toward his raj piece on the chatur game board. He knows it will be a decisive move that will end the game quickly, yet his mind is only half on the game. He suspects his opponent has a different game in mind. Her move won't be on the game board, and he prepares for it.

His opponent, Thyne, coils her muscles to spring. In her mind she reviews an ancient technique that brings sudden and—she thinks it unfortunate—painless death to the victim. She wonders what the captain would think if he knew he had but moments to live. She suddenly banishes the thought under her utter concentration. The time to strike has come.

In the hallway beyond their door, the wizard Djan and Localyte Trevis Fel approach. The magic is already growing in Djan, though he remains weak. Trevis leads the way not knowing or caring what business the stranger brings.

Four decks below them, Krith lays the limp body of a young girl on the deck and takes up a handcannon. He sets his jaw, moving purposefully down the debris-strewn compartment to the forward end of the gun deck. "It's time, lads!" he cries. "When we takes the temple, we owns this ship! Down into her belly, boys, and not a delver stop till she's ours!" He returns a volley of cannon shot up from the now-smoking stairwell and plunges into it.

No one notices the body of Snap suddenly and quite silently disappearing as a clouded mist at the back of the ruined compartment.

Delver Gennithna Parquan stands watch on the bridge, clasping and unclasping his hands nervously behind his back. Something was wrong. The trap they had laid for the Loyalist rebels had sprung, but the conflict should have ended long before this. He turns his head toward the watch-operations officer.

"Obres! What the *Hesth* is happening below! I thought those weapons had all been secured!"

Obres strains to hear the words coming up through the enunciator tube. The hollow sound of repeated cannon fire doesn't help the clarity of the excited voice from far below. He turns toward Genni. "Sir, the reports are fragmented. I . . ." he begins to say. Then, as Obres looks up, his voice stops mid-sentence. His eyes grow wide, fixed and horrified at some sight in the stars behind Parquan.

Parquan squints at the face of Obres, increasing alarm growing on his own features. "Master Obres?"

Mistress Ordina has nearly isolated the suspected contamination virus to the main optics trunk six leading to the main gun deck. Waves of force hammer against the isolation seals trying to reunite with its parent silverfire in the Transentstone of the altar. She pulls a hand ax from the wall and climbs the ladder to the walkway bordering the High Vaulting next to the offending optics conduit. "Cut now—fix later," she murmurs. She hears the muted sound of cannon fire outside the deck two compartment hatch behind her. "I wonder who's winning." she says to herself as she raises the ax over her head.

Cardinal Sabenth wipes sweat from his bald pate for the fifth time in as many minutes. The cannon fire is coming closer, he is sure. "Where is that wizard, Djan Kithber?" he wonders aloud to himself. Kithber should have been aboard to stop just such an occurrence as this. Sabenth looks at his companion Thrund. The hulking creature sits absolutely still. "How can you be so calm?" the Cardinal asks as he wipes his brow. He waits for a reply.

Hruna Nruthnar does not hear the Cardinal. She is in a deep trance, preparing herself for battle. Though she is an Kmissary of the Pax Galacticus and, therefore, supposedly a bringer of peace, she is now and has always been a member of a warrior race. The Cardinal is necessary for the ultimate plans of her people to succeed. The Cardinal is also, as the Thrund realized long before, something of a helpless old idiot. Therefore the Thrund must protect the Cardinal. Hruna prepares for the *Khuruch* . . . the way of dervish battle. In only a few moments she will be ready to fight in the Cardinal's defense with a bloodlust unknown among humankind. She hopes the Cardinal will stay out of the way. . . .

Delver Pol Vidra sleeps rather noisily in his bunk. His shift was over hours earlier and now it's time for rest. So deep is his sleep that not even the rumbling cannon fire below shakes him.

Elsewhere on ship the complexity of life continues. A delver picks at her meal in the common room as she worries for her friends fighting below decks. A Loyalist is thrown against the bulkhead from the impact of a cannon volley.

So, too, throughout all known space do people live, fight, love, and die. Children are born to a thousand worlds though their universes will not be the one into which their parents thought to bring them. Love blossoms and wilts across a billion more lives. Billions shake their fists at injustice and inequity. Billions count themselves fortunate. Quadrillions live this moment unaware that it is the last that they would recognize as their history.

Interrupt. The continuum of time focuses to a frozen moment.
Ever else will all be different.
Never again as before.

Mind-searing light erupted amid the stars Obres saw beyond Master Parquan, brighter than a sun so close as to fill one's entire vision. Its brilliance seemed blue with its intensity. The stars vanished in that moment, overwhelmed even in the darkness by the power of their new Brother.

Delver Obres never finished his sentence. The searing light burned through the bridge dome and into his eyes, engraving its stark, painful image seemingly to the back of his head. He had a vague impression of the deck heaving beneath him and the bridge crew diving for where they thought the deck should be.

Obres shook his head. The image remained before him— painfully white and persistent. He blinked his watering eyes repeatedly but without success. Even with his eyes tightly shut it was still there—still the blinding and ever-present point of light filling his vision. He staggered backward, away from the light that never moved.

The delver stumbled and fell.

The light would never go away.

Genni had instinctively fallen away from the flaring light behind him. For a moment he was disoriented; the floor seemed to be falling with him. He opened his eyes in his confusion and slammed them shut at once. The all-encompassing brilliance was still around him.

He seemed to fall forever through the brilliance piercing his closed eyes. When at last he slammed hard against the planking, the floor was slanting queerly, suddenly twisted into a form that he was not prepared for. Flailing his arms, he at last grasped the ship's wheel and locked his arms around its supports. The deck was continuing its list from the onslaught. . . .

The onslaught of what? he thought.

The glow beyond his tightly shut eyelids had suddenly subsided and again Genni tried to open them. The bridge was buried under charts and debris from the sudden lurch of the ship. Not surprisingly, the bridge crew lay tangled in a jumble with the debris. He realized with a start that many of the delvers around him were crying out with the pain of their injuries and wondered why he hadn't heard them before. The delver he had been talking to just moments earlier was lying on his back, rolling back and forth with his hands clawing at his eyes.

The still-pitching deck settled into great heaving rolls beneath him as the silverfire keel restored gravity and, with it, order to their senses. The ship still listed heavily to port, the keel again seeking its natural alignment with the darkwind passage the ship was following. The stars, wheeling in the dome overhead, soon settled into more familiar patterns. Genni pulled himself up the wheel housing and, not without fear, turned back to face what had just announced itself so forcefully.

He first noticed the clarity of his vision forward. The great darkwind sails that had been projected from the fore- and main-masts no longer glowed between him and the stars. The force of the gale had torn the matrix of the sails and stripped them from the mast projectors. The matrix could be rewoven by the shipwright—given time. As he looked beyond the masts to the stars, he suddenly realized there may never be time for much of anything.

Off the starboard forequarter, Genni saw clearly what could not be—a nova star had suddenly appeared where there had been no star before. The initial brilliance had subsided into a seething, huge star surrounded by an expanding ring of blue. The ring obscured the brightness at its center with a soft blueness but grew larger with a knife-sharp edge. The explosion of the nova—or whatever it was—had caused a secondary pressure wave to form from the cast-off energy. They had already experienced the first wave—primarily light—and seen its effects. This second wave would be of stellar matter accompanied by any interstellar dust and debris it picked up in its path. If the light wave had been a gale, Genni knew, this second wave would hit like a solid mountain.

"Clear the deck!" Genni shouted in his fear and excitement, although there was only the sound of moaning from the injured crew on the bridge. "Secure all hatches and get the crew to weather stations! Delver Nereth . . . I want you . . . to *Dreth*!"

The blue ring expanded beyond the scope of his vision. The black space filling the bridge dome dissolved into a soft blue. There was no time for anything. The wave was here—now.

Genni spun the wheel toward the menacing wave. If the pressure front caught them abeam, then he figured they were all dead men. The keel answered his summons lazily as the bow came about to face the new star.

The blow fell wide. Thyne cursed as the deck heaved beneath her feet and tossed her across the room. She collected herself at once, trying to stand on the still-unsettled floorboards without much success. The light washed over her like a solid thing. She turned her head away, groping in the brilliance for something—anything—that might be used as a weapon.

Serg instinctively rolled with the sudden motion of the ship, but the deck lurched unpredictably and he rolled painfully against the wall only a few feet from his attacker. It wasn't where he had intended to end up; this was one enemy he preferred to deal with at a distance. He locked his arm around the brass wall railing as some security against the slamming motion of the ship. It meant that he would be a stationary target, but as he couldn't see through the garish, all-encompassing light, he assumed that his assailant couldn't either.

Hesth Dranath! he thought. *What has happened!*

The keel was beginning to settle again. He remembered his opponent. It was time to make a few extra moves of his own. He blinked his eyes tentatively as the blinding flare died beyond the dome.

The compartment was a shambles, as, he suspected, was most of the rest of the ship. Chatur pieces were scattered all about the floor, mixed with remains of shattered carved chairs, a pair of broken tables, and a number of cushions. The debris shifted and slid about as the deck continued its unpredictable gyrations. He planted his feet carefully as the deck began to settle beneath him. Serg's eyes darted desperately about the room, searching out a familiar shape that he knew was his best hope.

Thyne blinked her watering eyes open and found her enemy near at hand. Her battle fury was again about to engulf her. She could feel the hatred gallop through her veins. Then she realized that he wasn't looking at her. She turned her head to follow his gaze. Her eyes saw it at the same time his did—the handcannon Dresiv had, no doubt, hidden under his chair lay nearly across the room tangled in the torn cloth of a cushion.

The two leaped as one, each with the same thought and goal, but the woman was quicker. She reached the cannon a moment before Serg. Grasping the gun with practiced ease, Thyne rolled over her shoulder and stood. In a fluid motion she turned and lowered the weapon.

But not quite. Her descending arm was suddenly blocked by Serg's upwardly crossed wrists. The Pax officer had recovered as well, crouching and then rising up to meet the weapon with his own hold. The weapon now stopped short of being able to fire at him, he slid his arms in scissors motion and grasped Thyne's wrist below the weapon. He turned under his own hands and threw his weight backward into his enemy. Thyne's own forward motion in anticipating the cannon recoil now worked against her and she fell forward over the top of the captain.

As Thyne fell, Serg rotated his hold with a viselike grip. The move should have stripped the cannon from the Loyalist's hand. Instead, the woman pulled the release.

A thunderous roar filled the room. Serg found himself surrounded by the acrid smoke of a discharged cannon. Serg started at the energy blast that had obliterated the floating dust into glowing specks just under his right arm.

Thyne didn't waste the moment. She swung both legs up around Serg's neck. The delver tried to counter but was too late. With a single pull, Thyne threw him free of his hold against the back wall.

He recovered, breathing heavily through the pain in his ribs. His feet slid against the slanting deck toward the corner of the room as he fell again. He rose slowly this time to face his adversary, knowing that he was probably going to be looking at his own death. Strange, he thought, how calm he felt.

She was silhouetted against the great observation dome, her tall form really rather beautiful, he thought, surrounded as it was by an expanding halo of blue light. He puzzled over that for a moment, then suddenly realized what the halo implied. He relaxed with the thought and smiled.

Thyne frowned behind the steady muzzle of the handcannon leveled at his head. "Now you die, Pax devil."

"Not too quickly, I trust."

She didn't answer—but she didn't fire either. The brilliant blue pressure wave continued to grow unseen behind her.

"They never die long enough, do they, Thyne?" Serg leaned casually against the back wall, belying the tension growing within him at the rapidly expanding sight behind his executioner. He could see that the ship was turning into the approaching wave—not, he thought, that it might do much good.

Thyne's unblinking eyes were fixed on the Pax officer leaning so casually before her.

"No," she said at last, "they never do." Her arms flexed as she discharged the cannon. The roar and flash surrounded her as the rushing wave of brilliant blue smashed against the ship.

The observation dome shattered behind her. The groans and

cries of the broken ship sounded like a thousand dead filling her ears. The hull splintered and twisted under the wave, the keel bent upward. Gravity shifted again, wavered, disappeared, and then reasserted itself directly aft. She fell from the floor as if it were a wall, slamming shoulder-first against the aft bulkhead twenty feet below her.

The rolling of the ship had subsided. Ordina willed herself to release the stanchion she had been grasping with bloodless, locked hands. Now, after the fact, they hurt from the effort. Deep within the ship's temple complex, darkness had engulfed her. The work-light globes had failed almost at once, and now only the green glow of the emergency lighting spheres cast their ghoulish illumination on the scene.

A glance through the dim green gloom below confirmed her fears. The Distribution Tree above the Transtator—usually alive with light—was now completely dark. The isolation seal at the base of the Transtator had ruptured from the explosion—or whatever it was. Now the virus was spreading unchecked through the distribution system, searching for the Transent core of the Ark. It might take months to unravel the tangled knot of the system contamination. There would have to be a purging canticle conducted over the Transentstone itself and a repurification of the silverfire base. The whole temple complex was, without doubt, a serious mess.

Ithilan was out of sight. She had been standing two decks below on the Clerestory dais surrounding the main altars moments before the ship had lurched. At least Tsara was still in sight.

"Tsara!"

"Allai," came the halfhearted reply. Her first assistant was sitting with her back against the starboard Altar of Knowledge, trying hard to drag herself up with her left arm. Her right arm hung limp at her side, lying at an unnatural angle. Several of the temple workers from the Triforum and Vaulting levels in the temple lay strewn chaotically over control altars, conduits, and platforms of the Arcade floor far below. Some were moving. Many more were not.

"Tsara! Where's Ithilan?

"Below I . . . I think." Tsara tried to reach the edge of the dais and peered down into the green-lit depths below. "I can't see her, but I was pretty sure she went over the edge. Ithilan! Ithilan!"

There was no reply. Tsara looked back up at Ordina and shook her head.

Ordina swung herself over to the ladder, sliding quickly down the outer edges to the dais below. She circled the slanting platform carefully, eyeing the indicators on each altar critically. "The Ark seems secure. There appear to be no cracks in the containment. The whole system is soiled by now, but there should be enough control left to limp us to the next stellar system."

"What about the darkwind sails?" Tsara was thinking hard through the pain of her arm. "Those optics aren't even feeding back now. The sails must be damaged or . . . or something."

"Or gone? It's possible. Still, the keel should give us enough directional stability to stay in the darkwind lane until we get the sails rewoven." Ordina looked at the unmoving forms around her. "I hope there are enough of us left to make this work. We could be here for a long time, Tsara."

A sharp slam sounded overhead. Ordina and Tsara both looked up at the noise, searching the Distribution Tree for some sign of further failure. Through the platform mesh of the high vaulting balcony overhead, she could see dark forms silhouetted against the emergency globes rushing through the now-open hatch. In an instant, a huge man swung down and landed heavily on his feet directly before the shipwright.

"Surrender now or die!" he thundered.

Ordina was barely over five feet tall. She looked up at the towering Loyalist brandishing a handcannon in her direction. Her eyes, set in her wide and unamused face, seemed almost bored. "Fine, we surrender. Care to help us pick up the mess you've caused?"

Krith, looking down at the woman, opened his mouth to reply and then abruptly closed it again. He didn't have a clue as to what to say. It was obvious to him that he could have reached down and smashed the woman like a ripe fruit—shouldn't it be obvious to the woman too? Her sudden capitulation had been followed immediately with a demand that he start sweeping the deck. He could have killed her, but it seemed unreasonable to do so after she had surrendered. And if she *had* surrendered . . . why was she ordering him about? He felt like a whelp still in school being politely agreed with by his teacher and then being taught the opposite lesson. He stood there, wavering, his handcannon still pointed at her, yet unsure as to whether he should kill her or pick up a mop.

She suddenly stepped up to him and stuck a small finger into his chest—a considerable reach for her. "Look, Master Loyalist-revolutionary-pirate type. You wanted to conquer the ship's temple and here you are. Fine! We surrender! None of my staff is armed. You win. But if I don't get this temple functioning again, you'll have pirated your way right to *Hesth*. This ship will never move so long as she's this badly off. Now, if you want to shoot me, do it or don't, but if you do, you and your idiot friends will die with me."

Krith blinked as she turned from him. Unexpectedly, the ship rolled heavily to port. Krith saw the little shipwright stagger suddenly under the unexpected movement, leaning precariously over the edge of the dais. He instantly grasped her around the waist and hoisted her back toward him.

"We can't have anything happen to you now, can we?" He smiled as he spoke down to her indignantly red face.

They both looked up at the horrific sound. Even in this dim light Ordina could see the bulkheads shifting between the decks under some terrible and unseen force from outside. They heard more than saw the compartments of the lower deck shift and splinter in the darkness below. The sounds of the tortured hull filled their ears with pain.

Gravity wavered, threatening to bounce anything loose madly about the huge temple compartment. The horrible tearing sound continued to grow. Ordina, still held tightly by the now-terrified Krith, wrenched her head around so that she could see below. The silverfire conduits to the keel were twisting in their mounts. As she watched, the conduits ripped through the decking and bent backward. Dust exploded around them as they fell against the back bulkhead with the shifting gravity. Krith held on with an iron will as the atmosphere turned into a gale.

Ordina dimly thought she could see the stars shining below them.

21

Into the Void

Serg's eyes flashed open. He stared wildly about him. His mind had at last decided to return to consciousness. It did so with a vengeance, trying to engage all his faculties at once. It couldn't get its bearings right. His balance tumbled unexpectedly in the surroundings that were both strange and familiar at once. His limbs flailed about in search of something on which he could steady himself.

That was a mistake. An overwhelming wall of pain from his left leg slammed through him, threatening to drag him again into the blissful dark forgetfulness. Serg was suddenly aware of his own screaming, and the surprise at his own sound caused him to become suddenly quiet. He closed his eyes for a moment to collect himself and, with supreme effort of will, forced them open again.

He floated amid the remains of the observation room. The crystal dome was no longer visible. The deck above had collapsed downward, crushing the dome under the cascade of broken timbers. Most of what had been the dome now floated as large, glittering diamonds about the cabin. Papers, cushions, and splintered chairs all drifted around the room. One chair had actually survived the concussion. It stood against the ceiling as though it had been placed there for someone's use. The absurdity of it filled Serg with an uncertain feeling.

"Please don't move, Captain, we're doing the best we can."

Serg stiffened at the sound behind him but knew the voice was familiar the moment he did. He spoke softly but didn't move. "Well, Father Trevis Fel. How nice to hear your voice. Seems your Farcardinal has brought a lot of grief to my ship."

A different, darker voice answered him. "You've caused your share of it, Captain."

Serg lifted his head slightly as his teeth clenched. "Such a pleasure to have you join us, Djan Kithber of Drevin." Serg's voice spoke of anything but pleasure. *The* dran *wizard!* he thought. *I should have known.*

"The *pleasure*, Captain"—the word was strangely emphasized—"is all mine. Your bottle was one of the finest I've seen."

"I take it you've seen your share."

"Indeed, Captain! Still, I don't think I'll be enjoying yours anytime soon."

"You never know, Wizard, what the future will hold." Serg looked down at his leg. The Loyalist's handcannon shot had been low and his own last-moment leap had gone a long way toward saving his life—though it had not done the leg much good. Someone had bound it for him while he was unconscious. The pain remained but was bearable as he floated without the strain of gravity—so long as he didn't try to move it.

He also didn't much care to have his back turned toward the wizard while he was making conversation. Serg began grabbing loose objects that floated around him, throwing them forcefully away from him. The opposing force began moving him from his stationary place toward his objective—the brass rail still mounted along what use to be called the port wall.

"You may have just traded in one bottle for another." Serg's progress was slow. He spoke as he continued tossing away anything within his grasp. "I don't know what it was you cooked up in there, but it must have been pretty impressive. There's no gravity in the ship—as you probably noticed—which means that the keel is gone. The ship's general power is out, but that's just a minor inconvenience for the time being. At least the emergency seals seem to—"

"Hey," Trevis cried out behind him. "Careful where you're throwing that stuff!"

"Sorry, Father." Serg smiled. He had built up a little momentum and was now drifting generally toward the railing. "At least the emergency seals are still functional. They'll keep us alive for an hour or so. There!"

Serg grasped the rail and carefully swung himself around. The green light gave everything in the room a sickly pallor, but he suspected that his uninvited guests would have assumed similar coloring even under more natural light. Certainly the cleric would. The young Localyte floated below him, clinging with fierce conviction to the back wall railing as though it were a holy icon. Djan fared somewhat better, he noted, with both feet hooked casually under the railing as he used his free arms to bind up the woman's shoulder.

Ah, yes, he thought, the woman. "What's happened to her, Master Kithber?"

The wizard didn't even look up as he spoke, concentrating as he was on his work. "My guess is that the failure of the dome pulled her toward the front of the room, then, when the gravity shifted, she fell against the back wall. Her shoulder was dislocated and her face is badly bruised. I can't decide if that was from the decompression or the fall." He tied off the bandaging that now held her arm immobile against her side. "There. That'll have to do until I can spend a little more time at it. At least she had a wall to fall against. Captain? . . . Captain, what are you doing?"

"Looking for the enunciator," he said as he began pulling himself along the rail toward the shattered front of the cabin. "There was a command set that communicated to the essential areas of the ship from the front of this cabin. If I'm going to save my crew—and your own traitorous hides by necessity—I've got to have a damage assessment."

Djan folded his arms across his chest, letting the still-unconscious Thyne drift free. His voice was flat. "I can give you mine right now, master Captain, sire."

Serg turned to look at him.

"You're missing fully the last half, maybe, two-thirds of the ship. The boy and I . . ."

"Stop calling me that!" Trevis whined.

"The boy and I were just coming to pay you a little visit

when—well, when whatever it was happened. We were in the corridor outside when the gravity shifted. Behind us quickly turned into *below* us—the hall turning suddenly into a vertical shaft. We found ourselves clinging to closed hatches to keep ourselves from falling. When that failed to work, I put a stasis field around us. There was a huge sound—rather like a thousand trees falling at once, I should think. The stairwell behind us collapsed into splinters and then there was nothing left but the cold of the stars to be seen beyond."

Serg stared back at them for a moment. When he spoke his voice was quiet and small. "The ship's back must have broken, probably at the ship's bay. The additional damage could have been caused by tearing members and beams." Suddenly he began his frantic search again, speaking with more conviction. "But the temple is in the bow. If the keel broke away clean, then the temple might still be intact. There's a chance of getting out of this if there's anything or anyone left in the temple. We could still rig a temporary sail and build a makeshift keel out of part of the temple silverfire . . ."

"Ho! You are an optimist, Captain! That would be a neat trick, indeed, now that we're in the Void!"

Trevis looked in shock at the wizard. Any remaining color disappeared from his face. Serg turned again in fury.

"The Void! *Dran* you, Kithber, and all your house! We're dead men. No one escapes the Void!" Serg seemed to deflate from his anger. There wasn't any point in it. His voice dropped its tone and sounded hollow. "Whatever you did to destroy this ship has caught you too. I'll at least have the satisfaction of knowing you will die with me in your own trap."

The wizard chuckled, drifting slightly with his feet still anchored about the railing. "So you think that I was responsible for this?" he laughed through his words. "You know, you really can be quite funny sometimes, Captain."

Serg was nonplussed. "I'll admit that it was impressive, quite beyond the powers of any sorcerer I have ever heard of. What I can't figure is how the Loyalists could have persuaded you to back them."

"You, too, are impressive, Captain. You do seem to have a knack for reading the politics of a situation and dealing with people's motives—other people's, at any rate. You seem to have made only one error that I can ascertain. You see"—Kithber

smiled warmly as he spoke—"I'm not 'in' with the Loyalists—I'm 'in' with the emissary and"—the sorcerer said, turning
toward Trevis—"your Farcardinal, boy."

Djan Kithber reached up idly for the drifting body of the Loyalist woman who was floating away from him. "Here, boy," he
said to the Localyte. "You secure this woman to the railing with
some of that cording while I explain the reality of the situation
to the captain."

Djan turned away to ignore the hurt remark from the priest
and looked directly at Serg. "You bottled the wrong wizard, Captain. That is why, I suspect, your power failed and allowed me to
escape. You'll have to look somewhere else to lay the blame,
Captain. You seem to be pretty good at that, at any rate."

Serg let the implied insult pass. He had to think of something,
anything, that might get them out of the Void. "Whatever or whoever was powerful enough to blow us out here might be able to
blow us back into the darkwind again. You say you didn't do it.
My crew certainly didn't do it. What about the Loyalist's wizard?"

"There isn't a sorcerer alive today that could have caused this.
If—mind you, if—the Loyalists had such a powerful wizard, then
I would have known about it during their internment on Brev.
No, I don't think you'll be able to ... Captain, something just
moved up there!"

Serg pivoted against the railing, looking toward what once
was the front of the observation compartment. The wooden overhead, walls, and floor planks had all been smashed downward.
Here and there, through the gaps of the debris, could be seen the
dim haze of the safety field. Beyond that the stars wheeled
slowly as the ship drifted in the Void.

Quite suddenly the stars vanished.

Serg peered closely through the gaps, moving his head from
one side to another, trying to get a better view through the debris.

The stars were gone.

Trevis was just finishing securing Thyne to the railing when
Serg began pulling his way through the debris above him. The
sorcerer pushed off from the back wall and sailed up to join him.
Within moments the two of them had dug a small passage
through the debris. Serg grasped both sides and sailed through,
followed closely by Djan.

The young Localyte waited. There was no sound from overhead. He called out.

"Captain?"

No response.

Trevis's mind raced ahead of his running fear. He wondered idly if he was getting used to terror. With a deep breath, he released himself from the railing and pushed away as he had seen the wizard do. He sailed across the room, missing the hole by only an arm's length and colliding with a cracked timber. Alternately swearing and repenting his words, he pulled himself through the opening.

The safety field had created itself from the prearranged magic laid on the hull of all ships. Its purpose was to seal breaches in the hull from the effects of vacuum space. As such, it had retained most of the compartment's atmosphere by shaping itself into a ghost of the room. The former dimensions of the dome, walls, and railings now flickered with transparent light as the magic struggled to maintain their form against the atmospheric pressure they contained.

Trevis saw the captain, one foot hooked in the debris so as not to disturb the field, gazing all around with both fists jammed firmly against his sides.

Trevis, too, looked up. For a moment he thought of his youth, lying on the ground under the open sky at night, watching the stars. Deep in the planetary atmosphere, the stars twinkled with ripples of the deep air. In the darkwind lanes, of course, no such effect existed. There the stars always shone with a constant and unwavering light.

Now the stars were twinkling.

More than twinkling. As he watched, an entire patch of stars would be blotted out as though by some great blackness. In his mind the blackness became a form that moved deliberately across the stars. Suddenly, a great black wave swept across the stars, obliterating the entire scene before them. Nearly a full minute of starless sky passed before the blackness receded again. A presence—unbelievingly huge—had passed overhead.

"Look." The captain's voice was almost reverential. "Most of them are holding a line of flight. I think . . . yes, there, that one. That one is deliberately changing course."

Trevis was suddenly aware of the wizard floating next to him, holding his position to a twisted length of metal and fiber conduit.

"I believe we have found someone to blame for the condition of your ship, Captain." Djan's words lacked any sting.

"I believe you're right."

"Sire!" Trevis's mind couldn't understand what his eyes were seeing. "What is it! What's happened to the stars?"

Djan turned to the Localyte, his words not unkind. "It's not the stars, boy, it's the ships passing in front of them."

"Ships, sire?"

"Yes, son, ships." Djan looked up and spoke in awe. "Thousands of ships welling up from that white hole. An incredible fleet springing existence from nothing. Ships so large we don't even have a clue yet as to their size. Ships that seem to ignore the darkwind altogether. Enough ships to fill this entire region of stars."

Serg shook himself with the cold implication of what he was witnessing, and spoke. "We've got to find the Farcardinal—if he's still alive. Master Trevis, where did you leave the Farcardinal?"

"He was in his chambers, sire."

Serg turned to the wizard and spoke thoughtfully. "In the bow section just aft of the temple. There's an excellent chance he made it."

The Localyte looked at the captain. "Sire, what can the Farcardinal do?"

Serg sighed. "He can warn the Pax. If this is the only entry point, then the Pax might be able to contain it. Otherwise . . ."

"Contain what, sire?" Trevis was very confused.

"The invasion." Serg turned his eyes back to the still-flickering stars. "I believe we've just been invaded."

Blackness again filled the sky.

22

Adrift

"Why am I not dead?"

The tendrils of that thought wove themselves slowly together in Shipwright Ordina's mind. Gazing with unfocused eyes into the dim green glow before her, she tried mentally to pull her existence back together against the pain that threatened to overwhelm her. Threads of consciousness seemed to drift just beyond her grasp in the bright green haze.

She was twelve years old. She could smell the warm breezes of the *Suthar* season rustling the tall grasses around her. The wing of her soaring glider was broken over her, coloring the light of the morning sun shining through the green fabric.

"Keri! Ke-ri!" Her mother's voice, drifting down from her own glider high above, settling down on her like the distant voice of an angel. In her mind she could see the clear sphere surrounding her native city drifting among the clouds high above them both. Her world was a garden left long ago for the peace the sky offered. She and her mother both loved to fall from the curved glass of the city gates to sail the currents and eddies of the atmosphere and gaze down upon the garden that their world had become. Only this time the winds had betrayed her for a moment and dropped her rather unceremoniously from her high-speed glide over the tops of the grass plain. It hadn't been much, but it was enough for her to have caught the runners in the tall grass before she could get back into the sky. Speed is life in flight, and she met the hard, warm earth with a shattering collapse.

We'll fix it, she thought of her glider. *Mother's the finest craftsmaid in the city. She'll help me.* She winced. Somehow she knew that she'd sprained her ankle again. Her father had threatened to end these expeditions if she came home hobbling one more time. He never seemed to understand that it was the soaring of the sky that spoke to her, not the city that floated stationary in it. No, the glider could be fixed but her ankle and, more important, her father, was another matter.

"Ke-ri! Keri Or-dina!"

She fought against the fabric. She wanted to see! Why couldn't she see?

The rushing overhead told her that her mother was circling nearer, looking for a place to land among the hills.

"We'll fix it, Mother!" she cried. "You'll help me fix it, won't you? I'm all right. Please don't tell Father."

The green glow continued to engulf her. Why did she hurt so much?

"I'll help you, child," her mother said. "I'll help you . . ."

"Mistress Ordina!"

Awareness flooded her mind. Her eyes closed as much against the green glow of the emergency globe shining in her face as against the pain that engulfed her. With a delver's instinct he groped for a handhold, fixed her hand around a smooth conduit, and slowly, carefully, pushed her face away from the emergency globe blazing with green light in her eyes.

"Mother," she murmured as she rotated, her eyes still shut tight against the offending light as it drifted away. She floated still, not wanting to open her eyes. Reality assaulted her, splintering the peace of unconsciousness and pressing against her lungs like a thousand atmospheres.

"Mistress," a voice shivered in a near whisper. "Please!"

Still she refused to open her eyes. "Tsara? Tsara, is that you?"

"*Allai*, Mistress." The voice carried little conviction.

A deeper voice continued. "*Hesth*, ma'am, I'm *dran* sorry at losing you—I mean, lettin' ya fall like that and all. You're only a slip of a thing and . . ."

Ordina's eyes flicked solidly open at the sound of the voice. The green haze cleared and she could see the huge Loyalist delver's face floating sideways before her.

"Loyalist," she whispered, "what are you called?"

"Krith, yer masterness—er—yer mistressne—er, ah—worship—ah, *dran*, it be Krith, ma'am, an' I be right full o' sorry for . . ."

"Krith?"

"*Allai*, ma'am!"

"Latch your tongue, *scrud*, it's flapping in the breeze!" she murmured almost to herself. Still, it was enough to get the big man's attention. Her eyes closed slowly once and then opened again.

"*Allai*, ma'am. Sopping me gob, ma'am." Krith fell silent, wondering vaguely why he was letting this diminutive woman tell him what to do.

"How bad, Tsara?" she asked, struggling to get her feet against the bulkhead and secure them under some foothold. Even as she asked the question, she knew.

The steady, dull green from the emergency globes was all the light that could be seen in the temple. The optic tree, transfer casings, and indicator glass embedded in the various altars around the temple—all of which normally displayed a rainbow of brilliance in the immense compartment—were dark. There was simply no power emanating from any of the altars. The sails were normally empowered via three separate and entirely independent optic busses, and the keel itself was driven directly from the Transentstone. They had managed to shut down the silverfire core to complete containment, though the silverfire was, no doubt, somehow contaminated by whatever initial invasion had corrupted the temple. Still, this should have left residual silverfire in the systems, which would have at a very minimum caused the buses to glow and the altars to continue telling them the status of the system. The fact that they could see no sign of light was ominously bad.

So were the stars.

She noticed their glow at once wheeling slowly past the terrible gash that had once been the floor of the temple. She reached out to a broken and now-twisted optic conduit and began pulling her way down toward the stars. She fleetingly wondered what conduit she had grasped. Though she knew every part of her temple with loving intimacy, its twisted carnage had become foreign and a stranger to her. She was glad to see that the safety fields had held—it was the only thing that had saved them.

Those who had been saved. She wondered for a moment, as she made her way through the contorted wreckage that had once been her beloved ship, how many of her sisters here in the temple had survived. She was vaguely aware of Tsara and the Loyalist *scrud* picking their way down after her.

She approached the blue, shimmering glow of the safety field. The contours of what had once been the lower deck continued to shine. She could even discern the outlines of what had once been the main feed shaft to the keel and, next to it, part of the ghostly image of the access ladder. Beyond that were the stars alone.

Ordina pressed her face to the very edge of the safety field. The lustrous outlines had formed a natural box where the wall and floor had once met. She carefully positioned herself so that she could look out over the exterior of the ship.

The keel was completely gone. The shearing force of whatever had hit them had torn away the keel and the three immediate decks above it. The keel was designed as the main structural member of the ship. It had nearly torn the ship apart when it left. Looking forward, most of the lower temple had departed with the writhing keel along with the bow of the ship as high as deck five. Looking aft was even worse.

"How bad is it, Mistress?" Tsara's voice floated up to Ordina from deeper in the temple. The shipwright smiled at the thought that her sister apprentice couldn't bring herself to come any closer to the safety field.

"Keel's gone with most of the bow. The ship's back is broken at the ship's bay roughly following the lines of the main access shaft. The hull's torn through the gun deck, but the temple and crew quarters look primarily intact." She sighed. "Well, we're missing the keel and the last half of the ship. There's a lot of wreckage, but I can't see any sign of the masts and the rigging twisting free and without weight. Not a spark of life from any of the optics that I can see."

Ordina spun herself around carefully and pulled her way back into the dimly lit temple. "Worse, the safety field is weakening. The glow is already shifting from blue into violet; it'll start leaking atmosphere soon." She stopped and looked about calmly, but there was pain in her eyes. "We'll have to abandon the temple and set up elsewhere soon. Tsara, how many do we have of the sisterhood?"

Tsara blinked twice.

"Tsara?"

"Ah, I, ah, don't know. The safety field took a moment to activate and the decompression of the temple . . . I saw . . . I mean, I think that most of them . . ."

"Tsara?" Ordina looked carefully into her assistant's eyes as she reached out slowly to grasp Tsara's shoulders.

The young apprentice before Ordina struggled with her own thoughts. "Ithilan! Oh, Mistress, I saw just a flash of her hair when the air exploded! She went—out." She began shaking. "There were others too. I just—don't know."

"Tsara! Tsara, hear me!" Ordina's eyes shone like green flame in the light burning through Tsara's pain. "We need to move quickly in order to live. Uncouple the Aft Wind Altar and the Lower Field Altar. Get whoever you can to help you and get those altars out of here. Take them up to the Healing Ward on deck A or somewhere else that looks secure. If you find an officer, fine, report, but don't stop moving for anyone. Then get back here. I'll have the Ark brought forward so we can move the silverfire." She continued to scrutinize her companion's face and finished quietly. "Tsara! We don't have much time."

Tsara's eyes fell from the shipwright's gaze. "*Allai*, Mistress. Aft Wind Altar and the Lower Field Altar. Take them to Healing and come back."

"Tell anyone alive you meet that they have just joined temple services. Everyone on this ship just became a shipwright!" She tossed the words to the already moving Tsara as she glided into the deep ruins of the temple. She could see some movement beyond Tsara deep in the compartment—there were other survivors. She hoped there would be enough.

She turned to the Loyalist named Krith. Her manner suddenly turned so cold that ice crystals might have formed in the air all around the tiny shipwright.

"What did you do to my ship?"

"Lady, I ain't done nothin' to account for the likes of . . ."

"Oh, latch it again, Master Krith, if that's your name. You

spend more air saying nothing than anyone I know. I don't have time or stomach to hear it yet. Do you want to live?"

Krith eyed the shipwright coolly, crossing his arms over his massive chest. "Aye, Ordina, I do."

"Then you need me. If I don't live, you don't, understand?"

"Oh, so you be proposing marriage, now, eh?" Krith's eyebrows arched over his bright eyes. "It's so comforting to me for having been asked, and at my advanced age too."

Ordina's eyes flashed as her face reddened perceptibly even in the green light. She looked as though she were considering saying something but turned instead and started pulling herself aft. Krith, now feeling stable again in more ways than one, smiled and drifted after her.

Ordina picked her way carefully around the base of the Altar of Command. It extended up through a platform overhead surrounding the Transentstone core. She could make out the Stasis Altar overhead as well as the Distribution Altar at the rear of the platform through the gridwork. She squinted and strained but could see no light from the jewels on those altars either.

A sudden nudge knocked loose her grip, and she began drifting toward the Transentstone itself. She caught herself and glared back.

"Sorry, Mistress," Krith said. "Just tryin' to help."

Without reply, Ordina pulled herself past the main distribution conduits and over the transmission base. The black Transentstone was normally dark, but the usual aura that surrounded it was gone. The Ark—a chest-shaped container designed to trap and transfer the silverfire in the event of such a catastrophe—was secured on rails behind the Transentstone. She glided past the assembly, inspecting it casually, when some motion caught her eye.

She gasped in shock and wonder, her life breath seeming to leave her. Had she passed the Transentstone on the starboard side, it would have been apparent at once, but her passage on the port side hid the sight until she was upon it.

The Transentstone was cracked wide. The breaking keel had wrenched the optic conduits with such force that the transmission base had shifted. The entire temple structure had been pulled out of alignment. With the keel swinging free, gravity shifts had then taken the already loosened components and altars and tumbled them freely about the temple. The resulting collateral damage coupled with the incredible forces of the keel separation had somehow shattered the unbreakable matrix of the Transentstone itself.

Now, even as Ordina watched, a stream of dull liquid silver flowed from the finger-wide crack into an undulating ball quivering in the air. It glistened as it folded into itself in a complex pattern of continuous waves. A nimbus of silvery light surrounded it as it grew, gaining volume from the stream that fed it.

"*Mont Hesth!* M'Lady, what be that!" Krith had joined her in wide-eyed wonder.

"That," Ordina murmured in awe, "my pirate *scrud*, is, I believe, silverfire."

With a cry, the enormous delver threw his arms up to shield his eyes. He quickly swung his huge body between Ordina and the writhing mercurial mass.

"Lady, save yerself! Flee! Flee fer yer . . . fer yer life! While there still be time! Flee!" Krith's efforts at heroics were, however, rapidly losing steam as Ordina wasn't moving and, more to the point, neither of them was dying.

" 'Ey, Mistress," Krith said with sudden and curious puzzlement, "ain't we supposed to be dead?"

Krith's huge body might have smothered her if there had been any gravity about. As it was, her round face spoke to him from around his left side. "Yes, absolutely."

"But—well, ain't silverfire *Hesth* incarnate when it's let free to roam about like that?"

"Yep."

"Don't it, like, eat ships, an' steal men's souls and drive 'em crazy mad just to look at it?"

"Yep. Technically it takes the order of the universe and accelerates its decay into entropy, thus providing a field of creationary chaos from which the power of magic is born."

"Eh?"

"It drives 'em crazy mad just to look at it," Ordina replied flatly.

Krith had almost lost the drift of the conversation but was now back on solid ground. "So . . . why ain't we chaosified, like you said. Why ain't we dead?"

Ordina shook her head in wonder. "I don't know."

They floated together there for a moment, watching the stream as it thinned and finally collected itself into the ever-shifting waves of the floating sphere.

Ordina finally shook herself from her stupor and began to move toward the Ark still secure on its railing. "I don't know why we aren't dead, but I do know that we all soon will be if we don't contain that thing and find some way to use it again. Quick! Help me get this Ark off its railing so we can capture that silverfire before it changes its mind and *does* kill us all."

23

Lost

~~~

Tsara's short scream shook everyone in the broken stairwell but none more so than the vision whose sudden appearance had inspired it.

"*Hesth*, girl, you've shortened my life a week with that screech!" the Thrund ambassador bellowed in three-part discord. The brown blood streaking each of Hruna's three talon "faces" had apparently unnerved the human. Tsara had only heard there was a Thrund on board. She had studied up on them for the mission but had not had an opportunity to meet the ambassador. From her cursory study, the shipwright suddenly remembered that the Thrund's own culture was warrior oriented. The ambassador probably believed it quite becoming of a warrior and therefore rather attractive. To Tsara, however, the impression of a bloodied cross between an arachnid and a dripping bird of prey had completely unnerved her.

"Calm yourself!" the Thrund chimed. "I demand to know what has happened!"

Tsara felt the color returning to her face, even though it would be unnoticeable in the green emergency lights. She'd seen more death in the past few minutes than in her entire life before.

The carnage of combat rarely penetrated as far as the temple Sanctuary. The battle had been won or lost long before it involved her personally. Now the Sanctuary was finished and her mistress Ordina was preparing to take the silverfire into exile— the shipwright phrase for abandoning the Sanctuary. It was a process she had studied but had never even heard of actually being done. She had found a pair of Sanctuary workers capable of helping her with the altars that Ordina had requested she move. She had found far more who would never be able to help anyone ever again.

Tsara had been maneuvering the altars out of the Sanctuary and into the forward access shaft, when the Thrund's three glistening faces had unexpectedly—and quite silently—appeared.

"Wha—who—who are you?"

"I am the Pax ambassador on a mission to Kilnar, I am the entire reason for this ship having any right to exist, and I am someone who is about to make your life a nightmare if you don't answer me! Report!"

Tsara vaguely wondered what could be worse than their current predicament but answered anyway. "*Lor*, Ambassador! I do not know what happened. There was an escape staged by the Loyalists. Still I cannot see how it . . ."

"Where is your captain?"

"There has been no word from the captain, sire. Now, if you will excuse me." Tsara didn't wait for the reply but turned to the altar floating behind her.

"I certainly will not excuse you!" The Thrund's discordant voices were like a steel edge sliding across slate. "I haven't even begun with *you* yet! You will stop this at once and assist me. The Farcardinal is in need of your . . ."

"Sire, with all *due* respect, go to *Hesth*," Tsara exploded. *What's she going to do,* though Tsara savagely, *kill me?* "If I don't get these altars safely up to the Healing Ward, we aren't going to *breathe*. That will probably put a strain on your diplomatic work, would it not?"

Hruna watch the temple worker struggle up the shaft from her trio of solid black eyes but spoke no further words. The apprentice shipwright was doing her job under the worst of all possible circumstances. Hruna turned back into the twisted corridor of the Sanctuary and made her way back to the Farcardinal's apartment.

"Sabenth! What are you doing?"

The Farcardinal was sitting in the large oak chair, his hands white from the frozen grip he had on its arms. This was all the more peculiar, because the chair was floating in midair, leaving the Farcardinal and his chair somewhere between sideways and upside down relative to the rest of the furniture. The effect might have been comical had the Farcardinal's expression not been one of stupefying terror.

The Thrund glided easily through the twisted frame of the doorway. Absence of gravity was second nature to the Thrund. "How your race ever conquered a third of the galaxy remains beyond me, Sabenth. Your people have no affinity for the ecstasy of true space. Unless you're in a gravity well, your people fall apart." Hruna had intended this to get a rise out of the Farcardinal—a man who the Thrund knew was fiercely humanocentric in his views and who believed blindly in humanity's destiny of interstellar rule. This in spite of the fact that the old holy man hated space travel in general and had a hard time sleeping during extended voyages.

Despite the barb, the Farcardinal gave no reaction. Sabenth and his chair both slowly rotated along two axes, occasionally bumping into something which would add a new vector to their complex joint motion. Yet as to the Farcardinal, he might have been a part of the chair for all his reaction.

Hruna moved into the room carefully. Most of the trappings in the room had been secured to the floor or walls during the construction of the ship, but even some of these had been jarred loose of their fittings. The numerous books had all taken flight from their cases and hung suspended in the room. The great woven rug that had once graced the floor now hung almost defiantly a handbreadth away from the planking, its surface rippled like a frozen sea. The support beams that ran the length of the ceiling were showing ominous cracks, one of them being splintered altogether. Hruna decided that the most secure route to the Farcardinal was along those beams and, almost without thinking, reoriented herself to the ceiling and pressed her way through the jetsam of the room.

Gripping the beams with her six gloved feet, Hruna wrapped the chair in two of her taloned necks, stopped it, and carefully turned it so that she could face the Farcardinal with her third eye. *The man had looked ill when she left him but he was much worse now,* she thought. "Sabenth! Are you damaged? Are you wounded?"

"What? Did you say something?"

The Thrund searched the Farcardinal's face with all the depth of her own shining black eyes. The man glistened with sweat. His eyes bulged slightly but were unfocused. Hruna could literally smell the fear which bordered on shock in the man. The Thrund examined him carefully as he hung suspended before her. There was a slight cut on the head and a rather ugly discoloring of the left side of the face. Hruna had reacted instinctively to the collision—or whatever it was—and had managed to secure herself quickly during subsequent concussions. The Farcardinal had fared far worse, having apparently stopped his fall with his face. Still, there didn't look like there was all that much damage to the human.

"What? Hruna? What did you say?"

"Sabenth! Sabenth, what is the matter?"

"Hruna? Yes, it is you!" Sabenth turned his puffy white face toward the Thrund, his eyes straining to focus. "It must be you! Oh, Hruna, it's so . . . loud! No, not loud, it's . . . so frightening and overwhelming, like a waterfall of anguish and thunder . . . and . . . I don't seem to be able to hear you very well. I'm overcome with a nightmare but my mind is awake. Everything seems so distant, so very far away. Are you here, Hruna? Are you with me?"

Hruna gazed at the quivering human. None of her eyes moved nor did her expression change with the disgust that she felt. Sabenth was weak, after all, and would die as many humans seemed to die—whimpering rather than fighting. How could they live with themselves, she thought, knowing that their fears can and often do take them over. Humans are a weak race to whom only providence seemed to have given them their "manifest destiny" to conquer the stars. Better that this pathetic creature should be left to die from whatever malady had overcome him than to help him live in shame. It was sick and perverted. She had little use for such beings in general.

No use . . . except to be used.

She shook him once roughly and then spoke in her smoothest and most calming voice, while staring into his still-vacant eyes. "Sabenth! I am here with you. I will take care of you and see to your needs! Everything will soon be fine. You will again walk the sands on fine worlds. Can you see them? Can you smell the sage in your future? Breezes will rustle your robes with their warm breath in the afternoon sun. You will again find rest in its light."

Hruna had heard the words from the Farcardinal's own mouth time and again as Sabenth had described his home world. Now he turned the words back on the holy man. They had their effect. The Farcardinal's face cleared with hope and calmed with the melodious voices of the Thrund.

"We'll find your Localyte and call for aid. After all," the Thrund clicked warmly, "with two such important personages as you and me aboard, there's bound to be relief soon. . . ."

The Farcardinal's face suddenly twisted itself in anguish, tears welling up over his eyes. He blinked furiously, trying to rid himself of the water which, without gravity, floated on his eyes and obscured his vision. The action sent small undulating balls of tears floating into the cabin.

"Oh, Hruna," he gasped, "the fear . . . the whole galaxy is screaming and weeping! I hear its cries pressing up into my mind from the recesses of my own soul. Cries! Inquiry? Wonder! Dread-knowledge-aware-flee-help-guidance-guidance-GUIDANCE!" The Farcardinal screamed and collapsed again into sobs. "I can't . . . I can't hear their words. They're pressing into my mind from the blackness like a . . . like a cascading torrent . . . like a . . . oh, *Lor*, like I'm drowning in thought. Uncounted souls—numbers beyond knowledge—are all crying out to me . . . to me! . . . and I can't . . . I can't hear them! . . . I can't hear them!" The Farcardinal sobbed uncontrollably.

Hruna suddenly realized why the Farcardinal had to live— why she would see that he lived. Without this weak-willed human they would have no contact with the rest of civilization. Rescue was not a priority for Hruna, but the ability to report certainly was. Securing her four-footed grip to the shattered beam, she gently lifted Sabenth from his chair and pulled the distressed man into the soft fold of her own robe. The physical contact caused her to shudder, but it seemed to calm the human. She shook off the revulsion. With a swinging motion she made her way across the ceiling and quickly opened the hatch.

"I rather suspect we will be needing your services soon, Farcardinal Sabenth. We must get you feeling better."

The human could only whimper once.

The forward access shaft was devastated, its main staircase contorted almost beyond recognition. In several places the torque forces had splintered the stair entirely. Shattered sections of wood drifted in the air, but the shaft held solidly against the vacuum outside the hull. The Thrund picked her way carefully through the debris while cradling the Farcardinal along. She vaguely regretted having to bring him. The battle blood still raged through her veins and the surroundings seemed to whisper to her of a warrior's glory.

The Healing Ward was near the centerline of the ship and was surrounded by decks above and below as well as compartments to either side. The ship's original designers had placed the ward purposefully in this location as a harbor for the wounded during battle. As a result, the Healing Ward seemed to be one of the few places where any remote countenance of the ship's original structure remained to be seen.

Hruna curled easily into the ward, holding the Farcardinal gently as she did. The compartment was small, Hruna noted, even in the best of circumstances. Hruna counted nearly twenty humans floating tethered about the ward with at least seven more apparently healthy crew members grouped closely at the aft end of the compartment. The exact number was difficult to tell with the poor lighting and the crowded conditions. Many of the injured were floating about the room secured only by whatever straps and ties could be managed under the circumstances. The floor-mounted beds remained vacant, their soft cushions rendered useless with gravity's loss. It was just as well, Hruna thought. The half-dozen beds would have been completely insufficient to accommodate the injured in the room. By the smell in the air Hruna suspected that death would soon significantly decrease the crowding.

The Thrund secured her footed grip on the door frame before releasing the Farcardinal and turning him about to face her. She was surprised. Sabenth's eyes focused on her. He was still sweating as though in a fever, but had managed a smile in her direction.

"Hruna, I'm much better now. Really. I know you have better things to do than look out for me." Sabenth reached out for one of the bunks and used its edge to hold himself steady.

The Thrund made her way carefully through the ward toward the group huddled at the far corner of the room. She could hear a voice, loud but somehow hollow and distant. Someone was speaking over the enunciator to the rapt attention of everyone in the ward capable of understanding. The words became clearer to Hruna as she moved forward.

". . . without communication to the bridge. Even the mechanical enunciators are without response. Our direct observations convince us that the aft end of the ship is sheared away from the primary upper access well aft. You say the keel is completely gone as well?"

"Yes, Captain. The base of the temple is now an open hole to space. Through that we saw that the keel is completely gone," Tsara reported factually.

The Thrund blinked all her eyes twice, slowly. The loss of the keel was the death knell of every ship.

"Well, we had expected as much. What about the silverfire?"

"Mistress Ordina is securing it now. We have brought several of the altars up to Healing Ward already. I expect her at any moment now."

"Very well." A muffled voice could suddenly be heard, apparently talking to the captain. When finished, the captain's distant voice continued to rattle from the enunciator grid. "Have you any news of the Farcardinal?"

Tsara flushed. "No, Captain. I, uh, met the ambassador in the forward access shaft and . . . uh . . ."

Hruna pressed herself carefully forward, speaking loudly in three-voice unison as she did. "Captain, this is the ambassador. The Farcardinal is here with me. He appears to be in a somewhat confused state. He was uncommunicative immediately after the—well, whatever happened, but now appears to be somewhat better."

The captain's hollow voice sounded light-years away. "Well, we're cut off from you and the Farcardinal's Localyte is here with us. Sabenth might be able to get in touch with his brothers, but without his Localyte present we would never know what he received. Even so, with this wreck adrift so deep in the Void, I don't know what good it would do to inform the Pax of our position. I *would* like to let them know about the fleet."

The hair on the Thrund's mane bristled. "What fleet?"

"A fleet of monstrously sized ships is sailing all around us— apparently independent of the darkwind and heedless of the Void. We've been watching them for the last ten minutes or so." The distant voice on the enunciator suddenly changed tenor and tempo. "Mistress Tsara, when Ordina gets to the ward, have her talk to me. If I can get to the bridge, I'll bring down a pair of signal lamps. If she can get me power, we'll start sending light patterns at those ships.

"What are your intentions, then, Captain?" the Thrund demanded.

"I am going to attempt surrender."

The hair on the Thrund bristled once more, if for no other reason than hearing what was to her a hateful word. "Surrender!"

"Yes, Ambassador, surrender. We're deep in the Void with no possible hope of rescue. These ships apparently sail the Void at will. If we are to survive this, they're the only ones—whoever they are—in whom we have any hope of being saved.

"I would suggest, Ambassador," called the captain's distant voice, "that you are about to demonstrate the abilities that your title suggests."

24

Passages

~~❦~~

"One-ONE. One-two; ONE-TWO. One-two-three; ONE-TWO-THREE. One-ONE. One-two; ONE-TWO. One-two-three; ONE . . ."

"Kid, do you have to do that out loud?" Thyne's eyes were framed by tan skin that was nonetheless several shades paler than usual. Every now and then the pain in her arm swept over her and blurred the universe. The rest of the time she simply floated in misery somewhere between anger and nausea. She reminded herself that one did not "throw up" without gravity so much as one "throws out." The prospect of graphically repeating the semantic difference between the two did little to calm her.

". . . ONE-TWO-THREE. One-ONE. One-two; ONE-TWO . . ."

"Hey, boy! Could you *not* do that *out loud*?!" Thyne's voice thundered.

The delver with the bandaged eyes roared. "Awe, Lady, will you just shut up and leave the kid to do his job!" A half-dozen other badly wounded delvers immediately added their voices with various levels of unenthusiasm.

Trevis was too frightened to care about what they were

saying—too frightened to do anything but what he had been told. He floated at the forward end of the shattered compartment, his legs locked under a bent railing. Floating before him was a huge brass lamp, its lens fit with an iris cover. The lever allowed him to close and open the aperture quickly, alternately showing and shuttering the light it projected. It was an old way of signaling—as old as delvers themselves—but it was new to the Localyte. Captain Dresiv had given him instructions on how to signal and the pattern of light to use but had left immediately after that with the mage. They were both now digging their way back into the wreckage, searching for others who could be helped and, hopefully, a way down to the remaining survivors in the Healing Ward.

In the meanwhile, Trevis followed his instructions to the letter. He'd pointed the great lens at each great blackness that passed close by, and begun the same sequence of one short flash followed by a long flash, then two short flashes and two long flashes, then a third set of three short and long flashes before repeating the sequence again. To the young priest facing death for the second time in a month, it became something of a litany prayer. It had become his faith. If he could just keep repeating this action—this phrase—then they would save him.

So the wounded behind him could say whatever they like. The captain had said that this might save them—so here he stayed, chanting with religious fervor as he worked the handle:

"One-ONE! One-two; ONE-TWO! One-two-three . . ."

"*Dran!* This one's blocked tight too!" Ordina heard Serg's voice with unfortunate clarity over her voxmitter.

Ordina spoke into her own voxmitter, draped around the back of her neck and over her shoulders. The device conducted the majority of the sound up through her own skeletal frame to her ears rather than through the air, so at least the captain's words weren't heard by everyone in the Healing Ward. She spoke quietly and confidently to Serg, still several decks above her. "The emergency breach doors must have been shut by a bridge command just before the wave hit. The whole ship has been twisted badly. My guess is that the frames have twisted around the doors."

"That means I'm not going to get them open, right?" The captain's voice sounded in her head.

"*Allai*, sire. I probably couldn't have welded them any tighter than they are now."

"That's what I thought. Ah, we've tried the main passages—those are all either vacuum breached or impassable. The secondary access shafts are all closed like this one. What about the service spaces for the silverfire conduits?"

Ordina ran her hands over the Altar of Granting. A glowing web burned its pattern in brilliant light onto its surface. Optics cables ran in huge bundles from altar to altar in the room, the largest from the silverfire altar. These in turn sprang from the altar she stood before into another mass of optics cables branching into a huge hole cut into the ceiling. Her equipment and altars had taken up the rear half of the Healing Ward, causing a crowded situation to become even more so.

Ordina glanced behind her. Yes, they were crowded, but not for long. Four of her own fellow delvers had died in the last half hour alone, their bodies each in turn pushed through the aft hatch to float in the ruptured compartment beyond. The ship's healer must have been aft at the time of the accident. No sign of him was found. His assistants also remained unaccounted for except for one. The sole healer they had found in the ward was himself dead—apparently from a simple head trauma caused as he fell backward out of his chair. It was a senseless death but no more senseless than hundreds of others elsewhere aboard what once was the *Shendridan*.

They had done what they could with the treatment supplies at hand, but the *Shendridan* was a ship of the silverfire and everything, including healing, was dependent upon it. Ordina knew it was urgent that she get the wizard Djan down to the ward before they lost anyone else to the Void.

So far, however, not a single passage they had tried came even close to being passable. Cutting tools were, of course, available, but with even the secondary power optics without appreciable power, most of those were of little use. Catastrophic failure on this scale was never supposed to happen. Their own emergency tools had been rendered helpless by the depth of their predicament. She had two delvers taking turns with her most elemental tool—the optics ax—but they were making very little progress against the mountain of timbers choking the most promising access shaft. Worse yet, without gravity not even the strongest of delvers could get enough strength into the blade to mark the wood. With nothing to press against, each swing divided its energy equally between the ax head, handle, and delver, propelling the latter backward from the intended blow. Action caused reaction and sapped the blade of any power. Crowbars had proved more effective, but the going remained slow.

"Captain, I'm still running feelers into the conduits to see if there's any continuity in them. So far I haven't been able to get power up to where you are, let alone any of our people. If the lines are severed, then the crawlways are probably cut too."

Serg chuckled. "You don't mind if . . ."

"Mind if you try?" Ordina hoped her smile carried over the voxmitter. "Why, Captain, I'd have been absolutely disappointed if you hadn't."

"*Allai*, Mistress Ordina," came the disembodied voice. "Take care for our precious silverfire and I'll get back to you when I know what I've found. Done."

"Done." The shipwright replied crisply as she reached up and touched the voxmitter collar to stand by. She turned again to the silverfire containment altar, folded her arms in front of her, and tried once more to fathom what had happened.

Silverfire is the embodiment of power and chaos. It naturally seeks its most entropic state. Without the reflective magic, not even the Transentstone can hold its form for more than a few seconds. Outside of the containment, it is more than volatile—it changes reality itself in its struggle to free itself from any semblance of order. It is in harnessing its madness, its chaos, and balancing that with reality and order that all the empire was built on. Contained, it conquers worlds and establishes a new galactic order. Unleashed, it destroys all order, turns on its former master, and shreds its surroundings down to its very existence.

So why, Ordina thought, was she alive?

The silverfire leaking from the cracked Temple Altar had distinctly demonstrated uncharacteristically stable qualities. Its form remained a liquid folding in on itself, a shape it maintained even after Ordina had moved it into the Altar in Exile. She had even questioned whether she had captured the Transentstone and its silverfire, but inspection of the cracked Altar of Containment showed itself empty.

She had set up the Altars in Exile in the Healing Ward by the proscribed sequences of the ritual. She connected the optics from the altars to the conduits running through the walls and ceilings of the ward. The action had primarily been an act of hope. Somehow, she believed, everything would work.

She was encouraged when the altar began exciting the optic power buss as it should. The silverfire was flowing. Yet her joy was short-lived. The silverfire was there, but the power levels were unbelievably low. Silverfire in the Transentstone is self-regenerative in the extreme. Now its excess output barely kept the local atmospheric rejuvenators and emergency lights operating. Nothing Ordina did seemed to make any difference to the altar. The field strength remained the same. Even under the worst circumstances, the silverfire transferred should have yielded an output of nearly thirty percent of the original temple system. Her current output was barely in the percentile range.

Perhaps the reflective magics had been affected during the collision and had stabilized the Transentstone into a liquid form, she thought. If she rewove the reflective magics and tried to dispel the original . . .

"Greetings, again, ma'am! Sorry to be disturbing your thoughts," Krith offered jovially.

Ordina mentally shook herself and slowly turned her cool gaze to the huge man who floated next to her. "Oh. Yes, squire rebel, I had forgotten that we had surrendered to you. Are we up to the 'rape and pillage' part now, or are you still working on the 'surrender or die' principle?"

Krith opened his mouth to speak but somehow wasn't sure just how to answer the question.

"No," Ordina said, turning her gaze back to the portable containment, her voice almost sounding bored. "I suppose we passed the surrender part and didn't die. Well, you're welcome to go a-pillaging, for all the good it will do you. Let me know if you find anything of value so that I can be duly impressed."

"Ma'am, I'm thinkin' you've got this old delver all wrong. I'm not about to go pillaging this here vessel. Wouldn't be 'onorable nor gentlemanly, like." Krith bristled his beard and did his best to look hurt but found it difficult to strike a dramatic pose with both feet planted firmly in midair.

Ordina floated a languid gaze at him from under her eyebrows that was as cold as the Void. "Honorable? I see. So you've never killed a man?"

"Well, now, ma'am, in time of war only such killin' as . . ."

"I see. So the 'surrender or die' was just a lie? Are you a liar, squire rebel?"

"No, ma'am, I'm no liar, it's just that . . ."

"So you would have killed my sisters and me in the temple if we hadn't surrendered?"

"No, ma'am, of course we'd not be harmin' a single hair on . . ."

"Then you did lie when you said that."

"Well, now, I suppose, in a manner of speaking, I did lie about that, but . . ."

"Well, since your threat didn't have much force, I suppose that our surrender doesn't either, does it? I mean, since you didn't really mean to kill us, then I suppose we really don't mean to surrender, do we?"

Krith wasn't exactly sure where he had lost control of the conversation. "I suppose so . . . I mean, I suppose not . . . but . . ."

"So"—she patted him on the hand and smiled with all the warmth and understanding of a tenured instructor trying to explain elemental truths to a slow-learning child—"please refrain from the 'rape and pillage' until we get this 'surrender or die' thing worked out. In the meanwhile"—her voice turned suddenly cold and precise—"get back over to that enunciator and let me know if anyone so much as whispers a word from the observation deck!"

"But I . . ."

"NOW!"

Krith floated against the wall, his huge, muscular form drifting with his ear next to the enunciator.

Ordina watched him settle where she'd sent him. He'd lost to her and they both knew it, though, Ordina suspected, Krith still wasn't sure how. He probably was wishing that Ordina would just quit surrendering so that he could go about his normal business. Ordina smiled to herself. She knew she was taking the fun out this whole rebel pirate business for Krith.

The shaft was seldom visited except on the most intensive overhauls. There was only a single main trunk optic that ran the length of the shaft—a massive brute that once fed the sails directly from the temple. The optic itself nearly filled the entire shaft but was normally laid to one side so that one person might be able to traverse its vertical length and make sure there were no flaws in the conduit.

Now, however, vertical was mostly a matter of personal taste and open to individual interpretation. Djan could imagine himself either hanging headfirst over the barely lit shaft or standing at its bottom and trying to peer up into the darkness. In practical considerations it didn't matter. It was only a mind game that Djan liked to play. Either way, he didn't like the way it looked.

The shaft spiraled down through the decks like a tortured thing, debris choking its passage. The captain had drifted into the shaft ahead of him. He apparently didn't care for what he saw. Serg had sighed, shrugged at the wizard drifting beside him, and began burrowing his way past the wreckage.

Djan watched him disappear into the remains of yet another shaft. His own strength was again beginning to return. He was fairly sure that the captain remained unaware of that fact and Djan certainly wasn't about to do anything to change that. Whether with opponents or allies, Djan found that a little reserve secret is always handy to have around. After all, opponents do change and allies often turn against you.

He had come with the captain to see what could be seen. What had happened with the separatist rebels below decks before their collision with—well, with whatever it was—had remained a mystery. Djan didn't much care for mysteries himself. He kept others in the dark about his own power and knowledge because he greatly feared the unknown and even minor mysteries made him uncomfortable.

Now Djan floated with both arms crossed before him. He called out into the shaft with slight impatience. "Captain?"

"Yes, yes, I'm fine." Serg's voice sounded hollow and muffled from the long, twisting cavity.

"Of course you are." The wizard, in a small, cleared area, allowed himself the luxury of placing his hands behind his head and drifting free. "Why are we alive?"

"This spar is bowed down here. If I can . . . just . . . . work it loose . . ." There was a crackling snap followed by what sounded like an explosion of wooden blocks. The loose debris in the conduit shifted slightly. "Yeow! *Dran!* I think I might . . . yeah, I think I can get through here."

Djan shifted slightly and allowed himself a low rumble of boredom from his throat. "This ship, if such you could call it now, is an unsalvageable loss. You could have sailed it straight into a mountain and it still would have looked better. So why aren't we all dead?"

Serg's voice tumbled up from far away. "I'd like to point out that most of us *are* dead. I don't have any way of making a detailed assessment, but only a handful of us seemed to have survived. Even at that our prospects . . . aw, now, how the *Hesth* did that happen?"

"What?"

"Oh, the optic trunk has coiled around itself. Filled the whole conduit frame. Maybe if I can just . . . ouch! *Dran!*"

"Look, Captain, do you need any help in there?" Djan offered in annoyance.

"Well, if you can cook up some of your pyrotechnics we might be able to cut through some of this and make our lives a lot easier."

Djan thought about that for a moment. He had gathered sufficient power to burn through a deck or two, even with the emergency fields activated. However, given their present situation, he doubted that getting through to the remaining crew would change their condition substantially. He preferred to keep things to himself.

"Sorry, Captain," the sorcerer lied. "Your bottle left me weak as a newborn. So, tell me anyway, why are we still alive?"

Serg had apparently stopped to ponder what to do next, for his voice had a distracted quality to it. "Well, you, sire, are aboard a vessel of the Pax Galacticus and she is designed to be an instrument of their policies. All compartments are individually shielded against breach and distortion due to damage as well as the hull in its entirety. The hull field obviously failed, but the compartment fields held fairly well. Rather like kicking over a stack of boxes—the stack is a mess but the things inside the boxes are pretty much all right. The *Shendridan* is . . . well, *was* a fighting vessel."

"An 'instrument of their policies,' eh, Captain? How about you? Are you also an 'instrument of their policies'?"

"No" echoed quickly and quietly up the dark shaft.

"No? A Tribune Exemplar of the Pax? *Lor,* Dresiv, I have heard that they still use tales of your campaigns as recruiting propaganda in some provinces of the Pax. Let's see how I remember it: Your ships were coming downspur into the Oyunth home system . . ."

"I don't need this lesson, Djan."

"Yes, yes, I remember. Your ships engaged their massive fleets of huge ships but they were outgunned and inexperienced. Their vessels began falling from orbit onto their own Groundling nations and cities with inadequate safeties on their containments. The devastation of the tragedy must have been horrible."

Serg's voice seemed more distant still. "I don't think this passage is going to work. . . ."

Djan continued speaking a little louder, pretending not to hear. "You, in the finest traditions of the Pax, ceased your own fire, sailed your ships—at considerable danger to your own fleet and victory—directly past the guns of the Oyunth fleet and began benevolent rescue aid to the Groundlings despite great personal danger to yourself. You *are* a hero of the empire by any standard of the word. *Lor,* Dresiv, you aren't an instrument of Pax policy—you ARE Pax policy!"

Djan absentmindedly spun a block of wood drifting in front of him as he spoke, keeping the block within certain arbitrary regions in a game he had only half formulated. Dresiv was born to the royal houses of the Pax. That didn't impress Djan. The tales of his heroism and compassion, however, did tell him that Dresiv was more than just old wealth and power. Yet the captain had given it all up. The official reports were that he did so out of modesty and honor. Bunk. Dresiv may be honorable, but modesty didn't seem to be one of his strong suits, at least not in the man Djan had come to know. Serg Dresiv had given it all up and Djan had to know why. As he finished, he arrested the block between his thumb and middle finger and waited for a response to his razor-edged words.

None came.

Djan hated mysteries that weren't his own.

Serg's muffled voice floated up from the deep blackness. The wizard couldn't make out the words, then they carried up the shaft clearly as the jetsam began again to move. "Djan! We've got to get back up to the observation deck. That Localyte of Sabenth's says the stars have disappeared altogether. I suspect that we've attracted some attention."

I wonder if that's good, thought Djan, who was now uncomfortably confronted with yet another unknown.

25

Belly of the Beast

———⟨⟨⟨◈⟩⟩⟩———

Djan followed Serg as they made their way back through the maze of the *Shendridan* to the observation deck. Through the opening, they could see that the stars had indeed vanished from the sky, engulfing their field of vision in impenetrable blackness.

"What happened?" Serg asked.

"C-captain! They came . . . they really came!" The Localyte Trevis was delirious with relief. "I couldn't believe it! I mean, I actually *saw* it! One moment I was flashing the lantern in those patterns—you know, just like you said—and the next moment they turned! I really saw one of those big huge ships turn in the dark!"

"Of course," Serg said, holding both hands up in front of him as if to ward of the Localyte's verbal assault. "Nice work, son . . . aaaugh! Kid, you just bumped into my leg!"

"Oh! Sorry, sire. I was just so excited—I mean, I just couldn't believe . . ."

"Yes, good work." Serg spoke the words through clenched teeth to the young man, but his eyes were fixed on the blackness through the shattered front of the room. He continued to speak as he pulled himself carefully forward past the boy. "You've done well. Thank you."

Serg pushed off the boy to move through the larger hole they had cleared through the wreckage. In the motion he pressed the still-babbling youth into the sorcerer. The youth apparently felt that Djan also needed to hear his story in all its detail.

"It was the most amazing thing I ever saw!"

Djan was more than slightly annoyed at the kid. "Yes, I'm sure it was amazing. . . ."

"It was just so wonderful—I mean, I just flashed the lantern and they came!"

"Marvelous. Now, if you will excuse me . . ."

"We're gonna be rescued now, right? I mean, that's what this is all about, getting rescued, right?"

The edge to the boy's voice rang an alarm in Djan, for he could feel the fear that engendered it. Someone like that could be dangerous. The sorcerer took the youth in a congratulatory fore-arm grip and looked him in the eye. "Yes, it could, and you have done well."

"Why, thank you, sire! I . . ."

"Yes, you have done well indeed, but there are other things to consider now."

"Other things?" The Localyte blinked.

"Yes." The sorcerer placed an arm around the Localyte's shoulders, made sure his own feet were well secured to the rail-ing, and turned the young priest to face the black opening. "For example, how long were you flashing that lovely light of yours?"

"Well, I don't know—for about ten or twenty degrees, I guess."

"Degrees?"

"Oh, sorry. Um." Trevis had to convert the time standard of his own home world to the delver's standard. "I guess that would be about twenty-seven or, uh, forty standard minutes."

"Right you are!" Djan's smile was carefully orchestrated. "And with all of space to look at and all the worlds around to see and visit, what a wonderful coincidence that they would see our dim little beacon and decide to rescue us?"

"Well . . . well, maybe, but . . ."

"I might suggest another possibility." Djan turned his ingrati-ating smile toward the face of the now-puzzled Localyte. "Would you like to hear it, Trevis—that is your name, isn't it, Trevis?"

"Er, yes—and yes, sire."

Djan turned again to the blackness before them. "In all the vastness of space, for them to come and engulf us with the huge vessel only thirty or forty minutes after we started signaling doesn't seem to indicate great fortune on our part."

"No?" Trevis asked quietly.

"No. They were looking for us."

"Nice assessment," Serg said as he came back from the opening, taking great care not to disturb his injured leg again. "I suspect that covers most of my thinking as well. Ujan! Welis! Are you two up for some light duty?" The two looked pale in the emergency lighting, but both responded, if a bit slowly. "Very well! Get forward into that opening and take watch. Let me know the moment you see anything at all. Ujan, keep flashing those intervals. Now that they've found us, let's make sure they aren't going to lose us."

Serg drifted skillfully over to the enunciator and spoke into it. "Ordina?"

"Sorry, sire, but the Lady has gone forward for a bit!" came the booming voice over the enunciator.

Thyne, still floating where Djan had tethered her, jolted awake at the sound of the voice. "Krith? Krith! Are you all right? How are the rest of the crew? What ... *dran*, someone loosen this line, I've got to get closer!"

Serg looked at her in amazement as Thyne struggled in the air against her tether. "Now, why in all *Hesth* would I want to let you loose?"

"What am I going to do, take your ship with one arm? I doubt there's enough left of this tub to fight over." Thyne winced again as her struggle tightened her arm bandage against her shoulder. She suddenly quit struggling and spoke quietly. "Captain, please—I have my own crew aboard as well."

Serg thought for a moment, then turned to the Localyte. "Master Trevis, would you please release Lady Cargil from her tether? What's the name of your man below, madam?"

"Krith. He's a merc-delver from Jekart. Can't you hurry that, boy? Haven't you worked a line before?"

"Sorry, M'Lady," Trevis responded as he fumbled with yet another knot in the line. "I'm a Jezerinthian Priest."

"Oh," Thyne responded flatly, "how nice for you."

Serg again turned to the enunciator. "Master Krith, have you been monitoring what's happening here?"

"*Allai*, sire—as ordered."

Serg couldn't be sure what the last of that meant, but there seemed to be an odd tone in the man's voice when he said it. He wanted to ask whose order it had been but decided it didn't matter. "Where *is* Ordina?"

"She's gone below, Captain. Gone to get out any of the poor souls that's left before we run into anything else, you might say."

"How many of my crew are with you there?"

"Well, Cap'in, that's a bit difficult to say, it bein' a bit crowded here at the moment. There's the four against the after rail near me and then there's . . ." Krith's voice faded as he turned from the enunciator and continued his count. As he did so, Serg watched the Loyalist captain, finally freed of her ties, start to move toward him. Using only her one good arm, she spun herself slowly around, grasped a second hold to reorient herself, and began making her way across the room to the enunciator. The motion was fluid and graceful in the weightless room—more graceful than he might have thought the tall woman capable of being. Without any wasted motion she settled herself along the ceiling over Serg and anchored herself by her ankles to an exposed equipment rail.

Krith's voice boomed again as he turned to face the enunciator. ". . . and the three healthy ones that went with her makes seventeen left of the *Shendridan*'s fine crew, Cap'in."

"Seventeen! *Dranath*, man, the last time I heard from Ordina, there were twenty-three . . ."

"*Allai*, sire, but I fear we've lost a few since then. Gained four—lost nine. We're doin' without a healer, don't you know."

"What of our own crew, Krith." Thyne spoke calmly, but there was an edge to her voice.

"Captain! Captain Thyne, blessed of the gods! By what miracle do I hear your schemin' voice to torment me again?!"

Thyne smiled warmly, a genuine and melting smile, thought Serg as he watched her. He had to remind himself that this woman was a machine of cold death when it came to his own crews' lives—or his. He wondered with sudden alarm just what had become of the handcannon she had used to nearly blow his brains into mush.

"Krith, you wouldn't want me to leave *you* in charge, would you? Who would follow you anyway?"

"*Allai*, Captain, and there's the problem of it." Krith's voice boomed, even over the enunciator. "Seven of our own made it forward before *Hesth* took the ship. There were many lost on the gun deck to the glory of the battle, M'Lady." There was a sad fire in Thyne's eyes at this. Though she was looking directly at Serg, the gaze was unfocused and distant. "Kerdan was taken in the first assault when we charged their guns. Snap ... well, Snap's gone too. Their tales bears the tellin', M'Lady, but I'll need more heart and a better stomach for it, if you take my meaning."

Thyne replied in a soothing, gentle voice. "It's all right, Krith. There've been many good delvers lost this day. They died that their dreams could live on."

"*Allai*, M'Lady. Well, then, Wethen, Yorki, and Ardo all made it. Berana's gone with the Pax delvers in search of more souls. Helisse's here and none the worse for wear. Ounthnar's in a bad way. There be a full accountin' of them that's made it of our own. . . . Oh, Cap'in Dresiv, sire. I beg to report that your crew has just dropped to sixteen on this deck. *Kern*, if any more of 'em drop off, this place would start to look absolutely roomy!"

Serg turned suddenly from the enunciator, his face set and grim. The abrupt action sent him spinning more than he had anticipated, slamming his leg against a shattered table and inundating him with pain. The injury served only to enrage further.

"Anything to report forward!" he barked as he pulled himself into the opening.

"Clear away, I suppose, sire," came the muffled voice forward. "I can't see a blessed thing."

"Well, keep that lamp working. If they want us, they have us, but they'll need to right well hurry if they expect to find any of us alive to meet their . . ."

". . . to report forward!" Serg barked, pulling himself roughly from his place by the enunciator and into the forward opening.

"Clear away, I guess, sire," came the muffled response. "I can't see a *dran* thing."

"Well, keep that lamp working. If they want us, they have us, but they'll need to *draneth* well hurry if . . . if . . . did something just happen?"

Serg turned back to the back of the observation deck. The look on everyone's face seemed to confirm his suspicions.

"Did you just repeat yourself?" Thyne looked suspiciously at Serg.

"Yes, not just the words but the actions as well." Serg and Thyne both turned their gaze to Djan at once.

The sorcerer folded his arms across his chest with a look of disgust. "Of course, blame the sorcerer. Isn't that always the way. Something strange happens, and who gets the blame. The sorcerer. Something vanishes into thin air and who's the cause—the sorcerer. Time loops back on itself and why is that—the sorcerer. Really, you people are entirely too predictable."

"Well, if it wasn't you—and the Loyalist's mage is dead . . ."

"Right," Thyne glared.

"Then who do you propose . . ."

". . . Really, you people are entirely too predictable."

"Well, if you didn't do it—and the Loyalist's mage . . ."

Thyne held up her good hand. "Wait a moment."

"*Dran*, it just happened again," Serg said.

"It's a temporal displacement of some kind," Djan thought out loud. "The physics of time seem to be altered, but our continuous memory of it isn't changed except for the displacement. It's got to be coming from our hosts."

"*Awas*, Captain!" Ujan called from the opening. "The sky is getting lighter!"

"Say that again?" To Serg's amazement, drifting objects began settling to the floor. Thyne quickly reoriented herself and slowly drifted toward the floor as well.

"Outside, sire! It's getting lighter—kind of a green color like the emergency lights. It's not coming from anywhere in particular, sire, sort of from all around."

"Can you see anything?" Serg twisted his head in an effort to peer through the opening. He spun around one anchored hand as he reoriented himself to move through the hole.

"It's all sort of greenish without—hold a moment. There's some . . . I can't quite make it out, sire! Little points of light directly ahead. They look like lamps or windows, maybe. They're in a pattern, though, hangin' sort of like on a cliff face, though I can't see no top to it."

"Where away?"

"Dead ahead, sire. Maybe a mile—maybe ten—can't say for certain, but we are getting closer. There seems to be a fog below us now, rising up toward us. There doesn't seem to be . . ."

The low rumble started below their feet, growing by the moment and covering Ujan's words. Soon the compartment was filled with a roar that sounded like a wooden waterfall. The ship heeled against its newfound gravity, falling ever so slowly to its side. Thyne grabbed quickly one of the ceiling rails as the room and its contents rotated beneath it. Debris tumbled slowly as though being rolled in a barrel, glancing lightly off the room's other occupants.

Serg rolled with the shift as well, trying desperately to pull himself out of the forward opening and managing to do so just as the cleared passage collapsed. The timbers and support from the shattered forward end of the room began raining down against the port wall, tearing additional support timbers loose from the starboard side. Serg drifted down, falling on top of one of his injured delvers, the pain in his leg increasing by the moment as the gravity increased. He turned, looked up, and saw the emergency field of the hull flicker suddenly, and disappear.

He grabbed instinctively for some handhold that would secure him against the sudden decompression of the compartment that was sure to follow. It took him several moments to realize that the explosive evacuation of atmosphere hadn't happened.

Ujan clambered over the mound of debris and looked into the compartment with amazement. Everyone was lying in a tumble of broken furniture, pillows, cushions, and other people. "Captain?"

Hanging by one hand from a rail now almost fifteen feet above the floor, Thyne swung slowly.

"Nice landing, Captain," she said.

As if in response, the perpendicular floor burst into flame.

26

Pyre

~~~

"Captain? Captain! *Dran* this thing! The enunciator's gone!" Ordina gave the silent tube a quick and vicious kick and tried again. "Captain! Anybody! What's happened?"

Ordina had extracted herself from the jumbled pile of delvers and debris. Her world was changing again. She desperately wanted to hear how it was changing from her captain.

Near her, Krith shook his great head before he realized what a bad idea it was. Three delvers lay sprawled on top of him. The rest of the compartment occupants had been tumbled unceremoniously against what once was the port wall of the healing bay—or what was left of it. Only the Thrund seemed at ease. She, at least, had managed to keep her feet—all six of them—under her.

Several of the bay's tables and bunks had broken loose of their strained mounts and slammed against the wall, splintering huge ragged holes in the bay's wall panels. Ordina guessed they'd start calling them *floor* panels from then on.

Ordina continued to beat hopelessly against the enunciator. Behind her, Krith's rough voice croaked. "Mistress Ordina, the gravity's back."

Her eyes flashed fierce anger at him. "Not possible!" she said, daring him to contradict her.

"Sorry, M'Lady." Krith shook his head slowly. "I'm afraid there's no saying no to it this time. Drop somethin' an' it'll fall. Worse yet, ma'am, we're afire."

There were many unpleasant smells she had experienced over the past few hours, but a new one quite suddenly bothered her. No, more than bothered—it came to call on an ingrained fear of all those who delved the stars. A second glance into the room confirmed Krith's words. The thin haze was already beginning to obstruct her vision to the far end of the healing bay.

Ordina looked as if she were about to reply fiercely, but suddenly her eyes focused on him as the fumes poured into her nostrils. Fire aboard ship was three times an enemy. Open flame running down the corridors of a wooden hull could alone kill delvers who were uncertain how to handle it. It could also destroy the structural integrity of the ship itself, and, if it reached the temple, could loose the silverfire from its chains. Yet even if a crew were capable of fighting the fire and kept it from the important areas of the ship, open flame could easily consume all the available oxygen before it was extinguished. Many a ship had been found adrift in space with its crew dead at their posts, deprived of breath before the flames themselves suffocated. In any fire it was a race against time—even under the best of circumstances.

Pax ships, however, had years before begun using the very structural emergency fields woven into the ship for fire suppression. In principle, the integrity fields were triggered by heat or smoke as well as concussion. The fire would be contained to a single space and, since the integrity fields were airtight, the fire would put itself out before it spread. This occasionally did lead to trapped delvers, but usually there was sufficient sentience woven into the magic of the field to allow them time to escape before sealing the room properly.

At least, that was the theory, Ordina thought. That's what was supposed to happen when everything was . . .

"The fields have collapsed," she stated flatly.

"Pardon?" Krith said with astonishment.

"The integrity fields have collapsed, otherwise the fire and smoke would be contained." Ordina was moving quickly again with the barest edge of panic in her voice. "Tsara! Get anyone who is able and make those altars portable. NOW! We're abandoning ship."

"Abandon ship!" Krith stumbled after her as she moved quickly toward the front of the now-sideways compartment, his voice more agitated by the moment. "Lady! Abandon ship to *where*?"

Ordina ignored him. "Madam Ambassador, how is the Farcardinal?"

Hruna's appendages were slowly returning to their normal orientation. She had steadied herself against the sudden onslaught of gravity by pushing against all the compartment walls, ceilings, and floors at once. All this while trying to keep the Farcardinal from slamming his head against the deck again and risking further damage.

Both Ordina and the Thrund turned to examine the Farcardinal again. Even from this distance, Ordina could see that his eyes were again unfocused and sweat had broken out on his brow. Ordina knew little of anatomy but strongly suspected that the Farcardinal was in terrible trouble physically. It might even be some sort of brain injury. That would effectively end his career.

Hruna turned back to Ordina. "The Farcardinal is in need of assistance, but I shall manage it alone. Where do you need me to take him?"

"Out, Madam Ambassador. We are abandoning ship."

Krith was being ignored and, feeling that a larger voice might be in order, bellowed. "OUT TO WHERE?"

Ordina whirled around and, in a single motion, grabbed the great delver's beard with both hands. With a single roar, Krith suddenly found himself bent forward with his face within an inch of the shipwright's nose.

"We are in gravity and the fields have failed. There was no decompression, therefore . . . ?" She yanked again on his beard when he gave no response.

"Yeow! Lady, please, ma'am!"

"Well? Therefore . . . ?" She gave another tug.

Tears welled up in Krith's eyes. "Therefore! Er, therefore there must be air outside?"

She let go so suddenly, the huge delver almost fell backward.

"Yes, air—if we're lucky. At least there's an atmosphere. There's a fire burning somewhere and that feeds off oxygen. If the fire can breathe, we can. Besides, what choice do we have?"

She looked around the compartment. The haze was thickening and it was already getting hard to breathe. "All right! Tsara, Emret, you—what's your name?"

"Helisse, M'Lady," the wiry Loyalist woman replied.

"You too, Helisse. Grab what you can of the assembled gear. Krith, you and the dark one over there take those chests out; we'll need what's in them! Tsara, organize whoever's left and bring the Altars in Exile and one of those optics chests." Ordina noticed the air getting decidedly thick with hazy smoke. "What shall it be, forward or aft?"

"Aft's fowled, M'Lady," Krith said. He reached down and lifted a chest without aid. Its painted handcannon markings made him smile as he lifted it. "We might be reachin' the crew bunks, but there be no way out from there."

"What about the forward stairwell?"

"No tellin' what damage the ship settling has done."

Ordina gave him her coldest eye. "You are simply a font of information, Master Krith. All right! Forward down toward the keel. Stay close, we don't have much time."

They ran through the milky-green mist. The ground below their feet was damp, and, it seemed, of the same pale green color that seemed to make up the air. It didn't matter to them. They were free of the wreck and with little time to spare.

Endless moments later, breathless, they stopped and turned. Their ship—what was left of it—was only a huge shadow looming over them in the sickly fog. Already the billowing smoke was staining black the perfection of the pearly jade haze. For a moment they were struck dumb by the sheer size of the hulk towering over them.

Flame gushed from the far side, rolling in increasing spheres of heat and light. Everything was obscured by the fog about them, giving a soft edge to their nightmarish vision.

"The emergency fields have failed," Ordina said in a voice of infinite sadness. It was her ship and, somehow, she felt she had failed her. "The heat has reached the wood."

The inferno suddenly lived. It reached around the veiled outline of the shattered hull, caressing its features, highlighting its broken lines even as it pulled them apart. Wreck that she was, the *Shendridan* remained proud with her bow high. She looked as though she would sail again, a ship of flame.

"*Dran* the smoke," Ordina sighed as she wiped her eyes.

"I'm wonderin' if any other souls made it out?" Krith asked aloud to no one in particular.

"Haloo!" Tsara cried out, her voice shaky but growing more firm with each call. "Haloo! HALOO! WE ARE HERE!"

The pause was filled only with the roaring cackle of the great blaze.

"HALOO!" they enjoined in a staggered chorus of calls filled with despair and hope. "HALOO! WE ARE HERE! COME TO US!"

Gray shadows began to emerge from the fog, some staggering, some limp and helped by others. From them came a most beautiful voice into Ordina's ears.

"Mistress Ordina! Do you have the altars?"

Her smile was warmed by the death of her ship. "*Allai*, Captain Dresiv. That I have!"

"Then," said Serg as he stumbled and fell breathless to sit near her feet. "I think your loud voice is the most wonderful song I have ever heard. Let's hear another chorus, if you please."

They called again. They shouted until they were hoarse. Their throats were raw and still they called out. From time to time one or two figures emerged from the smoke-stained fog.

An hour later, when the ribs of the hull collapsed into a glowing rush of embers, they fell silent. Of the *Shendridan*'s original hundred and twelve crew members, only fourteen had survived. Nine of the Loyalist prisoners remained alive of the thirty-six they were transporting. Miraculously, all four of their passengers—if you could count Djan Kithber among them—had survived. They numbered twenty-seven.

They were all that were left.

They sat quietly for many minutes, each with his own thoughts. The loss weighed heavily on them, each in his own way.

At last, Serg stood up.

Genni looked up at him and quietly asked, "What do we do now, Captain."

Thyne raised her head slowly. "Yes, oh, great, courageous Captain, just what do we do? Where the *Hesth* are we anyway?"

Serg placed his fists on both hips as he spoke, his voice distant as he continued to think. "I believe we're inside some kind of ship. We've been seeing a number of ships moving about us for hours now. One of them turned in response to our signal. Whatever it was, it seems it has encompassed us."

Thyne raised her eyebrows. "A ship? This size? Great! So now that we're inside, just what do you propose we do?"

"Well," Serg continued to think out loud. "Our hosts have provided us with a gravity and atmosphere environment—a rather thoughtful analysis of our needs so far, considering the possibilities. So . . ." Serg let the sentence hang suspended in mid-thought.

"So?" Thyne urged.

"So—we walk."

"Walk?! Walk *where*?"

Serg turned, his eyes scanning the fog about them. "Just before we made landfall, we saw bright lights—there! That glow over there. If there is anyone for us to contact, it's going to be in that direction."

Thyne scoffed. "Now, *there's* some fine reasoning for you. We are engulfed by some dark mass. You see some lights. You don't understand the lights. Ergo, the lights must lead to an advanced civilization. I suspect, Captain, that there are some gaps in logic."

Serg turned to her, smiling strangely. "Something's caught us. The light is the only indication of direction we've got."

"Ever hear of a moth, Captain?" Thyne said.

"What's a moth?"

"It's a small, stupid creature that's attracted by light to its own destruction."

Serg's smile was frozen but still in place. "Never heard of it. Do *you* have a better suggestion?"

Thyne took the handle on the side of a food container and stood up. "Lead on, courageous moth."

Ordina was beginning to feel Genni's panic as the two of them walked across the seemingly endless plain. Worse, she identified with that panic all too closely.

The great, pale nothing seemed to stretch eternally about her. Her countless steps across the soft white plain left her unsure of her progress. There were no objects about her by which she might gauge her motion. If it weren't for the delver accompanying her, she might not be moving at all. Ordina wasn't sure whether she was moving over the ground or whether she was, in fact, holding still and the ground was moving backward under her. For that matter, she couldn't honestly be sure if she was suffering from claustrophobia due to the omnipresent oppressive white fog or from agoraphobia due to the vastness of the space she suddenly found herself in.

She looked up again. The pale green light at the horizon was a goal that never gave any indication of getting closer as it glowed constant in the fog. It was the one feature that any of them could distinguish. The captain had ordered them to move camp toward that light in the hope of contacting their hosts. She and Genni had been operating as the second set of scouts. Now, four hours into their march, she wasn't sure that they were any closer to their goal. The light simply hung there in the fog, unmoving, encouraging, and tempting.

"This can't be a ship," she muttered to herself. "Who would waste this much space in a ship? I don't know what the captain saw, but I don't think it was a ship!"

The claustrophobia she was feeling suddenly rushed in on her, seeming to sap her of her breath. She stopped and placed both hands on her knees as she sucked in the air. "Master Parquan. A moment, please."

"*Allai*, Mistress Ordina," the delver said flatly. He didn't come to stand by her—but he did stop.

It was all she could expect, Ordina thought. In the best of times Genni had never much cared for the shipwright. She had run her temple with a convert's passion. Genni had once been assigned as a liaison under Captain Mandrith to the temple and lasted only three weeks before Ordina finally convinced Mandrith to let him out of the assignment. Ordina had struck a bad chord in Genni. She had once overheard him talking about her. He told his mate that he had heard tales of small animals with deceptively fierce dispositions living on obscure planets, but until he had met Mistress Ordina it had never quite been real for him. Now he was working for one.

Still, they had one common ground: They both followed their orders and saw the reason in them. It was this alone that allowed them to work together. Everything else was just more sand poured among the gears.

She gazed down at the ground—if it could be called ground. Its pale color cast a sickly green tint in this light and had a rather spongy quality, like a well-cared-for lawn. Yet while it seemed fibrous, it was also contiguous, like a weave without a break. It was also slightly warm to the touch. Like all delvers, she had heard and done her share of storytelling about the great space monsters that lurked between the stars. They always lived in the Void and swallowed ships and their men whole. Such delvers— except for the teller of the tale—were never heard from again. She, too, had done her share of telling the tale and had embellished it where she and the audience felt it needed more strength. Standing here now, however, Ordina had the thought that some of those tales might have been true. It was not a pleasant thought. The captain said that they were on a ship that had picked them up, but standing there as he was, the idea of invisible space dragons seemed far more likely.

"Mistress Ordina," Genni offered in real concern. "Are you certain that director is functioning properly?"

She pulled the small wooden box from her tunic and opened it. The device carried a minor magic of its own that allowed her to know the distance and bearing of her device from every other like device in her vicinity. It was almost toylike in its simplicity to her but was invaluable in this fog. She knew the answer to Genni's question, but the exercise would buy her a few more moments for rest. "Yes, Master Parquan. The director checks out just fine. We have been heading toward that light pretty much directly since we left the group a few hours ago."

"We must be fifteen kilometers from the ship by now," he said, a strange edge in his voice.

"*Allai*, what's left of her is probably that far behind us." Genni was getting at something, she thought. "What's your point?"

"We should have found something by now! Something— anything."

"Look, you saw that light on our approach. You were up there. Where else do we have to go to look for these things that rescued us except there? Serg's orders were—"

"Specific. Yes, I know. But if they wanted to hear from us— well, it is their ship! You'd think that they would have found us by now! You'd think they would have said *something*! All we're left with is that great sickly green haze and a flat earth of something that seems alive!" Genni was sweating profusely. Ordina noticed a strange fever in his eyes just as he turned away and began stalking off toward the light. "Fine! The Big Captain wants us to find the ugly light, then I'll find it for him!"

"Master Parquan," she called, fumbling to close the case on the director again. "Wait!"

The form of the delver was a vague outline in the greenish mist. "Where do we end it?" he called back to her. "Is this the place we settle down with the provisions we have? How about over here? Maybe ol' Serg would like this spot better. It's so *unlike* anything we've experienced so far."

Genni turned again, a shadow prancing at the limits of her vision. "Maybe over here. I'm sure that you'll like—Wait one more moment! I see something! It looks like I've found . . . hey, M'Lady? There's something . . . oh, goth! GOTH!"

Genni suddenly disappeared.

Ordina shook with a start at the sound of the scream. Genni's scream. It exploded her anger into shards falling like crystal around her naked fear. "Parquan?" she murmured.

A voice howled in the mists, speaking to the blackest recesses of the mind.

The paralyzing chill that had held her broke, and suddenly she was moving. "PARQUAN!" she yelled. She was running now, running toward where last she had seen him. As she ran, she fumbled to release the safety strap on the handcannon slapping crazily at her side. She looked down as she ran, finally dragging the weapon free. She was a Daughter of the Temple and Master Shipwright. She wondered vaguely somewhere in her mind if she actually remembered how to fire the thing.

"Parquan!" she shouted as she ran toward the now-gasping sobs. "Parquan!"

Dark shapes suddenly loomed ahead of her, and she slowed. The forms were quickly defined as she approached more carefully.

Her mouth gaped open.

A corridor. A ship's corridor appeared. Brass railings polished but twisted. Overhead were beams, some of them splintered but many of them intact. It was a ship. A corridor from a Pax ship. Yet it was all wrong. The same green mists floated above the open ceiling planks. Stranger still were the doors that lay open into rooms. There were letters on the doors marking them as well as signs on the walls, but the letters made no sense. They were a jumble of meaningless letters carefully placed in neat lines. Odder still were the paintings, their frames beautifully ornate but all of the colors on the canvas a jumble without portraying anything at all.

She cautiously made her way toward the end of the twisting hall. She could see rooms on either side filled with furniture but without evidence of any reason in its placement. The rooms themselves were a nightmare jumble of utilities. A stateroom faced what appeared to be a conduit access room filled with lusterless optics. Next to these was a mess hall without any sign of a galley nearby. Then an altar room without any connecting conduits at all.

The senseless hall ended at an intersection. Ordina turned toward the sobbing.

She found Genni sitting against a partial wall. Over him hung another senseless painting, the purpose of the wall apparently being only to support the artwork. The delver's knees were drawn up to his chest. He appeared badly shaken but was calming down.

Ordina swallowed hard and tried to steady the cannon shaking violently in her hand.

Genni sat opposite a door. Ordina quickly stood with her back against the wall opposite Genni and next to the door. She remembered vaguely having once seen the move in a Praetorian Theater presentation. It seemed like the right thing to do. She turned the corner of the door carefully and lowered her weapon.

Humans—naked—covered the floor.

They were all dead. Hundreds. Thousands. They lay in a vast chamber resembling the ship's boat bay, a jumble of arms, legs, bodies, and faces stacked casually as though tossed there by an uncaring child who had tired of toys.

"Goth!"

Ordina turned away from the scene, her eyes riveted open. Her breath came hard to her, and suddenly the corridor seemed small and oppressive.

"Parquan!" she gasped out, and then gained her voice. "Parquan! Genni! Listen to me! We've got to get out of here—NOW!"

Genni lifted up his head. His eyes were unfocused and he seemed to have a hard time hearing her. Great beads of sweat streamed down his face. There was fear there—but she also felt the heat of his skin. He was suffering from more than just the horror they were experiencing. Something was making him seriously ill.

Ordina pushed herself away from the wall, deliberately standing between him and the door. It blocked his vision and, gratefully, kept her back to the scene as well. She grabbed the delver by his tunic and dragged his face toward her own.

She pronounced every syllable as clearly as she could. "Parquan! We must get out of here NOW!"

Genni's eyes focused though he was still fevered. He blinked at the face filling his vision. "M'Lady . . . M'Lady, yes, *allai*, M'Lady." He struggled to his feet.

Together they turned back and rounded the corner to the adjoining corridor. It had been only thirty feet long when they had first entered it. She should have been able to see the end of it even in the mist.

Now the corridor ended in a door.

"Oh, *dran*!" she whispered in awe and fear.

Genni, eyes wide, dashed for the door and found it jammed. He drew back, the fear and rage building in him, and slammed bodily against the door, which splintered and gave way.

The room looked like part of the temple but had no ceiling. Altars circled the room. Their design was familiar, but, as Ordina went to each in turn, none of them even made sense let alone was functional. A large spiral staircase climbed up into the mists through what should have been the roof.

Genni tried each of the doors in turn, opening one after another in the room. There was a hysterical edge to his voice as he reported more at Ordina than to her. "Corridors, every one of them! More compartments! Now what!"

"Shut up, delver! Get a hold on your line!" Ordina held up the director. "We haven't moved that far! The reading on the director shows us to have moved just as we should have. If the terrain is changing on us, it won't matter. We can still find our way back!"

Genni looked at her and then at the director.

"Hey, Genni," she said with a sly shrug. "At least now you have something to report, right?"

Genni caught the smile playing around the shipwright's lips and suddenly laughed. The release was complete and he hung his head, shaking it. "*Allai*, M'Lady. It's nice to feel like you're making progress. Still, what's going on here? Halls and corridors that go nowhere full of . . ."

"Yeah, I know what they're full of. There's changes going on, Master Parquan. I'm going to find out why. Look."

He followed her gaze to the great staircase. As he had suspected, it literally went nowhere. She could now see the top of it suspended in the air.

The mists were dissipating.

"Stay here!" Ordina ordered as she scampered up the staircase. The structure swayed under her as she climbed, but she knew how high would be safe. When she had gone up as far as she dared, she stopped and looked.

The mists had cleared. In the direction from which they had come she saw a huge white clearing. The clearing lay in the middle of—chaos. As the mists parted, she could see a forest of debris extending outward to the horizon. Here and there in the refuse could be seen a partial ship's hull or a complete superstructure jutting at odd angles from the carnage. The great green lamp in the distant horizon shone clearly beyond the debris.

She wiped her forehead with the back of her sleeve. As her hand crossed her brow she felt the heat of her own increasing fever. She wondered vaguely if what she was seeing was an illusion caused by her sudden illness, then feared it was not.

Everywhere she looked, huge gray mounds of rotting corpses dotted the wreckage.

27

Out of Touch

———◆———

Djan Kithber crouched over the gray body with a critical eye. "Dead? *Hesth*, Lady, the thing never lived."

He had found yet another mystery, this one more puzzling than the ones before. The twisted and shattered walls that had sprung up around them as they walked had unnerved him and continued to do so. There was something about its mix of familiarity and total disregard for logic that left him considerably uncomfortable.

Ordina leaned over him for a closer look. She apparently found little comfort in the three flanking delvers who stood watch around them, their handcannons drawn and ready, although nothing had moved in the strangeness Djan had come to call "the maze." Ordina had returned with this detail only after a short but rather vehement discussion with her captain. The tension still sounded in her voice. "What do you mean, it's never lived, Squire Kithber?"

The sorcerer looked up. "That's *Lor* Kithber, Mistress Ordina—and what I meant was just what I said: Not only are these lumps of flesh dead, but they were never alive in the first place. Every living thing generates an aura—some cultures call it nimbus, others call it a soul. Whatever you call it, some trace of it remains even in death. There is no aura residual from any of these things that I can detect . . . and"—he held up a hand to stop her interruption—"yes, my powers are sufficiently recovered to detect such a remnant. The bodies haven't decayed sufficiently for a total absence of aura. Furthermore, there's another observation that I would like to make and I don't even need magic to do it."

"And that is, Squire . . . Lor Kithber?" Ordina asked.

He reached down with his gloved hand. He roughly turned one, then another of the bodies over, dragging them by an arm until they lay faceup side by side. Ordina shuddered but looked.

"They're identical," he said, his open hand pointing to each in turn. "The faces have the same general bone structure. The builds and size are the same. Haven't you noticed that they *look* alike. Yes, they're male and female but it's only cosmetic. *Hesth*, Mistress, there are some in there that are *both* male and female and an equal number that are neither.

"More than that, their minds have never been used— absolutely virgin brain cells. In all the dead there is at least some pattern of their original thought process. Oh, nothing that you can read or comprehend or anything—just changes in the way their synapses are aligned and connected, showing some evidence of brain work. All the synapses in these minds are aligned identically! Lady, I tell you that these people never thought a thought. They never lived."

"Yet here they are," she said.

"Yes, here they are—but why?" Djan stood up, absently wiping his hands on his trousers as he looked over the corpses. "Why are they here? Why is any of this here? Why the broken hulls and meaningless words on walls? Why all this ghastly green light?"

"I hate it," Ordina muttered half to herself. "It reminds me of the light from our emergency globes. I wish the shipwrights guild would come up with a better color for emergency lighting on . . ."

Djan turned suddenly to look directly at her. "What did you say?"

"I said that I wish the shipwrights guild would . . ."

"No, before that. You said the light was the same as the emergency lights."

"Yes. I think it's making me ill. Why would anyone want to construct such a monstrosity?"

Kithber smiled. He surveyed the dreadful carnage again, this time with a new insight. He hadn't noticed before, but the broken ship pieces all seemed to follow the same design as the *Shendridan*. Not exact copies, but all the pieces were of the same type and pattern as their own broken ship.

"I think, Mistress, that someone is trying to make us feel at home."

". . . hundreds, possibly thousands of bodies piled in various places—if my observations are correct. I climbed a staircase as well as the two masts after that. Everywhere I looked, it was pretty much the same."

"A chaotic jumble of shattered ships—everywhere?" Serg wasn't sure he had heard the words properly. He hadn't been feeling well since they had fled the *Shendridan* wreckage. There was a dull aching in his head and he was having a hard time concentrating. He had also started sweating profusely, although the room seemed cool to him. It seemed to make it all the harder to concentrate on what Ordina was saying. She seemed to be talking at him from very far away. He was dimly aware of the wizard Kithber lying with his back against the almost vertical floor in the corner. Thyne Cargil, the Loyalist captain, stood opposite him, eyeing the sorcerer warily.

He himself leaned heavily against an upturned Altar of Command which lay upright inexplicably in the center of the room. The room itself was a sleeping compartment that might have been considered luxuriously appointed except for the fact that it was completely laid on its side. It was a duplicate of the Farcardinal's apartment with the addition of the anchor and chain that was a major fixture coming up through the floor.

When the mists had parted to reveal this madness, the survivors of the *Shendridan* suddenly found themselves walking into their own ship's mess hall turned upside down. The tables suspended overhead were in some cases suspended from flooring—in others they simply hung in midair. They were still recovering from this when Ordina and Genni burst breathlessly through the far hatchway.

The excitement and horror evident in both of them fairly screamed for discretion. He quickly found his bedroom through a sideways-mounted door on one side of the mess hall. It was the most convenient place to hear Ordina's story out of earshot of the rest of the survivors.

He'd calmed her down and somehow talked her into leading Djan back to investigate her discovery. Something in the back of his mind told him that this may not have been a smart idea, but he couldn't seem to get his mind to work properly. By the time they had left, his health had deteriorated to the point where all he wished for was sleep.

Now Djan and Ordina had returned to report. It was all he could do to stand as they spoke.

"*Allai*, sire, a field of ship sections and parts all merging as perfectly as if they had been connected by the finest shipwrights of the Oipan nebula. I couldn't have merged some of the joints that well. Yet none of it—well, none of it makes any sense."

"What?" Serg closed his eyes, rubbing the bridge of his nose on either side with his hands.

Ordina opened her mouth again just as the compartment door slammed open next to her. The only entrance to the room was through the wall that led to the mess hall. However, the heavy door was situated sideways with the hinges on the lower edge. Each time anyone opened the door, it swung falling into the room, slamming against the wall that now served as floor.

"Sorry, sire! I understand you need me?" Tsara was red-faced.

Serg held his head, the impact of the door still rattling between his ears. "No!—yes, Tsara. Have you had any luck with our Altar of Knowledge?"

"Yes, sire. The Altar of Knowledge in Exile appears functional, but I'm still having trouble getting the optics properly powered."

"I'll have Mistress Ordina to you momentarily," Serg said. The assistant shipwright disappeared as she laboriously dragged the door upward to close it again. Serg continued to look at the door, his head pounding.

"Captain!" Ordina leaned forward, placing both hands on the altar between them. Her voice was getting hoarse and she had to clear it twice before she could proceed. Her arms ached as she gestured, but it was the only way she knew how to talk. "There are whole sections of ship out here that are joined together as though they were one ship, but none of the sections make sense. Temple conduits running directly through sleeping quarters and then terminating in a closet. Free-standing equipment without any optics connections. Signs, Captain, signs labeling everything but not a single one of them is legible. They use our alphabet and the letters are all perfectly placed, yet they form no words.

"Then there's the bodies, sire."

"Bodies?" Serg croaked.

"*Allai*, sire, bodies." Ordina shivered.

Leaning against the wall to Serg's right, Kithber sniffed behind watery eyes as he quietly spoke. "Yes, sire, bodies. Flesh and bone but no souls. Never alive, Dresiv. Just legions of dead flesh. By any of our standards, it's a nightmare of unimaginable proportions, yet I wonder . . ."

"Wonder what?" Serg was more tired than he remembered ever being.

"I wonder if maybe they aren't trying to make contact," the sorcerer sniffed again. He coolly noted to himself that whatever was affecting his health seemed to be affecting everyone else as well. "This display didn't arrange itself. Some intelligence obviously set it up. We are interpreting it as an uncomfortable manifestation . . ."

"It's grotesque!" chirped Ordina.

"Yes, it's grotesque, but did you notice just how much of our own circumstances that mess resembles. When we were captured, our ship had been shattered and twisted. That wreckage out there *looks* like us!"

"But it doesn't make sense!" Ordina cried. "None of the pieces fit together. And what about those—you know! What the *Hesth* are they doing out there?"

"I don't know." *Lor*, he was tired, Djan thought as he leaned his head back against the floor that was a wall and closed his eyes. "There's a pattern here, just the hint of one. If I could only see it. The one thing I'm sure of is that whatever brought us here is somehow trying to make contact with us. I just don't see how yet."

The door tumbled open again with a resolute bang. This time the plunging door dragged a ragged Loyalist sprawling into the room.

"What now!" Serg bellowed, and was instantly reprimanded by the pounding of his skull.

"Sorry, yer master, sire! Master Krith asks that I convey his—

er—compliments and bids me informate you that them Exile Altars has all been set about just as Mistress Ordina asked."

"What is he babbling about?" Djan demanded.

"I've put the Loyalists to work with the temple survivors," Serg replied. "Most of the terrorists were still aft of the break when the disaster hit us, so their numbers are about even. They've been helping get the Altars in Exile set up in the next compartment."

"Do you think that wise?" The sorcerer raised his eyebrows in a supreme effort.

"I'd rather keep them busy than leave them time to work up more trouble on their own. Besides, where would they go?" He turned to Thyne. "Right, your ladyship?"

"Indeed, great Master of the Pax, where could we go?" Thyne replied quietly.

Serg looked at Thyne sharply. "Nowhere. There is nowhere for you to go. Those lights on the horizon are our only hope— yours as well. I don't understand this bizarre turn of events, but we've got to keep trying to connect with whatever or whoever pilots this craft. Work with us and we might make it out of this alive. Do something stupid and we all die without furthering your 'cause' along one bit. You understand?"

"Of course, Great Captain, without question." The Loyalist smiled so wide that Serg thought he could count all her teeth from where he sat. Still, she turned to her crewman and said, "Yantha, give the word. We'll be cooperative *kidikers* and help the nice beneficent Pax until I personally say otherwise."

The Loyalist delver bowed deeply as he backed from the room, as much falling out of it as he had fallen in. He slammed the door solidly shut.

Serg rubbed his temples. "*Lor*, I wish I felt better."

Ordina sighed. "Nearly everyone has this sickness. It seems to affect different people in different ways.

"Well, Wizard, is this something we should worry about, catching a disease from alien creatures?"

"No. It doesn't seem to be that severe an illness." The wizard closed his eyes again.

"But what if this . . ."

"Aw, please—ask me in the morning," the wizard said as he drifted off to sleep.

"Captain," said Thyne with honeyed words. "If you'll excuse me, I'd like to help my crew about their tasks."

The tall woman moved with unexpected grace through the hatchway. In five quick strides she crossed the green-tinged mess hall to join the workers laying out the altars. Several of her own crew moved purposefully and cheerfully about. Each flashed warm and genuine smiles at their Pax counterparts as they worked, the very essence of cooperation.

"Master Krith." Thyne's suddenly melodic voice carried well despite her feeling ill. It's got to be a good show, she thought. Just keep it up. "I understand they've put you to work at last! I trust you won't mind telling me what it is that I can do to help. I'm a captain, of course, and not accustomed to actual work!"

This, and her bright, wide smile drew hearty laughs not only from her own crew but from many among the Pax survivors as well.

"*Allai*, M'Lady Cargil." Krith smiled with her, crouching down behind the Altar of Communion and pointing to the optic connection points. "Let's be startin' with this little gem over 'ere, eh?"

Still smiling, she kneeled down with him.

"Well, Krith, let's have it." Thyne's eyes suddenly blazed. She'd stood side by side with the Pax *draneth* through the day, urging her companions along in cheery cooperation. She'd had her fill of cheery cooperation. Now out of sight and with her companions' loud banging about and shouting voices, she was ready to give vent to some of her rage.

"M'Lady! I've been cartin' about a chest full o' them Pax handcannons. They's charged and ready for yer service, ma'am. All them that's with ye stand ready to move on yer word."

"No less than I expect, Krith. Any ideas as to why all this horror has sprung up?"

"Some o' them Pax boys have some ideas, especially that there sorcerer fella. I don't suppose there be any among them that might consider changing their careers right soon . . ."

"Krith, I'm going to eat their hearts, every one of them. Speak up, man, before I burst!"

"*Allai*, M'Lady. It's the hosts of our hosts you might say that's causing all this strangeness; at least so them that thinks says."

"The masters of this huge vessel we're in?"

"*Allai*, M'Lady." Krith looked sideways. "The wise one thinks that they be trying to speak with us but just haven't found the right words yet. Still, to my way of thinkin', they can't be too terribly far off. They built that horror out there, didn't they? That means they gotta have some idea, don't they?"

Thyne pondered the green-cast wreckage that lay about them. If every kind of ship's part were duplicated out there—down to a dead crew—then perhaps there would be a pantry included without thinking. If there were a pantry . . . she turned slowly, wearing yet another, more genuine smile as Tsara, one of the temple Acolytes, passed near.

"Master Krith? I think I understand that now. What about that altar over there? I think . . . I . . . oh! Oh!"

Thyne collapsed into a faint, Krith managing with some difficulty to catch her in his arms.

Tsara rushed over. "What's wrong with her?"

"Nothin', ma'am, I'm sure," Krith said with as much worry on his face as he could muster at the moment. He was still struggling to find his balance with Thyne unexpectedly in his arms. "I suspect it's just this little sickness goin' about now. I'll just put her down over here for a bit and give her some rest."

Krith waddled a few steps before he got his legs under him. With concern in her eyes, Tsara watched them go.

"Cheap trick, M'Lady," Krith muttered as he walked on.

"The *drith* fell for it, didn't she?" Thyne said for his ears only.

"I suppose you have found us a way out of this"—he shifted her in his arms to get a better grip—"or did you just want a ride?"

"The sorcerer says that the wreckage was put there by the masters of this giant ship. He says that whatever or whoever brought us here is trying to communicate."

Krith reached the pallets the altars had been brought on and began carefully laying Thyne down.

"No! Not that one! The one on the far end!"

Krith groaned as he straightened back up. "Gettin' choosy in our age, are we, M'Lady?"

"No madness without purpose, Krith." The huge delver settled Thyne down behind the broken table she had indicated—out of sight but not conspicuously so.

"At the change of watch, start rotating crew out to visit me." Thyne spoke quickly as Krith knelt next to her. "We'll each in turn set out for that main spar sticking out from the wreckage of the ship's bow."

Krith pointed with his hand, but Thyne was adamant.

"No, not that one, the closer one on the right! While they're busy feeding their stomachs, we'll make our break."

"Pardon me askin', M'Lady"—Krith began scratching his beard, his face itself a question—"but, what's out there that we ain't havin' here?"

There was a glint in her eye as she spoke. "THEY are out there, Krith. They who brought us here. They who don't yet know the words to speak. They're learning though, I'm sure of it. The sorcerer says they're trying to find the words. Do you want them to start their dialogue with His Highness Captain Pax Butcher over there, or me?"

Thyne turned to look toward the chaotic wreckage beyond their chamber. "No. When they gain their voice—we'll be there to hear them, not the Pax dogs. That light in the distance remains our best bet. We can travel faster than these Pax squealers can—we aren't burdened by their precious altars that don't work. We'll find these strange hosts first, and when they know how to hear—it will be our words they'll listen to."

"We're going to have very powerful friends, Krith. Very powerful indeed."

"Captain?"

Serg turned slowly toward the voice with an absolute minimum of effort. He lay with his back pressed into the corner of the room. Each movement threatened both nausea and vertigo to his fevered mind. He closed his eyes and waited for the motion in his head to stop. When he thought it safe, he dragged his eyelids open and gazed dully in the general direction of the sound.

"Captain? How are you feeling?"

The face wasn't focusing for him, but Serg was pretty sure that the voice belonged to Genni. He allowed his eyes to fall shut again. "What is it, Genni?"

"I just thought you would want to know. The Loyalists have disappeared."

"*Dran! Dran! HESTH* and *DRAN*, Genni!" Serg worked himself into his anger, using it as a crutch against the physical weakness he felt. He grabbed the wall railing now overhead and pulled himself up until he stood. The room spun around him and

the pain that sleep had blissfully blocked from his mind now
rushed over him as a tidal wave. He fell forward, catching himself on the altar in the center of the room. He should have known
his own debilitation would be all that was needed for Thyne to
do something stupid.

"How long have they been gone?"

"Not long, sire, but they went straight into that mess out
there. I don't see much hope in finding them."

Serg fell back into the hammock. "Break out the handcannons
and distribute them to the crew. Better get some to the temple
workers as well. There's no telling what those Loyalists will find
out there. Get the crew ready to break camp. We've—we've got
to beat them to the—to the—"

Genni waited for a minute before realizing that the captain
had passed out. "It isn't looking good, Serg. Not good at all."

28

Discoveries

Djan Kithber raised his head from the prism and closed his tired eyes. *Lor,* he thought, *I wish it were easier than this.* He pressed his open hand forcefully against his eyes, trying desperately to clear his vision. His hand came away wet from his fevered head as he sighed and turned to look into the augmenter glass once more.

The illness had set in just as they had crashed—or so it seemed to him. There were the few that were violently sick— including the captain. Then there were some, like himself, who had only a mild discomfort. There seemed to be no pattern to the illness. There was no apparent common denominator among those who had or did not have the disease.

Of course, it had fallen to him to figure it out. Who else? The company would march to exhaustion through the horror of the maze and then stop for rest. The lack of night and day were quickly having their effect on everyone. Without a cycle—even an artificial one as was imposed on the silverfire ships of the Pax—human minds quickly became numb. The periods of walking, he noticed, were getting shorter and the periods of rest longer as time went on.

Still, Mistress Ordina found comfort at each encampment in ritualistically setting up the Temple in Exile. Her novitiates—such as had survived—carried the Silverfire Ark to the specific place designated by the outstretched hand of their Mistress and set it carefully on the ground. Then, in turn, each part of the temple, the Enunciator Altar, the Distribution Altar, and the Knowledge Altar were set to form a ring in the most clear and level place available. When all was ready, the shipwright and her assistants performed the mystic rites and the circle was linked together.

Each time, Kithber watched closely. Each time, Ordina finished and sighed. Everything was as it should be. Nothing worked as it should. At that moment he could almost feel the baffled despair as her mind once again raced through all she knew about silverfire and the Altars in Exile and the accident for that one item—that one key of knowledge—that she was sure she had missed. She knew, somehow, that it was something she had not done—some small thing she had overlooked or forgotten. Kithber understood. He was sure that he would feel the same way—if he ever overlooked anything.

Then, with his own ritual, Kithber would ask Ordina's permission to enter the ring and work. Each time, Ordina would nod, her eyes focused elsewhere, her brow furrowed in troubled thought.

Kithber then would spread his own instruments near the Altar of Knowledge in Exile. He, too, took care in their placement and in their relationships with each other. He was no shipwright, but he knew his own craft well. He was no Farcardinal of the Holy Church, but he could practice the healing arts—better apparently than old Sabenth, who day by day seemed a little farther from the edge of reason.

Directly before him he set the crystal sphere atop the Altar of Knowledge in Exile precisely between the markings on its surface. Three times did he pass his open hands in circles from his chest to encompass the sphere.

Three rings in honor of the Elders and their all-encompassing truth. The words came into his mind unbidden, for the ritual was as much a part of him as his own hands. Both hands moved smoothly to cover his face. *Hidden from sight the pain at the death of our home. Forever to wander.* The image of a world blue and inviting floated unfocused in his mind, fading to black and brown in its death. Thus does all his house remember the Purges that made all the universe the house of the wizards and yet no place their home. As it did each time, the vision of Lost Home gave him his center and focused the powers of chaos and nature that he drew upon. He felt the conduit open in his mind, cutting through the fever of his illness like a shaft of brilliant light in a dark cavern. He was prepared.

Without looking, he then reached back and took each of his instruments in turn, arranging them also on the altar as proscribed by the pattern cut in its surface. Then, with infinite care, he took from the hard leather case he carried a series of glass bottles—each holding a sticky red liquid, carefully labeled. He set them in a line before him, then pulled a clean bottle from the case. Without passion, he then opened a wound in his wrist, spilling at once his own blood into the vial. He sealed the wound at once with his arts. Armed with these samples, old and new, he would then begin his work.

With familiar gestures, he touched the altar. The carved symbols glowed green on its surface—a color which had begun to annoy Mistress Ordina all the more—and floated tendrils of wispy light up the framework of the crystal sphere until the connection was firm and the sphere glowed with power. The crystal would work without the union, of course, but was completely inadequate for his current purposes. He was no physician—he needed the Knowledge Altar and its powers to find his way through the labyrinth of human biology.

The same tendrils would then weave their way to the lampgem and shine into the focusing mirror and through the primary prism. Their alignments were crucial and it often took him nearly half an hour before he was satisfied. The visionprism closed the loop and connected itself again to the crystal sphere.

With all now ready, he would pass each vial in their turn through the prismatic light and observe the act through the visionprism. The alignments and intonations were toward precise function. Take everything that is uncommon and discard it. Take all that is common and highlight it. The trick was in determining just *how* common to make what you are looking for. It was not unlike trying to focus a magnifying lens by finding just the right distance from its subject.

For the last three days he'd been taking samples, analyzing them, and trying to find that focus. Even with the increased number of samples, over time it was beginning to look like an impossible task. The problem was in the enormous complexity of human blood, let alone the human anatomy in its entirety. Biology was not his forte.

Worse still was the poor performance of the *dran* Altar of Knowledge. Like every other piece of Pax temple that was brought with them, this one, too, was acting up. In the middle of analysis, strange visions would cloud the crystal. Disjointed and hazy, they would occasionally come into clear focus. The face of a human girl. A city burning. A ship. None of it seemed to connect. The mindstream that he maintained with the crystal was normally the cascade of analysis data that he expected. Yet now and then voices would intrude in the stream with vague phrases murmuring in his mind. One particular phrase would occasionally slam full volume into his mind that would jar him from his train of thought and—

Wait a moment, he thought.

He had just passed a vial through the miniature rainbow of light with yet another alteration. He was reaching out to gesture yet another alteration when he stopped himself. He wondered for a moment if he had just imagined it. Slowly withdrawing his outstretched hand, he ran the vial again through the multicolored light.

"By the Name of Valiz!" He murmured the most effective oath he knew. He passed the vial again and peered closer into the flat surface of the prism. He straightened abruptly, opening his palms toward the array, scanning it with his mind to secure each placement, angle, and turn of his equipment. Then once more he passed the vial through the light. In fluid motion he began passing each of the other vials through the rainbow circle of light. With each vial passing, his cry increased in tempo and strength.

"Yes! Yes! By the Name of Valiz, yes! YES! YES! BY THE NAME OF VALIZ, YES!"

His head fell back in a cry of joy and wonder. Its primal sound reverberated through the shattered halls about him.

In an instant, a red-faced Mistress Ordina appeared to confront him. "Sorcerer, the conditions of your use of these altars was specific. You are violating the sanctity of our most cherished—"

"Ah-ha! Good Mistress Ordina! You are gloriously mistaken. It is not I who have been doing the violating!" He stepped toward her and suddenly swept the diminutive woman up in his arms in a dance common to his people. "Ah, good shipwright, they are here—they always were!"

Ordina's own people must have developed their own forms of dance more along the lines of graceful poses and morally acceptable intervals. Ordina's reaction to his sudden embrace seemed somewhere between a date and some form of assault. In any event, the sorcerer had affected complete surprise, literally lifting the suddenly panicked shipwright completely off the floor in a whirl of motion. "Put me down! Put me down!" was all she managed to bleat out.

"Of course, Good Mistress. Don't worry, the sanctity of your temple is safe from me. How fares the captain today?"

"Much better, I think." Ordina cocked her head to one side, eyeing Kithber curiously. "I believe that he has begun eating again."

"Then *send for him*!" Kithber grabbed the shipwright's shoulders, pulling his face uncomfortably closer to hers and staring into her eyes. "We've been wandering this horror, looking for them—I'm here to tell you that they've been with us all along!"

"Captain, our hosts have made contact."

Serg stared at the sorcerer through watery eyes. Somehow he knew that his mind wasn't functioning well. He passingly wondered how he could know that his brain wasn't well if the only measure he had was taken by that same brain. He also knew that his mind was wandering. He blinked, trying again to focus on the words that were coming at him. The room was full of people, but he was only dimly aware of them.

"What, Master Kithber?"

"We've been trudging toward your lovely lights in hope of making contact, but, judging from this, they have been attempting to contact us for the past three days."

"Who?" Serg's mind struggled toward full consciousness.

"The invaders! Our hosts! You understand? Whoever or whatever guided us here!"

"And you say that they've been in contact with us for three days?"

Kithber folded his arms across his chest, relishing the opportunity to lecture Dresiv. "Yes, in their way they have been trying to communicate for at least three days—probably longer."

Serg mopped his forehead with his tunic sleeve and looked around him. The Thrund was there, having set herself carefully on a brilliantly colored rug. Her strange faces were unreadable to Serg even in the best of times. No clue there. The Farcardinal sat near the Thrund, but he was of little more use. Sabenth had begun talking to himself after the first day of their march, laughing occasionally at a joke that he alone heard. At least Genni was there to support him, as was Mistress Ordina. Unfortunately, both of them looked just as puzzled as he was—a thought that somehow reassured him.

"It's really very simple." Kithber didn't bother to mask the superiority in his voice. "I set out to find out what had caused our illness—why it was so violent with some early on and left those who contracted the illness later with much more minor symptoms."

"Maybe we were getting used to it?" Genni interjected.

"Used to it?" Kithber snapped. He was well into his lecture stride and didn't care to be interrupted. "Something this virulent doesn't give time for immunity to develop. No, I began by looking for similarities between those who didn't contract the disease first. That may have been my mistake, for if I had concentrated on comparative anomalies first, I might have—"

"This is all quite interesting, I'm sure"—Serg rubbed his temples—"but just what conclusion are you coming to?"

Kithber just stared at the captain for a moment. Serg stared back. The sorcerer, he thought, looked like a mother whose child had just asked for dessert before the main course. Serg waited him out. It seemed easier than arguing.

After several moments passed, Kithber sighed and spoke with the exaggerated patience of a parent to a dense child. "That the sickness we are experiencing is, in fact, the first efforts of the aliens to contact us. Their emissaries are inside each of us now, no larger than a single cell in size in most cases. It is these emissaries inside us that is causing our illness."

"You mean," Serg said slowly, "that we are imprisoned in an unimaginably huge ship—built by a disease?"

"No! *Lor dran*, how can I help you understand?" The sorcerer shook his bowed head as he reorganized his thoughts for another assault on the fever-slowed mind of the captain. "Look. When I finally did find a common denominator between those who were sick, it turned out to be the most astonishing thing I had ever seen. You have no conception of it, captain. It was a small creature—not unlike those that cause normal illness in us—so in that sense I guess you could call it a disease. The astonishing thing is that they are partially organic and partially mechanical. I can't even begin to imagine a mechanism created that is so small as that. Yet there it was, before my eyes. Even as I watched, it was propelling itself between cells, examining them. You see"—Kithber smiled broadly—"they are looking for us—they're just looking at the wrong scale."

"What?" Serg questioned.

The Thrund behind him began to laugh her deep chortle in the background as though her entire race supported her in her humor. "Ah, the vanity of humanity. Your race is the most impertinent and self-important of all space. You drive your ships hard with the darkwind from star to star, glancing at planets and discarding them if they are unsuited to your habitation or are populated by anything other than races roughly similar to your own. Did you know that over a thousand new worlds are discovered each day by the great ships of the Pax. Only three each year meet the requirements for use by your humanocentric Empire of Peace. Is it because there is no life on those thousands of worlds? No. You toss them aside because the life on them is not 'your kind' or is 'incompatible' or 'not understood' in human terms. The galaxy seethes with life forms that you turn your back on."

Serg flushed. "What has this to do with . . ."

"You just can't understand, can you, racist!" The Thrund elevated her heads so as to look down slightly on Serg, her voices resonating in a minor key. "You think that life is always about seven hands high and walks on two legs. At least *our* hosts are considerate enough to go looking for life at all levels. I don't know what the two time distortions we felt were about when we first were taken into their ship, but I'd bet they were some kind of examination for life at the most basic level of physical composition. Then they took a step up and began looking for us at the level of cells, blood, and bone. Our bodies reacted to them as though they were an infection—it must have looked like a war to them. They may think that they *have* made contact. These things inside us may, indeed, have built this ship—"

"No," Kithber said flatly, drawing the attention of the assembly. "I've made a careful examination of them—now that I know what to look for and where. They show signs of intelligence but only in a limited way—rather like a clockwork device. They respond to stimuli but they do not seem to *learn*. From recent tests, I've noticed that their activity is diminishing—that's why we all seem to be getting better. No, I'd say these were more like information gatherers, designed to find intelligence and then report back to whoever sent them. We have met the emissaries not the . . .

". . . reacted to them as though they were an infection—it must have looked like a war to them. They may think that they *have* made contact. These things inside us may, indeed, have built this ship—"

"No," Kithber stated flatly as everyone turned toward him. "I've made a careful examination of them—now that I know what to look for and where. They show signs of intelligence—did everyone experience that?"

Time had once again folded on itself. It was only a moment, but it was enough for whatever purposes their captors intended.

Kithber spoke with some urgency. "Listen to me! The things inside our bodies are leaving us—my tests prove that. They didn't find us among our own cells. All those dead, rotting corpses they created may have been intended only as additional housing for us if we were in fact the size of cells. *They are looking for us!* When did the first crewman get sick?"

Serg said, "Just after we got here."

"That was after those first two time displacements, right?"

"Yes."

"Well," Kithber said. "I think they just decided to look at a larger scale. This time they just might find us."

Serg smiled. "We've got to get in touch with the Pax somehow. They've got to know what we know. Master Fel, is the Farcardinal able to establish a link?"

The young Localyte wore a pained expression and was about to speak, when Sabenth himself spoke.

"Of course, I am able and willing!" His pale face gave lie to the enthusiasm in his voice. "I not only am willing, but I demand to do so! There is an Altar of Communion brought into exile that will do quite nicely. Give the word and it shall be done!"

Serg hesitated, but the old man seemed determined. "Very well. By the scepter, so is my command. Master Fel, you will, of course, assist. Mistress Ordina, inform all parties when the altars have been made ready. All others should take this time to rest. We may find ourselves in need of it before long."

Ordina stood next to Kithber as they watched all that remained of the *Shendridan* crew drift wearily off to whatever places of rest they had arranged for themselves. It was only after all were out of earshot that the shipwright turned her back to the sorcerer and lay both hands on the Altar of Power.

"You know," she said quietly, almost to herself, "the silverfire output from the altars may not be sufficient for contact."

"Oh, I wouldn't worry." Kithber canted his head toward her as he spoke. "The Farcardinal has a considerable reserve of his own. He'll manage. Still, I'd feel much better about my own results if this *dran* altar complex were working properly."

Kithber could feel her bristle at the implication of something amiss in the shipwright's temple. He smoothed it over with "There must be something wrong with the altars themselves. I've been getting the strangest feedback through the knowledge crystals."

"What sort of feedback?"

"Visions of places and people and things that have no place in the knowledge stream that I am working on at the time. It's as though someone else were fighting me for control of the crystal."

"That's impossible," Ordina said with some interest coming back into her voice. "There's only one knowledge access symbol on an Altar in Exile, and this is it. Besides, it's a closed system. Anyone can see that."

"Exactly," the sorcerer said, his mind already moving toward another problem. "Still, that's what it seemed like to me. Interruptions of visions and other places from another mind."

"It's obvious that the silverfire itself has been corrupted. That was established when we found it loose from the containment . . ."

Kithber's eyes widened in fear and astonishment. "The silverfire core had escaped containment? *Lor!* What did you do?"

Ordina frowned deeply. "Do? Nothing. The *dran* stuff had contained itself."

Kithber frowned. "I do not appreciate your joke."

"No, it's no joke. The stuff kept folding in on itself until we maneuvered the emergency containment around it. It hasn't worked the same since. We'd had some corruption feedback down one of the main optic feeds just before the collision. I wish I knew what it was." Ordina just shook her head.

Kithber began gathering up his tools, replacing them carefully in his case. "Well, Mistress, I have no insight on that. All I know is that the *dran* thing keeps saying the same thing to me over and over. It's a word rather than a sound, I'm sure of it, but it doesn't make sense."

"So, now my altars are talking to you!" Ordina rubbed her hand forcefully over her tired eyes. "So what do they say?"

"Just one word," Kithber replied. "They just keep saying 'Snap.' "

29

First Blood

"Where the *Hesth* are they?"

Thyne's back stiffened ever so slightly, her soul bristling at the panic in the words behind her. She'd expected it from the more transient members of her band, but Krith was a new addition to the choir of frayed nerves. She wondered vaguely what was wrong with them—with her. Her clothes clung to her with a cold sweat that had come suddenly upon her and had shown no signs of leaving. *Lorn,* she wished she could think straight. A threatening headache sat just behind her eyes, bothering her only enough to blur her vision and sap her concentration. She wondered vaguely if she was coming down with some illness.

"They're out here, Krith, it's just a matter of time." Thyne sighed as she pushed her weight against yet another twisted doorway with the forced motion of distaste for what almost certainly lay ahead. "Everything else is out here, isn't it?"

"Excuse me, M'Lady, but yer doin' me work, if you'll be recalling." Krith gently pressed Thyne aside and thrust his head into the now-open doorway. He retracted it much faster than it went in. He slammed the door shut. "No exit, two stairs leadin' up, but they be goin' nowhere. Pile o' them rotting things on the floor."

"Unlived?" Thyne couldn't think of anything else to call them after hearing the report from the sorcerer. That had been four days ago—at least she thought it was four days. Lack of any night was beginning to tell on her as well.

"*Allai*, M'Lady, them Unlived. They just lay there staring up and rottin' away. Couple of Thrunds in that bunch too."

Thyne's lips pressed into a thin line as she edged her way past the huge delver and continued down the wrecked corridor to the next door. After their initial sprint into the maze—as she had come to call it—they had taken their time in searching the ruins, trying to find some edge to defend themselves against either pursuit by the Pax or their first encounter with their unknown captors.

It would have been helped if they had felt better. Four of the crew had come down with this mysterious illness, although, so far, the other five had not. There were too many to leave behind but not enough to stop them altogether. So they dragged their companions through the horror of the maze in the hopes that somewhere, somehow, they could find a way to make good their escape. The spinning in her own head she forcefully ignored. If she fell, there would be no crew.

They had been fortunate with the handcannons. Within an hour they had found a weapons cache—adjacent to a kitchen, of all things. Their current problem was to find a pantry or larder so that they could have the strength to fight as well as the weapons. So far they had little luck on that score. Thyne vaguely wondered if she should start looking for a weapon shop that might have food attached.

The corridor suddenly ended in a huge open bay. The remains of several small ship's boats lay scattered about the floor, indicating that this area must have represented a launching deck. Not a single small boat was in any working order, each of their keels having been broken. Six separate corridors wound their way out of the room in several directions. The great green blur that was the sky shone through the partial roof. Several temple altars were set carefully around the bay, some connected to the others, some connected only to themselves, and others connected to nothing at all. Massive conduits extended upward and through the hull, giving the appearance that they might work—but not quite.

"Ardo! You take that one on the right. Yorki! Wethen! Take the two on the left. No! One each, you kettleheads! Berana!" Thyne turned to the mercenary woman with the short-cropped strawberry hair.

"*Allai*, M'Lady." Berana fingered the grip of her handcannon with nervous anticipation.

"Take the middle one to the left . . ."

"I'll bag one for you, M'Lady. How many pieces do you want it in?" There was a burning brightness in her eyes which Thyne mistook for battle lust.

"One! *Dran!* Only one! You all get that? We're not out here stomping out these things! This is their ship, and if we're ever going to survive to save our own world . . ."

Berana grinned. "You mean save *your* own world . . ."

Thyne turned to the mercenary. "Yes, Berana, my own world—a world you are supposed to also save. You've been paid enough for it."

"I was never paid for this," she said, gesturing with her handcannon at the shattered room.

"None of us expected this to be in the bargain, but here it is. Continued breathing beats the alternative. Life is the best offer I've got for you right now. If we can find these—whatever they are, then it will be our terms we're negotiating, not those of the Pax." Thyne turned again to Berana. "Would you rather that Pax *trig* back there do your negotiating?"

Berana's lip curled. "Would I rather cut off my hands?"

"Well and good," Thyne said, not without some relief. The tension of their escape into the maze had only been heightened by the chaotic horror of the maze itself. Holding her crew together—how good it felt to think of them as her crew again—was a major problem for her. She could only hope to find some evidence of their new captors before the Imperials did. "Krith, what's the bearing on our Pax friends now?"

"*Allai*, Captain." The giant delver checked the director he had quietly borrowed before they left. "Their base is about two leagues in that direction. You wouldn't be thinkin' about goin' back, now, would you?"

"No, Master Krith. I just am trying to keep some sense of bearing in this madness." Thyne smiled. "Besides, I rather think they wouldn't be very good hosts if we did return. Everyone! Hear and comply! Proceed down different corridors into no more than three compartments and then return here. We'll determine which one to follow after that. Leave those who can't walk here. Yunta—you stay with them for the time being."

The dark delver nodded, lowering Ounthnar gently to the ground before helping Ardo and Wethen with their charges.

"Well, Master Krith?" Thyne bowed deeply, her sweeping arm indicating the way.

Krith returned Thyne's smile and moved to take his own corridor. Thyne gave him a rather sloppy salute and ducked into her own hall. She took one look around at the companions she was leaving in the large room and then moved into her own passage.

Rich wood paneling, beautifully stained and finished, lined what might otherwise have been considered an elegant hallway. The ubiquitous green globes lit the hall. Thyne pressed down another nauseating thought concerning the color—and ended in a heavy and ornate door.

Thyne shuddered as she approached the door. The images, she knew from previous experience, would be a jumble of the beatific, horrific, and obscene. None of these would have upset her individually, but the collective effect was one of subconscious dread. She had seen enough ghastly images behind such doors today, each one unexpected and each stranger than the last. She took a breath and pushed open the door.

Rows of bunks lay scattered through the room. It was a moment before she realized that no bloated corpses lay in them. The walls were all fitted with portholes, but they were all dark. She knew from experience that they looked out only into other rooms. There was a shallow pool forming in the middle of the room, its surface disturbed from time to time by falling drops. She looked up.

The low ceiling sagged just a little toward the center. There the wood dripped constantly in various places, collecting on the floor. The entire surface of the ceiling was soaked, jewel drops of water hanging precariously before giving way to gravity and plunging to the floor.

Thyne cast about quickly for some kind of tool other than her handcannon but found nothing available that suited her. For a wild moment she considered discharging the weapon into the ceiling, but at the same instant realized how stupid that would be. Not only would it upset her crew, it might unduly tell the Pax delvers just where she was. So she took the best alternative available. Grasping the handcannon firmly, she swung as hard as she dared against the ceiling planks.

The dull iron ring of the handcannon connecting with the plates was heard twice more before the plank splintered. The weight of the water above fragmented the wood even further as it bowed down, seemingly relieved of the weight it had been forced to bear.

Water cascaded from the broken plank in a rushing torrent.

Thyne grinned broadly, cupping her hands. The clear liquid looked potable, but she had sailed too many seas to take that for granted. She sniffed at it, examined it, and, at length, after she was satisfied, risked a drink.

Again she smiled and stepped into the spraying waters. Days had passed since she had been able to wash properly, but it was more than simple relief that drove her. It was the feel of the water itself, so familiar and so much a part of her, that not only quenched her thirst but fed her soul as well. The sensual luxury of the water coursing down her neck and through her clothing washed more than dirt away. It gave her back her life.

She convulsed with the sudden echo of a cannon shot, throwing slivers of water about her.

She blinked once, not sure that she had heard the report properly, or perhaps it was some trick of the water rushing about her ears or even—the second thunder rang through the contorted structure. She was running before its echo died in the hall.

She ran back along her path, picking her way through the now-familiar shredded hull sections that littered the corridor without reason. The dark, leaning walls rained loose debris on her, shaken free now by the ever more frequent concussions rolling down the passage before her. She discerned cries amid the fire and could not tell if they were born of order or pain. She lunged forward into a sprint, half stumbling through the wreckage, nearly out of control in her haste.

She stopped just short of the archway, falling behind cover just long enough to insure her own protection before she looked.

The ship's bay she had just left was well lit by emergency globes and the same light pouring through the partial ceiling. Chaos reigned in the room. From the corridor to her right, Yorki and Wethen were both running with a speed that had even surprised Thyne. Both leaped at slightly different times, each clearing the broken hull of different small boats in a desperate act in search of cover. To her left, Ardo sprinted easily into the room as though someone had just called some drill.

"Hoi," Ardo said, resting his handcannon on his hip, "Who's using the . . ."

The wall to Thyne's right suddenly collapsed. Ardo, eyes suddenly wide, fell at once behind the nearest protection—a table just to his left. Splintered wood and dust filled the room. Thyne struggled to see what had caused it all.

As the wood chips fluttered to the ground, two dark shapes began to take form. As the circles gained definition, the Loyalist commander marveled. They were like nothing she had ever seen before. Two metal balls, Thyne thought, made of curved armor plates that spiraled into themselves. They must have been thirty . . . no, forty hands across, floating slowly into the room just above the height of a man. She thought, *Could these be our hosts?*

"Hold the fire!" she shouted. "Hold fire for the captain!"

"Allai, Captain." Wethen's response was quick, but Thyne noted that it lacked some enthusiasm.

"Captain! Just what do you be wantin' us to do with the beastie?"

"Yorki, shut up! I want to talk to these folk!" Thyne turned her attention back to the floating metal globes. *I want to talk to these folk! Now, just how do I suppose I'm to go about that!* She felt that her plan was their only chance to survive, but she hadn't confronted the real question of how she might go about communicating.

Suddenly, both metal balls began to slowly uncurl. Thyne watching in open wonder. The motion was natural, not at all mechanical, as she had expected. She had hoped that this would be one of their captors, but the metallic plates seemed to suggest that it was some kind of vessel. Now, watching the smooth motion, she wasn't sure what she was facing. As the plates flattened backward, the thing's underside was revealed. Parts of it glistened—sweated, she thought—with the struggle of life, while other parts shone with the abrupt angles of machines. A huge bulbous casing emerged at what Thyne assumed was the rear of the thing, judging from its direction of travel. The casing was the nexus of a tentacle mass. The individual tentacles were too numerous for her to count on first examination, but they seemed to all be of different sizes and mass, as though for different uses.

Many seemed enmeshed with strange metallic tools. Thyne admitted to herself that she couldn't tell where the machines began and the creature ended. Forward, tucked under what appeared to be a set of huge curved plates, a veined red mass could be seen behind a clear encasement. Mucus secreted from between the plates, stringing itself into sticky strands as the thing stretched itself. Small mounds of the icor fell to the ground with a sickening, soft thud. Thyne shrunk back behind her cover. In all, it was the most hideous thing she had ever seen.

Three of the thinner tentacles were stretching out from the main mass. Their ends were splintered into what might have been the veins of an old leaf in autumn just before it crumbles to dust. There was a lacelike quality to the network—something indefinably delicate in so brutish a structure. The tentacle lace waved through the air, searching. It was soon joined by another tentacle, this one ending in some sort of cup with metal fittings.

Both were pointing at Yorki.

The moment that Yorki realized it, he began raising his weapon. It wasn't meant to be. A bluish aura enveloped the cupped tentacle in an instant before flashing in a wavering stream, itself an extension of the tentacle, around the face of Yorki.

Without a single sound Yorki gazed into the light with unblinking eyes. He was frozen, transfixed by the light, in rapture or agony, none watching could tell. Their cries fell like silence on his ears—if they ever reached him at all. It was only a moment in time.

Then the light stopped. Wethen was screaming nearby, but it never bothered Yorki. The delver's handcannon reached the floor a moment before he himself fell as lifeless as the Unlived.

The tentacles moved again. The lace again fluttered through the air. Overhead, the great, gleaming mass turned slowly toward Wethen. The delver scurried through the debris on the floor, throwing odd bits of wreckage behind him. He couldn't stop screaming.

"Dran! Hesht and *dran!"* Thyne shouted through her shock, trying to pull reality back together in her mind. "Krith! Krith, where in *Hesth* are you!"

The booming voice of the delver sounded out of the corridor to her left. Krith wasn't too far from her after all. "I be here, M'Lady! *Lor!* What be that beastie?"

The second creature—what else could she call it?—was mov-

ing forward, apparently to get into a better position on Wethen.
A huge mechanism of some kind swung out on the thing's largest
tentacle. Thyne hadn't a clue what the thing was, but she also
wasn't about to wait and find out. It was time to rethink this
plan.

"Delvers! To me! We're leaving the field!" she shouted. Suddenly she remembered the sick crewmates she'd left behind in
the room with the dark delver. "Yantha! Yantha, where are you?"

Motion caught her eye and she turned toward it. Krith had appeared against the wall, clawing his way toward her through the
rubble. Ardo, too, moved instantly, bounding in a half-run from
one pile of rubble to another as he made his way toward the
sound of her voice. Yantha answered her call—he remained on
the far side of the bay. Thyne had the impression that the dark
delver was helping his charges find better cover.

New motion chilled her. Wethen had heard the order and
sprung up, running toward Thyne. He took only three quick
strides before the light enveloped his head. He tumbled from the
momentum onto the floor, but the tenuous snake of light tumbled
with him until he came to rest on his back only thirty feet from
Thyne.

At that instant Berana burst from her corridor into the bay,
screaming obscenely at the creatures. She raised her handcannon
and began emptying it, bolt after bolt, toward the underbelly of
the first monster. Her first shot went wide, but she corrected as
she fired, walking the bolts forward along the creature. Three
bolts flared into the tentacle mass. The final two shattered the
clear casing, pulverizing the red mass forward. The blue light
flickered out as the huge creature began to sink to the floor.

Berana didn't see the huge tentacle from the second hulk that
swung suddenly and with incredible deftness to point toward her.
Thyne had tried to call out a warning. There had been no time.

It was a rushing sound at first. She wasn't really sure that
she had seen anything at all. A single line, invisible except for
the pronounced distortion of the air around it, extended from
the huge tentacle of the remaining creature through Berana.
Thyne saw a look of indescribable pain come to the delver's
face. At that same instant Berana struggled to flee, but the invisible line seemed to hold her in place. At the next moment the
woman folded into herself. Bones cracked and shattered, flesh

curled, imploding into a sudden red mist before that, too, collapsed into the invisible line.

The line disappeared with a thunderclap.

So had Berana.

A heartbeat passed in the horror of what they had witnessed. Suddenly cannon fire erupted simultaneously throughout the bay. Ardo, still moving toward Thyne, now opened fire on the run, discharging his cannon sometimes without even looking toward the mammoth hulk gliding overhead. A stream of volleys came from across the bay. Yantha stood—clearly visible now—firing into the creature. Other volleys came from a hidden place near him. Even the wounded were getting into the fight.

Krith fell into Thyne's corridor, rolled over, and discharged his own cannon into the melee. "Nice to see you, Captain!"

So much for diplomacy, thought Thyne as she pulled her own cannon into firing position.

This time, however, the creature was prepared. Curling defensively in on itself, the plates now shielded the underbody from their assault. Each plasma discharge smashed against the plates—although from her position Thyne thought that some of the shots were hitting against something before they reached the plates—and dissipated without apparent damage. The only exposed area left on the thing was the single giant tentacle suspended below the curled plates. She shifted her fire downward in desperation as the monster turned toward where she had left her ill crew.

Yantha saw the huge weapon swing with deceptive ease in his direction. Again the impossibly thin line distorted the air about it. Yantha had anticipated it and fell sideways. Thyne could see only a swirl of dust and debris, which was followed by another shattering blast of thunder as the line weapon abruptly stopped.

It was the opening Ardo had been waiting for. As the creature turned, Ardo changed course abruptly and dropped, rolling next to the fallen Wethen. Thyne had to admire the man's courage. The move had taken him under Krith's cannon volleys and brought him dangerously close to her own. Now, however, they could concentrate all their fire. Ardo used the momentum of his roll and stood in a single motion.

He was bringing his weapon up, when the impossible happened. With a speed that was unthinkable in a being that size, the creature turned the weapon in a sudden flick toward Ardo and fired. The line ripped through the air with surgical precision, penetrating Ardo's head in the exact center of his face and passing without impediment through the back of his skull into the corridor where Thyne and Krith knelt, firing their weapons.

The line split the air between Thyne and Krith. Dust and debris exploded into a whirlwind around them, centered around the access of the deadly line. She glanced up and saw the silhouette of Ardo dancing like a broken marionette, suspended by his own head for a moment before his legs, arms, and body folded impossibly backward with a crackling sound before they, too, imploded into a fine red mist. That, too, fell at once into the invisible line.

Thyne felt herself begin to slip. She was being drawn in by the line as though by some attraction. *Gravity?* she thought. *A gravity weapon? How in* Hesth *am I supposed to fight gravity!*

Her momentum increased as she began to slide. Frantically, she began clawing at the debris with her good arm and both legs, searching for any handhold that would stop her fall into the cyclone around the line. Sudden pain jabbed her stomach, and she was pressed against the wall of the corridor.

A thousand thunders sounded two feet from her face as the line disappeared.

Krith shouted at her, but she couldn't hear. His huge, booted foot was still pressing her against the wall. She couldn't hear what he was saying but knew that he had saved her from falling into the line. She turned back to the bay, shaking her head, trying to hear again.

The now-quiet world looked different to her. She saw the line appear again, plunging this time down where she thought the hidden crew lay. The cannon fire from that side of the room stopped. Thyne sucked in two shuddering breaths as the creature hovered silently across the hall. Then the thing uncurled again, the lace waved, and the blue light again plunged down.

In the silence, Thyne was quaking, her resolve shattered. Two more of the spiraling balls were descending from above the far wall.

Yantha—miraculously safe—appeared moments later, tears flowing down his obsidian cheeks, skirting the debris. She wouldn't know until later what he had seen. Or that his friend Ounthnar had fired their remaining charged cannon until the monster had obliterated him. Or that the other weapons held by the wounded were empty, as was Yantha's. Or that the black delver had watched helplessly as the light again descended, but this time their victim cried out in horrific pain. She was ever grateful for having been spared that sound.

All this did Yantha try to say to Thyne—all this she could not hear. She could only gaze up into his beautiful black face, into the deep, painful well of his eyes and feel what he felt. She sobbed without control, her own sound lost on her.

Someone shook her and she stopped, because her father had done the same when she was a young girl crying over a dead pet. Krith's face floated before her, blood trickling from one ear. He held the director in his left hand, pointed to it with his right, and then gestured as if asking which way to go.

The creature was shifting toward another victim in the rubble.

Thyne sobbed once more, tapped the director with her finger, and fainted.

30

Silence

———❦———

Sabenth hadn't slept—that much was obvious to even the most casual observer. The Farcardinal's eyes drifted into vacancy from time to time, a watery blankness floating in dark wells. Small things, however, would make him start back into consciousness with a flurry of blinking—a word, a noise, or a motion.

This time they had stopped in what looked like a cross between a gun deck and a reception lounge. Everything had blurred for them as the constant green light gave no hint of time's passage. Night was unknown—so, too, was any knowledge of good sleep or wakefulness. The constant light was beginning to break them all.

Serg, arms crossed, watched the Farcardinal move toward the Temple in Exile, his young Localyte supporting him with each step. Something was obviously wrong with the old cleric, but for the life of him he couldn't figure out what. Even in the worst of the clockwork plague—as he had popularly dubbed it to the great annoyance of the sorcerer—the Farcardinal seemed slightly ill but never really came down with the worst of it. Following the last temporal disturbance, the minuscule things that had invaded them had miraculously disappeared. Now the Farcardinal looked worse than ever while everyone else had been suddenly cured.

Well, not entirely cured. The defense mechanisms of the body, in full rage against their foe, had suddenly been confronted with the lack of any enemy to fight. The body was taking time to recover from the onslaught, but with the exception of a dry throat or occasional cough, the effect had been miraculous.

The Farcardinal, however, remained worse than ever. Serg suspected the Farcardinal was still holding back something that he already knew. If Sabenth did have such knowledge, then its effects were telling. Sabenth had aged beyond years. Serg wondered if he really wished to know what could wreck such a powerful man of the church.

Trevis—Jezerinthian Localyte—conducted the Farcardinal to the Altar of Communion. Lor, *this man is heavy,* he thought, and at once cursed himself for his lack of charity. *I am here to serve,* he thought to himself in a more correct frame of mind. It wouldn't do to screw up this communion. Though his own life was at stake, his mind wandered into thoughts of his embarrassment at failing to perform well at such a critical time. Again he cursed himself even as the thought formed.

The communion was a different procedure in minor respects from the usual communion that he had helped Sabenth with many times in their journeys together. There would be no communion chair this time—the Farcardinal would have to lean over the Altar of Communion and rest his hands on its sides in order to draw the needed power from the temple. Trevis would stand at his side. Once the communion link had begun, he would weave his own conduit into the stream flowing through the mind of the Farcardinal and dictate out the information that was being received. He began rehearsing the patterns in his mind for yet another untold time.

What are you worried about, another part of his mind told him. *You've done this a hundred times before. What could go wrong?*

Sabenth settled before the altar and relaxed. At last, he sighed inwardly, something familiar, something he knew. Here was a relief he had not suspected—almost euphoric. He was going to be one with his brothers in the stars again—more real than poetic—

and in being one regain the loss of self that seemed to be eating at him daily.

He had no notion as to where his drive had evaporated, nor any name he could call the numb fear that spun unbidden in the back of his mind. He knew it was there, however, lurking at the fringe of his consciousness, crouching at the edge of a thought, waiting. Waiting . . . for what? It was shapeless. He could do nothing more than feel its presence ready to pounce and devour him. All that was left him was to beat it back with vague mental notions and reassurances that never quite struck the mark.

Yet the altar, ah, the altar was real! Its chill surface was alive to his mind, a partner in their great calling. With its help he could join his mind to his brothers and in so doing make himself part of the greater mind they all shared. That was the great solace of his kind. So he knelt at the altar. His hands joined gladly to each cold side. There wasn't much power there, but it would be enough for his purposes.

He smiled. It was time to begin.

His mind moved through the Void.

". . . once established, grant this servant communion with our brothers though the stars separate us."

Serg shifted uncomfortably. He had heard it all before, of course, for the litany never changed. Space faring for the Pax would be a sight uncomfortable let alone glacially slow without the ability of the Farcardinals and their order to communicate findings and needs back and forth across the stars. Still, there was something just mildly unnerving about the mystical practices of the church that made him uneasy even on the best of days. The Localyte was new and it wouldn't do to offend him just when we needed him most. He forced himself back into the appearance of thoughtful concentration.

Trevis continued to speak, his arms now raised in the final motion of the rite. ". . . our thoughts and dreams, O Father of the Sky, be your will and destiny." He turned to Serg. "Are your questions ready and your answers in your mind?"

"Yes." Serg said—simple and direct. *Get on with it!*

"Very well, sire, then it is time and place well destined." Trevis turned smoothly to the Farcardinal. "Oh, Father, does the wind answer?"

Trevis waited. No response.

Trevis blinked, his brow wrinkling into a question. He spoke a little louder. "Oh, Father, does the wind answer?"

Serg turned to the Farcardinal. Something was wrong. Normally the cleric would, after establishing contact, form some sort of answer in response to this basic question as a cue to the Localyte that he was ready. Serg looked closer. Sabenth continued to kneel, still as a stone, but it was his eyes that attracted his attention. They were locked open, the pupils darting from side to side. There was a look of terror in them.

Trevis continued. Perhaps he had seen some sign in the Farcardinal that Serg had missed. "As ordained," he said, and inclined his head toward the kneeling Sabenth to read his thoughts and, as per his training, be the medium that gave voice to ideas from far across the Pax Galacticus.

It started in his eyes. They widened until white shone completely around the dilating pupils. Then the face muscles tensed, contorted into unspeakable pain. The Localyte's jaw sprung open wide, the head snapping backward in a painful arc. Then the body locked muscle against muscle in primal response. Instinctively expected, the howl still did not come. The contorted Localyte dragged air into his lungs through his gaping mouth. Only then could Trevis give vent to the scream within him.

A Farcardinal of the Church of Sky is never alone.

It was like immortality, really. When one cell of the brain died, the rest of the mind continued to function. Even should one of their number disappear, there was comfort that their thoughts and self would somehow become part of the great communal mind that they shared. Nothing was ever lost, for it could always be found in the mind of one of their order. He would live forever in the common mind. It was what had appealed to Sabenth about that high order even when he was a novitiate not much older than his current Localyte. Of course, he never would have followed the Jezerinthian codes—he felt himself much too practical for such strictures—but his own Order of Gondrim was sufficiently lenient in its rules to allow for someone of moderate ambition to rise through their ranks. He had, as he had always known he would, made the best of it. First as a Localyte and then later as a System Priest, he continued his carrier of service to both church and empire, always somehow in touch with the greater will and mind of the church. It was a gift, really, and one he used often. From that time onward he was always *aware* of his fellow practitioners of the communion. Their minds always touched his. They whispered to him even when he didn't think of them. They murmured as he slept without care. Some part of his mind, beyond thought, always listened lest someone should call his name and require action or knowledge for himself or his companions. The voices, with practice, had faded beyond conscious thought. He didn't think of them, yet he was never alone.

So, when the voices began dying out in his mind, far beyond thought, he didn't notice. He had only a vague notion of absence. It wasn't that no one had contacted him—it was rare enough that a specific Farcardinal would get a message—but the half-realized quiet that began to grow in his mind.

The universe was growing silent.

On over a billion planets scattered across the glowing mist of the galactic spiral, the Orders of the Sky—Jezerinthian, Gondrimite, Lady of Light, Saint Lorkin, and a dozen others—were hunted and died.

In their deaths their minds cried. Hundreds of such cries were common each day in the mind, and their loss was accepted and absorbed by the whole. Yet with a billion minds across uncountable planets being systematically destroyed, there was no one left to cushion the blow.

Sabenth had felt it happening in his own mind but refused to acknowledge it. Yet the galaxy had grown silent even as he denied it. At last, having convinced himself that no such disaster could have happened, Sabenth took hold of the altar and opened the conduit like a great well.

The galaxy had grown silent, only to be filled with the death pain of uncounted billions. It was a well with no bottom.

He was alone with its infinity.

His mind fell in.

Trevis realized he was screaming. It was his first self-aware thought. He was screaming. He couldn't stop. He was screaming. He couldn't . . .

"MASTER FEL!"

He was screaming. He . . .

"MASTER FEL!" The open hand slammed hard across his face. Somewhere inside he knew it hadn't been the first. He was screaming and he—

No. He stopped. He couldn't focus his eyes. He'd been standing, but now he wasn't sure. Vague shapes moved over him. He squinted, unsure.

Knowledge slammed forward in his mind like a dark wave, clearing his vision. He began to breathe quickly, shallowly. His eyes moved unbidden from side to side as his mind groped to comprehend the incomprehensible.

"*Lor Makan!* Master Fel! What happened!"

Trevis turned to the sound. The Captain. It was the captain who had saved him from the—who were they, they seemed so far away—oh, yes, the Loyalists. The captain held him now. *He'd saved me once,* he thought, *perhaps he can save me again.*

The Localyte suddenly gripped the front of Serg's tunic in his two fists, burying his face in the man's chest.

He wept without shame.

Time passed uncounted. Threads of himself began to reweave themselves into a cohesive whole. He pulled his face away and looked up at the captain. His face was gray, but there was in those eyes, thought Trevis, compassion and concern.

"Father." Serg spoke in a quiet, steady voice. "My questions are ready and my answers in mind."

Trevis blinked. Something was familiar. "Are your questions ready?"

"Yes, and my answers in mind."

". . . and your answers in mind," Trevis mimicked.

"Yes . . . Father, does the wind answer?"

Trevis snatched a shuddering breath. Chaos spun through his mind, but he checked it, concentrating on the words of the ceremony. *"Father, does the wind . . . answer?"* *Lor,* he thought, *how can I answer that question?*

"Sire, yes, the wind answered."

Serg sighed. "What was the answer?"

Rage burned through Trevis's horror. "That there *was no answer*! The entire galaxy's gone silent! All that's left are raging images of death—the soul cries of a billion clerics ringing like an echo through the void. They're all dead—dead or not answering the call at all."

Trevis paused. He expected another question, but none of the group surrounding him seemed inclined to pose one. They were going to wait for him.

"Look," he said, "the whole thing was so catastrophic that my mind is having trouble sorting it out. Only parts of it make sense. Whoever or whatever invaded didn't just appear here—it appeared everywhere."

"Everywhere?" Djan asked.

"Yes, everywhere—at the same time, too, it would seem." Trevis shuddered again. "Throughout the Pax and any of the known states we have—or had—any contact with through the church, it's the same: huge fleets of ships appearing out of the Void."

"A fleet of ships invading an entire galaxy—at once?!" The size was beyond comprehension. "From where? For what?"

"I don't know. They seem to find the clerics first—somehow they center on them. Perhaps the communion process is recognizable to them. I don't know."

"You say they center on the clerics?"

"Yes, they came to the worlds of the Farcardinals first. Then visited the others."

"And when they found them?"

Trevis looked directly into Serg's eyes. "They kill them."

"Dran!"

Trevis looked down. "Not just them. There are *trillions* of dead on over five million worlds in the Pax alone. They are indiscriminate, without compassion for any thinking being. They seem drawn to those who participate in the communion first."

Serg's eyes were locked on the Localyte, his mind trying to grasp with little success the implications of what he was hearing.

"One other thing." Trevis gasped. "They're looking for something—some piece of information that they think we might have. Only we don't know what it is. They keep looking for an answer to a question we don't understand—and they're killing worlds to get it."

Trevis buried his face in his hands. Serg stood up and turned to Djan. "If these things are looking for communion people first . . ."

". . . then we've just shouted in their face!" Djan finished. "We've got to leave before they find us."

Serg became suddenly animated, as though hit by an electric bolt. He quickly moved through the survivors, touching each as he spoke—somehow believing that his touch would anchor his words to their souls.

"Ordina! Strike this temple site *now*! Genni! Fold camp!

We've got to move! If you can't carry it, leave it. I don't care if . . . No! *Dran,* we've got to clear the area now! Madam Ambassador"—he turned to the Thrund—"give Mistress Ordina whatever assistance you can with the altars. If we don't have those, we are finished."

The Thrund stood, crossing her legs to sit in defiance of the human's instructions. "I shall assist the Farcardinal," she stated flatly. She moved to stand next to him as he continued to kneel before the Altar of Communion, his arms outstretched to either side.

Serg turned back again and knelt quickly opposite Sabenth at the altar.

"Sabenth." Serg spoke urgently even as he began disconnecting conduits from the altar. "I'm sorry, Father, but we must act at once or else . . ."

It was then Serg looked up into the face of the Farcardinal. Sabenth remained posed as before, each hand on either side of the altar, his eyes wide as he knelt. Yet already the eyes were beginning to fog over. He grasped him carefully by the shoulders and slowly lay him down on the ground.

"Lady Ambassador, the Farcardinal does not require your assistance."

"I should think he could answer that for himself."

"That might be difficult. The Farcardinal is quite dead."

The flurry of activity suddenly stopped as each delver's gaze rested on the still form next to the altar. Serg stood in the silence. Here was our last link to the universe they knew. Now both Sabenth and their universe were suddenly and terribly gone.

Thin wisps of his own white hair danced across the Farcardinal's lifeless eyes.

Djan's voice was suddenly harsh in Serg's ear. "We must go *now*, Captain!"

Serg snapped. "But the Farcardinal . . ."

". . . is *dead*!" Djan finished. "As will the rest of us be if we don't leave at once."

Serg looked up. "Madam Ambassador! I am sorry for the loss of your friend. I'm afraid we have not time for a ceremony."

Hruna nodded with all her heads. "It is just as well. He would not have wanted to live without his brothers. He always feared being alone. Let us move quickly before—*BY AMSHAH!*"

The green mists, pervasive since their arrival, suddenly vanished as though a dream. The maze dissolved with it, replaced in the blink of an eye with trees, rocks, and shrubs. The horrors had been replaced with something even worse—familiarity.

Djan's murmur was nevertheless heard by all. "Pax Prime environment. Trees. Grass. They now know that they're looking for humans. That means us."

Serg yanked the last of the optic cable free of the altar. With both hands he lifted its mass heavily and began running awkwardly toward a copse of newly appeared trees, calling out as he moved. "Follow me—NOW!"

31

Shipmates

————— ❦ —————

Thyne ran. She ran wildly, leaping obstacles, falling, tumbling, rolling, and scrambling, only to dash again through the newly formed underbrush. Trees flashed by her, rocks battered her shins, and brook water erupted from its surface tranquility into white froth about her churning feet.

Thyne saw little of it. She clung to the director, her eyes fixed to its steady needle.

Don't look back, she thought. *If you look back, you'll see them and stop. If you stop, you're dead.*

In fact, she had no need to look back. Behind her, the discordant thrum of the monsters was clear enough. The remaining creature of the two they had first encountered had pursued them quickly. It was soon joined by at least two others, judging from the sound behind her. It was difficult to tell as she fled, especially with the cacophony being raised by the remaining members of her crew immediately behind her.

The creek down which she had been running abruptly ended. Thyne tried to stop, but her momentum was too great. In an instant she tumbled down the waterfall, landing wildly in the pool below.

Thyne surfaced, gasping for air. A large wave washed over her, burying her again in the foaming water. Near panic, her tunic tightened around her as a huge fist dragged her again to the surface.

"*Lor,* Thyne. Where're we goin'?" Krith held her up, standing chest-deep in the churning water.

"Krith, we've got to keep . . . Oh, *Lor!* They're here!" Thyne's eyes were wide as she looked up.

Through the spinning mists of the thundering falls, three huge, obscene shapes sang overhead. The rising and falling sounds fought against each other in deafening chords. Their shadows blotted out the brilliant, sunless sky. They had uncurled again, their long feelers twisting in the air, searching . . . searching . . .

Krith cast about for cover. There was none. All he could do was watch.

Yet they didn't stop. In moments their shadows had passed, leaving only the brilliant, sunless sky overhead.

"*Lor-o-dan!*" Krith murmured. "Not so much as a 'By your pleasure,' and they pass on! What do you make o' that?"

Thyne shuddered. The adrenaline was still slamming through her system. "Krith. How many? How many did we lose?"

"Lose? Well, now, isn't that the question, M'Lady? If you're meanin' 'lose' as in misplace, then I'd say that counts for just about everyone but you and me. If you're askin' in the sense of givin' up the troubles of this world and dyin'—well, that I'm not prepared to report." The old delver eyed his captain critically, judged that she had her legs under her again. He let loose of her tunic and began slogging toward the water's edge. "Yantha was behind me and I was behind you. Whoever's left is scattered about in this here fairy forest. *ALLAI!* YANTHA!"

"Krith! No!" Thyne's eyes were shining with wide fear above her pale cheeks. "Don't yell . . . they'll hear you!"

"M'Lady, if them creatures from *Hesth's* abyss are looking for us, I would think that they would have taken us sooner than this." Krith clambered up onto the short ridge bordering the stream. "I can still see them, M'Lady, moving off in that direction. They ain't paying a second thought to me with all my lungs. YANTHA!"

Though her hearing still suffered from the assault, Thyne heard a faint voice drift toward her from the far side of the ridge.

Its deep rumble was the sweetest thing she thought she had ever heard. She slogged onto the sandy edge of the stream, exhausted from her panicked flight.

"Stop bellowing, Krith. *Lor!* Bad enough to listen to it on our own ship ... must I endure your braying even in the midst of doom?"

"Ah," smiled Krith, "and sure it is good to see you as well, old shipmate!" The huge delver, his huge arm around his spindly thin companion, walked with him down the slope toward Thyne.

"Master of Fates!" cried Yantha, his eyes rolled toward the heavens, partially in spiritual plea and partially from the pain of Krith's grip. "I have been saved from the monsters of the night only to be assaulted by a friend."

Thyne looked up. The hollow might have been quite peaceful in other circumstances. The clear cascade of water from the overhang covered the pond before her in a gentle blanket of rushing sound. The trees and brush were, she had to admit, from about every different climate zone imaginable—coexisting here without apparent contradiction. Most of the species she couldn't even attempt to identify. She could only assume that they were from worlds she had never visited. Yet the few that she did know were both lovely and impossible at the same time. Desert plants sprang in full blossom next to rain-forest ferns. A group of conifers bordered a palm-tree-lined grove.

"Krith, we've got to find somewhere to rest." Thyne was shaking again and somehow couldn't seem to stop herself.

"*Allai,* M'Lady. Well, now, this here is a lovely spot. Water, trees, some fruit that looks almost appealing. Seems to me that you've already had yer bath ..."

"No. Not here. Somewhere more defensible. This is too low and open."

"Lady—Thyne—beggin' your pardon, but what's the point? We can't possibly defend against—"

"Not here!" she snapped.

The huge man stopped in midsentence and released his breath. "Right! Well, there's a clearing up top o' that ridge. Approaches are steep enough that it's a chore to climb. You can see well over the countryside so as no one will be coming on you sudden like. If they do, then you've a good route of escape." Krith pointed to the distant ridge. "Will that suit you? Thyne?"

Thyne wasn't looking. Her eyes were on the darkening sky.

The stars had come out. They were *moving*.

When she first fled from her troubled world on a darkwind ship, she found the flight disappointing. Her experience was with the sea—the rush of the salt spray and rumble of the wind. The ships of the silverfire traveled at wonderful speeds on the darkwind, yet the stars are beyond any comprehension of vastness. Never was their velocity such that actual motion could be perceived by even the most diligent observer. Even in the closest of stellar groups it was like trying to watch the minute hand on a timepiece move.

Now she was truly awed. The local stellar groups were moving at a rapid pace while even distant groups were demonstrating motion. They streamed overhead like a rain of stars sweeping past her. She thought she recognized one or two of the classical navigational clusters, but their positions were all wrong. If they had been traveling at such velocities for days . . .

"*Lor,* where are we," breathed Krith at her side.

"We are far from home, my friend." Her voice was hushed and reverential. "Very far indeed."

Crack!

She kept her eyes closed.

The noise had awakened her instantly where she lay. Yet revolutionaries learn quickly that surprise is their greatest strength and patience their finest shield. Panic, she knew, could kill you quicker than any enemy. So she lay perfectly still and kept her eyes closed and waited.

A gentle swish of leaves might have been mistaken for the wind, had there been any wind. She knew her prey—it never would do to think of oneself as anything but the hunter—to be downhill from her.

It was distance enough. She opened her eyes slowly into slits. The streaming stars overhead were blocked in patchwork shadows by the leaves of the huge fern she lay under. It was a natural shelter beneath the fronds. Good solid cover. With infinite patience she began to move, each position carefully calculated. Each muscle moved with measureless care. Even after she had come to a full crouching position, it took her four slow breaths before her weight was fully down on her extended left hand. A full four breaths more, and her right hand was secure around the handcannon grip. She was a predator in the night. She was the hunter. She was ready.

Through the dappled streaks of starlight she could see the approaches to the knoll. The ferns, bushes, trees, seemed to shimmer slightly beneath the strange sky, occasionally flashing under the light of a too-close passing sun. In the distance she could still see the light on the horizon, now also flashing under the light above. For a moment she wondered if the dome was a membrane that had turned clear, or was it only another illusion placed there for their convenience? She could not know. Her crew was, for all purposes, gone. All that was left in her was to survive.

There! She was sure she had seen it. Shadows moving amid darkness. Perhaps . . . no! There! Now she was sure. Whatever it was was coming, this time no longer in the air but moving through the brush. *Clever,* she thought. *The creatures have decided that an open approach is too costly. Now they're coming through the brush. Well, things are going to be a bit more even this time around.*

The shapes—there were five by her count—were moving up the hill. They moved slowly, picking their way through the brush. It was quickly evident to Thyne that they were heading directly toward her.

Her nerve began to falter as questions surfaced in her mind. Do they already see me? Why are they coming directly toward me? She glanced around, checking for an escape if she needed it. If they could see her, would they spot her escape as well? She felt trapped. Suddenly the great fronds seemed to be of no protection at all.

Just then the leading shadow emerged from the brush into full view on the knoll's clearing. In the flickering starlight it could barely be seen, yet to Thyne it was hideous. It had the body, arms, and legs of a humanoid creature, but its head was grossly misshapen with deep, sunken eyes. The details were obscured by the partial darkness, making its appearance all the more horrific in her mind. She imagined the Unlived now, somehow animated by their captors, coming to them like obscene zombies.

The huge head turned toward her, staring directly at her. It took another step.

With the howling of a ravenous beast, Krith exploded from his own hiding place, charging directly at the apparition. The stalking creature turned suddenly toward the sound, seeing only a blur as the mountainous delver ran full force into its body. Both of them continued on, tumbling into the underbrush. Krith's howls continued, now beyond Thyne's sight.

Thyne raised her handcannon, hoping somehow to get a shot at the monster which, no doubt, was even now sucking the life out of her huge friend. So intent was she that for a moment she didn't sense the shadow falling over her shoulders.

She felt her hair move. Crouching, she spun, raising the handcannon. The hideously misshapen head loomed above her. She tripped the release, leaning against the recoil.

Thnickt. No discharge. The cannon was spent.

Thyne, compensating for the blast that did not come, leaned toward the shape standing over her. The creature's arm slammed outward against the handcannon, knocked it from her grasp, slamming her sideways as well. All balance lost, she fell to the ground on her back.

The shadow swung back toward her. Instinctively, she kicked at its legs, her feet connecting just below the knee joint. The effect was hardly what she desired, however. The force was so great that it knocked the thing's feet out from under it. With a muffled groan the shadowy figure fell forward, landing directly on top of her.

She screamed at it; swore at it; howled at it. Her primal self had taken over. There was no thought. No plan. Only experience. Only training. Only survival.

She tore at its horrific head. Grasping its ears, she pulled with all her strength.

With a great sucking sound, it came off.

Her eyes filled with horror, yet she could not bring herself to look away. As the stars again began to thin into a brightening, sunless day, she slowly came to realize what she had done.

Still holding the Pax Battlehelm above her head as she lay, she stared up into the still-grimacing face of Serg Dresiv as he reached down to rub his throbbing shin.

"My apologies, Lady Thyne." Serg pressed the words out between his pain-locked teeth. "It's good to see you again. I had lost hope. . . ."

Relief flooded her face as she let go of the helmet. She suddenly saw in this human face some light of hope.

She grabbed his face roughly in her hands and in a single motion pulled their faces together. Strong, impassioned, she kissed him.

He drew back from her. "I . . . er . . . would you . . . does this . . . are you proposing a truce?" Serg smiled warily through his question.

Her fist threw his smile at least five feet.

32

Flight Dynamics

LOCATION: LLEWELLEN SECTOR / ANCR16732(?)
ESTIMATED FROM STELLAR OBSERVATIONS

Serg fell sprawling on the ground. Thyne scrambled to her feet, crouching warily. She wasn't sure what had possessed her to kiss him. Not that she had she felt that her right uppercut would somehow put them back on more familiar terms.

Serg, however, sat up slowly. He watched her carefully as he moved, pulling his knees to his chest. "Well, I suppose this doesn't mean a truce." He rubbed his jaw as he moved it from side to side. "You'll have to tell me about the strange customs of your homeland sometime."

"Why waste my breath! The Pax wasn't that concerned with my homeland's customs when it left us to murder each other in the name of unity." Thyne's voice was ragged. "What do you want from me, pawn?"

Serg looked up. The brightening sky had obliterated the streaming stars of just a few minutes before. Someone, somewhere, had decided it was going to be day for a while. He shook his head. "Want from you? Thyne, not a thing. That little locator you're still holding not only allows its user to find the ship again but also allows us from the ship to find whoever has it. It wouldn't do to have a member of the Pax Imperial Fleet wander off and be in need of some assistance, would it? We've been using the battlehelmets for seeing our way through the dark. We just happened to pick up your signal."

Thyne straightened, placing both hands on her hips. "I suppose you're going to tell me that I'm once more in custody?"

"I don't think so." Serg, groaning, pulled himself up by the huge fern fronds until he stood. "You see, there really isn't any Pax left for you to hate. It's hard to believe. I don't believe it still. But all our evidence suggests that our civilization has ceased to exist."

Thyne's sleepy eyes were all skepticism.

"I see. How about this, then," he said with a broad flourish of his hand and an exaggerated bow. "As the highest-ranking citizen of the Pax Galacticus in the known universe, I hereby absolve and pardon you from all your crimes. You are free to exercise your own agency without malice or prejudice of the Imperial Senate."

Suddenly the sarcasm left his voice. "We know what's happened out there, Lady Haught-Cargil. We've been invaded—all of us. *Lor Amsha*, can you even conceive it? A fleet of these ships fills our galaxy. Its presence alone would be enough to cripple the Pax economy, maybe even bring down the entire government, but that wasn't enough. They've systematically ravaged all the known worlds. They've destroyed everything.

"There were over five million inhabited worlds in the Pax alone, each connected by a fabric of starship wakes and the whispers of Farcardinals' communions on the wind. Now that fabric has dissolved and the whispers are as silent as the graves their clerics now fill."

Serg suddenly hung his head. "Your revolution is over. My empire is over. The war—if there was one—is over. Everything . . . everything is over."

Silence fell suddenly between them.

Thyne let out a long, slow breath, her eyes staring into some distant place. "My world." She breathed. "What was happened to my world?"

"We were on our way between Brev and your world when this fleet appeared," Serg said as gently as he could. "The invasion ships have since visited nearly our entire galaxy. Your world would certainly have been among the first to have been visited. I am—dreadfully sorry for us all."

The Loyalist captain suddenly looked up, her eyes large and moist. "Now—now where will I go?"

Serg stood slowly. "We could start again. Come with us—let's find some way to live through this."

Thyne gave a single humorless laugh.

Serg felt his jaw clench. "Stay here or come with us. It is a matter of complete indifference to me. You may do as you will, Lady Haught-Cargil, but I cannot afford the time to chat. These things—whatever they are—are on to us. They are looking for us, and unless we can find a way out of here soon, they'll find us." He turned his head toward the brush and called out. "Genni! Ordina! Are you out there?"

"*Allai*, Captain." Ordina's voice floated up from the brush just off the ridge. "I'm holdin' two of your Loyalists here. The quiet, dark-skinned gent and the large, overtalkative one. Genni's gone back down to help with the march. He wants to know what direction you want them to take."

Serg smiled and called down. "Tell him I'll give him a bearing in a moment. Go ahead and let your prisoners go, Mistress Ordina. I've just pardoned them."

"As if you had any say in what we did!" Thyne sputtered her words out, their venom sapped by the awful possibility that her reason to live had vanished into the cold night.

Serg lifted the long glass from its shoulder case, held it to his eye, and extended it with both hands. He continued to speak to her though his sight was on the horizon.

"Again, as you wish, Lady Thyne, but your political discussions have little weight in our current circumstances. By the way, you've picked an excellent spot for defense as well as observation."

Krith emerged from the underbrush, walking toward them. His eyes did not meet Thyne's, however.

Thyne asked airily, "What happened to the little Imperial you jumped?"

"Ah, Thyne!" Krith still didn't look up. "Turns out it was that little troll of a shipwright lady. I didn't feel right about hittin' her, seein' as she's so small and all. I guess she kind of got the drop on me when I was bein' polite. Yantha's with her. He's waiting for the Word."

"The Word to do what? What can I . . ."

The motion of the telescope glass suddenly stopped. "There

they are! Treetop level about five miles off. They're crossing laterally—that means they're still following our original path. That should keep them busy for a while yet."

"They'll find you," Thyne said in a hollow voice. "And when they do, they'll kill you."

"Yes, I suppose they will," he said, closing the glass and stowing it. He walked over to the helmet lying on the ground and picked it up. "Of course, they must find me first. What do you say, Lady Thyne? Your kiss was delightfully alluring—although the left cross that concluded it was a bit more impromptu than I might prefer. I like your company, and we desperately need your skills.

Thyne folded her arms and gave a remarkable impression of an immovable object.

"Besides," Serg concluded, "when they do kill me, I would have thought you would have wanted to be there."

Serg smiled, turned his back to her, and strode down the hill.

Krith rumbled behind her. "Kiss?"

Thyne shrugged. "The Word is we follow the Pax delver until he gets himself killed. I just hope his death is worth the price of admission."

Thyne suddenly walked down off the hill, following Serg's path.

Krith followed in turn. "Eh! 'Ere now! What's this about a kiss?"

". . . the flying creatures passed over our heads. They must be the same ones you've been tracking—we haven't seen any others. We decided to hide out on the hilltop until the light came up again—if the light came up again. That's pretty much where you found us."

The remaining *Shendridan* crew had stopped in small meadow surrounded—to the delight of the Thrund ambassador—by the towering Ordach trees of her home world. Her delight, however, had turned to somber reflection when Serg pointed out that the presence of the trees probably meant that the worlds of the Thrund had also been visited by the creatures.

Silence drifted through the circle of listeners as Thyne finished her tale. The images of the Loyalist crew falling below the focused gravity weapons or the columns of projected light were struck into their minds. That their own fate seemed inevitably similar was all too evident.

Serg had listened without interrupting, his arms folded across his chest, head cocked slightly to one side. After a moment he stepped into the circle of silence.

How could he express to her the thoughts that were raging through his mind? He knew Thyne's hollow pain. The great darkness within him—never far from him—threatened again to overcome him. How could he tell her that he shared her grief, that he, too, had walked that road? How could he soothe her wound? Yet in the end there was little he could say.

"Lady Haught-Cargil, we thank you. We grieve with you."

She raised her head proudly, her nostrils flaring. In her eyes was again contempt. She could not believe that he would understand. He knew that nothing he could say then would convince her. So he turned to the assemblage.

"We've all heard what happened to the balance of Lady Haught-Cargil's crew. From their direct observations and from what the Localyte has told us about the state of the galaxy, there is much we can surmise.

"Whoever or whatever these beings are, they have appeared throughout the known galaxy—all at the same time. I could not guess how such a massive thing is possible. Where could they have come from? What is their purpose?"

"Their purpose is pain, Captain." Yantha spoke, his soft, deep voice heard by all. "I have fought them with these hands. I have watched delvers and mates torn and folded into so small a space that not even a drop of blood was left to be seen. I have seen the light hit men's faces. The first ones were robbed only of their life. The later ones were robbed of their minds, tortured with insanity. Captain, truly, these are devils of the Void, come to take delvers' souls!"

A paralyzing chill ran perceptibly through the circle of delvers.

"No," Serg stated emphatically. "These are not gods of the Darkness. Were that so, then how is it you brought one down? No, these are not immortals. They can be stopped, but not here. We've got to get off this vessel. What are our options?"

"Well, we'll need a ship," Genni offered.

"Yes"—Serg shrugged—"but built out of what?"

Hruna spoke up from her low perch in a tree. "My ancestors'

first spaceships were built from the wood of Ordach trees. To this day they remain a primary component of our starcraft construction."

"Ordach wood makes for tall ships, that is true," Ordina spoke up. "If we had any, it would be perfect—now, wait, Ambassador. I said, if we had any. The tree you are cradled in so fondly isn't real. None of this is—that's the problem. It's all some sort of make-believe that's being provided for us by our jailers. It isn't a matter of finding materials to build an escape craft—it's a matter of finding anything *that is real*."

Krith sniffed. "Well, them skybugs is real enough for my mind. They dealt death, and I'm for tellin' ya that my shipmates knew their end was real!"

There was a moment as Thyne and Serg looked at each other, then turned to Ordina.

Her puzzled look suddenly melted into incredulity under the gaze of the two captains. "You can't be serious!"

"Why not, Ordina?" Serg coaxed. "It's real!"

"Serg! It's . . . it's . . . I don't know!" Ordina stuttered. "What if it *is* one of them?"

"Ordina," Serg said, "if it will help, we'll boil it down to the bones and then use the bones. It's all we can count on existing outside of this ship."

"You want me to build a ship *out of one of them*?!" The shipwright's voice broke at the end.

Thyne spoke up, adding her enthusiasm. "We don't *know* it's one of them. Even if it were, it's the best chance we've got now! I've heard you're a pretty fair shipwright."

Ordina stood suddenly, her short legs in a wide stance. She gave the immediate impression of immobility. "Great! Let's go gut the carcass and see what's left. But I *still* have no idea how we're going to power the thing. The silverfire's been acting strangely ever since your people attacked. The power keeps folding back in on its own mass. Stable silverfire might have gotten us a research grant from the Pax Institute, but it won't do sand worth of pushing a ship down the darkwind."

Serg's brow drew together. "You've had no luck with it?"

"Well," Ordina sighed, "I haven't had a lot of time to work with it. We were occupied both with the march and with healing our sick. After that we've been hiding while we tried to figure out what to do. Maybe if I had a little time . . ."

"Very well!" Serg turned to the Loyalist captain. "Thyne, do you think you could find this thing that you cannoned down?"

"Yes, I suppose I might. The terrain changed just after we started running, and it seems not to have changed since then. I suppose I can get us close . . . but . . ." Thyne's tall, strong form seemed to get smaller.

Serg understood. Softly, he said, "Your crew is there."

She drew herself up again. "No matter. I can get us there."

"All I'm saying is that we need to communicate!"

Ordina had heard it before and wondered how many more times she was going to hear it again. She and the young Localyte had been detailed to the litter bearing the silverfire altar. Through the various jungle, forest, and underbrush that they had encountered, she had been forced to listen to his ceaseless arguments about the creatures that held them there. He speculated (without wisdom), he advised (without experience), and he gave his considered opinion (without any basis in knowledge). Trevis just wouldn't shut up. When Serg asked for a detail to recover the locators, Ordina had gladly gone. Now that she was back, Trevis had picked up the argument from where he'd left it off. Sitting by the silverfire Altar in Exile under a huge lilac bush, he began speaking as Ordina returned with Yantha following.

"It's time to start moving again," Ordina directed, ignoring the comment.

The young man got quickly—if awkwardly—to his feet. "Did you have a chance to talk to the captain? I mean, did you, you know, ask him about talking to—well, whoever it is—that's chasing us?"

Ordina glanced with an almost pleading look at the dark form sitting deeper in the shade of the lilac. The sorcerer looked back placidly, shaking his head.

"I've been listening to him for the last hour. It's your turn again." Djan smiled.

Ordina grimaced but turned again to the young man. "Pick up your end, there, Master Localyte. It's time we moved on—and, yes, I did mention your concerns to the captain."

"What has the captain decided? Are we going to attempt contact?"

"Look, noviciam, I've got my orders and . . . hey! Watch where you're pushing us!" Ordina staggering suddenly with the weight of the wildly swaying altar, found herself pressed against the trunk of a mango tree. "Whatever these things are, they have systematically destroyed your Brotherhood and, by your account, every civilization they have touched. The captain is of the opinion that it may not be in our best interests to associate with folk like that. It *might* be unhealthy!"

Yantha, walking with them, spoke. "My brothers died most horribly. Some were dragged into nothingness—others felt the light in their faces and lost their minds to the enemy. These are devils of the Void!"

Trevis stopped so abruptly that Ordina nearly lost her grip on her end of the altar support rods. "Devils of the Void, indeed! It is such superstitions that keep the outer provinces in the sorry condition that they are in. . . ."

"Master Fel! Brother—Brother Fel!" Ordina's round face was turning a deep red as she struggled with her temper. "You will respect the customs and faith of others in my presence. Close your mouth and still your tongue! I for one will appreciate the silence for a space. I'll walk. *You* will follow!"

Trevis's mouth gaped open only a moment before he slammed it shut. Well, thought Ordina, sullenness and hurt at least kept the whelp quiet. "Let's get on. The rest of the crew is moving out of sight."

She couldn't bring herself to ask where they were going. She was afraid that no one knew the answer.

Djan listened to the low conversation as it moved off through the brush. His drawing in the dirt would seem random to those who might have casually watched him, but to him—and any other mage—they were important divining symbols. They told him how powerful he was.

Each day he had fought the urge to use his abilities. The conservation brought him greater power as he absorbed the ambient power of the universe, even from deep inside the huge ship that now contained him. It was his magic that had served him all his life. It had brought him power and position and, he was sure, it would do so again.

Of course, he knew, it was not just about raw power. He had met many wizards who had used their abilities in crude contests of brute strength. He despised them. Once, as an apprentice at the Lyceum on Jarba-thei, he had tried to bully a younger boy with his abilities. Though the child was a full two years younger than he and his power accumulation was far inferior to his own, the boy, in the end, had beaten him. It had taken weeks and their battle was fought not on the field of magical confrontation, where Djan would have easily bested him, but in far more subtle fields of influence, alliance, and position. It was a hard lesson but one he never forgot. You can win your battles if you can choose where, when, and over what you are fighting.

He had waited for a time to act—now was the time.

Thyne, it would appear, had the right idea but at the wrong time. The first among us to communicate with the aliens would, of course, have a significant advantage over the others. He wasn't sure what the renegade had done wrong—Thyne certainly didn't seem to be any master of subtlety so far as he could see. Yet, perhaps there was something in their encounter that could be used—by him.

Yantha had said something about—what?—light? Yes, light in their faces. The early ones simply fell dead while those who were later hit by the light were left apparent idiots. Well, if it wasn't subtle, at least that was a moderate improvement over . . .

Djan suddenly smiled. Of course.

The aliens—whatever or whoever they are—are trying to communicate. They are probably even desperate to communicate. That's why they have been searching for intelligence at any level necessary. With such an infinite diversity of life possibilities, they simply are running through all the possible combinations, looking for contact.

They just aren't very subtle about it. They use raw power and raw, crude structures to make their contact. They aren't necessarily evil—just clumsy.

Djan smoothed the dirt beneath him and began drawing new tracings. They were far more complex in their examination of himself than the simple evaluation of his powers. The tracings were maps of his own mind.

When at last he was done, Djan stood quietly and took a deep, satisfied breath.

Let the captain run blindly through the woods, he thought. *I'll confront this faceless terror. I know how to shield my mind, to close it and open it systematically. I have the power to hold off their crude attempts until rapport can be established. Then it will be I who makes the deal. If the empire has collapsed because of these creatures, what of it?* He held no great love for the Pax. No, there would be a real void—a power void—and he had in mind someone whose ambitions could fill it.

With a smile he turned quietly away from the line of march and entered the woods.

33

Face of the Alien

―――――∾⧉∾―――――

Thyne hesitated. The world around her was far different from what she remembered. She had been able to follow the line of march up the brook from the top of the waterfall. She remembered some of the rock and tree formations, but the details were getting more vague. The world had changed around her as she ran, and now the way back was unclear.

"What is it, Lady Haught-Cargil?"

She turned to the Pax captain. "You may call me Thyne. It is my name, but I give you permission to use it."

His eyes smiled as he arched his eyebrow at this thought. "Very well—Thyne. And you may call me . . ."

"Sire, I suppose?"

Serg lowered his eyes, shaking his head. "No, Thyne. With only fourteen of my own crew left and there being only two of yours, there doesn't seem to be enough remaining for even a good brawl, let alone a war. You may call me Serg if it pleases you."

"It does not," she said, turning from him. She glared at the landscape, as though daring it to change again. "But since it is your name, I suppose that it will have to do."

Thyne struck off a few paces again and stopped, looking back in the direction from which she came. She remembered the panic she had felt. Vaguely, she remembered the first few moments of her flight. She thought she had run in a straight line, but who could tell? In the distance she could see the stand of trees she had run through—she remembered that much. Beyond that lay the rock field and the stream through the rain forest. It should be somewhere in there—

But the last time she had crossed this area, it was still the maze; broken ship sections and filled with the Unlived. Now she found herself hip-deep in still grass with towering raintrees blossoming a brilliant white around her on slender trunks nearly two hundred feet high.

"Krith!" she called behind her. "Did we pass this way?"

The giant wove his way through the trees to her side. She noted that beyond him the rest of their diminished expeditions was picking their way through the trees to join them.

"Well, Lady, that be a bit difficult to know. I mean to say that we must have passed through here, ma'am, only I think I remember it lookin' sort of shiplike at the time. Them critters have changed things considerable since you and I crossed this ground, M'Lady."

Thyne nodded and sighed. Turning her face up, she could see the light of the evenly brilliant sky diffused by the thin white leaf-petals of the raintrees. They formed a gossamer lace canopy overhead. She had never seen their like anywhere on her world and wondered vaguely what world their form had been stolen from.

"Thyne." Serg spoke her name, and it sounded hollow and strange in her ears. "Are you certain this is the way?"

Thyne shook her head. "No, the only thing I *am* certain of is that I am not certain. We followed the path pretty well up to here, but it's changed. All we can hope to do is maintain our line and hope now that we come across it."

"Well, let's at least search properly." Serg turned to the rest of their group. "Genni, take Master Klar and Master Feth off in a direct line to our left, then move forward with us. Let us know if you see anything as we move. Ambassador, will you join us in our search?"

The Thrund moved quietly forward—surprisingly quietly for a creature as large as she was. *Nature must have been the preferred element of the Thrund,* Thyne thought. *I'd hate to have one of their warriors sneak up on me in the open.*

"Of course, Captain. I shall take your right side."

"I'll be off to the right as well," Thyne said, not quite being able to use the captain's first name without choking. "Krith, you can come with me."

They quickly deployed among the towering trees, wading through the tall grasses like small ships in a green sea. They pressed forward under the lace canopy high overhead. Soon they were enveloped by the forest, losing sight of where they had come from. The gentle light that reached them brought a hush to their usual chatter. It was a silence that was peaceful in the shimmering forest light. Thyne suddenly felt weary of fear and terror—letting it drop away into the grasses that surrounded her as she walked. She could almost remember places of beauty and joy where once she had walked in her youth. They seemed so far away—so dreamlike. She was heartsick for them and for their return. Just for a moment she wondered if she would ever have a life of her own, unfettered by the memory of her dead father and his crushed dreams. How she longed for a place of peace, like this, she thought. *In a galaxy so vast, is there no place for me to rest?*

She looked up as she walked. *The trees are beautiful, but they are false. I am getting too old for illusory wonders,* she thought. *I want something real and permanent. Something that won't vanish in the morning with the sun.*

The space between the trees had grown smaller as she walked, but ahead of her she could see a small clearing filled with the same tall grass. She remembered a cathedral on her home world that she had visited in what almost seemed to her to be another life. It felt much like this, she thought. Even the tall grass was still, although, she noticed, there were patches where the grasses had been matted down. They formed what appeared to be holes in the even surface of the top of the grass.

Slowly, like a dream, she walked to them, peering down over the tops of the grass between them.

At first the figure she saw matting down the grass seemed asleep, curled as he was on his side on the grass. Thyne reached down slowly to touch him, somehow not wanting to wake him. Then, in a moment, she knew that the stillness was too perfect—and that her friend would never wake.

So she stopped and knelt. She was filled with sorrow but not with tears. She knew then that she had shed too many tears and had seen too much. In the peace of the soft grotto she felt only the ache of the loss, not only of this young man's life, but of her own life as well. She had been robbed of any real life—so she mourned for the boy and for herself. In the manner of her people, she tilted her face to the sky and covered it with both hands.

She felt as dead as they.

Krith stood at Thyne's side. He had seen her stop and went to her. Now there was little else to do but stand silently by her as the rest of the group came toward them.

Serg called out as he ran toward them, "What is it there? What have you . . . ?"

Krith looked up sharply at the captain, the pain evident in his eyes.

Serg abruptly slowed to a careful walk. In moments he had come to stand next to the large delver just as Hruna arrived. He took it all in at once.

"Lor Amsha!" he murmured. "Is this your crew?"

"Allai, sire, what be left of 'em." Krith's voice was husky and raw with emotion.

"Is there . . . is there anything that is to be done for them?" Serg offered though he somehow knew the answer.

"No, sire, I fear not. They've passed to new stars, they have. But, sire . . . My Lady, she'll be needin' a little time of her own now."

Serg looked at Thyne. Her face remained covered by her hands as she knelt silently. He nodded solemnly.

Behind them both, a gentle chorus floated softly to them. "Leave us," it sang. Both Krith and Serg turned toward the Thrund's voice.

"Leave us here—I will attend to her and her pain. Do not look so skeptical. One of the talents that make Thrunds excellent ambassadors is their ability to deal with other races' pain. Surely you have something else to do? Leave us to our work."

Serg nodded and turned away. The giant delver, however, remained still.

"Krith."

Krith stood over his lady, surveying the figures of his fallen comrades. His thoughts tumbled. What did they die for? Where is their cause now?

"Krith," Serg called again.

With a shrug of his huge shoulders the delver turned and joined Serg as he walked through the grass.

"I need you to think now. Those were your wounded, weren't they?"

"*Allai,*" Krith sighed. "Them were the unlucky ones that was wounded. That creature just came up on 'em and dispatched 'em quick as you please. Bad way to leave your life, if you take my meanin'. I wouldn't want my brains vacuumed by no vile monster."

"I get your point," Serg continued, "but where were you when all this happened?"

"Oh, we was over there about twenty meters." Krith pointed off to his right. "We was having a terrible fight of it. Old Berana, before she was sucked up by that there gravity weapon, she was blazing away just about—oh, *Lor,*—just about where that depression in the grass is now."

Serg kept watching the delver. "And the creature that Berana downed it would be . . ." He let the question hang.

"Oh, well, sire"—Krith lifted his arm without thinking and pointed just ahead of them and slightly to the right—"it would have been about—*Lor Amsha!* Will you look at that now!"

Serg followed Krith's pointing arm.

Through the dim light of the closely growing trunks, lying in a depression, Krith's eye caught the glint of blue metal.

The shipwright stood at the edge of the twenty-foot-deep ravine. Serg, Genni, and the large Loyalist stood with her, each waiting for her evaluation. Ordina gazed down and shook her head. The alien—thing—lay on its side. Nothing looked farther from a ship of the stars than that lying hulk did to her practiced eye.

"Well . . ." Serg's comment hung precariously in the air.

The thing *was* huge, she noted. Its curved back plates of blue metal rose above the ravine nearly as high as it was deep. It certainly was big enough to be a ship. It was made of metal—mostly—and her mind was already figuring on the points where she might mount a makeshift sail.

It also stank.

"Are you going to tell me that our happy crew is going to willingly climb into this thing—assuming there *is* an inside to it—and try to sail this monstrosity to some harbor?"

Genni gave a short, embarrassed cough.

"Keri," Serg began, "it may not be the most advantageous of building materials . . ."

"Advantageous? I think the thing's still moving! You're asking me to build a starship out of an overgrown animal and sail its carcass on the darkwind!"

"It has one advantage over everything else around us!"

"What?"

"It's real."

Keri Ordina turned again to eye the monstrosity with a more objective eye. After another contemplative moment she shook her shoulders and said, "Fine. Let's have a look at the beast."

The slope was precipitous, but there were a number of exposed roots that provided ample foot- and handholds. It reminded Keri of her time "before the mast"—when she was an apprentice to her craft and spent much of her time in the forward optics riggings of the ships on which she served. With little effort she reached the uneven floor of the ravine. She was soon joined by the others.

"You say this was the top of the thing?" she said, pointing again to the curved metal plates.

"*Allai,* M'Lady." Krith tried to stand protectively a little in front of her, eyeing the thing with distrust. "We killed the beast through its soft belly—round the other side."

Keri found Krith's protective streak endearing in a minor way and annoying in a major one. This broad back kept getting in the way of her observations. With a deft move she skirted around him, moving quickly on her short legs around the "front" of the thing.

She nearly gagged at the sight of the other side.

The creature lay partially uncurled, its gleaming wet underside exposed. A series of mechanical servos and hydraulics ran in parallel frameworks back from the forward end through a series of metal gill-like structures. Running around and through these were a network of—impossible, she thought—blood arteries and muscle fiber. The main mass of these organic structures wove together, combining at a central point near her. There, the fibrous mass passed into what was once a clear hemispheric case of some type but which has since been burned black and shattered. Black icor hung from its raw edges.

"Krith, is that where . . ."

"*Allai*, mistress. That's how poor Berana brought the thing down." Krith's voice sounded dry.

The case frame was taller than Keri. She was no healer and therefore not versed in the arts of biology. Still, she could see a pattern in a system better than anyone—even if that system involved anatomy.

"Must have been some sort of sensory system—or, perhaps, control. Hard to say yet," she said aloud to herself.

"Well, Ordina, do you think— *Lor Amsha!*" Serg said as he and Genni rounded the front of the creature.

"Look," Keri continued, pointing to the various parts of the monster. "There are the other burn marks you described. Looks like those hits fell on the metal mechanisms—not much damage there. Your Berana was a good shot. The horizontal structures look to be a supporting framework—that's good for our purposes. It's the biologicals that I don't understand. There appears to be something like a nervous system or network of blood veins—maybe both—running just under the framework. It's not an infestation, because there are specific passages cut through the metal frames to accommodate them. One network comes together here around this burned-out dome. The other appears to lead to that tentacle mass at the other end—you can just see it exposed behind the curve of those last plates. Oh, and there's that weapon you were talking about also."

Serg let out a long, low whistle.

"Hey, Captain, you wanted a ship! This one will at least have the benefit of being unique." Keri started walking along the underside, examining it in detail. "So what I want to know is, how do we get in to the . . . ah!"

About five feet above her, the gills of the support frame formed a larger, circular structure. There, a metallic iris, gleaming with lubricant, lay partially opened.

"Krith, lift me up there, would you please," Ordina said in a voice that otherwise would have been a command.

"You must be pullin' my leg, woman!" he said. "You ain't seriously thinkin' about goin' in there!"

"Someone must, Krith, and it has to be me. Want to join me?"

"Mistress," Krith said with a little too much honesty, "I've thought about gettin' you in a dark place, but this ain't it."

Ordina was, for the moment, speechless at what the giant delver had just suggested. Serg coughed into the sudden silence and said, "Ah, well, mistress, do you recommend we continue moving or stop here?"

The shipwright shook herself from her thoughts and answered. "Captain, move everyone down here. If there's room enough in the belly of this thing, then we have the perfect hiding place—it is, after all, the very last place where they would think to look for us. I only wish I had a healer to help with the anatomy. Does anyone know where that wizard went to? I couldn't get rid of him, and now, the one time I need him, and he's missing."

"Missing?" said Serg.

"Yeah. 'His Master of Magic' is usually right on back of my shoes, but now that I need him, he's nowhere in sight."

"Strange," Serg said, but thought otherwise. "If Djan is missing, he's up to something. Djan never does anything without a reason."

Keri turned back to look at the hulking—ship; yes, she admitted to herself, she was beginning to think of it as a ship. She smiled. "If the Gods of Night are with us, who knows? We may even be able to figure out why my silverfire keeps saying 'Me Snap' all the time and actually have a chance."

Krith shook visibly, as though a chill wind had just passed over him.

Ordina eyed him curiously. "Are you well?"

Krith's voice shook. "Did you say 'Me Snap?' "

"Yeah." Ordina watched as Krith's face turned pale. "Whenever I use the console for any length of time, it starts displaying strange images and says 'Me Snap.' It's like it has a mind of its own."

"Oh, Lor!"

34

The Mind's Eye

LOCATION: HERATH SECTOR / ANST26783(?)
ESTIMATED FROM STELLAR OBSERVATIONS

Djan watched the dome of the sky darken again as his unseen hosts apparently determined it was time for night to come again. The pattern, he reflected, was about standard for a Pax Prime world—somewhere around twenty hours. This, he thought, added more evidence to the argument that their captors now knew that they were looking for humanoids not much different from himself.

He stood at the edge of a copse of trees cresting a hill. For a moment, as he stared down over the large clearing before him, his resolve wavered. Although he had heard them described by the Loyalist woman, he was unprepared for the experience of seeing them.

Drifting silently toward him in the purpling sky above were five of the great machines already moving into the area where Dresiv and his crew had all been just an hour earlier. Even from this considerable distance he could see their metallic plates flexed along their spines, laying open their glistening underbellies. The appendages snaked out from beneath the hindquarters of the beasts, writhing almost hypnotically. To either side of this group, extending as far as he could see in the gathering darkness, additional groups of five were moving as well. They moved as one, combing the ground with swift and terrible patience.

They hovered, less than three times his own height above Djan's vantage point, on a bulging column of opalescent light. This cushion, as it passed over the ground, melted away the constructed forests, rocks, trees, and other familiar surroundings almost instantly into the same gray blankness on which the *Shendridan* had met her end. As they continued past each place, the seeming featureless gray of the floor was left devoid of the more familiar surroundings of flora and fauna. Beyond the line of flying beasts there was now again the even, flat desolation which, he guessed, now extended to the limits of the vast compartment.

Djan flashed a smile to himself through the wonder and horror at what he was watching. "It's all staging," he murmured to himself. "They're just setting us up."

The mage shook himself from his reveries. The hulking things were moving more swiftly toward him than he had expected. In a few moments they would overtake his position and he needed the time to prepare. He reviewed again the curving, intricate renderings that he had worked out in the so-called dirt a half hour earlier, brought his hands forward to cover his face, and released the tracings from his mind.

At that instant he lowered his hands and knew his mind was prepared, receptive, and secure. It was time to meet the enemy.

Djan stepped from the trees into the strange night, walking down the hillside toward the rapidly advancing glow of the columns. He stopped at the base of the hill, placed both hands on his hips with his feet set wide, and waited.

The grass beneath him melted to flatness as the column of light washed over him. He was nearly surprised that there was no sensation at all when the dim light passed over him. He raised his face toward the titan that floated over him, eager and expectant.

The light left him. The alien hulk had passed over him without slowing down.

Rage filled his mind. They hadn't considered him important enough to stop! What makes them think that some poor *slonk* of a Loyalist bastard is worthy of communicating while they just pass him up without so much as . . .

The light columns suddenly blinked out of existence, dropping him suddenly into darkness. Only then did he realize that they hadn't ignored him, they had merely surrounded him.

He quickly checked his mental defenses once more and gauged them sufficiently in place. The power of his magic flowed into them and he knew that he was safe. He could reach with his mind but that part of him that was himself was now securely locked away from them.

He gazed upward. Only the black outlines of their huge floating shapes hung against the streaming stars of the night above them. He thought of those stars for an instant, wondering idly just where in the galaxy they actually were. The black silhouettes hung above him for a breath of time.

White, brilliant and pure, flooded over him—through him. His body unraveled from his mind. His physical self fell behind him like a discarded shell blown to dust in the hurricane raging through him. Thought only was he, climbing, falling, whirling, tumbling towad the streaming nova that he would join and be lost . . .

. . . No, not quite lost. Burning somewhere in the center of his thought, flaring against the assault was the core of his Self. From it the Self looked out—watching the rest of that which was Djan Kithber unravel from the fabric of his mind. Memories, dates, images, smells, feelings, impressions, abstracts; they all spun out into the brilliant void, picked apart expertly and carefully. Each strand was examined, considered by the Greatness that surrounded the Self, and then tugged at carefully again, only to be discarded for the new thoughts that had been undone. Images burst in on the Self as Djan's mind was dissected, obscuring the sightless vision of the Self with a cascade of painfully clear sensations of being in his own past. His life history roared through him in an avalanching cacophony of forced impressions. Power. Deals. The Academy. Lost love. First love. Mother. Home. These rushed out from his Self in flight, sifted, considered, and catalogued as they whirled into the bright nothing beyond.

In the end, all that was left was this Self. The tendrils of the searing slight assaulted it, burned it, electrified it, pummeled it, knocked, and begged for admittance. The Self stayed locked within, never answering nor speaking. Self lay still and hoped to be ignored and forgotten.

An instant of eternity passed as the light considered, then, grasping the Self, hurled it into the brilliance. Self fell—and began its simple, desperate task. It looked beyond its Self and saw the threads of its own thoughts falling carelessly abandoned with it into the light, random and unorganized. The Self tumbled in the void, grasping at the thoughts that once made up all that Djan was, desperately trying to gather memories and responses, that it might begin reweaving the fabric of Djan's mind.

The Self became aware as it careened down through the alien mind. As it did, it understood, for the magic of the Self continued to do its job. With its newly recovered self-awareness, the Self continued its work at a fast pace. The scattered thoughts were coming together into a whole pattern again. The process was nearing completion when Djan, knowing suddenly why he had come there, asked a single question into the whiteness around him: "Who are you?"

The question soared away from him at the end of a blue filament in his mind. It wheeled like a bird through the brightness beyond him, searching for some connection with the mind that had so completely understood his own. All that he had ever known and had ever been had been examined by this being. All he asked in return was a simple answer.

The thought turned suddenly into the brillance.

In an instant, he KNEW.

His mind shook to the core. The knowledge pounded through him complete and unquestionable. It was existence beyond anything he had ever known in life. The five senses palled in the face of its fullness. He pulled away, truly afraid now, for he couldn't hold with his mind the experience that was raging into it like the waters of some titanic broken dam. Still the connection would not be broken.

The galaxy, his galaxy, flashed through his mind in complete detail. In an instant he could recall every race on every world in known existences—and lost the knowledge in the next moment. Not just at that moment, but he knew that the galaxy he was experiencing was now dead for more than a hundred millennia. Yet he saw it with such vivid detail that it was alive in his mind and he sensed its life from those uncounted centuries now gone.

His mind in flashes spread through the stars now long dead, each passing him at such speeds that fear entered his mind for the first time. He saw the galaxy united under one rule which . . .

Oh, *Lor*, his mind wept.

. . . which killed without remorse, which expanded without merit. He saw each of the trillions of worlds fall before the ruthless fleets of unimaginable size. Far, far worse, all at once he was each of those worlds, and each of the nations of those worlds, and each of its cities and . . .

No, please, he screamed without voice.

. . . each of the inhabitants of those worlds. He felt their horror and their pain. He *was* their horror and pain. He was the child burying his face into his mother's breast, hiding from the death that unfeelingly stalked him. He was the mother, face turned upward to confront their joint death as she held the child. He collapsed with her and her child into oblivion, only to know another death. He was the father dying powerless far from his home and love. He was the family suddenly trampled to oblivion under their machines.

Each death he did not just feel—he *was* that death.

A trillion deaths on a trillion worlds ran through him in one eternal instant. He longed for his own death, but the magic of Self preserved his mind, stubbornly working against his own will. So the full experience raged in him as a seemingly never-ending hell.

The Arch'tra ships—he knew their name!—held the galaxy in their steel grip long before his ancestors made their presence known on his own home world. Djan bled with star after star as its life and hope was dragged into the Void, the Arch'tra taking without thought and giving nothing. He wept to fill oceans as he tasted the cries of the survivors, the slaves of those worlds. Bereft of future and faith, comfort or need, races willed themselves out of existence while others, Djan knew with horrific clarity, struggled on.

Then creation turned itself inside out and in the moment he was not the universe looking in but the Arch'tra looking out. Djan was the constant thrumming of its mechanism. He danced with the rhythm of its purpose in a cold metronome of precision time. His Self sped suddenly through the mind of Arch'tra and knew in the moment the vastness of its collective intelligence. Uncounted individual minds united through unnatural space to form a single living force. The seamless integration of nature and machine. The perfection of its single-eyed will. The Self spun inward on its own, seeking companionship. There it found the core of the Arch'tra also. Cold power and survival were its roots; it held disdain for all else.

Djan knew its logic and its perfection. The cold of iron certainty closed about his soul. The mind was absolutely right and unquestioned in its right. There was no other view than its own. It was purpose and progress incarnate and it owned the stars.

The Self flew upward into the light of the Arch'tra intelligence but felt a burning darkness in the frigid light. The black fire burned in the mind Arch'tra and consumed it, destroying it. Unbidden, the Self fell into the black flame. The frames of night engulfed the Self and, with the horrific clarity that Djan had come to expect, he knew—he KNEW—what it was that threatened the existence of these titans and what had destroyed them so completely in an age so distant that no written history in all the worlds of his time had mention of them.

Drowning, the Self swam against tides of black toward the light that he knew was there. He burst through the barrier, flung in a sweeping parabola above the stars until he encompassed the entire galaxy filled with the Arch'tra fleet. There was a shadow flash and the stars wheeled again as he fell through uncounted millennia back to his own time.

And they were there with him.

He KNEW why they had come, how they had come, from where they had come and when. He KNEW that they would stop at nothing to assure their survival and the survival of their race. He KNEW that they could be stopped and how. He KNEW that they must be stopped or that everything that Djan held as true would vanish in the blink of an eye. He KNEW . . .

At that instant, the Self smashed against an immovable wall, shattering into a trillion shards of consciousness.

The hulking Arch'tra devices passed on, floating quickly over the ground on their pillars of dim opal light. The things themselves were but silhouettes against the streaming stars of the sky overhead. As the pillars passed, the flat gray ground remained free of trees and ferns, and, where the clearing had been, tall, soft grasses were found no more. All that was left was the plain of monotony.

Unknowing, uncaring, the Arch'tra hulls continued on, leaving a sole dark figure, cold and unmoving, to mar the perfection of its surface.

35

Autopsy

LOCATION: HERATH SECTOR / ANSV28722(?)
ESTIMATED FROM STELLAR OBSERVATIONS

". . . just as yer fellows was returning fire. We was cooked, ma'am, though our lads was makin' a good fight of it. Then we sees that the conduit fer the silverfire was broke just above our mage. I tries to call to her—to warn her off, like—but she'd have none of it. Next thing I know she's shining like a warrior queen, only she's having trouble holdin' her shape, like. That's when I knocked her loose o' the conduit, but when we fell she were dead . . . least, so's I thought."

Both Serg and Ordina listened intently to Krith's tale. Ordina was openmouthed with astonishment.

"You mean to tell me," stammered the shipwright, "that this mage connected with a main power buss that was still active?"

"Yes, ma'am. I'm thinkin' she had in mind to use the power to smite yer crew."

" 'Smite' my crew? *Lor,* Master Krith, she could have turned the ship and everyone on it into slugs or just about anything she wanted—if she could harness it." Ordina shook her head. "The poor thing had no clue what she was dealing with. I've never heard of a case where a living person has harnessed that kind of power."

Krith's eyes cast down to the ground. "Well, ma'am, it's not like she was particularly successful, if you know what I mean."

Serg turned to Ordina. "Is this possible? Could this person be the cause of your silverfire behaving so strangely?"

Ordina considered carefully, her answers more to herself than to her captain. "We were getting a corruption feedback down the main power buss about that time. There was a break in one of the mains, but we couldn't isolate it. Silverfire kills people who fight against it." She shook her head and focused on Serg. "I've never known anyone to *join* with it though."

"I'm tellin' ye, ma'am, that I am knowin' this person," Krith said. "Sure as I thought she was dead in that little difficulty we had on yer ship, ma'am, she's in that there altar makin' fun with yer silverfire."

Just then Genni returned from the top of the ravine.

"Well, the rest of the crew is coming, although I don't know as they'll much like where they're coming to." The delver looked critically up at the stinking hulk. "The light's fading again. I suspect we'll be in dark soon. Tsara's having a little trouble getting the altars down from the lip of the ravine, but she says she'll take care of it. The rest of them should be here in a moment."

"Right." Serg nodded then turned to Ordina. "The silverfire is critical to getting us out of here on our own. I'm not sure I buy everything that this Krith is telling us—I don't even think he believes it. Still, if this Loyalist mage has somehow corrupted the silverfire, is there any way of purging her from it and getting the power back?"

"I don't know yet. There simply are no procedures set up to deal with such a possibility. If I had a full staff in a functional temple, then perhaps we could divine how to exorcise one from the other. As it is, who knows?"

Serg thought a moment. "Maybe this Snap does."

Ordina sighed. "Fine, we'll ask her later. In the meanwhile, I've got to turn this carcass into something starworthy and you need a place to rest the crew safely." She unconsciously pushed up the sleeves on her now-filthy matron's tunic. "You get everyone down here. It's time I go in."

Krith squawked. "No!"

Serg smiled, ignoring the huge delver's complaint. "As you wish, Lady Ordina. Genni, let's give Tsara some help with those altars—it would appear that they might offer us some salvation after all. Master Krith!" The red-faced delver turned to him. "Please render whatever assistance the Lady Ordina might require in her examination of this—well, soon-to-be starcraft. We'll return soon."

Krith turned, wide-eyed, toward the captain, his voice a little too eager. "*How* soon?"

Serg was already climbing the steep side of the ravine toward the shadowed outline of the survivors waiting above. He called back without looking, "Soon enough. You find us a place to sleep and we'll all get out of sight."

Krith's reply was interrupted by a slap on the back.

"Well, Delver, give a lady a hand here, if you would please," Ordina said. "There's equal parts animal and metal in this thing, but it's all we've got. See if you can force open that iris and we'll have a look inside."

Krith turned again to the putrid hulk and, with a single shudder, began to scale the metal framing to the partially open iris five hands above him. The iris lubricant made his handholds precarious as he climbed. The iris itself was about nine hands in diameter and there appeared to be some kind of rubbery—or muscular, he wasn't sure which—filaments that were used to seal the aperture. Whatever they were, they lay lax and the center of the iris looked to have opened to a width of about a hand and a half. Hoisting himself to the next section of framing, he was actually able to look in. The blackness he saw beyond gave him little encouragement.

"Beggin' your pardon, M'Lady, but why don't we just quarter this beastie and be done with it?" With a second shudder Krith grasped the aperture with both hands and tested it. It bounded back, but he felt it had given a little. He continued speaking to keep his mind off the smell and feel of the thing. "Cut the meat off this carcass and use the parts that's, well, useful?"

Ordina spoke from below with both hands planted on her hips, eyeing his work critically. "It's a good thought and one that I'll entertain—later. For the time being, we need a little more study and a little less carving. I want to know what does what on this thing before I start cleaving it up." She cocked her head to one side. "You know, I think if you could just release the pressure in that line by your foot . . ."

"Would you be meaning this one here?" Krith reached down and pointed to what he hoped was a red pressure hose.

"Yes, that's the one. If you could just cut a little . . ."

Krith immediately drew a short blade from his baggy pants and, holding himself up by the iris opening, slashed downward against the artery. The tube, already under pressure from the large man's weight against its trapped liquid, exploded in a crimson rush. The iris sprang suddenly open, falling with a rush into the recesses of the ring around it.

Krith reeled backward. His handhold suddenly vanished from his grip. Overbalanced, he fell without grace as a sprawl of arms and legs mixed with the thick crimson fluids spilling on the ground below.

He looked up mournfully from under the thick red gel covering him to see Ordina clambering through the now-open portal.

"Thanks!" she called back. "I think I can make it from here."

Ordina pulled her torchwand and shook it. The chemicals inside mixed and, with a sudden flash, gave off a soft amber light. It wasn't particularly bright—emergency wands never are, she grimaced—but the warm glow surrounding her gave her a degree of comfort. There was little else around her that could.

The exterior iris had opened into an interim chamber of some kind. The walls were lined with hundreds of—arms? She wasn't sure. They looked like armor-jointed tentacles, the ends of which split into seven smaller digits not unlike her own fingers but with metallic armatures. All those on the floor lay like a flaccid carpet of chrome while those overhead hung down toward her, their digits seeming to reach for her. Still, her job was her job and she never shirked her duty. She could already dimly see on the far side of the chamber a second iris valve lying almost completely open. With a testing step and then two quick and gingerly bounds, she crossed the metallic worm-carpet to the second iris.

The second section was a slightly twisted tube formed by a series of stainless-steel rings. Each ring was connected to the others with complex, articulated joints at spaces of about three feet. At equal points around each of these rings were mounted nine wheels, each with a supported drive mechanism. The space between each of these ring sections was filled in by some sort of dull-ivory synthetic membrane. Ordina could clearly see the weave of the fabric underfoot.

"I have to walk somewhere," she muttered to herself. She took a careful step onto the mesh.

With a great metallic groan, the mesh contracted under her feet. The rings shifted, twisting the tunnel around her even further. Ordina leaped backward onto one of the rings and held fast to one of the articulated frameworks. Within a moment the motion subsided.

Ordina was panting heavily. "Very well," she breathed out in short gasps, "I suppose I could just stick to the rings."

It looks like I'm walking down a leviathan's throat, she thought, and then quickly shoved it out of her mind. *It's just a machine! See the bolts and the rods and the wheels. Those aren't natural! Someone built this thing!*

Steadying herself, she stepped to the next ring. She concentrated. One ring . . . next ring . . . next ring . . . and then there were no more to cross.

She stood on the brink of a large chamber, laid on its side. The walls were smooth and metallic, clean and polished, reflecting her dim light back to her. It opened up an area about twenty-five hands across and an equal area up and down. The apparent floor on her right was about fifteen hands from the ceiling that was on her left. Both the floor and ceiling as well as the two walls both above and below seemed to be featureless except for an occasional access panel of wildly varying size.

The back wall, however, was different. From a large circular aperture cut in the wall's center, a tangled mass of huge, deep red tentacles hung limply intertwined with what appeared to be dozens of sickly-white fern fronds with oversize stems. Ordina could just make out three dull gray orbs mounted into the wall. *Sightless eyes,* she thought as she gazed at them. *Those meaty things look like they might be able to reach clear back up the throat of this thing, dragging anything that those hands got earlier the rest of the way into the creature's belly. . . .*

Something touched her shoulder. In panic, she grabbed for it, finding her fears confirmed by the cold, slick feel of it as her hand fought to free it from her. Without thinking, she dropped the torch, her only desire being to free herself from the thing's grasp.

As her only light tumbled into the chamber, her nerve left her completely. She screamed, desperate to get out, to get away, to get back under the open sky. The thing blocked her exit; still, she frantically beat at it, clawing to get past it. It slipped and fell into the chamber and she pushed around it, its mass falling atop the cool chemical torch and instantly snuffing out all light.

She ran up the throat of the beast, the mesh groaning and twisting around her as she ran heedless of her step. *Light, oh, Lor, I can see light!* She leaped from the inner iris, clearing the first chamber entirely . . .

. . . and collided with Serg just as he was entering.

The two of them fell as one. The crowding survivors below broke their fall as several of them were also knocked to the ground.

Serg groaned from the succession of impacts that left him on his back on the ground, Ordina on his chest.

Ordina's vision cleared, the adrenaline still pounding through her. "Captain! Oh, *Lor,* Captain! Begging your pardon, sire!"

"Ordina!" Serg groaned again.

"Yes, Captain!"

"Please get off me."

The shipwright rolled off at once. Several hands hoisted Serg to his feet.

"Mistress Ordina." Serg felt the need to restore a little dignity to the proceedings after the shipwright's rather undignified exit. "What did you find?"

Ordina still hadn't quite recovered herself. "Oh, sire! It grabbed me! I mean, it . . . it . . . it grabbed me. I was down the throat and looking in the stomach and . . . and . . . and it grabbed me!"

"Grabbed you?" Serg repeated with concern. "You mean there's something ALIVE in there?"

A hollow voice echoed deeply from within the bowels of the creature, its voice drifting out through the now-open iris.

"Yes, there be something alive in here, though it's not for the lady's lack of trying to snuff me out!" Krith yelled from within.

36

Wall of Light

~~~~~

LOCATION: HERATH SECTOR / ANRD34951(?)
ESTIMATED FROM STELLAR OBSERVATIONS

A gentle breeze stirred the vaulting raintrees as the evening dimmed. A gentle, warm mist fell from their lacelike leaves, bringing their fragrance with it. The mist drifted around two unlikely figures as it lightly flirted with the tall grass and the ground. One was a woman who might have been tall had her shoulders not been bent under some invisible weight. The other, a Thrund, her six legs smoothly pulling her next to her companion, left a wide swath through the tall grass behind her.

They walked in a silence filled with memories. There was nothing left for them to do but walk those unspoken thoughts. They had shared everything and yet knew nothing of each other.

At length, Thyne spoke. "Thank you for taking on my pain."

The Thrund laughed deeply. "I have taken nothing on. Pain isn't something you can steal from someone else. Pain is sometimes forced on us and sometimes caused by us and not occasionally held on to by us for reasons of our own. Nevertheless, it is never stolen. What you do with your pain is up to you, Thyne. In fact, I would say that your pain has served you very well."

"Served me?" Thyne looked up at the Thrund as they walked. "How?"

The Thrund gestured with forward leg appendages all about them. "Well, bringing you here may not have been in its best interests ... but I am not completely unfamiliar with your cause. I would say that ..."

"My cause!" The old fire kindled in Thyne's eyes as she took a step away from the Thrund and stopped. "What can you possibly know of my 'cause.' YOU were a part of it. YOU serve them, you Pax *thrish*!"

The Thrund stopped also. Her forward appendages crouched down even as her heads reared high overhead. Her eyelids closed to a thin slit.

"I helped cause it? Stupid humanoid," she hissed in triple discord as she towered over Thyne, "always in the center of creation. What is it about your species that demands it be the foundation of all the universe? What do you know of me or my people? Answer me!"

Thyne was suddenly shaken from her mood by the aggressiveness of the response. She took a step backward. "Nothing, I suppose."

"No, I suppose not." Hruna suddenly looked up at the darkening dome. The stars had again come out, flashing past in their unnatural speed as they went. "We, too, sailed the stars. We, too, had our own culture, art, music, history, and honor. We were proud of who we were and what we had accomplished. In our own way, we, too, were warriors and conquerors. Yet, for us, there was always the Runes of Fire, carved into the Mountain of the Sky, telling us who we were and how we should act. Yes, it is true that we took by conquest, but we honored the slain and cared for their conquered survivors as our own."

The trees had become a silhouette in the dimming light against the universe of stars.

"And when at last we encountered the Pax and warred with them, we were humiliated. Our dead were defiled and our people subjugated. We were not honored for valor. Admiral Starchis"— the Thrund spat out the name—"put our so-called rebellious people under marshal law, deprived us of our governments and temples. He shamed us by destroying our fleets. Oh, Thyne, what works of art those crafts were! Some were a thousand years old. . . ."

Thyne watched as Hruna fell lost into some private reverie. When a moment passed, she watched as the Thrund lowered her cold black eyes to her again.

"Without honor there is no victory. Without victory there is no end to the war. We do not 'serve' the Pax as their most able ambassadors. We, humanoid, are only continuing our war in much more subtle and different ways."

Thyne stood looking at the Thrund for several moments, then took a step back toward her. "Then, Hruna, I thank you again. I now see that we are sisters."

Hruna's mandibles twisted visibly into a Thrund smile. "Yes, I believe I would like a sister. There is much that we can offer each other once all this is done with. It would be—wait!"

Thyne froze, still looking at the Thrund.

"They are coming—very quickly now! *Lor,* can you see"—Hruna pointed—"there through the trees!"

"I can't—all I can see is that light. It look like a wall of light."

"A wall: yes. They are looking for us in earnest now." The Thrund suddenly began to move at a speed that Thyne would have thought impossible just moments before. She called back behind her, "Thyne, my sister, follow me! There's no time to wait!"

Thyne began to run too, moving swiftly through the tall grass as she picked up speed. She cried out, "Hruna, where are we going?" The trees fled past her now as she ran. The Thrund was moving at a speed Thyne would not have thought possible for a creature her size. Even at a dead run Thyne was having trouble keeping up with her companion. In the thick trees Thyne suddenly lost sight of her.

Panicked, she stopped and looked around. The wall of opal light was much closer now. Having reached the edge of the copse, the trees were now dissolving before their solid line. The darkness was complete now with only the streaming stars above and the shifting glow of the wall behind her to light her way. She could see nothing beyond the light—*perhaps,* she thought, *there IS nothing beyond that light!*

"Thyne, this way!"

The words echoed all around her in the trees. "Where!" she cried. "Where are you?"

"Ahead of you," came Hruna's silk-voice reply, "about thirty degrees right of your course. Hurry!"

Thyne didn't wait. She plunged again headlong into the now-dark forest. The dim shadows of gigantic tree trunks loomed before her in her flight. She dodged, leaped, and sprang across the uneven ground, sensing somehow that the light behind her was getting brighter as it closed on her. Still she bounded toward the darkness with feverish determination until the ground suddenly disappeared under her. She slid now down the steep hillside into darkness. She had decided that she rather preferred the dark. As she sensed the hillside leveling out, she rolled to her feet again, prepared to run ... prepared to run all night if need be....

A tree limb caught her, or, at least, she thought it was a tree limb, but it suddenly wrapped itself around her and hoisted her into the air, throwing her sideways. She screamed obscenely as she fought it. She might have been trying to fight stone. The limb pushed her into a cavernous hole and then in the next instant filled that hole with its huge bulk, cutting off all trace of the dim light behind. The closeness of the place pressed in on her, she could hear the sounds of many breaths.

Something grabbed her shoulders. She struggled fiercely, landing several blows until the arms wrapped around her, pinning her own, and the words sank into her mind.

"Thyne! Thyne! Stop it!" Serg said until she relaxed, still shaking and taking her breaths in short, stabbing pulls.

"Silence!" Not a tree limb but the powerful leg/arms of Hruna that had caught Thyne and pushed her into the opening of the dead enemy craft. The mass of the Thrund in the first chamber shifted, revealing the glowing ravine beyond. Hruna's soothing voice came to her. "Silence! They are here!"

A curtain of soft light swept down the side of the ravine. At its touch, the world dissolved into a featureless plain, the hillside gently melting into flatness. The shifting pastel colors seemed bright against the darkness that had gathered.

Serg leaned forward, fascinated by the display. He had only heard reports of these creatures and how they moved. He'd had little time to examine the dead one in which they now were hidden. He slowly released Thyne and moved into the round outer chamber, bending down so that he might get a better look at the underside of the—

A thick leg encased in natural bone slammed in front of him, barring his way. "No," murmured Hruna, "they hunt us. If they find us, then we are finished."

Stillness descended on the interior of the alien craft. Serg stopped and listened to the slow breaths that his companions took behind him, each one not daring to move lest he give away their position. He concentrated on the shifting lights over now-flat ground.

As he watched, an area brightened as one of the craft descended. He saw the brilliant edge of light crawl onto the still-open iris before him, slowly creeping into the chamber. The Thrund withdrew her leg quickly and silently. Serg seemed mesmerized by the light, and it fell over the metallic-plated manipulators of the outer chamber. It moved slowly in the direction of his foot.

The captain lurched sideways, grasping the limp arms lining the side of the chamber. His stomach lurched at the feel of their cold slickness, but he pulled himself against the side and out of the path of the light. Turning, he looked back to warn the rest of his companions.

They needed no encouragement. Thyne had already pulled her way through the partially open inner iris valve and fallen flat behind it. Some of the others followed her lead. Still others slowly eased their way back up the "throat" toward the inner chamber and out of sight.

The light came full into the chamber, spilling onto the inner iris and beyond to the first bend in the "throat." Serg closed his eyes. Either they would be seen or not.

The light shifted this way, then that, as its source moved. Searching the surface of the thing. Questioning. Wondering.

Then it left, and with it went the wall of light. Serg could see it through the opening now: a solid wall cast down from the machine-things overhead. Their number was so great that the wall seemed to march forever into the distance. Unquestioned, in Serg's mind, was that it extended from wall to wall of the vast chamber, leaving only a flat grayness on which their carcass-spaceship now rested.

Genni made his way up to the outer chamber, watching the receding lights of the light curtain. "Serg, when they get to the opposite wall . . ."

"When they get to the opposite wall, they will know that they have missed us. And, yes, Genni, they will come back."

"And when they do," Hruna added, "they will have very few places to look."

"And there will be no place to hide?" Genni sighed.

"And there will be no place to hide." Serg turned away from the opening and found himself looking into the faces of the survivors. The *Shendridan* had started with a crew of a hundred and twelve. The inclusion of the passengers on the trip plus the saved crew from the Loyalist vessel brought that up to over a hundred and fifty. Now he was looking into the faces of the nineteen that were left. The Loyalist captain was looking away from him, staring into some distant vision of her own. The other faces looked to him. The Localyte was still frightened to the bone. The look on his face was one of utter hope and faith—that Serg could somehow get him out of this. Genni knew better but looked to him to lead. Ordina, Tsara, even the Loyalist Krith, were waiting for him to make the move, lead the way, and, somehow, with his words make everything come out right.

So, what do I tell them, he thought. *Tell them that I'm just a man on the run. Tell them that I'm no hero with spectacular powers that can wave his magic wand and make it all good. I am no savior and never was,* he thought. *But the empire needed a savior and turned me into one. I've been running ever since.*

So, without hope, I have to give hope to them. I'm powerless, but they won't hear that. It's time to lie once again and make them believe that it'll be all right.

"There will be no place to hide," Serg said with confidence and calm that he did not feel. "So we have no choice but to make this carcass into a ship. Ordina, what's the status of the silverfire altar?"

"Sire? Well, Krith here thinks he knows what's corrupting it—rather, who's corrupting. That's a start."

"Good." Serg put on the hero façade as though it were old and familiar clothes. "Ordina, you and Krith see about getting that silverfire purged. Hruna, Genni, and I will see about rigging projectors into the plates of this thing. Tsara, you take the others and get the altars arranged in that large second chamber so that we can set up some atmosphere sealing and air processing."

"What about me?" Trevis asked earnestly.

"You are to stay here and keep watch. We must know if there

is anything approaching. Let's go, we have much to do and not much time to do it in."

As the others disbursed back down the corridor, Genni leaned his head over toward Serg and whispered, "You realize, of course, that this is hopeless."

"Of course," Serg replied under his breath. "But what else can we do. There's nowhere else to run."

37

Full of Thoughts

~~~

LOCATION: HERATH SECTOR / ANST26783(?)
ESTIMATED FROM STELLAR OBSERVATIONS

"*Amrasha,* M'Lady, I just can't do it!" Krith's temples pounded like huge drums of pain on either side of his head. It seemed to make it hard to hear. "I'm not cut out fer this type o' *tsik.*"

Ordina had been tutoring him for nearly an hour, and the big man's patience had long since run out. He was no Holy Father to go about communing with sacred altars and such! Yet if Snap were somehow caught in the silverfire as Ordina said, then he might be able to get her out of it. He didn't understand it all and the understanding of it that he *did* have had given him this headache in the first place. The only thing holding him in check was the fact that the angrier he got, the calmer the shipwright became.

Most frustrating of all, there were a few times that he really thought that he had it. It wasn't that he made any contact through the devices arrayed before him in the hollow belly of this terrible beastie. There had been no big connection for him. Yet he was almost convinced that he *had* heard snatches of words just outside his hearing or witnessed images that flashed ethereally at the edges of his vision. Yet the moment he turned to look or hear it was as though it were never there.

"Ma'am." Krith looked up, gathering his patience from the bottom of his soul. "Why can't you be doin' this yerself? You've got the knowing of this *dran* thing."

"I've tried, my renegade friend, and it's no use. There are certain keys—combinations really—that allow a Temple Priestess access to the silverfire itself within the Transentstone. I've tried those keys, but the locks remain shut." The small shipwright leaned over the Altar of Knowledge and pointed to a framed instrument. "Look, do you see the writing that's floating here in this lens?"

Krith groaned and peered into the glass. "*Allai,* Mistress, that I do."

"Can you read what it says?"

"*Allai,* M'Lady, that I can. I ain't no slop that don't know his letters and such!"

Ordina straightened her back. "Well, *I can't!* That writing is Kilnaran, if I'm not mistaken—the language of your own world."

Krith looked up at her, puzzled. "What for be that Pax using Kilnar Script in its altars?"

Ordina sighed. "We don't, Master Delver Krith. Somehow the display's been rewritten—apparently by someone who *does* know your Kilnar Script."

Tsara had been observing intently from one side of the altar array. She spoke up quietly. "Mistress Ordina, if the displays are being rewritten, then perhaps the Altar Keys have been as well."

Ordina shook her head. "Those keys are concept keys, not literal keys. Even if the language were rewritten, the concepts themselves would remain intact."

Krith spoke up. "Beggin' yer pardon, ladies, but what be these 'concept keys'?"

Ordina turned to him with the smile of a teacher relishing her instruction. "The ships of the Pax range over a tremendous variety of worlds. The language barriers—even with the establishment of Pax Common Speech—are overwhelming. To keep the fleet running efficiently, we use concept keys in certain areas. These Pax concepts allow many different worlds access to the temple without troubling too much about dialects."

Tsara wasn't put off so easily. "Yes, but what if the concepts themselves had been changed?"

Ordina blinked. "Of course! If both the concepts and the language were recoded, then there would be no way to enter the proper command sequence regardless of language. Further, you wouldn't know what the problem was because the language change would make it impossible to understand what the problem actually was in the first place! I've tried those keys—and thought that the stone wasn't responding. Now, however, I think it likely that the stone just doesn't understand either my words or my concepts!" She turned suddenly to Krith. "THAT, delver, is where you come in!"

Krith nearly jumped up from the altar. "You mean you're wantin' me to talk to a stone?!"

Ordina leaned closer to him, smiled, and patted his hand. "No, Krith, I want you to talk to the silverfire *inside* the Transentstone."

"But that there silverfire don't even understand yer Lady Mistress o' the temple!" Krith sputtered. "How is that there stone ever gonna listen to me?"

"It just will, Krith, if you can figure out the ideas that will allow you to talk to it." Ordina was in earnest now. "I think that this is because there is not enough common language AND common concepts between this Snap person and myself. Here, this time, try translating my instructions into your own language and into your culture's context—that may break down the wall and get you access to the silverfire core."

The huge delver sighed again, beaten. "*Allai*, M'Lady. I'll hear ye and think me own thoughts, rather native like." He settled down again to perform the ritual Right of Access yet again. He was equally convinced that this time, by translating everything he said into the common tongue of Nereth, he would enjoy an even greater level of failure.

With an infinitely deep sigh, he placed his hands on the carved surface of the altar, twisting his fingers and hands so as to touch the prescribed positions properly. In Ordina's case, this gesture was second nature. To Krith, a delver with huge, brutish hands, it was excruciating.

"Now," said Ordina, "just follow my words, only this time translate them into your own tongue."

"Might we not be tryin' it with me tellin' you what to say for a piece?"

"Hush! Just do as I ask. Sometimes temple problems are simply a matter of adjusting for language difficulties. If this Snap person has somehow corrupted the access system of the silver-fire, then the only way to find out what is happening may be through your own culture's language and ideas rather than mine."

"Right you are, ma'am," said Krith, not a bit convinced of it.

"Very well. 'Skyfather, we custodians are of the silverfire.' "

Krith groaned. Ordina punched him in the back.

"Right! Right!" Krith snapped. He again arranged his fingers on the altar. *Skyfather? How do I translate that?* he thought. He decided to use the most common deity forms from his home world and hope that it wouldn't offend whoever was running the silverfire. "Arga, Goddess of Night . . . er, *Arga, Khar-alantith! Sum havarni metarish wo.*"

"Grant us thy wisdom and knowledge in this our dark existence."

"Nurvarshi eo Nurkagdani karangot wo ava keadan wo."

"Serenity it the key."

Krith thought a moment. *Serenity* could either be rendered as *Kuman*, meaning outward serenity, or it could be rendered as *Peran*, signifying peace within self. These religious folk, he thought, always are big on inner peace. That decided it for him.

"Peran eo gaf."

"Order is the way."

"Jisth eo farani."

"Heaven Beyond is our reward."

Heaven Beyond was a Pax concept. Forget that, he thought. The Halls of the Dead were more his idea of reward—a palace ruled by Arga, who, if the tales were told properly, was an appreciative and talented goddess whose rewards to a valiant delver were not restricted to mere blessings by the gods but were handled on a more personal level with pleasures and skills unknown among mortals. *Herutkas,* he thought, *now, that was a place for a Kilnaran!*

"Herutkas eo jejan wo!" Krith said heartily.

Ordina rubbed her tired eyes as she spoke. *"Allai,* my Lord, thy will within our actions we devote."

"Allai, thurindrish-an wo cordali pakh." Krith turned toward the shipwright. "I told you it wouldn't . . ."

Ordina was gone. The strange belly of the alien thing had disappeared as well.

Instead, the world had been completely replaced by a vision immediately recognizable to anyone who had even the most shallow understanding of the historical culture and mythology of his home planet, Kilnar. Yet such a place as he now inhabited, some part of his mind screamed at him, did not exist and was only a place of fables and stories told to children to help them sleep at night.

He found himself staring down the length of the Hall of the Dead.

Trevis was cold despite the temperature. There was a bleakness to the landscape stretching to unimaginable distances beyond the aperture. The now-flat gray-white expanse clearly stretched to the distant vertical wall now a hazy blue through the now-lit atmosphere. Not a single blemish on all that plain. The vast chamber's first incarnation of the maze had been horrifying. The forest form it had taken had been deceptively treacherous. Yet this almost limitless nothing filled him with dread and slowly rising terror. It chilled him as he sat, knees to his chest, just inside the opening of the creature thing and watched. Watched and watched.

Even if he could see what was coming, he wasn't sure it would help. He imagined himself sitting there as the monsters came slowly across the plain. They would know that their prey was somewhere around and that the only place to hide was where he sat.

Worse yet, he suddenly realized, if they come from the other side of the ship, opposite the opening he had been charged with watching, then there would be no warning. They could approach without ever being seen. They might even be there now. . . .

He glanced furtively around him. The limp tentacles in the aperture quivered to some unseen impulse. His mind filled with the image of sitting in the mouth of a huge, sleeping carnivore. The chamber seemed to contract as a answer to his thoughts— closing tighter and tighter around him. The air became hard to breathe.

All four limbs moved at once, pushing and pulling him toward the opening—toward light, space, and air. At the iris hatchway he moved to jump, but his foot caught on the casing. He flailed at air. He tumbled through space.

His lungs emptied with the impact. He lay dizzy on the too-warm ground, gulping air. Pain swirled the edges of his vision.

He rolled over and felt the ground. He froze.

The ground was—alive. There was a pulsing warmth to its

touch that reacted ever so slightly to him. Its surface had the distinctly unpleasant feel of raw fowl meat that he had once been asked to prepare for a ceremonial dinner—slick yet it clung to you when you touched it.

He pushed away from the mess with a sticky tearing sound. He grimaced as he pulled his hand away from the surface that was reluctant to let it go. "Eeugh!" he muttered to himself. "Why did I think this would be better than inside?"

"I don't know," came the sepulcher reply.

Trevis jumped to his feet, his heart suddenly racing as he turned toward the sound. There stood Djan Kithber, the sorcerer, next to the front of the derelict alien machine as still as iron.

"Sire!" Trevis ran up to him in relief. "Captain Dresiv was worried about you being all out there in—"

" 'Captain Dresiv' I don't know," came the hollow reply.

Trevis stopped a few feet short of the robed man. There was life in his eyes, but it was well back, distant, and dim. The pupils darted here and there, fixing on some vision far from them both and unseen by the Localyte.

Trevis cocked his head to one side. "Master Kithber, are you well?"

Djan's eyes suddenly focused on Trevis. "The soul-magic held against their onslaught. The Self was protected, you see, from their mind-spooling force that disassembled my mind for storage and assimilation into their own collective . . ."

Trevis's eyes widened. "They disassembled your mind?!"

The sorcerer's face fell blank again. "I don't know."

Trevis stood silent for a moment, considering. At last he asked, "So, what happened next?"

Doubt crossed Djan's face. "I don't know."

"I mean, what happened after they disassembled your mind?"

"I don't know."

Trevis had the rising feeling that the man he was speaking with was dead. He shook his head to clear out the image. "Sire, are you sure you are well?"

Again the eyes focused on Trevis as Djan spoke with inflections and tones that were identical to the first time. "The soul-magic held against their onslaught. The Self was protected, you see, from their mind-spooling force that disassembled my mind for storage and assimilation into their own collective conscious. Part of my mind must have been assimilated when the soul-magic attempted to reassemble my mind. It tapped the Arch'tra conscious and tried to assemble it in my own mind as though it were part of my being. The thoughts and memories of their entire race began pouring into my mind, filling it with foreign thoughts. The soul-magic did its job too well. I realized the danger finally but was unable to stop the flood of information before my mind was complete . . . completely . . . I don't know!"

Tears welled up in the eyes of the sorcerer, pressed out by some unseen pain.

Trevis whispered. "Completely . . . full?"

The sorcerer's eyes lost their focus. "I . . . don't . . . know."

Trevis thought about this for a moment. He'd studied about soul-magic and how it was used by sorcerers to prevent their minds from being read by Localytes. It was a subject of considerable amusement to the novitiates in the priesthood, since the idea that a Localyte would ever spy on someone else's mind was ridiculous. Or so it had seemed back then in the seminary. Farcardinal Sabenth made him realize that the real world was much different.

So the soul-magic had saved Djan's mind where the Loyalist crew's had been lost. Yet something had gone terribly wrong as the magic tried to reassemble his mind. It had somehow connected with the mind of . . .

Trevis faced again the sorcerer. "Djan! Where are we?"

Djan's eyes suddenly focused sharply. "We are aboard Fleetcommand vessel Ka'ardoch, 5,278,919th Command T'khar of the Imperial Arch'tra Dominion."

Trevis smiled excitedly. "What is Arch'tra?"

"Arch'tra is a collective society of biotechnological beings who ruled the disk of the galaxy and seven of its adjacent globular clusters six million cycles prior to the present epoch. They are pragmatic in all things and . . . and . . ." Again the sorcerer's eyes welled up with tears, his face contorted into incredible pain. ". . . and they are without compassion. They take that which they need. They kill without reservation. They strip societies bare of all value and then enslave them. The world of Ulu'un cried out for their lives, their mothers left their children and walked into the slave ships of the Arch'tra in the vain hope of saving them, but . . . but . . ."

"But what?"

"I don't know."

"What happened to the children of Ul . . . Ool . . . whatever it was?"

Djan rocked gently back and forth behind a blank gaze. "I don't know."

"Stop!" Trevis was sweating. He decided to try a different tack. He turned to the mammoth hulk lying on its side and pointed at it. "What is this?"

The sorcerer followed the Localyte's finger and spoke clearly. "That is spar J'kan-842, the port support frame of assembly 722."

"Not that part! The whole thing!"

"I don't know."

"What is this entire assembly?" Trevis forced himself into a specific question.

"Arch'tra Bioprobe."

Trevis smiled and turned, walking quickly toward the iris aperture in the side of the—Bioprobe. "What is that assembly called?"

Djan looked up. "Primary sample exterior hatch."

Trevis climbed up to the hatchway and pointed to the tentacles lining the interior. "And what are these?"

Djan didn't even look up. "Secondary manipulator muscle filaments. Look, I don't have time for this, I have to . . . to . . ."

"What?" Trevis said in surprise. "What is it you have to do?"

"I have to . . . I have to . . ." Djan pressed his hands to his temples, pulling back his features sharply. "I don't know!"

"Dran!" Trevis exclaimed quietly, ignoring the sin of the utterance in his excitement. "You know all about this thing, don't you! I'll bet you even know how it works! You may just save us yet, Master Sorcerer! What do you think of that?"

Djan only stared back at him.

"I don't know," he whispered.

Trevis jumped down from the opening. Grasping the sorcerer's shoulders, he looked into Djan's eyes and spoke quietly. "No, you don't know—and yet you know everything. Your mind magic worked too well, Master Kithber. Every corner of your mind is full of their knowledge—so much so that there is now no room in your own mind for being Djan Kithber. I have little hope that you will ever know anything again, my poor friend. But the one thing *I* know is that you may have just saved us all. Please follow me."

"I don't know."

Trevis sighed. "Will you follow me?" he questioned.

The sorcerer walked toward him.

38

Dark Past

LOCATION: HERATH SECTOR / ANMK46728(?)
ESTIMATED FROM STELLAR OBSERVATIONS

"Captain! Captain! He's in! I can hardly hope to believe it, but
this big lummox actually made in it!"

"Ordina! Ordina, calm down!" Serg thought the small shipwright might start jumping up and down in her excitement.
"What are you talking about?"

"This lumbering Loyalist," Ordina practically screeched, "has
just merged with the Altar of Knowledge—he's in direct contact
with the silverfire containment. We've not been able to do that
before now. As soon as we extract him from the process, he can
tell us how he did it. Then I can go in and fix whatever is wrong.
That Localyte can help us get that far, at least. . . . say, where is
he?"

"Master Fel!" Serg bellowed, "You are needed . . ."

"No need to yell, Captain, here I am." Trevis beamed. Serg
wondered just what the youthful priest had to smile about. "I've
found something—rather, someone—whom I think you will want
to talk to!"

Trevis turned and began assisting Djan Kithber from the iris
opening to the chamber floor.

"*Lor!*" What happened to him?" Serg exclaimed. Serg looked

closely into the vacant, distracted eyes of the sorcerer. "Are you all right?"

"I don't know" was Djan's distracted answer.

Thyne had been observing Krith in his trance but on seeing the sorcerer stepped carefully over the conduits to the small group. She turned to Trevis. "What is the matter with him?"

"It's fascinating, Lady Thyne. Master Kithber was trying to contact the aliens. They used their light rays on him just as Lady Thyne reported. But this sorcerer was better prepared for them. He used an old mind-management technique. It's usually used to keep out unwanted mental intrusions, but in this case Djan used it to try to keep himself sane through the process. It apparently was only partially successful and backfired."

"Backfired?" Serg said. "How?"

Djan suddenly spoke, his eyes animated as though someone had just brought him to life. "By asking a question of the mind-probe during the link, I unintentionally activated a memory cascade dump into my own mind, becoming linked and one with the collective mind of the Arch'tra and their invasion fleet. Their history, experience, thoughts, plans . . ."

"Plans!" Serg and Thyne said nearly as one.

". . . technology, and sum of their existence was incorporated into my memory through the self-magic," Djan continued. "I knew I had to report to Serg Dresiv what I had found. I attempted to break the magic at that point in order to protect . . . protect . . . I . . . don't know."

Trevis spoke up. "What he's saying is that the memory cascade was too much for him. Every corner of his mind is now taken up with those thoughts, memories, and information—so much so that there is no room left in his mind to process and understand what he had learned. He'll never be able to learn anything new because . . . well, there just isn't anywhere left to put it."

"Who are these—what did he call them—Arch'tra?" Serg asked.

"Arch'tra is a collective society of biotechnological beings," Djan intoned, "who ruled the disk of the galaxy and seven of its adjacent globular clusters six million cycles prior to the present epoch. They are pragmatic in all—"

"Stop!" Trevis cried out.

Djan stood quietly.

Trevis responded to Serg's questioning gaze. "It gets a little, well, emotional from here. Suffice it to say that these creatures ruled the galaxy six million years ago with complete disdain for all other life. We can get it from him later if you wish, but I suspect that a complete answer might take him days to complete. You have to be kind of specific in your questions, or the answer will be either overlong or make no sense."

Serg thought about this for a moment, then nodded. "Djan, what are the Arch'tra doing here?"

"I don't know."

Thyne spoke to him. "What are their military plans?"

"I don't know."

"Is there a way out of the ship that captured us?"

"I don't know."

"Where are we?" Serg asked.

"I don't . . ."

". . . know!" Serg finished with him. "This is not getting us anywhere!"

Trevis shook his head. "You don't understand! He can recall specific information but can't *process* it. There's no room left in his brain to sift through it and bring the different part of it to any conclusion." Trevis gazed at Djan in wonder. "Rather amazing, actually."

"Hey, how about the Localyte"—Thyne spoke to Serg as though Trevis weren't even there—"doesn't he read minds as part of his job?"

Trevis bristled. "Madam! I do NOT read minds—as though it were some parlor trick! When I searched the mind of our beloved and now-lost Farcardinal—may his spirit find peace in the night—I was doing so at his invitation. It's against all the Jezerinthian Codes to go 'rummaging' around in someone's mind unbidden! Why, the very thought of it makes me . . ."

Thyne turned to the vacant-eyed Djan. "Yo, Master Sorcerer. Do you know of any reason why this Localyte shouldn't explore your mind?"

"I don't know."

Thyne beamed with a triumphant gesture. "See! Now you've as much as got his permission."

"Lady Thyne!" Trevis sputtered in outrage.

Serg chuckled, holding up both hands as if to calm the Localyte. "Master Fel, I don't necessarily agree with our Loyalist captain in her method, but if Djan knows what you say he knows, then it may be his knowledge that saves us."

"Why can't we just question him directly until we get the right answer?" Trevis complained.

"Because," Thyne finished, "it could take us days to stumble onto the solution."

"Look," Serg said, "you tell us that his brain is packed to the gunnels with information—so much that he can barely tell it to us. If you use your communion techniques on his mind, the open spaces of your own mind could process that information for him—and for us."

"You certainly have plenty of open space available for the task." Thyne smiled as she tapped the Localyte's head.

"We need the information now. Otherwise it will be too late. The creatures will reach the other side of this huge place they've been keeping us, and when they do they'll be back—much faster and with far fewer places to look."

Trevis sighed. "Very well . . . I see your point and our survival may depend on it. Still, I—"

"Good." Serg cut off the Localyte's argument. "Do you need the Altar of Communion?"

"No, not for this technique. The altar would be used only for communion over distance."

"Of course," Serg said as he led the Localyte closer to Djan. "Whenever you are ready."

Trevis took a deep breath, hesitated once more, then put his crossed hands before his face. "O Lords of Night, we bring ourselves together in supplication to the will of the universe. We bend our minds one to another in the Unity of Life that our minds may be open to one another and, once established, grant this servant communion with our . . . our . . ."

"Go on," Serg quietly urged.

"With our brothers though the stars separate us. This then is . . . is . . ."

" 'Our brother,' " Serg prompted again.

Trevis shuddered. "Our brother Djan Kithber, who stands before us w-willingly to accept and share our thoughts and dreams, O Father of the Sky be your will and destiny."

The Localyte was sweating profusely as he concluded and turned to Serg. "Are your questions ready?"

"Yes." Serg and Thyne spoke again as one and tossed annoyed glances at each other.

"Very well, sire, then it is time and place well destined." Trevis sighed.

"Father, why are the Arch'tra here?" Serg asked.

Trevis turned away, a look of pain crossing his face. It took him a few moments to answer. "The Arch'tra race died of a Mnestugan virus plague that ravaged their race six million cycles ago. No cure was found on any of the conquered worlds of the galaxy at that time despite an exhaustive search. The virus remains dormant for several generations before attacking the genetic coding of the host and rewriting the memory synapse of their brains, causing hallucinatory effects and madness within . . ." Trevis opened his eyes. "Their entire race died, Captain!"

Serg asked. "When did their race die?"

Trevis squinted as though trying to remember a long-lost fact. "The Arch'tra race died approximately five million nine hundred ninety-nine thousand nine hundred fifty-seven cycles before the present time, given plague propagation data, size of the empire, mortality rate—"

"Stop," Serg said.

Trevis again opened his eyes, sweat pouring down his forehead.

Thyne shook her head as she spoke to Serg. "This makes no sense. How can we be invaded by a race of creatures that's been dead for six million cycles?"

Trevis overheard the question and somehow thought it was directed to him. His eyes closed slowly and he began to recite flatly, as if from a manual. "The Arch'tra Galactic Fleet utilizes a transfinite drive system that propels their craft with equal felicity through either time or space. These drives were utilized to displace the entire Arch'tra fleet forward in time in order to facilitate the Imperial Collective's plan to salvage their race and domination. The principles of the transfinite drive center around the nature of space-time as it relates to quantum superstring structures which negate the mass—"

"Stop!" Serg commanded.

Ordina was indignant. "Captain! That was just getting interesting. . . ."

"You can have him shortly, Mistress Shipwright," Serg said.

"Trevis, what was the —*dran*, what did you call it,—ah, the Imperial Collective's plan to salvage their race?"

Trevis, eyes still closed, spoke as though he were delivering a report on current rainfall. "The Collective determined to send their invasion fleet forward in time, utilizing an initial temporal transit of six million years followed by three-million-year intervals thereafter. At each temporal invasion point, their fleets would ransack all intelligent life for the knowledge that would end their plague and cure their race."

"Stop! What if the knowledge was not found?"

Trevis continued smoothly. "The civilizations of that epoch would be crushed in order to make room for new civilizations in the next time period. This would be accomplished by the death of all sentients on a predetermined number of worlds which—"

"Stop!" Serg's eyes were wide with the horror and magnitude of what he was hearing. "How close are they to achieving their goal?"

Trevis cried out suddenly, bending over in some pain. Thyne lunged forward to catch him, but he straightened up and continued. "This epoch campaign is nearly complete. At the time when Djan made contact, the Arch'tra fleet was preparing to jump within ten days."

Serg asked again. "Have the Arch'tra found the knowledge that will save their race?"

"I don't know." Trevis responded too quickly.

Thyne shook her head again. "You're asking wrong, Captain. Trevis, did the Arch'tra find the knowledge before Djan was contacted?"

"No," Trevis intoned immediately.

Thyne turned to Serg. "Even with Trevis's help, the man can't speculate at all. Everything he knows will be from before they contacted him."

Serg nodded. "According to their plan, if they do find the knowledge they seek, what is their next step?"

"The fleet will then return to their own time period, utilizing the same three-million-year transit periods backward to reach their own time. These periods are required to allow the ships to recharge their engines between each transit. This recharging takes place by the intermixture of certain bulk compounds—"

"Stop!" Serg commanded.

Thyne shook her head. "If they don't find what they need

here, they just go ahead again in time. Then they have to come back the same way they came. Serg, they'll be passing this way again!

"When the Arch'tra reach their own time, what will happen?"

"The plague will be stopped. The Arch'tra race will remain dominant in their galaxy, going from power to power in their conquest of neighboring galaxies and mandated by the Decrees of—"

"Stop." Serg was suddenly quiet. "Wouldn't that change history?"

"Histories for events after the fleet's transit through time would be changed forever with the fleet's return. All that had taken place after the fleet's return would not take place." Both Djan and Trevis smiled the same smile.

"If the Arch'tra fleet succeeds," Thyne whispered almost to herself, "then everything we have known will be gone. We will never have lived at all!"

Serg shuddered. "Trevis! My questions are done!"

Trevis shook himself and sat on the floor. He looked as though he were going to cry.

Serg turned to the shipwright standing next to him. "Ordina, we've got to get out of here."

"With what?" Ordina cried out. "Captain, I don't have anything to work with here! Sure, it looks like we've access to the silverfire now, but I don't understand anything about how this horrid-smelling monster worked!"

Trevis spoke up. "Sire, Djan knows this thing—he calls it a Bioprobe—inside and out. I thought that the shipwright might be able to use him to somehow get us out of here using the Bioprobe."

"Tsara!" Ordina called over her shoulder. "Keep an eye on that pirate that's using the Communion Altar. At the first sign that he's either in trouble or coming out, yell for me." Ordina came forward, taking Djan by the hand. "Djan, please come with me—I suspect we're going to have a very interesting conversation."

39

Meeting of Minds

LOCATION: HERATH SECTOR / ANMK46728(?)
ESTIMATED FROM STELLAR OBSERVATIONS

Krith caught his breath, his eyes blinking as though to clear a vision from his eyes that his mind could not accept as real.

It was incredibly beautiful, horrible, frightening, calming—a peaceful chaos that raged around him. The length of the hall could not be determined, for its far end disappeared to a single point of perspective, an eternal procession of pillars supporting a roof that must have been a thousand hands high. Delicate glass vines wound their way up the pillars, punctuated by stars that served as flowers. The hall itself was almost four hundred hands wide. Delicately carved shrubs formed the walls that filled the hall with a sweet and bitter smell. Vertical windows could be seen set into these shrubs. The windows were composed of standing sheets of water whose surface rippled from an unfelt breeze. Arching fire formed the ceiling, glowing with moderate heat, yet frozen and unmoving. A great promenade circled the hall with long, wide cloud-steps leading down to the central floor. There, trees walked nervously about, forming copse and meadows at their whim, taking their turns uprooting animals and replanting them wherever they thought most esthetically pleasing.

Yet it was the inhabitants of the hall that caught his attention.

There men and women lounged—each wearing ceremonial robes of the Kilnar priests. Yet on closer inspection there were horrific differences between many of those he looked at, for each was in various states of life and death. Three badly burned corpses, their flesh nearly boiled away from their bones, lay basking in a newly formed clearing as they spoke with great animation to each other and occasionally bit into some red fruit. A young, beautiful woman whose breathtaking shape could furtively be seen through the folds of her diaphanous robe sat on a bench, laughing heartily. Her companion seated next to her was badly decomposing, his gray flesh clinging precariously to his frame. He was trying to tell a story, but his head kept falling from his shoulders to land—still speaking—at his feet. Both the woman and the corpse seemed to think this terribly funny. In a grove to his right, three strong men with swords fought three other men in armor. Behind each group stood three women. The armored men pressed their attack, rending the strong men with their own swords. Blood gushed and spat over them as they stepped over their fallen enemy and raped their women savagely. Then the armored men stepped back as the strong men rose up from their mortal wounds and attacked again. The armor was crushed in a crimson spray. The strong men then savaged the women behind the armored men. Then the women took up arms against each other, raping and humiliating their foe's men. Then the women took up arms against the men. All the while, to the side of the bloody conflict, a skeletal cleric in tattered robes kept score on a huge, blood-coated slate. . . .

Krith found it hard to breathe. He closed his eyes tightly, crying out, "What the *Hesth* is happening! *Lor Amsha!* Help me!"

The voice behind him was like a whispered thunder.

"Me Snap, stupid Krith! Me help."

Krith turned suddenly toward the sound, his eyes wide. There she was, the slight girl he had known with the eyes that were too big and too eager to please. When he had last stared down into those eyes, they had been cloudy and gray with death.

"You little *shikth*! You scared the *Hesth* out of me!" Krith was shaking now, concentrating on his anger in hopes that somehow rage alone will bring to him some sense of stability.

"Hey, me Snap! Me no hear this *shikth* from Krith!" As he watched, the child suddenly changed. In a moment she towered over him, fully three hands higher than his own head. Brilliant armor replaced her tattered tunic. Sunlight streamed from her helmet, making it impossible for Krith to look directly at her. The Shield of Honor was slung at her left, while in her right hand—*Lor,* he thought—she held *Justik,* the legendary sword of vengeance and just wrath. "Me lord Hall of Dead! Me prove self in battle!"

The dead in the hall fiercely applauded her speech.

"Snap, I'm right sorry for my harsh words, so to speak. I didn't mean nothin' by it, really." Krith hunched over, less from supplication than from a desire to save his eyesight.

The young healer mistook the gesture as one of adoration and worship. She seemed truly touched. "Krith no must worship Snap! Snap understand all. Snap queen Hall of Dead now! Krith no worry! Hey, Snap want know. How you die?"

"Well . . ." Krith let his voice trail off. He had no answer for that, really. Truth be told, he wasn't all that sure that he wasn't dead. Maybe that temple altar-ma-bob had not liked the way he'd talked to it and zapped his brain stone dead. Maybe this *was* the Hall of the Dead.

Yet while it was true that he had little idea about what the afterlife would be like, he was pretty sure this wasn't it. All of this seemed a great deal more than a little off plumb to him even if it wasn't a subject he felt he had to dwell on much in the past. The things that he had seen so far were so utterly common and yet so utterly bizarre that it just couldn't be true.

"Krith not worry. Not important how Krith croak. You here now." Snap was again her familiar, slight self. Suddenly her eyes flew open wide and she shrieked, "No! No! No! How time and time me tell you! Flower not sing! Birds not smell pretty! Put back! Put back!"

The small healer dashed down the steps to the offending flowering bush. The petals stopped their chorus in mid-discord while the birds quit swaying in the breeze.

"It constant struggle," Snap sighed as she shook her head. "Outside always want in. Snap no rest. Hard for Snap keep order in world."

Krith looked around again. The hall was huge, but it wasn't endless. There were doors leading out of the hall, but each was heavily barred and barricaded from the inside. The great windows were heavily draped and shuttered.

"What of the outside, Snap," Krith asked. He moved up the

steps toward the drapes at the side of the hall. "What be outside the Hall of the Dead?"

"No!"

Snap's small, thin hand fell with surprising strength on the arm of the giant delver. It felt cold on his flesh, cold as the corpse he had held in his arms not so long before. He quaked at the thought, wrenching his arm free of her in an instant.

Snap recoiled from the gesture, her lower lip quivering. The legions of dead behind her hid their faces. Willows throughout the hall wept blood.

"Snap sorry," she murmured, her eyes averted. "Snap not hurt Krith. Snap not touch Krith."

Krith's face suddenly softened as he looked down on the slight girl cowering before him. All she'd ever wanted was his approval. He had taken her in when no one else of the crew could stand her nuisance ways and her constant chatter. They hadn't understood that the butchered Pax speech she effected with such enthusiastic abandon was driven by a conflicting knowledge of how hard it was for her and the consuming desire to fit in. Yet he had known. With a sigh, Krith turned toward her and extended his hand.

"*Amsha,* Snap, I didn't mean nothin' by it, really now. It's just—"

The curtain behind him exploded. Krith flew with the blast and smoke, tumbling in the air only to slam suddenly against something semi-soft, pressing the air from his lungs. The hall was filled with dust and smoke but was clearing quickly as he gasped for air. He looked up.

He lay on a bank of pillows strewn against the opposite side of the hall from where he had last stood. He was left with only a moment to wonder how those pillows had gotten there. Chaos, literally, had broken into the opposite side of the hall.

The wall was gone, shattered by the force of a huge horned head more than three times his own height. It had no eyes, but, he somehow knew, could discern the hall better than he himself. The smell of it offended him to the core of his being. Ten sphincters lined the razor-edged orifice at the front of the scaled head, each twitching in anticipation of prey as it writhed through the wall. Pillars fell as it pulled forward on four titanic human arms. Leathery wings beat frantically beyond the opening. Beyond that . . .

Krith turned suddenly, slamming his eyes shut against the vision he had seen. He buried his head in the pillows like a child terrified in the night. He wept again, this time in fear of his own insanity.

Beyond the wings was the heart of the silverfire.

"Krith!" A voice called to him from far away. "Krith! *Dran,* Krith, come back!"

"Krith! No leave me!" Snap screamed. He heard the sound of swords rattling against the scales of the beast. The creature roared.

"Krith! Come back!" Voices raged somewhere in his mind. They called distantly to him, urging him here and there. He lifted his head.

"Krith!" Ordina shook her head, then suddenly grabbed his head and shook it. "Krith! *Dran and Hesth!* Krith, come back!"

The blank face of the huge delver suddenly contorted in pain. His eyes slammed open, then the pupils dilated and suddenly focused.

Suddenly he stood, yelling incomprehensibly. His arms flailed, catching Ordina fully under the chin and sending her sprawling to the deck. He scrambled backward, fell, and began crabbing away from the altar, babbling. His eyes darted from place to place as if seeing things that only his eye could discern. His head jerked sporadically as he moved.

Thyne and Serg had been watching Krith since his apparent success in accessing the Altar of Knowledge. She moved quickly, following him across the floor, taking up Ordina's calling to him. "Krith! It's Thyne, Krith, stop!"

Krith's wild motion halted only because he had run directly into the forward bulkhead of the compartment. He pressed himself upright against the wall as his legs continued to work against the floor. His breathing was heavy as he gulped air.

Thyne stepped close to him, batting down his flailing arms as she yelled into his face. "*Lor Amsha,* Krith, come back out of it! Krith!" She slapped him hard across the face.

Instinctually, blindly, he hit her back, his mammoth hand knocking her to the floor.

Serg slowly pulled out his handcannon. He glanced at Thyne, however, and saw her hold up a hand, signing him to wait.

Thyne stood up; her lip was bleeding as she stepped back up to Krith.

Her right cross came almost from the floor.

Krith's head snapped back as she connected. "Krith!" she screamed in his face.

His eyes suddenly focused with rage. He grabbed her by the shoulders, lifted her off the floor—and suddenly knew where he was. Panting, he let her down gently, then slid quietly down the wall, spent.

Serg smoothly holstered his handcannon. "Well," he said, "I can see that discipline is not a problem in your command, Lady Thyne."

Thyne dabbed the back of her hand at her mouth, stanching the trickle of blood. "It had its moments," she said quietly. "What about it, Ordina? Did he make it?"

The shipwright knelt at the huge man's side with more concern than her station warranted. She pushed open one of Krith's eyes as she spoke. "Just a moment, Captain! He made it all right! But unless we get him back, it won't do us much good." She grabbed his beard by both hands and pulled his face within a handbreadth of her own. "Krith!" she yelled. "Wake up, you thievin' *dresth*!"

The delver continued to lie on the deck like a mound of wet sand . . . but his eyes opened.

"Sure, lass," he said, smiling weakly back at her, "your face is the prettiest I've seen tonight"—suddenly his thoughts collected in his mind—"but not the only one. *Lor!* What a terror that was! If the Hall of the Dead be aye'thing like that place, I'll be put'in' in for a worse life from now on! Thank the One I be back alive! Ye wouldn't be believin' it yerself if you'd have been there, ma'am! Monsters, there was! *Allai!* And things so strange as to go beyond the tellin' . . ."

A shadow fell across them as Thyne appeared over Ordina's shoulder. "Krith? We think we've found a way out . . ."

Krith continued his visionary cascade, barely taking notice of their words. ". . . leagues long, it was! Yet the windows, you see, they was entirely boarded over against the beast ragin' outside . . ."

Serg's head appeared over Ordina's opposite shoulder. "Master Krith! We've not much time, you see, and it would appear that you are the only one who can . . ."

". . . oh, and the terror of it! I found her, y'see, just as she were in life, only she were dead! Dead as stone! Then she turned into the goddess of death and I'd sure have been blind, only I couldn't see already . . ."

"Krith!" Ordina said.

". . . and the rotting dead swarmin' about me ready to eat my flesh at a moment . . ."

"Krith!" Ordina tugged again on the beard.

". . . and then the beast broke into the hall, rending me own flesh with its dripping . . ."

"KRITH!" Ordina filled both hands with beard and hauled sharply back with all her weight.

Tears sprang up into his eyes. "YEHAS! Belay that action, wench! This beauty took me many a year to grow!"

She let go of the beard but continued to look him in the eye as she spoke. "Krith, the things are coming back . . ."

"Oh, *Lor!*"

". . . but we think we know how to get out of this place."

The delver relaxed and smiled. "Aye, lass, I knew that you could do it! Put that mind to anything and there's no stoppin' you, is there?"

"It will work, but we need your help."

"Right you are!" He struggled to his feet, then pulled down his tunic to straighten it and look properly heroic. I've been to *Hesth* and back today already. Nothing could be worse than that! What be yer need?"

She looked up at him from where she still knelt. "We want you to go back."

40

The Quick and the Dead

———❧❧———

LOCATION: HERATH SECTOR / ANST26783(?)
ESTIMATED FROM STELLAR OBSERVATIONS

" 'You and yer brilliant mind, Mistress Ordina!' " Krith mocked to himself as he walked behind the shipwright. The giant was sweating profusely now. "I'm takin' it back, you hear! I'm taking all of it back!"

The mammoth man followed the shipwright as though he were a reluctant child, straining backward from her leading hand yet not daring to resist too strongly. Her grip on his hand was firm as she rushed them back toward the Altars in Exile.

"It's not as though you're going alone. This time you're taking me with you." She paused. "Think of it as a holiday."

"Holiday! I'd sooner suck particles in the Void as go holiday in that place again!"

"Yes," she countered patiently, "but you'll have such good company. Now, wait here while I prepare for the full ceremony."

He growled menacingly but stayed where she had placed him. It was the same altar that he had fallen from earlier. He knew that he and the mystic stones were somehow on bad terms. Still, he stayed.

"All right! Listen, delvers!" Ordina's clasped her hands together loudly. "We're going to get this beast into the sky. We need your help doing it. I want the Temple Acolytes here securing the altars to the deck. Pry those plates off so we can run the cables around the framing. Localyte Fel, we'll need you to assist us. Madam Ambassador?"

"Yes, Mistress Ordina," chimed the Thrund voices.

"We are in need of some rigging in here to give us all something to hang on to when we move. I can't guarantee gravity or inertia fields, so we'll need something to keep us from bouncing around the compartment. I believe that your race are rather adept at such devices?"

"Madam Shipwright," the Thrund intoned with great solemnity, "the internal rigging of our ships is known throughout the stars as the finest protection against acceleration changes short of magic itself. I myself am most adept at the art."

"As I would have expected, Madam Ambassador." Ordina bowed slightly, then continued to address the group. "The sorcerer stays with me—the rest of you assist the Thrund in rigging the interior of this compartment for acceleration. That's all! Move it!"

As the crowd suddenly moved into action, Ordina quickly but purposefully moved from altar to altar. Her hand motions were sure over each altar, yet there was an urgency in her actions. Time was against her.

"How is this going to work, Mistress Shipwright?" Serg asked as he moved behind her from altar to altar, trying desperately to stay out of the way. Ordina bent to rearrange the conduit strung again between the altars.

She frowned but continued working. "I've got an idea, sire, just an idea. Djan has given me access point to the nervous system of this monster as well as the main power feeds. The trick is not getting the equipment to work but controlling it once it does. We have to go through the Altar of Knowledge to get control of the ship systems—and *that* means that this Snap woman will be controlling the ship."

Serg frowned. "A dead ship captained by a dead woman?"

"Yeah." Ordina smiled as she worked. "Rather hard for us living to have much faith in that. The thing is—she'll be thinking she's piloting her imaginary ship on some voyage to her people's heaven. Translating that will require the Localyte to be in mental communication with this girl through the altar. We tell him what we want done—he tells the girl through his mind link, and she executes her commands in her little dreamland. Meanwhile, Krith goes back in to make sure the girl carries out our instructions."

Serg's face contorted into a skeptical grimace. "Just how sure of all this are you?"

"Sure? I'm not *sure* of anything, sire. At least now we have a chance—now that I understand how this Bioprobe works. It was fortunate that Loyalist shot hit the central nervous center of this thing—it brought the beast down without damaging its peripheral systems. If we can run our own direction impulses through that tentacle mass at the back of the compartment as well as power feeds into the main conduits, we have a chance of getting some life into this dead spaceship."

"Yes, but will she fly?" Serg said not without concern and with a slight urgency in his voice. "What will you use for projectors and rigging for the sails?"

"If what Djan tells me is true, we won't need them. These things fly off something called a transfinite drive that shifts infinity around the drive core. It's the most *dran* thing I've ever heard of." Ordina shook her head and laughed. "That Localyte wanders back in here with a sorcerer who can't add two pair into four yet can tell me the name and function of every piece of muscle and hardware in this beast—and beast it is, you understand. There's as much biology at work here as there is mechanics. These Arch'tra—as Master Djan calls them—seem to use a smooth melding of organic life and machines. Sometimes it's hard for me to tell where one ends and the other begins. There are entire systems on this craft that are comprised of both. Oh, I've played the question game with Djan, all right! You can't just ask him a question, you know, you have to—"

"Yes, you have to ask him specific questions he can answer with facts." Serg grabbed an uncooperative conduit and shoved it back into place without a thought. "He's incapable of forming conclusions or even following a conversation."

"Sad to think he'll never be able to change that sparkling personality." She smiled ruefully as she straightened up. "That's it! We're ready."

"How long will this take?" Serg moved quickly toward the forward corridor. *Lor,* he thought, *I wonder if there's enough time for this?*

"How long?" Ordina asked incredulously. "Hah! I've no idea. What we are attempting is crazy to begin with. I'm going with

Master Muscle-Bulges over there"—she pointed with her thumb toward Krith—"into some fantasy world existing in the silverfire. There we're going to talk to a dead woman in the hopes of convincing her to connect the silverfire conduits to a half-animal starship that is also probably dead. And who is going to show us how to make this impossible union? A sorcerer who can no longer add up the fingers on his own hands!"

"Simple as all that? Where's the challenge, Ordina?" Serg smiled and then turned to pull himself up into the corridor. "I'm going forward to see how long we have for you to perform this little miracle before our hosts arrive."

"Captain, did anyone ever tell you you were a real pain in the—"

"Ho! Whoa!" he called out as he disappeared into the darkness, his voice echoing into the darkness. "Sorry! Can't hear you!"

"Witness, sire!" Ordina yelled after him. "I can't even tell you if this leviathan will fly no matter what we do. If the beast is dying—and my nose tells me that much of it is already dead—then there may not be much working even if we do figure out how to make it happen!"

Ordina turned smartly. "Tsara! Bring that sorcerer over here and lead him through the ritual of granting. He knows it, but he won't know to do it until you tell him to. It's time we see if we can resurrect this monster."

"Where? What do you mean, where! Everywhere!" Thyne said in exasperated tones. Her arms flailed about to indicate the horizon, nearly toppling her from her perch in the open mouth of the dead Bioprobe.

Serg squinted. "*Dran!* How many can you make out."

"Thirty—perhaps more. At this distance it's hard to tell but—*Lor,* look at them move!"

As she spoke, the vague blur in the distance was even then becoming discernible as the humped shapes of the Arch'tra "inquisitors" as Djan had called them. They bobbed slightly as they moved across the flat white floor of the containment.

"We were so close! So *dran* close!" Serg swore under his breath.

"They're coming straight here, you know." Thyne's voice

sounded quiet and resigned. With the illusion of their surroundings now gone, there was, literally, nowhere left to hide.

"We've got to buy some time—slow them up somehow." Serg drew his arm across his wet brow. He looked frantically outside the opening. "Ordina's in there now, trying to get this hulk to move, but she needs TIME!"

"Buy time with what, Pax dog." Thyne's protest lacked energy or even interest.

Serg stood and turned to face the Loyalist. "Lady Thyne, I hand you the scepter . . ."

"What?!"

". . . and you now hold the scepter of command. The command is thine. Get our people out of here if you can. You've got to get Djan to the Pax Core worlds—if there's anything left of them. The Farcardinal said that the universe had gone silent. Everything that we knew before is gone—including the Pax Galacticus that you hate so much. Still, if they did somehow survive, then they may be the only ones who can use Djan and his knowledge of these Arch'tra to end their invasion." He turned back to the opening, hands on his hips. "Take care of our crew, Lady Thyne. They all deserve better than this."

"So just what do you intend to do?" Thyne asked incredulously. "I don't suppose you're going out there to reason with them? Perhaps you'd like to try to negotiate a truce?"

"You're in charge here, Thyne. You need a little time, and I'm going to buy it for you."

"You're going out there? And do what?"

"Run like *Hesth*."

"You're crazy."

"Let's hope I'm fast."

Thyne opened her mouth to speak, but somehow the words didn't come.

"Now, THAT is something I had never hoped to see." Serg smiled. "Farewell, Lady Thyne. Take care of my . . ."

Thyne spoke softly. "Captain, I . . . I just wanted you to know that I admire your leadership. I think . . ."

"I really don't have time for this—but thanks." He turned, placing both hands above the opening, preparing to jump.

Pain slammed through his head. The world went suddenly white and he had the vague impression of tumbling for a long, long time. He was unconscious before he hit the ground below.

Unnoticed, Thyne landed on the ground next to him, holding the handcannon she had just swung full force into his head. "Captain, I have just given back the scepter of command," she said.

Then she ran.

"Snap understand . . . Snap understand that you crazy!"

The problem with talking to the dead, thought Krith with a weary sigh, is that they never know when to give up. Death seems like such a final thing to the living, an impenetrable void that seems to be the great finale of all existence. An entire life summed up in the final flash and the curtain drawing to a conclusion of one's presence on the stage of mortality. So think the living, never seeming to take much thought of the existence after the curtain falls, except in some religions, where shining existence is filled with harps or wings or clouds or waves or flutes or any other state of constant bliss.

Yet Krith had decided, as he stood before Snap with a rather spectral and formidable-looking Ordina at his side, that the dead were ill prepared for their new existence by all of this religious talk. Being dead didn't seem to be all that different from being alive, for all he could tell. Indeed, Snap seemed to accept this strange space of existence where everything changed at a whim as though it were the way things should have been in life.

And Ordina was certainly not making any headway.

"We are not crazy!" she rumbled with a voice that was barely under control. "We are merely trying to get you to understand how we wish for you to interface with the outside, real world!"

"Me leave real world behind," Snap countered. "Me great warrior-goddess in the Hall of the Dead now! Me already attain my reward. Now me do great and wonderful work for the Gods of Night. Me tend to Hall of Dead! Keep clean! Keep in order for when they return! Then me be more powerful than ever! Me be even greater goddess than before!"

Krith looked around. Snap sure had tidied things up since the last time he was there. The exploded wall had been rebuilt and she had asked the trees to reorganize themselves into much more interesting ranks. Some part of him hoped that the gods would be pleased when they got back—though he mentally shook himself back to reality as he realized they were inside a silverfire world that did not exist except through the will of a dead companion.

"Look, young lady"—Ordina's voice rose in pitch and volume—"you are dead and . . ."

"Yes, me dead! Me now in Hall of Dead! You pretty slow for shipwright!"

Ordina sucked in a long breath, closed her eyes, and held herself back for a moment while the anger washed over her. She slowly released her breath, blowing the rage out with it before she continued. "Please listen to me—Snap, isn't it?"

The slight figure leaned forward in concentration. "Yep, me Snap. So far I follow good."

"Right. Snap, what you have done here is astonishing! I've been a priestess of the High Temple for over ten years now, and in all my experience with silverfire, I've never known anything remotely like this. Through the will of your own spirit you've tamed the chaos that rages through the silverfire and created this incredible, stable island of ordered existence from the very heart of entropy."

Snap frowned. She wasn't following very well, but what she was following she wasn't sure she liked. "It not look all that stable to Snap."

Ordina smiled. "Well, take my word for it, compared to silverfire in its released state, this is remarkably controlled. Now, you want to be a hero . . ."

"Me already hero."

"Ah, yes, you want to be an even greater hero, right?"

Snap's eyes flashed. "Of course, what other purpose for mistress of Hall of Dead?"

Ordina had to admit the young girl had her on that one. "Of course. Now we need you to do a great and heroic thing. All of this isn't real. We are actually inside the silverfire. The silverfire is inside the Altar in Exile. THAT happens right now to be inside the belly of an ancient probe craft of an invading army. We need the silverfire guided to interface with this alien craft for guidance and power so that we can escape these enemies and hopefully warn our people of the invasion. There! What could be simpler?"

Snap looked at the woman for a heartbeat. "Boy, you nuts!"

Krith rolled his eyes back into his head.

"That one whopper of tale!" Snap raved. She turned toward Krith. "Thanks for laugh, Krith! This one really lost it somehow when she die. She comes and tell Snap she not dead but in dead beast. That rich one. I like play you two, but Snap have to rearrange seating for death banquet. Rocks always barging in. Water not like having to sit next to fire and always complain."

Krith watched the young girl stomp off. *She's never going to believe the shipwright,* he thought. *She's just a child and knows only child things.*

Ordina gently touched the large delver's arm. "Krith, she's our only hope. If we don't get through to her, we're done."

The mind of the huge delver worked feverishly. *She knows child things.*

"Hey, Snap! Come back!" he shouted.

Ordina looked up at him in surprise. Krith turned suddenly toward her, grabbing her by both shoulders as he looked into her face. "Can you bring that burned-out sorcerer in here?"

"Well, I . . . I think he's in the communion network." She closed her eyes for a moment. "Yes, I can see him there. But whyever would you want . . ."

"Just follow my lead, lass. It'll be hard to weather, but hold to my line and I think we may just be gettin' through this." He turned back to Snap. "Snap, my great warrior woman of the dead! I've come to you with a message from the gods!"

The girl stopped and turned halfway across the hall. A congregation of the putrid dead had gathered to follow her in search of salvation. "What nonsense you speaking now, Krith?"

Krith folded his arms across his massive chest. "The Gods of Night have seen your sacrifice and accepted it. They have sent me here to come and get you. You will cross the Sea of Heaven to come and dwell with the gods themselves."

Snaps eyes grew wide. "Truly?"

"It is what you want, is it not?"

Snap ran back across the hall, abandoning the corpses to stand milling around on their own. "Oh, Krith, me become greatest hero of all!"

"Yes," Krith said softly as he looked down on her, "you will become the greatest hero of all."

"When we go? How we get there?"

"Two people have come to help ye. First, this crazy woman who's been talkin' of strange things." He could feel Ordina's fists close behind him, but went on. "She'll be helpin' you build a Neffi . . ."

Snap caught her breath. "A ship of the gods!"

"Yes," Ordina inserted. "A ship of the gods—only not too big so that only three of us can cross, ah, to where the gods are." She turned to Krith, muttering under her breath. "A smaller area of order in the chaos will give us more power from the silverfire."

"*Allai,* Snap, and a grand ship she'll be. You'll not be crossin' the Sea of Heaven without guidance though, gal. Them are treacherous winds, they be. So the gods have sent another to help ye."

Ordina's eyes closed once again. A tall, thin man in robes suddenly appeared next to them.

Snap fell to the ground in worship.

"Lay yer eyes on the Prophet."

Snap gazed up worshipfully into the burning, vacant eyes of Djan.

41

Flight of the Neffi

━━━━◆◆◆━━━━

LOCATION: HERATH SECTOR / ANST26783(?)
ESTIMATED FROM STELLAR OBSERVATIONS

She ran.

One leg after another pounding the ground. Left. Right. Again. Again.

She had looked back only once—when she had first left the broken alien behind, half hoping that Serg would recover from the blow with which she had felled him and somehow make her stop. As she had turned, she had a glimpse of the huge machines drifting silently and weightless over the milk-white plain. The dark shapes were in sharp contrast to the featureless surroundings, the curved blue of their metallic hulls mirroring each other as they turned toward her. Eyeless, she could nevertheless feel them look at her. They wheeled together with one mind, one thought—and that thought was her.

Then she knew that there was no point in looking back, that the menace would be there whether she looked or not. There was only going forward, doing whatever she could to keep moving and stay on her feet. There was, after all, little point in looking backward. She had fought in combat many times and had known what it was to have an enemy at one's back. She could already feel the huge mass of them behind her, closing still and suddenly too close.

She turned with her handcannon and fired—blindly. It flashed through a lightning of illumination across the surface of one of the probes, its glistening curves flaring in its light. The shot struck no mark, but in the instant she saw the giant behind her bob easily clear of the particle beam.

They had learned to avoid that one, at least.

They were within a hundred meters of her and closing fast.

Instinctively, she ran toward the only other objects she could see—realizing too late what they were. The bodies of her crew were suddenly all about her, no longer covered in the illusion of the meadow nor with the peace it bestowed. Bereft of cover, they lay clinically cold and somehow obscene on the stark white ground that stretched to forever around her.

"They were mine," she thought. *"Where have I led them? What good were their deaths?"*

The hair on the back of her neck rose suddenly. On instinct alone, she leaped for cover behind the bodies before her.

Silent white light split the air over her head. She rolled once for better position and rose to fire. Thyne conserved the shot, knowing that the handcannon had a limited number of blasts. As the handcannon roared twice, it occurred to her that it might not matter how many rounds she expended now, but she was loath to think of herself in the midst of these things holding a useless weapon.

The shots bolted true at the nearest of the machine-creatures, slamming hard against the side plates before dissipating. The lead was within ten meters now: Five more were close behind with more still seen stretching to the horizons in both directions.

She fired again, three bolts and lower this time as she'd seen her crew do earlier. The lead creature ducked smoothly—effortlessly—to deflect the blow.

It wasn't until then that she noticed the others moving silently to flank her on both sides.

She jumped up, firing twice again, more for cover than precision, and ran again, nearly tripping over the body of Yorki as she moved. She was in full flight now, her lungs shot with pain in the effort. She screamed long and hard in desperation. At the edge of her vision, the blue-black forms were passing her on either side. A shadow passed over her, blocking out the gentle glow overhead. In an instant, five more of the creatures fell as a curtain before her and her flight was at an end.

"NO!" she growled as another of the beasts turned toward her. She sidestepped quickly, just as another white beam from the tentacle mass cut the air where her head had just been.

She dodged and weaved, running back on her path in a staggered pattern. White columns of light flashed about her as she moved, panic curling into her mind like the roots of some hideous tree. She fought it back, firing her handcannon randomly now, trying somehow to frighten the things away from her, to keep them at bay. Still, they closed on her, the circle about her tightening. It was hard to breathe. Her lungs were raw as she turned again to fire.

The light caught her face.

Suddenly the world changed about her. Her vision flipped crazily. She saw herself. She vaguely knew that many in her clan told tales of people who had nearly died and claimed to have seen their body left behind them as they went on to the great spirit. Was this death? Where would she go? She thought of her father and wondered if his spirit was too far from her to find it again. She suddenly saw her father and his entire life playing before her, around her, through her. She was with him, she was him, and all he had ever said to her raged through her mind, being replayed, and listened to, watched and experienced by ... by ...

By the creatures, she knew. They were taking her mind.

She raged and rebelled, but strand by strand her thoughts were being taken and her mind was being violated. Not just her thoughts, but everything her father had taught her, and she knew that he was somehow being violated too. She would have wept, but the tears belonged to another body and so she had even that comfort taken from her.

She floated again on the seas of her world. The wind rushed about her, spraying the salty mist from the bow into her hair. Dolphins played about the bow wave. The sun shone warm on her body. It was the joy of freedom she had once enjoyed. It was the time of innocence when all was right, and there was no fear or hate to consume her spirit.

And they were taking that from her too.

A huge creature came up from the stern, tearing the waves behind her. It leaped over the stern railing and suddenly, for a moment, became her father with outstretched arms. She reached up for him.

"Pampa," she said innocently. "I've tried to be good. Please help me."

Her father took her arms as she fell out of the sunlight. She fell upward toward the open mouth of the great fish, pulled by her father's powerful arms. He turned his head back and shouted into the depths of the leviathan.

"Now, Ordina! We've got her! Get us the *Hesth* out of here!"

The zombie ship rolled abruptly. Serg still held Thyne with both arms, while Genni tried desperately to steady him. The delver lost his footing in the abrupt spin, and the three of them tumbled free against the side of the creature's throat. Serg scrambled for a handhold amid a mass of slick, leathery tentacles. The world outside the gaping opening next to them whirled sickeningly as the ship corkscrewed into a vertical position and shot skyward.

The iris opening slammed shut as the ship accelerated. Serg held Thyne with a single arm, desperately groping with his free hand for a hold somewhere in the tentacles that lined the interior of the opening. His hand twisted into the slick, cold flesh. Tightening his grasp on the unconscious Thyne, Serg looked across to Genni and saw a rather pale face. As one, both of them looked down.

The horizontal ribbed corridor that had once been behind them had suddenly turned into a vertical shaft over which the three of them now painfully hung. The impression that this was the beast's throat was now complete. It yawned open, beckoning them below.

"Hold on, Genni!" Serg cried. "Don't look down."

Genni continued to stare downward. "It's a little late for that, don't you think? *Josth*, Serg, we must be doing better than a gravity in acceleration! If we fall forty feet to that back wall—"

"No! Genni, just . . . just . . . *dran!*"

Serg's own handhold was giving way. The slick tentacles offered little resistance. The throat yawned open below him.

Suddenly Serg held very still.

"Serg!" Genni's voice was hoarse. "Let the Loyalist go! You can hang on—she's finished anyway and . . ."

"NO!"

"*Dran,* Captain, you can't save her. She was hit by that light—you saw it! Her brains have got to be little more than vegetable broth by now. You can't do anything for her, but you can save . . ."

The look Serg gave him froze his blood, but the delver continued on.

"*Dran,* Serg, it isn't going to bring those kids back."

"*Dran* you, Genni! *Dran* you and all of you to *Hesth*! I don't need your *frasith* forgiveness or your—"

With a sickening sound, his hold gave way. In the moment, he plunged into the waiting darkness below, still holding Thyne.

The darkness engulfed him, as, Serg thought fleetingly, it always had since that day.

He could still smell the clean bridge on which he had walked. Pax ships were usually well-ordered affairs, but he had taken great pride in the *Scylan*. It was his second ship but his first flagship. The fleet under his command as a Tribune Exemplar of House Cantra was arrayed about him with equal order. Order was, as Serg understood it, a philosophy whose trademark was owned by the Pax.

The outreach mission they were pursuing was a part of that policy of establishing law and civilization wherever they went. They had made numerous contacts with new worlds and cultures but were becoming increasingly aware of a pocket empire coreward of the Haven States that appeared both enigmatic and worrisome. Inhabited worlds became more and more infrequent, eventually disappearing completely as they moved down the Fourth Arm of the Galaxy.

Worse yet had been the silence from his own scout ships. Not a single one had returned to report. Under Pax policy, as representative of the Imperium, he would then be required to perform a reconnaissance in force followed by the bulk of the fleet. As per his orders and those of the established protocols for the Pax, his fleet rearranged itself into its new pattern and spun down a heavy darkwind spur into the stellar system in question.

The lead echelon moved into the system first, passing the outer planets without incident. Serg had ordered the bulk of the fleet to follow and take up a disbursed observation pattern to examine the system and its planets more efficiently. The lead groups continued their penetration of the system.

Then *Hesth* itself broke loose throughout the group.

The Oyunth, star-faring natives of the system, appeared suddenly in swarms of ships from the inner asteroid belt. They pounced on the lead grouping, encasing it in a spherical maneuver before the Pax scouts could turn, let alone regroup. As Serg watch in horror, two of the ship's keels were suddenly ripped open, their silverfire wrenching free before turning suddenly on their previous host and obliterating it in a chaotic flash.

"Localyte! Signal the other ships to form on us! No, belay that order!" He thought furiously for a moment. "Tell them each to attack independently around the periphery of those ships. Two of us can play the game of spheres, after all."

The bulk of the fleet opened sails as one, their silverfire trails forming great rainbows in the darkness. From their hemispherical observation positions, their attack hit the Oyunth defense boats from all sides, distracting them from their more immediate prey. They turned outward.

In moments the battle was joined. Iridescent rods shot in parallel bands from the Pax main cannons in raging broadsides, splintering hull sections from the sides of the Oyunth ships. Strange blue tongues of flame erupted from the Oyunth in return fire. Where they touched, superstructures shattered and erupted into flame on the Pax ships.

"Pol, what are they using?"

"The diviners are working on it now, Captain."

"Bring it to me as soon as we know, delver."

"*Allai*, Captain."

Serg half turned to his Localyte. "Stay with me, holy one, or we may yet lose this one." He turned to the Altar of Seeing and touched its carved surface after the pattern he had been taught. Above it, a glowing globe appeared with his own ship mirrored in ghostly image floating at its center. He expanded his vision slightly to encompass the ships around him. Already they were disbursing into their own hemisphere pattern, cupping around the myriad ships that had risen to attack them.

"Sire, the diviners have some answers for you."

"As you wish, Master Vidra."

"Sire, the ships we are engaging come from the second and fourth planets of the system. They are individually approximately four times the size of our capital ships by volume and five times by mass."

The ship suddenly staggered under an impact. Serg held fast to the altar until the keel settled beneath them.

"Anything else, Master Vidra?"

"Sire, they are entirely technological in nature. They are firing what appear to be magnetically jacketed streams of anti-protons and anti-electrons. There is no trace of the silverfire nor its use in any of the opposing ships."

Serg smiled to himself. "Then I rather think we have a chance against them, Pol." He turned to his Localyte. "Instruct the fleet to maintain distance from the home world. I don't want their civilization below disrupted just because some hero up here wishes to make a name for himself by being blown to atoms."

Serg stood with legs wide apart on the bridge, eyeing critically the great globe that hung before him. There was the battle arrayed before him floating above the Altar of Sight. At a gesture he turned the globe moving his vantage point in and out of the battle, examining it from all sides. The Localyte at his side stood ready at each moment to will the directions of the fleet commander to the others of his brotherhood set on similar bridges throughout the fleet. Satisfied with the course of events, Serg pulled back a cupped hand to get a larger perspective on the battle. The numerous individual defense ships that had floated like lightning flies before fell back into a cloudy mist as the perspective changed. So intent was he on the conquest of the enemy that he had forgotten about the original lead group that had previously been surrounded.

He blinked.

"Genni, what do you make of this? What is that?"

His aide moved beside him to look into the great sphere. "Where?"

"Here, downspur toward the planet." Serg gestured.

"Is that Sewar's Echelon?"

"Where does he think he's going?"

Echelon Tribune Erendrith had been chosen for the mission because of their leader, Windcaptain Sewin. Windcaptain Sewin was a tenacious if not particularly clever man who lived by the rules of the Pax. There wasn't a procedure or guideline that he didn't know or follow. He was ultimately predictable—he never varied from his routine or the mission profile orders when it came to that. He was a tall man with a rather ferretlike face, awkward but imposing. His small eyes could cut steel with a look, so his delvers always said. It was his often-stated opinion that creativity was the excuse others used for their lack of commitment.

His orders were to take his echelon into the heart of the system, discover the home world of the Oyunth, and prepare for the coming of the fleet. Granted, the attack by the system defense ships had been somewhat of a surprise, but he had responded, characteristically, by deferring to the Standing Operational Orders and taken a defensive position.

However, the enemy disengaged his smaller group to take on the larger fleet. This left Windcaptain Sewin with a dilemma as to what he should do next. It was fairly obvious to him that the fleet would be victorious without his further intervention.

And so he continued on, tacking his ship with the darkwind and spinning her down directly toward the home world of the Oyunth.

Even as Serg watched, the milky mist of the Oyunth attack formation collapsed suddenly toward the planet.

"Localyte!" Serg yelled. "Contact Windcaptain Sewin! Instruct him to move to . . . to . . . *dran,* where's that system chart . . . instruct him and his ships to take hard into the 427 spur and ride it high out of the system. Get him away from that planet!"

The mists condensed into a funnel, its point driving toward Sewin's position—with the planet directly beyond.

"Any contact with Sewin?" Serg barked.

"Sire, Windcaptain Sewin sends his compliments . . ."

"Get on with it!"

". . . and states that he will comply as soon as conditions warrant. He states that he is currently under attack and cannot comply."

Serg turned back to the globe.

"Pol, how large did you say those things are?"

"About four times the size of our largest ships."

"Right, and about five times our mass. You said they're firing jacketed anti-protons as their primary weapons system?"

Pol nodded.

"Then they're carrying jacketed antimatter as their weapon source if not their primary power." Serg went white.

"Sire?"

"Genni! Hard open all sails! Helmsman, ride the darkwind full downspur! We've got to get between this fleet and the planet!"

The ship surged forward suddenly. The stars shifted about the bridge.

"Genni, you know Sewin. What will he do?"

"He'll follow standard attack procedure."

"And what is that?"

"Fire on approaching enemy with the intent to disable."

"Correct and right out of the book." Serg looked up again at the globe and took a shuddering breath. His own ship was passing the lines of the Oyunth defenders, several of whom were so surprised to see a Pax ship moving in their same direction that their few shots fell wide. "And if Sewin disables these huge ships as they run full speed into their own gravity well?"

"Well, the ships will fall uncontrolled into the atmosphere and . . ." Pol faltered.

"And each of them will break up, releasing their jacketed antimatter streams high above the surface—about ten to twenty kilometers, I presume, considering the size of those ships."

"Lor Amsha!" Pol murmured.

"Localyte! Contact Sewin! Tell him that under no circumstances is he to open fire upon incoming enemy vessels. I personally order him as Tribune Exemplar of the Pax to—"

"Captain, look!"

The great planet hung as a blue crescent now, nearly filling his vision. Against its night backdrop he could almost make out the ten ships of Sewin's echelon . . . and the brilliant blue beams as they fired their first coordinated salvo.

"Localyte! Tell him to stop! Now! Tell him to . . ."

Already the glittering tumble of titanic hulks began to glow red in the night sky below. The Localyte finally connected with Windcaptain Sewin and dutifully his guns were silenced.

An eternity lapsed as Serg traced the glowing lines across the dark side of the world until he had almost begun to hope. Until there might have been a chance. Until . .

Two dozen suns erupted one after the other across the night face of the world.

Serg stood in what had been a courtyard and gazed fixed into the nursery. The Oyunth cared for their communities as related clans, each town raising its youth in community centers that were social gathering places and bonding locations for extended families. Even in the mountain communities such as the one where Serg stood, a sense of social belonging was evident in the layout of the town—concentric streets around the common park and nursery.

The nursery was collapsed, as were all the other buildings so far as he could see. Beyond the rubble of the central township, the mountainside fell sharply away to the great western plains.

He looked up for a moment with closed eyes and tried to imagine what it might have been like to stand in that commons on a summer night and look down onto that plain. There was a city that would have blazed with light and life there, streams of light from the ground conveyances that shuttled across the world. He heard the echoing laughter of a dozen families all bound together by their common heritage, history, and joy. Visions of the living Oyunth cascaded around him like ghosts.

He opened his eyes. The nightmare remained. The overpressure of the nuclear explosion high above the nearby plain had crushed the structures as though some enormous hand had fallen from the sky. The city was no more. Its culture and its dreams had now disappeared forever.

So, too, had disappeared the children whose broken bodies were scattered through the nursery rubble like carelessly discarded dolls. He had thought he had seen one move and frantically pulled the rubble aside. An unseen rodent was tugging on the arm of the child. Serg screamed, frightening the creature clear of the lifeless body. He drew his handcannon and obliterated the creature in several needless shots.

He was still holding the body of the child when Pol found him.

42

Into the Night

~~~~~~~~~~

"Now, Ordina, We've got her! Get us the Hesth *out of here!"*

"Hold on!" Ordina cried as the ship jerked upward into a spiral. The iris at the front of their compartment suddenly slammed shut. She could hear the air rushing around the outer plates with an alarming roar. *"Dran,"* she muttered to herself, "it's working!"

The Altars in Exile remained in place, lashed to the exposed framework of the probe. The conduits for the altars she had carefully woven made their way through a makeshift maze of lashing cables and ribbing lines between the altars themselves and the connecting points Djan had shown her. There the conduits terminated either in exposed access areas or in the tentacle mass at the back of the compartment.

The rigging for the crew was a marvel, for it was of classic Thrund design. Original Thrund ships had no gravity or any really accurate inertia compensation—consequently, their race had devised internal rigging designs that allowed them both ease of movement and protection during flight. Hruna had not lost the art of it, for the rigging she had laid out in the compartment was ingenious. It would work well for Thrunds but its effect on humans remained to be seen. There was a ball-like structure in the center of the compartment suspended to the eight corners of the room with special cabled knots that allowed the central "cage" to absorb motions of the ship around it. Hruna had even woven special harnesses to the altars so that Ordina, Tsara, Djan, and Trevis could all remain at their stations. One final harness was made for Krith, the huge man's body holding firmly to the Altar of Knowledge while his mind was deep within the silverfire.

The great roaring outside increased.

Ordina twisted in her acceleration harness to look into the face of the Localyte. He was pale and wide-eyed, welded to the Altar of Communion before him, it seemed, by his bone-white hands as his legs, with a mind of their own, sought some hold in a world turned suddenly on its side.

"Trevis! Tell her to slow this thing down!" The shipwright's words were unnoticed by the young cleric. "Hey, Localyte! Snap out of it!"

At the word "snap," he turned toward her with a jerk. "Where are we going?" he screamed.

"Dran!" She reached down slowly through the acceleration rigging, taking hold of the sorcerer's arm as he swayed in his own harness next to her. "Djan! Can we see out of this creature?"

"I don't know," came the sepulcher reply.

"Hesth and *dran*, you worthless sorcerer!" She took a huge breath, pushed away images of their newly revived craft rushing toward a solid wall, and turned to Djan to try another tack. "Sorcerer, does the probe have eyes?"

"The probe has a full-spectrum imaging system that translates a complete dimensional representation of its surroundings to—"

"Stop!" She was gratified that the command seemed to halt the continuation of his explanation. "Where are we now?"

"We are suspended in the main specimen chamber of the Arch'tra probe located just aft of the access shaft—"

"Stop! Is there a—*dran*, what did you just call it—ah, imaging system in the, er, specimen chamber?"

"There is an imaging system in the specimen chamber that is used to create false representations of more familiar surroundings. These images are used to extract information from the—"

"Stop! No, not the *dran* shadows they've been fooling us with, I mean—wait! Is it possible to reroute the eyes of the drone to the imaging system of the specimen chamber?"

Djan's eyes were turned toward her, but they remained unfocused on her features. "Yes, there is optical fiber that is rerouted through its neural trunk that is often used to conduct dimensional imaging directly into the specimen chamber. It requires a sequence coding of . . . of . . ."

Ordina shook the sorcerer. "Don't freeze up on me now!"

". . . of seven combinations of numbers transmitted in sequence through the eighty-fifth neural buss of the main optic trunk. The sequence is . . ."

"Hold!" She turned to the Localyte. His hands remained riveted to the altar. The sweat pouring from his forehead was a dead giveaway of the strain he was under. "Localyte! See what Djan sees and pass it down into the mind of the girl."

Trevis shook visibly. "This is obscene! I'm linked with the mind of a dead woman! It's against the Jezerinthian Codes to go running about other people's thoughts as though we were in some kind of . . . of . . . amusement!"

"Boy, if you don't do this, we'll be running into something a lot more solid than an amusement! The sound outside is getting softer; that means the air is thinning out! We're *inside* one of these Arch'tra ships and soon we'll find the wall if we can't SEE it first! Now, SEE WHAT THIS MAN SEES AND MAKE IT HAPPEN! NOW!"

Trevis blinked hard once, then screwed his eyes shut.

In an instant the specimen chamber around them and, indeed, the entire Arch'tra drone vanished.

The imaging system in the specimen chamber was designed to fool captured sentients into believing that they were elsewhere. As such, it represented everything holographically in a projection that completely surrounded the specimen. The probe's "eyes" were also full-spectrum imagers that gathered information in a similar holographic way. They were a perfect match—too perfect.

To Ordina and the rest of the crew, it looked as though the Bioprobe had disappeared. It seemed as though they were all suddenly hurtling skyward in a net suspended from thin air.

Ordina's scream was involuntary, and she quickly choked it off. *What a view!* she thought. She looked behind her. The rigging hurtled higher above the plain they had just left. Directly below them, several Bioprobes were following them, vapor trails rippling behind them. They were closing quickly. Ordina felt suddenly completely exposed in their flying net which appeared to be attached to nothing at all. She looked up and—

"Stop!" she yelled at Trevis. "Stop the boat!"

Through the thinning air, a massive wall of steel gray stretched into infinity directly in their path, solid and formidable. Ordina twisted in the rigging from the sudden deceleration, hanging, it seemed, momentarily upside down. Several delvers tumbled free of the rigging, spinning into the open air, slamming hard against the seemingly invisible forward bulkhead.

"Now, THAT'S imaging," Ordina murmured. Below her, the foremost of the drones suddenly leaped much closer. Beyond them what first seemed like a gray cloud but now appeared to be countless more of the drones were rising up to meet them.

She turned back to the Localyte. His eyes remained tightly slammed shut. She spoke just loud enough to be heard over the shouts of the delvers around her. "Brother Fel, turn the ship ninety degrees to port and . . ."

"Can I open my eyes now?" he whimpered.

The drones were slowing, closing to within a hundred yards of them.

"Ah, no, not just yet. Have the girl drift the ship slowly ninety degrees to port and—"

"That's to the right, isn't it?"

"Uh, sure, fine. Have her drift ninety degrees to the right very slowly. Then I want you to have her get ready to move very, very fast."

The great wall turned slowly away from them. The seven drones nearest them were moving slowly—unsure of their suddenly stopped quarry. They moved to encircle it again, tighter now so that it wouldn't escape them.

"NOW!" Ordina yelled in his face. "NOW, OR WE'RE AS DEAD AS THE VOID! GO! GO! GO!"

The wall suddenly rushed past them. Images of steel, muscle, and veins sped past them in a blur. The pursuit probes were a moment in realizing what had happened, but the moment was enough. They soared below the ceiling of the enclosure.

Ordina yelled in joy. To make it happen! To make it work! And, oh, to fight and live! She was no longer a victim of the faceless unknown. She had conquered them!

Suddenly her face fell. Four more of the creatures bobbed directly in her path. She felt the numbers climbing and the odds dropping. There had to be something they could fight back with. There just had to be something.

"Localyte! We need something . . . Localyte?"

The young man's eyes were wide—locked in fear.

"*Lor Amsha!* Ordina!" Krith yelled to the seething sky, "Get me the *Hesth* out of here!"

His huge arms were wrapped around the mast. The golden deck bucked violently beneath his feet. The starlight sails were secured to the crosstree, battened down against the fury of the storm. They rippled angrily against their moorings, straining against the gossamer filaments of her standing rigging. A rain of thick, warm blood, driven by the howling winds, swept the decks crimson, only to be followed by sobbing tears that washed everything clean once more. The surface of the sea, frothed and wicked, formed a sphere around the ship, threatening to engulf him given any opportunity.

Krith turned again to look back at Snap. She held to the helm tightly, yet the look on her face was nearly one of rapture. She had seen her promised land in her mind and was making that final journey into the arms of the Nightmother. She had attained the utmost in salvation, the greatest glory that her people could conceive. Nothing would stop her.

Krith looked away and hated himself.

It had started as a simple game, just to please the shipwright. He'd certainly never expected to find a comrade's spirit trapped inside the *Hesth* of the silverfire.

Now things had decidedly gone too far. Snap was so innocent and decent. She'd always needed looking after and he had considered it his duty to see to her. He had always liked that innocence in her, that wild and wide-eyed belief that anything was possible for her and that death was something that happened only to bad people—or far, far away.

Then they had used her. They were using her. Snap's faith was the tool they had used to resurrect another dead thing—the Arch'tra probe ship—just to keep their own miserable existence continuing. He wondered if they were saving their lives just to lose their souls.

Trevis was racked with misery. The union that he had been coerced into making with the sorcerer—morally repugnant as it was—was little more than an inconvenience compared to what he was enduring in the mind of a woman younger than himself who was many days dead.

His talents and his training were all directed toward the service of the Jezerinthian Localytes to the Farcardinals of the church. They walked the minds of the Farcardinals as guests—invited and welcome to further the ends of the church and the empire at large. Such intrusions—shallow as they were—were always with willing participants. The Jezerinthian Codes—established from the very birth of their order—prohibited contact with those outside the church as being both morally and ethically abhorrent.

Yet it was this very thing that he had been coerced into doing. It had been necessary to link with the mind of this Emilithia woman, using Krith as a guide to the center of her mind. He had managed to establish a link, but now the woman thought that his voice was some sort of spiritual source of inspiration. True, he had thus been able to establish direct contact between the dead woman and the real world. It had allowed a good part of the silverfire power to be restored and helped the shipwright to establish links into the dead hulk of the machine-thing.

Yet it was getting out of hand. He was no warrior. He was no commander. Now he found himself at the center of all that was happening, asked to walk the minds of innocents and manipulate their understanding so that they might, somehow, escape from their enemy. The laws of survival and his faith collided within him, waging war on his soul that he had neither the time nor the ability to fight.

So it was, as he contemplated his own misery, that he suddenly was aware of the menace to his existence. Four dark shapes looming up to steal from him all that he was or ever was or might ever be. In that moment he panicked, instinctively reacting to the fear of this most terrible prospect. Without conscious thought he reached into the mind of the sorcerer, found what he needed, and used it.

"Krith!" Snap shouted above the wind. "How passengers? They fine?"

"Er, ah, *Allai,* Captain," he shouted without much conviction as he gazed down into the hold. Snap had insisted that they take along as many of her "dead subjects" as could fit in the hold in

an effort to save their souls as well. She was about to make the
ship larger to accommodate them all, when the huge delver had
convinced her that it might anger the gods. "They be doin' fine,
though I suspect that some of 'em are a bit sick, even for them."
He wondered vaguely if zombies had any breakfast to lose and
decided that he really didn't want to know.

"*Allai*, Master Krith. It not long now. Me can see way to
promised home."

A hundred blue arms reached out from the white-capped
waves about him, groping for the deck with long fingernails. In
an instant they were set upon by howling, slashing teeth which
dragged them back into the waves.

The ship heeled over violently, its crystal oars bending against
the tossing waves. The waters washed the deck, its slender fingers wrapping around Krith's ankles, stroking them, beckoning
him to come back with them.

The ship suddenly bounced in the water, slewing around as
Snap leaned hard against the tiller.

"We under attack, Krith!"

"What? Again?"

"*Allai*, Krith! Daemons closing in on us from the darkness.
Them not want Snap soul-saved. Not worry! Snap save everyone.
Gun crew already on deck."

Krith groaned as he turned to face the forecastle. Snap's gun
crew had been hastily assembled a few minutes before. They had
seen far better days. Their flesh fell in wet globs from their bodies no matter how carefully they moved. Several were little more
than skeletons, as it were. Others occasionally had to stop to pick
up an arm or leg that had fallen carelessly from the main of their
bodies. They looked embarrassed each time they had to do this.
However, Snap had given them sharp new uniforms of red and
gold which effected both an increase in morale and assisted in
keeping them somewhat together as they moved.

The ship suddenly righted itself in the storm. The forward
cannon, now manned by the gun crew, swiveled around and discharged repeatedly into the raging sea that encased them.

Thunder shivered through Trevis as he aimed the weapon of
their Bioprobe and discharged it. He saw the first of the great
curled monsters suddenly explode into black blood, steel plates,
and torn muscle. An instant later it collapsed into itself.

Trevis was aware of the Alter of Knowledge and his own blood oozing between the bone-white fingers gripping its edges. His eyes were wide and locked. His mouth worked continuously, making sound without words, words without meaning. The world rotated around them, around him. Yet he was also aware of ever so much more.

The thunder of the gravity weapon he now commanded became a mountainous staccato, wave after wave of pounding sound beating one on top of the other without relief. His enemy—as now the pursuing Bioprobes had truly become—fired back with carefully placed shots. Yet the Localyte had lost himself into his own instinct, merging in the moment as one with the knowledge of the mindless sorcerer and the power of a dead girl. He *was* the ship and the ship was him. He could feel it dying around him as part by part it continued to succumb to the damage it had taken so long ago at the hands of the Loyalists. He could reach out and touch its extremes. It opened to him and his will. He bucked and weaved to avoid the shots coming at him, firing his own great spinning singularity whose gravity tore the atomic structure asunder and truly obliterated one's foes. The shots pounded from the uncoiled tentacle below him as though it were his own arm and fist.

The numbers of his foes were increasing rapidly. His shots began falling wild.

He awoke from his frenzy only to hear Ordina murmur, "What have you done?"

Trevis looked forward. In his blind panic he had stuck piercing line of the singularity upward, directly into the great wall overhead. The metal and tissue of the wall puckered inward with a terrible wrenching sound, twisting in on itself. The gravity weapon was drawing more and more power from the silverfire core—the core giving it whatever it demanded to destroy the wall.

The Arch'tra pursuing probes had backed away, circling like pack animals around their suddenly dangerous prey. Yet they suspected that now was their opportunity. Again they moved closer, now completely encasing the desperate quarry. The soft light disappeared, dropping them into darkness.

Stinging pain across his face suddenly shocked Trevis back to himself.

"Let go, *dran* you!" Ordina screamed. "Turn the weapon off!"

His eyes suddenly focused on her and, by reflex, he obeyed.

The hull of the Arch'tra ship, no longer straining against the singularity, suddenly ripped open into a huge gash. In an instant the explosive decompression of the compartment tumbled the Bioprobe and its host of pursuers into open space.

43

Dance with the Daemons

———◦✦◦———

Ordina was pressed hard against the nonexistent wall of the specimen chamber. Impressions bounced into her mind of stars wheeling about her and a huge blackness filling half the sky.

The Arch'tra mothership, Ordina realized. *We have escaped!*

In an instant the stars steadied. Sudden explosions erupted all around her among the stars, illuminating a swarm of alien probes dancing around them in the darkness.

The shipwright turned to issue orders through the Localyte. She opened her mouth but stopped short of making a sound.

The acceleration harness continued to hold the limp young Localyte. His hands had fallen loosely at his side—no longer in touch with the Altar of Communion in Exile. He was either dead or unconscious, and either way there was little she could do.

They had lost contact. There was no way to communicate with the world of Snap. Without Snap they had lost control of the probe.

She had run out of ideas.

"Where the *Hesth* is the captain!" she called.

• • •

"Daemons too many, Krith. Snap run for it."

Two of the starboard oars suddenly snapped, calling Krith's attention sharply toward the sound.

"That ain't supposed to happen," he murmured.

As Ordina had explained it to him, this Neffi ship he was riding on was some sort of manifestation of the real ship they were on. The oars were silverfire filaments controlling movement, he'd gathered. The tiller accessed directional control. The cannon—maybe some kind of weapon like the godless thing he'd seen destroy his shipmates. If parts of this nightmare ship were coming off, then . . .

"Captain!" His normally deep voice broke to a squeak as he cried out. "I think we be takin' damage from them daemons o' yours!"

"No daemons. Daemons at bay, circling around to capture Snap soul. Ship dying," she said casually.

"We ain't takin' damage?"

"Krith not pay attention." Snap blinked, a look of worry crossing her bright eyes. "Ship not just wood; ship part alive. Parts alive now dying. Snap hurry or never make promised home."

Krith suddenly remembered the Arch'tra probe ship. They had killed the brain that had effectively brought down the ship and allowed them to use it. Yet, Ordina had said that much of the ship was a blend of machines and living things. If those living things died off, then the ship would stop functioning—wherever it was they were now. His stomach suddenly felt hollow.

"Snap not leave now. Snap not survive trip to promised home!"

The slender girl pressed with all her might against the tiller at the back of the ship. The Neffi groaned under the load, the aft end leaning in against the turn. Krith had the sudden impression that the ship had spun to point straight down. The wind screamed through the delver's ears.

"Master Krith!" Snap's voice carried calmly over the gale. "Unfurl the sails!"

"*Lor!* No, Snap!" Krith twisted his head back to look at her. "You set them sails in this blow and we'll lose the mast sure as—"

As he spoke, the starlight sails suddenly released from the yard overhead and snapped open in the gale, straining the stays at once. The ship surged forward against the waves.

"Me see home, Krith!"

Krith shouted again into the storm. "Ordina! What in the name of *Amsha* are ye doing!"

"This is IT, everyone!" Ordina called out. "Hang on!"

The stars spun wildly again, their glory becoming increasingly diminished by the growing specks of black around them. Again, they were being encircled.

They'll be careful this time, Ordina thought. They'll take us apart bolt by bolt until they have us and steal our thoughts. She took in a shuddering breath.

A low throbbing hum reverberated through the cabin, gaining in intensity and strength as she listened. Soon its vibrations were shaking the rigging itself. The Altars in Exile danced in their places.

In an instant, the sound exploded into a cacophony tumbling around them like a waterfall. The stars around them fore and aft compressed in a moment into a single rainbow band of light. Ordina's jaw dropped in awestruck wonder. It was one of the most beautiful sights she had ever seen, for the band was not entirely featureless. At the forward edge she could see points of light suddenly springing into existence in brilliant violets before joining the great glowing ring. Trailing the ring, other points would fall away, drifting from red into nothingness. The huge mothership and the pursuing probes had disappeared behind them.

"Lor Amsha!" she whispered in awe. "Those are stars! What speeds must we be making?!"

Just as quickly, the great rainbow band around them suddenly expanded again into the familiar stars against the black velvet night. Ordina knew that the sky had again changed and that they would need to figure out all over again where they were. Yet these thoughts were suddenly banished from her mind. Tears welled up unbidden and spilled down her cheeks at a sight she had never hoped to see again.

A brilliant star, so close now that its sphere could have been distinguished, cast its rays on a world that drifted below them. In a moment, through her watery vision she took in the continents and oceans, the blue horizon and the towering white clouds. It was a home. It was a port in the storm. It was their salvation. They had found a place to rest.

An oval appeared in the middle of the stars. The access throat to their chamber must have been closed earlier. Now that someone had opened it, it interfered with the perfect representation of the invisible ship around them. Genni's face suddenly popped out of the throat—and turned white at what appeared to be the *Shendridan* survivors standing about in completely open space five hundred miles above a world.

Ordina wiped her eyes and laughed. "Hey, Genni, what kind of a delver are you? You look absolutely green. Don't you like the pictures we make here?"

"*Lor,* Ordina, what's going on here?"

She smiled and moved toward him, avoiding the conduits and rigging that remained visible as she walked. "This is an imaging system, I understand. All I wanted was a window, and look what I got."

"Yeah," Genni said, still a little unsure. "Nice view."

"Genni, where's the captain?"

"Here—so's the Loyalist captain. We pulled her out just before you took this thing ballistic. They fell down the throat here. I think there's a couple of broken ribs. Captain's busted his forearm pretty bad. I've got it wrapped, but I think it's gonna need something more than that."

She thought for a moment, then spoke. "Tsara?"

"Yes," came the quick reply.

"Get that sorcerer over here, we need his advice."

Within moments the Temple Priestess freed the wizard from his acceleration harness. Without another word Djan moved toward the oval opening.

"Genni, give me a hand up and then help 'King Personality' back there up as well." Ordina clambered up into the throat.

Serg lay at one side of the tunnel, the bloody wrapping around his crooked forearm lying across his stomach. Genni hovered over him, unsure of what else to do yet wanting somehow to do something. Thyne lay against the other side of the throat, unconscious but breathing.

"The Scepter is thine, Captain," she said, smiling, "although I'm not all that sure it was ever mine to begin with."

Serg smiled weakly. "You may have to hang on to it for a little while longer yet. What happened?"

"We're not entirely sure, Captain. Somehow the gravity weapon was activated and tore a hole in the side of our host ship.

It blew us out into open space." As she spoke, Djan knelt down next to her. "Master Kithber, what should we do to repair this man's arm."

Without a word, Djan skillfully began unwrapping the bandage.

Serg grimaced against the pain. "Go on. You were in open space . . ."

"We lost control of the ship at that point, but apparently Master Krith activated some kind of drive that took us out of danger. Quick as that we found ourselves above a planet—and, oh, Captain, it's beautiful and I believe we can call it port for a while. Long enough to hide out and get ourselves back on our feet again."

There was a snapping sound. Serg's eyes suddenly lost focus and he cried out. Djan began rewrapping the wound.

Ordina waited until Serg spoke again.

"You were surrounded three times by these Arch'tra probes that are in a lot better shape than we are, and yet you weren't destroyed?"

"I don't understand it myself," she said. "They should have taken us out. Why haven't they destroyed us by now ten times over?"

"Because," said the quiet, dull voice beside her, "they believe we have the answer that they are searching for. As they took my mind apart, I lied to them, telling them that the answer they sought was found in someone we had brought with us."

Ordina turned in horror toward the sorcerer. "Do you know what you've done?"

"I don't know."

"*Dran,* they'll never give up on us! Even if we get out of this." She suddenly looked up. "We've got to get out of sight!"

"Lady Ordina!" Hruna's voices chimed a full dissonant chord with an urgency she had never heard from a Thrund before. "Come quickly!"

She turned quickly and looked out the oval access into the image-complete specimen chamber. Her blood turned to ice at a glance. Dropping herself into the chamber, she scrambled through the rigging toward the Altar of Communion, yelling as she moved, "Krith! Let me in!"

An Arch'tra probe floated next to them only ten yards away.

Its steel-blue back plates shone under the light of the nearby star, uncurling as the tentacle mass was revealed.

Ordina grabbed hold of the altar, looking up at the still form of the big man wrapped in the acceleration harness, his eyes closed as though in sleep. If she were where he was, then maybe she could help. They were so close, so close to haven and home. She chanted the communion, but the silverfire would not let her in. Only Krith knew the way. She screamed, "Please, Krith, let me in!"

Five points of light suddenly flashed in the sky nearby. Five more probes appeared.

44

The Golden Shore

LOCATION: NEW COLONIES SECTOR / ARPX15348 / ORBITING
WORLIN 5 ABOARD THE BIOPROBE / INSIDE THE SILVERFIRE

The death-gray waters surrounding the Neffi suddenly abated
into an infinite sea of glass. The stars shone reflected on the
smooth surface across which the Neffi sailed with quiet serenity.
The air was still without a trace of wind. The remaining oars
dipped silently into its surface, making perfect concentric ripples
across the perfect plain. No sound disturbed the peace and tranquillity, save for the gentle padding of bare footsteps across the
deck.

"Krith furl sail with Snap," came the gentle voice. "Krith almost home now with Snap. No sorrow at lost life. Time to move
to next life."

She moved quietly to the halyard and lowered the yard. Krith
dutifully began gathering the sail which felt like the lightest of
silk in his hands, shining softly in his arms. He fastened the stays
almost absentmindedly to the yard, holding the sail in place. The
sudden quiet and peace were shocking to him. He watched in silence as Snap padded over to the ratline and climbed the mast. It
took him a few moments before he could bring himself to speak,
to break the incredible beauty of the silence that had so suddenly
graced them.

"Snap," he said at last, his voice sounding harsh in his own ears. "I think it's time I was leavin'."

Cracking echoed from underfoot. The deck below was suddenly rotting beneath his feet. He stopped and gingerly pulled his foot from the hole it had just made.

Snap stopped and looked down at him with serenity and understanding through the tarred lines. There was a peace in her eyes that made him turn away, ashamed of all that they had lied to her about. He wished desperately and with all his soul that his promises to her of everlasting life would come true, that the Nighthome was there for her and all that she had tried to do for them. He knew, somehow, that he, too, would soon be truly dead and had no hope for further life. He also knew that some great part of him wished that her dreams came true and that there was more to his existence than today's meal and tomorrow's profit.

"Snap, I've got to be tellin' you the truth now, gal." Krith drew a deep breath and made himself continue. " 'Tis true now that ye be dead—and right sorry I am for it. I held you, gal, in my arms when you went and, *Lor,* how I wished it had been me 'stead o' you there. I'd 'ave given my soul then just to see you smile and walk and chatter on and . . . oh, *Lor,* Snap, I ain't fathomed why you had to go and die like that, but you did, *dran* the night, and there weren't nothin' I could do about it."

Snap continued to look at him, her eyebrows forming questions over her piercing brown eyes. "Krith, why do you make with such speech, we are almost to Nighthome."

"No, Snap, yer just not followin' my line. This ain't the truth, none of it is. There ain't no Nighthome and Amsha ain't waitin' for us on the other side o' this pond. This is a lie and a dream you've made for yourself and, *Lor* help me, I've been here helping you believe it."

"Oh! Krith just mean that Snap is inside the silverfire," she said calmly with a slight smile.

"*Allai,* I mean the . . . Snap? *You know?!*"

Snap swung down from the ratlines and landed softly on the deck before him. "Krith such big man. Krith always protect Snap. Keep Snap alive. Always know what to do when Snap mouth get too big. Snap not stupid. Snap always know what was real and what was not."

She took his hand like a child, leading him forward. Two of the mainmast backstays suddenly snapped, their lines coiling snakelike into the sky. The mast shifted as they walked along the creaking deck. The water continued to slide quietly by as they moved toward the foredeck and the short ladder up to the forecastle and looked up into the velvet sky.

"The Bioprobe is dying. We have not much time. Snap always grateful to Krith. Snap loves Krith for what Krith tried do. Now is time for Snap to say farewell. Snap is almost home."

Krith looked down at her with love for the child and pain for the truth. He softly placed his hand on hers and turned to look down at her.

"Snap, my gal, I'm trying to give it to you square. There ain't no Nighthome."

Snap climbed the short ladder, still holding the delver's huge hand inside her own fragile free hand. He followed her unquestioningly upward.

"Krith not understand. Silverfire temples not understand. Ship priestess not understand. Silverfire chaos touch many worlds, many times, many creations. Silverfire not a tool of Pax. That all mixed up backward. Truth is other way around. Silverfire touch the spirit creation. Silverfire touch afterlife and before-life." She stopped them both on the forecastle rail and gestured past the bow. "See, Krith. Nighthome."

On the horizon off to their right, dawn suddenly sprang into being. Silhouetted against its morning light, towers sprang skyward from the thin line of a golden shore. The grace of the buildings struck awe in his heart and joy in his soul. He yearned for it as one waking from a deep sleep and remembering suddenly that he was home.

"Krith," Snap whispered to him. "These are last waters we cross. Neffi ship dying and Bioprobe dying. Snap can hold both together until we reach shore with silverfire magic. Snap cannot both pilot ship and hold bucket together." She looked up at him with her eyes wide. "Krith, pilot our ship to Nighthome."

He looked down on her with tears in his eyes and whispered down to her. "Snap, love, I don't believe in Nighthome."

She smiled knowingly at him. "Snap believes in Nighthome. Not needful that Krith believe. Only needful that Krith believe in Snap."

He gazed into the shining, bright face. She knew. She knew where she was and why she was. And something else. There was something more that she saw—saw beyond what he could see.

He knew, somehow, that this lovely, placid lake and the shining shore was something Ordina had cooked up. More than likely it was a way for her to trap Snap's spirit or mind or whatever it was that existed there to rid her of her precious silverfire forever. And wasn't that only reasonable and just to Snap, he thought. This was no life, no real existence for the little spirit who had been so free in life. If he were to send her off, best that he should send her as she would go—willingly and joyfully.

"*Allai,* Captain!" he said as he kissed her on the forehead. He suddenly sprang down the ladder, breaking several rungs on the way. The ship was falling apart beneath him. He moved gingerly aft to the tiller. Somehow he didn't feel his great mass and bulk as he moved. His heart had buoyed him up, his smile carrying him nearly weightlessly aft. He shouted with joy. "Give me yer course, Captain, and I'll bring yer home!"

Serg struggled back through the oval opening, his eyes sadly resigned to their obvious fate. They had come so close. The world hung above them now as they slowly spun in orbit, a siren whose song they would all too willingly answer if they could. It seemed to them that they could almost reach upward and touch the brilliant blue surface that promised shelter, freedom, and peace.

It was a peace they would never reach. The sky was alive with light. As he watched, a dozen miniature suns flashed into momentary existence. Arch'tra ships, unimaginably huge, fell from their light.

Serg gazed down at the shipwright. Floating in the illusionary chamber, Ordina clung to the Altar of Communion, sobbing. Behind it, the huge delver—he remembered his name as Krith—stood straight as a statue in his harness, his eyes closed in the reverie of the silverfire. Momentarily, the image of the Temple Priestess pleading in earnest supplication to her towering idol crossed Serg's mind. He knew at that moment that they had lost control of the Bioprobe.

Serg sighed. He gazed at the few survivors of the once-promising crew. He saw all their faces before him—more ghosts to add to the many that still haunted him. Soon, they, too, would be gone—and he would have failed them as he had failed so many other lives in his hands.

He glanced down at the Loyalist captain. At least she was unconscious. The end would come in the quiet night of her mind and she would not know the regrets and failure that he felt. He envied her that.

He closed his eyes and longed for home. He had lived so many years among the stars that he did not even know where such a place might be. Where could he go to soothe his wounds and calm his soul? He had fled from himself and his ghosts into the night. He had searched for that halcyon shore with every port. Now he thought his soul already too scarred and too long-lived to even remember what tranquillity was like. He closed his eyes, not knowing if such a place could even be.

His eyes stung with regret and remorse.

Take me home, he prayed from the depth of his soul.

"Snap see rough water. Krith steer with heart." Snap turned to face the shore. She smiled to herself as the backstays rewound themselves in shining silver light.

Silently from the water a black shroud rose up directly in their path to tower over them. Faceless, its arms reached out for them.

"Hard a'starboard, Master Krith. This it! This last shore! They not stop Krith! Steer for shore, Krith!"

Krith leaned hard against the tiller. The ship slew across the glassy surface as the golden shore hove to their bow. The ship picked up speed quickly, as though the shore were pulling them toward it.

More shrouds slipped out of the water, drifting toward them with arms outstretched. He ignored them, weaving between them as needed, his mind on the glimmering line against the sunset. The ship's speed continued to increase eagerly, spray flaring over the bows. Snap sang with joy in its showering cascade.

Flame sprang to life about the bow of the ship. Within moments its fire raged blue with its flame, howling around the forecastle where Snap stood, pushing the flames aside as the golden shore came ever closer.

It was time for Snap to go home.

Serg grabbed the suddenly shifting framework of the opening. The Bioprobe had suddenly sprung to life again, spinning about its axis and rushing forward toward . . .

Serg's heart sank. They were plunging directly toward the planet.

There was little point to further action. It would be over soon now. Not a bad way to leave, he thought vaguely. He watched the Arch'tra ships move about around them. *They must also see how hopeless it is,* he thought. *At least my mind is my own. They won't have that.*

The ship buffeted as the atmosphere surrounded them. Soon the howling rose to a deafening crescendo. He could see the sheets of flame and heat grow in front of them and then surround them as they slammed into the atmosphere that had previously called them so enticingly. Metal plate cried under the pressure. He could see flaming parts of the Neffi begin to fall away behind them.

He thought of the survivors in the chamber before him. *Make it quick,* he pleaded to the sky. *Make it quick for them.*

The image flickered suddenly and then died, plunging them into a darkness lit only by the dim glow of the Altar of Communion.

The Arch'tra probes in the Worlin star system—as it had been known to its former inhabitants—recorded the events individually. The data was transferred by courier probe to the lead command elements of the 57,238th Expeditionary Fleet. The data was reviewed, analyzed, reconstructed, and compiled. The results were conclusive.

OPEN MEMORY: At 5 dur 92 sep into jump 1 of the expedition, an Arch'tra probe ship forced its way out of the containment of the 82nd research vessel. It was thought to have been commandeered by one of the five thousand subjects of investigation on that vessel. Prior information indicated that one of the specimen subjects in that containment may have had the information sought by the expedition. The ship then jumped through nonspace. Arch'tra-controlled probes pursued to obtain the desired information. Probe 6782 discovered the commandeered probe in the Worlin stellar system above planet five of that system.

The target had been previously badly damaged in an earlier encounter with the subject specimens, its condition deteriorating rapidly. At 5 dur 182 sep into jump 1, the subject vessel tumbled suddenly and fell toward the planet's atmosphere. Attempts by the pursuit probes to prevent its fall failed. No explanation has been forwarded as to why gravitic attractors failed to lock to target vessel.

At 5 dur 184 sep into jump 1, the external friction heating of exterior hull plates reached critical failure. The subject vessel is determined to have broken up under aerodynamic pressures.

Subject specimens on board were determined to have been destroyed.

Worlin system planet five was previously investigated (See Memory ref: 8108AD/38) and local life-forms uncooperative. Planet sentient life was previously terminated.

No further investigation warranted. END MEMORY.

45

The Arms of Amsha

The flame was intense. Its heat seared his lungs and dried his mouth. The mainmast bowed back toward him, its peak dancing in the flames that engulfed it.

Krith stood determined at the tiller. After all, he thought, what else was there to do? The ship continued to come apart piece by piece. The cannon on the foredeck tore from its mounts, flying backward in a sudden molten state. It sailed past Krith as he dove under the tiller. The bulwark around the deck was shredding into the fire, falling behind them as raging embers into the tranquil sea now devoid of shrouded figures. The tiller even seemed loose to him, and he suspected the rudder was pulling away from the skeg. Stanchions were pulling free, allowing lines to flail backward free. The ship was coming apart under the flames, yet Krith held firm to his tiller—and his purpose.

The light raged before him, screaming its venom. The ship shuddered under his feet. He could barely see the silhouette of Snap, still standing at the forecastle, her arms outstretched. She embraced the fire, taunted it. The light screamed into white fury.

The ship lurched suddenly to a halt as inky blackness exploded around him. Despite his strength, Krith was torn from the tiller. He fell slowly, tumbling through the air like a leaf in a breeze, his movements slow in his mind. It was some time before he landed, softly and quietly, facedown on the softly glowing golden sand.

He lay still for a moment. Absently, he watched his outstretched right hand gather in the moist grains and release them, gather them in and release them again.

The bright laughter brought him out of his reverie.

"Krith, you fun. You arrive on Nighthome shore and all you want do is play with sand."

The huge delver pushed himself over on his back. Over him stood the shining figure of Snap.

"Snap," he rasped. "Are we home?"

"*Allai*, Krith. Snap is home."

"*Lor Amsha!*" he murmured.

The girl frowned and looked away from him. "Snap sorry, Krith. It time for Snap to go."

"Right!" Krith sat up and began brushing the shining sand from his trousers. "Where to now, gal? I suppose you'll be wantin' to visit in town for a while, eh? I'm happy to oblige you. Where are ye wantin' to start?"

Snap looked down shyly at the shore, her brow wrinkled. "I am very sorry. Snap must now go home. Krith must go back now."

He smiled up at her. "Oh, right you are, gal. An' just where are ye thinkin' I'll be going back to?"

"Krith must go back to living."

"Ah, so that be it, then. Tired of playin' with ol' Krith, is it?" He stood up and stretched, amazed that he didn't seem all the worse for having just run an imaginary ship against the shores of the gods. "*Allai*, ma'am. I'll come and see you again soon in your little play-box. Things here in the silverfire ain't so bad once you get use to 'em."

Snap took his hand. He looked down at her puzzled.

"No, Krith. Snap will not be here. Snap is going home."

His face froze. "Snap. This ain't real, gal. This is just some new illusion cooked up by that *dran* shipwright. She's used you, gal, and now she'll be throwin' you away just so's she can get her precious silverfire back."

She shook her head. "Krith not understand."

"No, *Hesth*, girl, it's you that's not understandin'! This ain't real, I tell you." Krith shook his head and decided on another tack. He gazed at the opal towers of the impossibly delicate city beyond the gates. "Snap, 'tis a beautiful place this. I've never hoped to see anything so beautiful. It sings songs to this ol' delver's heart that he feels must have been forgotten. Just don't leave! So long as you're here, there's hope."

The gates swung open. Brilliant light, soft and inviting, sprang from within the portal. In its radiance, a single willowy figure in a flowing gown walked through the air toward them.

"Amsha!" Krith swore under his breath at the sight.

"Allai, Krith," Snap confirmed. " 'Tis *Amsha.*"

She let go his hand.

"Snap! Please, gal!" Krith begged. "Don't . . . don't leave me here."

She turned to him and smiled. "Krith understand soon. This was the only way to save Krith. The only way to save Lady Thyne. The only way to save everything. Be a hero, Krith. You fly the stars. You will come home soon enough."

She turned and walked into the outstretched arms of the Mother of Night. Amsha enfolded her. Krith, gazing from afar, felt the total fulfillment and joy in the embrace. He began to cry, both for the joy that Snap attained and for his lack of it. He felt he was somehow being left behind.

The gates shut and impenetrable darkness fell around him. He felt suddenly dizzy and disoriented. The air grew stifling. Someone was calling to him from a very far place. He couldn't quite hear it. He drifted toward it. Suddenly he knew that the reason he couldn't see was that his eyes were closed. He opened them.

The blur before him suddenly coalesced into the face of the shipwright hovering over him.

"Krith! Can you hear me? Krith, come out of it!"

He closed his eyes again, hot tears squeezing out from under his eyelids. *"Dran* you, Ordina," he muttered.

She smiled, a reaction that rather puzzled him, but then, he thought, he never did understand her.

"That were a lousy trick you played on my mate, you *brethis* shipwright," Krith sniffed. "I'll not be forgivin' you for that one."

Ordina shook her head, not understanding. "What are you talking about?"

"Right after the cannon fire, woman! We set sail and the next thing I know we're riding the calm seas 'round 'bout Nighthome." The anger welled up in him and consciousness returned. He sat up, gathering in her tunic at the shoulders with both huge hands and pulled her face menacingly toward him. His eyes were filled with tears. "Then you go creatin' this faked-up goddess so's to lure my friend out o' yer precious silverfire! She comes waltzing out o' godhome just as pretty as you please and takes my friend to oblivion!"

Ordina trembled. "Krith, what are you saying?"

"I'm saying we used her. We robbed her faith and her hope with lies and illusions!" He shook at the thought, tears streaming down his face. "I'm saying we stole her trust an' then tossed her overboard just so's we could breathe a little longer. She believed, Ordina! You showed her salvation and freedom just to get your precious silverfire back, and she believed it!"

Her eyes steadied on his as she spoke. "Krith, we didn't do it."

"What?" he sobbed. "What?"

"Krith, listen to me." Ordina continued to look through his eyes to his soul as she quietly spoke. "We didn't create that. The Localyte collapsed just after the cannon fire. He hasn't been with you since then. We haven't had any contact with you since we were blown clear of the mothership. Whatever happened in there after the gunfire didn't come from us."

Krith slowly released his grip as he thought. "You're sayin' you didn't make that up."

"*Allai*, Krith."

"The Localyte didn't make it up?"

"He wasn't there then."

"Well, if you didn't make it up, and the Localyte didn't make it up . . ."

"We tried to reach you," Ordina said.

Krith suddenly looked up.

"*Lor Amsha!*" he said, and, for the first time, meant it.

He looked around. They were still in the Bioprobe chamber, where he had started his journey into the illusionary world of the silverfire. It was dark inside with only a single dim lantern lit. Only Ordina and her assistant were there. The others were missing. "Mistress, what happened?"

"You saved us," she said, taking his arm as they walked toward the aperture leading out of the chamber. "You brought us home—well, to this shore, at least. It might end up to be home, though, not that I mind." She looked up at him fondly, wondering if the huge man sensed her setting her trap for him.

"I were no hero, ma'am. It were Snap's doin'. Pardon me, ma'am, but just where are we?"

"Planetside, Krith. We're safely down—for a while, at any rate."

"Planetside? How in *Hesth* did that happen?"

"We're not sure." Ordina smiled. "We were falling planetside pretty fast. The heat from the entry should have blown us apart more than a dozen ways, but somehow the ship held together."

"Held together," he murmured, and shook his head.

"We weren't able to see for a while. Next thing we know we're rolling over in the tops of trees. We set down hard, settling into the bottom of a deep forest. Everyone made it though."

"We reached the shore." Krith smiled.

"Allai." Ordina smiled, thinking Krith was talking to her. "We did at that."

He turned to the shipwright. "Snap said that her leaving were the only way to save everything. She told me to fly the stars."

Ordina shook her head. "Not likely now, Krith. Without the silverfire, we'd be here a long time."

"Try it, M'Lady," he said to her.

She gazed at him quizzically, then walked over to the Altar of Communion. "You know I've done this a hundred times since the accident."

"Allai, M'Lady, but I've got faith. Do it again."

In each touch, the pattern was repeated. She could do it in her sleep. The arms moved in their rhythm and their paths over the altar.

Glorious light suddenly filled the chamber.

"Krith! It's back! It's free!" Ordina sang from the depths of her soul.

"I hear tell," Krith said as he laughed, "that you can make a ship out of anything . . ."

". . . with silverfire," they finished together.

She turned in the lustrous room and threw her arms around him as far as they would go.

Krith held her. Snap had freed them, he thought. She had freed them all.

Epilogue

The Silence of Night

LOCATION: NEW COLONIES SECTOR / ARPX15348 / UPDRIFT FROM WORLIN 5 ABOARD THE *NEFFI*

Serg leaned carefully against the railing and looked over the side. The cloud masses below swirled in their silent dance over the pleasant blue-green of the surface. Here and there he could still make out the regular lines of transport routes and irrigation fields. Metal and glass occasionally winked at him as they sailed ever higher overhead.

"Sorry to leave it?" said the familiar voice behind him.

"Yes," he replied as he continued to look over the horizon. "It was a good place to be—and a sad place."

Thyne moved forward and joined him at the railing.

"You mean the cities?"

"The cities were terrible and frightening, of course. I kept thinking that someone would come out of the next door or look at me through the next window. Everything was pretty much intact, at least in the city we visited. Everything pretty much in order—except for all the dead. It's hard to believe that anything could be so efficient in its killing and so uncaring about the result."

Thyne gazed down on the beautiful world retreating below them. "Yes, then it truly is a sad place."

He turned to her. "Yes, but it wasn't just that. This world was a thriving civilization. There were eight billion thinking beings on this world only a few cycles ago. They had no concept of the time we now live: a time everything that they knew—everything that they were—would be gone.

"How many more worlds are there like this one? The Arch'tra Fleet was a galactic fleet of oppression—both in their own time and in ours. It must have been so immense to occupy the entire galaxy at one time. If this world is any example of their work, then civilization as we knew it is at an end."

Thyne turned and leaned her back against the railing. She wondered at the vast sky surrounding them. She hadn't thought of her home world for some time now, occupied as she had been with her survival and the survival of those around her. What had happened to her own home among the stars?

For that matter, where was her home? They had traveled blindly for the most part while in the Arch'tra ship and found themselves—somewhere else. Dresiv had told her that he figured they had traveled possibly as much as a four-degree arch around the outer spiral of the galaxy. That put her months from home—even if they had proper charts. They were sailing uncharted drifts of the darkwind amid the Void. It was a new galaxy to explore so far as they were concerned.

The Thrund's velvet voices intruded on her reveries. "Sire, Lady Thyne, may I ask when we will be fully under way?"

Serg stood and turned to face Hruna. She had been careful these last months not only to be of general assistance but, he noted, to keep herself as clean as possible. In a Thrund it was a sign of good mental health.

"Madam Ambassador, we shall be getting under way directly, although we do not yet have any clear concept of where we are going or of how we are going to get there," he replied.

"I'm sure you realize the urgency of reporting our findings back to the central Pax Forum. The sorcerer remains a primary source of information. Without him it will be impossible to prepare our defense!"

"Yes, Madam Ambassador, I understand. I'm not certain that there *is* any Forum to receive our report nor any Pax to prepare to defend. Nevertheless, we shall try," Serg smoothly responded.

This seemed to satisfy the Thrund, who slipped quietly away on her six legs.

"What was that about," Thyne asked.

"She made it her task to try distilling information out of Djan. You yourself said that they would be returning once they had found a cure for their race's disease. If they are on schedule, they left the galaxy entirely five days ago."

Thyne stood up and folded her arms against a nonexistent chill. "What happens if they find it?"

"You mean *when* they find it." Serg turned back to the planet. "It's only a question of how long it takes to get the right combination of time and distance before they find the cure. When that happens, they will return—in the same three-million-year intervals—to their own time."

"So they *will* be back through our time—again."

"Yes. There is a difference. This time we know they're coming. Look, I know it's not much, but it's better than we had before. If we can find some way of defeating them, then we can keep history from being changed in our own past."

"And if we don't."

Serg took a deep breath and let it out while he thought. At last he said, "I just don't know. If there's anything left of the Pax, they may be our only hope. We'll sail into the Imperial Core and see what's left. If not—then I guess we're on our own."

She thought for a moment, then smiled. "At least we have a ship and stars to sail."

He looked about. The *Neffi*—as Krith had named their rebuilt ship—still bore a faint resemblance to her Arch'tra ancestry. The curving plates now formed the bottom hull instead of the top. A new deck had been fitted and laid over it from the woods into which they had fallen. Ordina had worked miracles over the past weeks, but it still amazed Serg what she had done with the *Neffi*. She had systematically cut away the dead flesh parts of the ship, demanding that each part be examined. Ordina insisted that the technology they would eventually salvage from the *Neffi* would be immensely important. The parts that weren't bolted together properly she reinforced with split rails. The mast, of course, had to be cut from tall lodgepole trees since they couldn't get the transfinite propulsion machines operational again. Ordina had even put the temple where the specimen chamber once stood. The *Neffi* would now fly again, but this time as a silverfire ship.

"Right you are, Lady Thyne," Serg replied. "Master Genni!"

"*Allai,* Captain!"

"Is Mistress Ordina ready to make sail?"

"*Allai,* Captain. Master Krith has given the word."

Krith smiled. "Well, Lady Thyne, it looks like there may be some unity between our two crews after all."

"Don't count on it," she said through her own crooked smile.

The great sheet of opal force materialized before the mast. The *Neffi* surged forward, climbing higher and higher, trailing the rainbow of light behind its keel. The darkwind caught its sails as it soared into the silent, unknown stars.

Tracy Hickman is the co-author, with Margaret Weis, of the *New York Times* best-selling *Dragonlance Saga, The Darksword Trilogy*, and *The Rose of the Prophet Trilogy. Requiem of Stars* is his first solo novel.